GREY HOOD

Detectives clash in this noir crime mystery thriller

JAMES DAVIDSON

Published by The Book Folks

London, 2024

ISBN 978-1-80462-282-7

www.thebookfolks.com

*GREY HOOD is the third standalone novel
in this noir detective series by James Davidson.
Look out for the others, OUTCAST SISTER
and ROUGH SLEEPER!*

*More details about James' other novels can be
found at the back of this book.*

Prologue

March 12th
Shush! Quiet please!

March 13th
*Was it his idea first, or mine? We must have dreamt
it together on one of those long nights under the river.
Our miracle, a fairytale, a cheating the world.
After you kill me… will I find you again?
But he had slipped away while I slept and dreamt of
him.
There's nothing left now in the world except to wait.
The skin prickles all along my arms, and the sky
crawls with expectation.*

March 14th
*Do others not feel it? They pass by in the street so
blankly. Their laughter is like cotton wool. They'll
never see the grey hood. I know it's wrong, but I can't
help despising them, with all their dull pleasures, their
gardens, their children. The spared.*

1

It started again.

'Who are you?'

He blinked and looked around the white walls of the hospital room as if seeing them for the first time.

'Where am I?'

Panic rising, he fingered the collar of his Armani shirt as if he was choking, but the buttons were undone, and his expensive tie had been removed.

DI Beth Krush studied his anxiety, not quite believing it. 'You really don't know?'

'Who… who are you?'

'I just told you my name. I told you ten times already. I'm the detective.'

'I don't understand. What happened to me?'

She did not respond this time. There was no point. It would all begin again in half a minute. In her silence, there was strange power over him, almost pleasurable.

'What…? Where…?' His questions petered out.

Still, she said nothing.

An unseen wheel turned. Just like before, and the time before that, he looked down and discovered the high-heeled shoe in his hand. Red, shiny in the bright light of this empty doctor's surgery with its posters of anatomy and hygiene. *Wash your hands.* As if water could make everything OK.

He gazed at the shoe. 'Is it yours?'

Krush kept her silence. She refused to play the game any longer.

He blinked, turning the red shoe in his hand. It was as if he had never seen a shoe before, but she knew better.

Five o'clock in the morning, she'd been dragged out of bed. A&E was crowded and noisy after a typical Saturday night in Liverpool. Burns, broken limbs, overdoses, panic attacks… the usual. But Krush was not a typical detective; and this man who sat on the examination table, trying to get up, but falling back, was no ordinary patient.

Damon Slate owned half the city, they said. Not that Krush paid attention to the nurses' gossip. The mayor himself had made the call to the chief inspector in the early hours. A matter of urgency. That was how Krush, the city's top murder detective, ended up in A&E, talking in circles to "the richest man in Liverpool". Without his memory, he might as well have been the poorest.

'Who are you?' His voice was tremulous with the need to understand.

'I'm the detective. Remember? I told you my name. We've been sitting in here for half an hour now.'

'You told me your name?' The strain of trying to recall showed in his fraught eyes. 'I have no idea. Please, help me. What's happening to me?'

His frame was muscular beneath his shirt, the Rolex on his wrist a symbol of status, but he was just a little boy in his terror.

'Try to think,' she said. 'What's the last thing you remember?'

In truth, Krush had been lying sleepless, alone in the dark, feeling the kicks in her belly, when the phone call came. To get up and go to work had felt like a miracle.

Slate shook his head. 'Where is this? How did I get here?'

'You were found in the tunnel. Do you remember the tunnel?'

'The *tunnel?*'

'The Queensway Tunnel. You came wandering out of the dark. You were holding that shoe. You've lost your memory.'

'But I don't… why was I in the tunnel? How did I–'

'We don't know. Mr Slate, please, try to remember. We're concerned about your wife. We haven't been able to contact her. Is that her shoe in your hand?'

'Iris…?' His frantic eyes contracted.

'You remember your wife, don't you?'

'Where is she? Is she here? What happened?'

'We don't know where she is. Try to focus. Is that Iris's shoe in your hand?'

He looked at the shoe and gasped but did not answer. She sensed she was losing him again.

'Please, Mr Slate. When was the last time you saw your wife?'

He stared at the poster behind Krush's back, a cutaway human body with its organs neatly labelled, and shook his head. Tears welled at the corners of his eyes, but they did not fall.

'Who are you?' he said. 'Where am I?' The unshed tears that rimmed his eyes were haunting.

'Not again.' She felt a twinge and rubbed her swollen belly. Five months pregnant, and she could not hide it.

Slate's teary eyes widened. His face changed. A glimmer showed as he watched her hand.

'You're pregnant,' he said.

'What?'

Something in his face was disturbing. She pulled her jacket around her stomach.

'We've met before, haven't we?' he said. 'Where was that?'

'It was right here, just now. You remember? Is your memory coming back?'

'Here?' He looked around the pale walls that seemed renewed every time he noticed them. 'No, it wasn't here. It was somewhere else. Where was it?'

'*Have* we met before?' Suddenly, *she* was the one who did not remember.

Yes, they had crossed paths in some place, but he looked different. He was almost unrecognizable, and yet…

'Where was it?' Slate said. 'It must have been before you were pregnant. Yes. I can almost remember, but… no, it's gone.'

'We don't move in the same circles, you and I. You're rich; I'm a police detective. You must have me mixed up with someone else.'

But the words did not ring true.

'It would be hard to mistake you.' The tears at the corners of his eyes dried, forming slug trails.

'Your memory's coming back, isn't it?' She sat forward, wanting to grab at the light before it faded. 'Do you remember the tunnel?'

He blinked. 'Who are you…?'

Strangely, she could not answer.

The shoe dropped from his hand.

2

DI Eleanor Rose ducked under the crime-scene tape and entered the park. The streetlights were still on, catching the budding trees and the drizzle in a dismal glow. Springtime in Liverpool. She followed the waterlogged path through pink and white petals strewn in muddy puddles. To one side, a play area had gone to waste. Rusted chains hung empty from what used to be a swing, and a weathered slide was bent out of shape, tinkling in the downpour.

The forensics team was crouched at work in a large patch of overgrown grass, what might have been a bowling green, illuminated by torchlight.

'Detective, over here!' An officer in a yellow high-vis jacket waved beneath his umbrella and waded towards her through the grass.

'Eleanor Rose.' She offered her hand. 'I came as soon as I got the call.'

'Derrick Jeffers. "Jeff", they call me.' He smiled, revealing a gap between his front teeth. 'The Marsh is my neighbourhood. I grew up around here. You can ask me anything.'

'Right, great.'

'Lived here my whole life. Lost my virginity in this park.' He pointed to a leaning sycamore tree behind the swings. 'The leaves were all around us. I could never forget. You'd be amazed at the things that happen in here.'

A chatty type, she thought. It was too early in the morning for this.

'OK,' Eleanor said. 'I'll give you a shout if I need anything. For now, please, stay by the entrance and don't let the dog walkers inside.' She started to walk away, but he kept pace.

'You know about… I mean… did anyone tell you?'

'What?'

He grinned, pondering the old sycamore tree. 'Never mind. Here I am yacking. Everyone at the station says, "Shut up, Jeff. Stop talking for five minutes."'

'OK.'

'Alright. I'll leave you to it then.' He headed towards the park gate.

'Fantastic.' Eleanor shrugged and kept walking.

She found the forensics chief, Jack Elliot, squatted down between two of his colleagues.

Elliot grunted, seeing her. 'No lie-in for you this weekend, either.'

'What are we dealing with?' She peered over his shoulder, but the body was hidden from view among tall stalks of grass. She felt the damp seeping through her trousers.

'We haven't turned him over yet. But it's a male, Caucasian, youngish. Well, he has a full head of black hair at least. His throat's been cut, right through the jugular. It's a mess.'

'Found a weapon?'

'Not yet, but the grass is thick; we'll have to search it one square foot at a time.'

'You think it was a knife?'

'It was sharp, that's for sure.'

'Guys, can I just interrupt?' Jeff popped up again behind her. 'The kids carry pocketknives, but you won't find it. They don't chuck them away. They're wild, the kids in the Marsh. All they do is ride bikes and cut things.'

Elliot looked embarrassed. 'Listen, what's your name? Jeff, right? We have to take care of this now. Why don't you go back to the gate? There's a crowd of people over there gawking.'

Jeff showed his tooth gap. 'Got it. Sure. Sorry. I don't mean to be in the way.' As he backed away through the grass, he gave a thumbs-up. 'Just give me a shout if you have any questions. I know this neighbourhood like the back of my hand. I was born here, just one street over.'

When he was gone, Eleanor crouched down next to the forensics chief. 'Talkative type.'

'He's a pain in the arse. Been hanging around my shoulder the whole time, chatting nonsense. Come on, let's turn the body over.'

'Alright.' She grabbed hold of the dead man's hip, while Elliot took hold of his arm.

The deceased wore a black tracksuit and trainers. He lay as if exhausted with one arm stretched out flat, and the other bent underneath his chest.

'Ready?' Elliot said.

'Ready.'

They pulled and rolled the man over onto his back through the soft, wet grass. His face was ugly, dog-like, caught in a snarl. The final, frozen emotion in his brain must have been hatred. A few petals and tufts stuck to his pores. The arm that had been pinned beneath his chest sprang free. A shoe dropped from his hand.

'What?' Eleanor reached but did not touch it.

A single high-heeled shoe, scarlet red, lay on its side in the grass.

3

'Where am I?' Slate stared around the white walls.

He tried to get up from the examination table, but he was too weak; he slumped back with a bump.

'Disneyland,' Krush said.

'What's happened? Why am I here?'

Krush took out her phone. 'I'd like to show you something. This video was filmed a few hours ago.'

She tilted the screen towards him, and he stared with fear. A blur of streetlight and darkness. She turned up the volume to maximum, but it was just confused laughter and shouts.

He peered. 'A tunnel mouth. Why?'

'Do you recognize it? It was filmed after midnight. Keep watching.'

The arching tunnel mouth was vast, a black hole that filled the camera's eye. A figure walked out of the tunnel. Unsteady, slow, he lumbered into the streetlight. Somebody was laughing. Distorted voices shouted, but the stricken figure did not appear to hear them.

'What is this?' Slate said.

'Those voices are students. A group of them were out late, wandering around drunk. They took the video.'

The camera zoomed in to show the figure in the tunnel close up. In one hand he clutched a red shoe. He wore an expensive suit. He blinked and squinted.

The video ended.

'Do you remember?' Krush said.

Before he could say anything, the door behind them swung open.

'Don't say anything!' A man in a green suit burst into the room, rattling a stethoscope on a tray by the door.

'Hey!' Krush jumped up. 'You can't be in here.'

'I'm Clive Mann. Mr Slate's lawyer. This interview is unlawful. We'll sue.' He stood in front of his client with arms folded.

Chief Inspector Linda Carver came through the open door behind him, carrying a large paper cup of coffee. 'Sorry, Krush,' she said. 'I tried to stop him, but he's right. We can't talk to his client without him.'

'This isn't an interview,' Krush said. 'There's been an accident. All I'm trying to do here is help.'

The lawyer wiped sweat from his brow. 'I know who you are, Beth Krush. You're not a doctor.'

Carver took a swig from the coffee and grimaced.

'Listen, Mr Mann. The detective is only here because your pal, the mayor, personally asked for my best police officer. Stand aside, please. This is a hospital, and your client has suffered a potentially serious head injury.'

Tall and imposing with her silver hair tied back, Carver's authority was only slightly blemished by strands of cat fur on her otherwise immaculate uniform. But perhaps Krush was the only one who noticed.

Mann smoothed his tie. Sweat patches showed on the white shirt beneath. 'Well, the mayor overreacted. It's because of that stupid video doing the rounds on social media. I've issued a cease-and-desist.'

'Good luck with that,' Carver said.

The lawyer kneeled beside Slate. 'Are you alright, Damon? I'm sorry I couldn't get here earlier. I was, err… I was held up.'

Slate blinked into the light. 'Where am I?'

'You're in the hospital. Don't you remember?'

'Hospital? Why?' Slate looked down and noticed the red shoe on the floor where he had dropped it. 'What's this?'

Krush was glad to let someone else answer these questions.

'It's alright,' Mann said. 'Relax. You're suffering from some kind of memory loss.'

'Memory loss?'

'I'm here now. I'll get you out. These NHS doctors are hopeless. It's a zoo out there in A&E. People are eating kebabs and selling *The Big Issue*. I'll drive you to the private clinic.' The lawyer took out his phone. 'I'm calling our doctor now.'

'You can't,' Krush said.

Carver tapped her on the shoulder. 'Come on. Leave them alone a moment. Let them talk. The mayor was emphatic on the phone: Mr Slate is a special guest of ours. We have to handle him with care.'

* * *

Outside in the corridor, the doctor was waiting. A young man with a strong Scouse accent, he was tranquil, in the way of hospital staff who have already seen everything there is to see, but he was unable to provide any answers.

'How's the patient?' He gave a sleepless smile.

'The same,' Krush said. 'He repeats the same questions over and over. I introduce myself, but a minute later he asks me again who I am. Has he had a stroke?'

The doctor shook his head. 'The brain scan came back clear.'

'But, to lose his memory like this… how is it possible?'

'We think he's suffering from something called transient global amnesia. It's actually surprisingly common. The patient loses their short-term memory. Like they're stuck in a loop, they keep asking the same questions. It seems scary, but patients typically recover within twenty-four hours.'

'And after that, what, he'll be back to normal?'

'Fingers crossed. He'll most likely never remember anything from today or yesterday. In truth, we can't say for sure. The condition is not well understood.'

As they were talking, two nurses came down the corridor pushing a man on a trolley.

'Don't look,' the doctor said.

Krush looked. The man on the trolley seemed dead. He lay motionless, covered in burns all over his head and torso.

'What happened to him?' she said.

'Gangs. Crossed a border he shouldn't have crossed. Some of the things we see in here are… indescribable.'

The trolley disappeared around the corner.

'Gangs.' She looked down at her notepad and saw the words she had jotted down. *Transient global amnesia.*

'What do you think caused Mr Slate's memory loss?' she asked.

The doctor sighed. 'We don't know, but his blood pressure is sky high. We've given him something to bring it down. With any luck, his memory will start to come back once the pressure is reduced.'

'Could he have had an injury, banged his head or something?'

'Maybe, but the brain scan didn't show it. More likely this was brought on by stress. Sometimes when a person is in a crisis, the body gets overwhelmed, the brain shuts down to protect itself.'

Noticing her cradling her oversized belly, the doctor frowned. 'Detective, sit down, please,' he said.

'Is it possible he could be faking?'

'What?' He looked confused, still pointing at an unused chair against the wall. 'Why?'

'I just need to know. Can you prove his amnesia is real? From the brain scans or something?'

He considered. 'Well… not one hundred percent, but his blood pressure really is through the roof.'

'Even so, could he be pretending? There was a strange moment before… he seemed to know who I was.'

The doctor frowned. 'That's not really my area. I only deal with things we can measure. Why would he want to pretend?'

'I wonder…'

4

The streetlights blinked off, and the park shimmered in muddy puddles. Eleanor crouched in the grass a few yards away from where forensics was bagging up the body.

'They dragged him through this way,' she called. 'There's parallel tracks where his trainers trailed in the mud.'

'It would take two people to carry him,' Elliot said.

She closed her eyes and imagined. 'Maybe one, if they were strong. Either way, they dragged him face down; the front tips of his shoes are crusted with mud.'

'Any footprints?'

'Bits of prints, but the ground is muddy, and the grass is trodden over. People must walk through here every day.'

Elliot looked doubtful, or perhaps just sleepy. 'It'll be a hell of a job sorting them all out. Still, we'll photograph what we have and process them.'

'It's interesting, there's no blood.' She snapped off a blade of grass and sniffed it.

'What do you mean?'

'If they cut his throat here, there should be blood.'

'They didn't cut it here,' Elliot said. 'A cut to the neck like that, it lets out a fountain. As it is, there's just a small patch in the grass.'

'So, he was already dead when they dragged him here. Why did they bother?' She carried on through the grass and mud, following the gouged spaces where the man's feet had caught on the boggy ground. 'They came this way.

Look at this.' She crouched at the path where the bowling green ended.

'What?' Elliot followed her.

'Bike tracks.'

'Fresh? I'll tell the guys to photograph them.'

'That local officer, the talkative one, said something about kids on bikes.' She looked through the rain to where Jeff was standing guard at the gate. 'Maybe he can help.'

'He doesn't know what day it is. I wouldn't pay him much attention.'

'Still, he's from around here. He might come in useful.'

'Excuse me, love.' A voice from behind made Eleanor jump.

A dishevelled man wearing a soggy dressing gown over a tracksuit came towards her with a Yorkshire terrier on a lead.

'You can't be in here,' she said. 'The park's been sealed off.'

The man grinned as his dog nosed through the overgrown grass.

'Oh, that's the witness,' Elliot said. 'He's the one who found the body. I told him to wait until you got here, but he disappeared.'

The man fished a packet of cigarettes out of his dressing-gown pocket. The edges of his tracksuit bottoms were coated with pink petals. 'I was walking the dog,' he explained.

'Alright.' Eleanor took out her notepad. 'You found the body. What time was that?'

'Well, let me think.' He checked his wrist but did not find a watch. 'It must have been sometime after four o'clock.'

'Why were you out so early?'

'On account of this one.' He nudged the dog with his foot. 'She's an early riser. Every morning, she jumps in my bed and starts barking. If I don't get up, she wakes the whole street. After breakfast we go for a walk. It's our little routine. I live alone, just me and the princess.'

'So, you were walking the dog,' Eleanor said. 'Then what happened?'

'The princess sniffed something and went running off. She wasn't on the lead. I usually let her off when we're in the park at that time. There's no one else around for her to annoy. I thought she was just doing her business, you know, dog business, but she didn't come back. It was dark. I called her name, but she didn't come – not that that's unusual, mind you. I started looking for her, but she's so small, I couldn't see her in the long grass. Then I heard her sort of growling. I went in the grass, and I could smell something. Something bad.'

'And you found the body,' Eleanor said. 'Did you touch it?'

'Oh, no. Thank Christ. I almost did. I crouched right down next to it. I thought it was a cat or something, but then I saw it was too big. I rang the police right away.'

'Alright.' She stared at the page in her notebook, it was empty. 'And did you see anybody? Was anyone else in the park during the time you were here?'

'Not a soul. People don't come here so much nowadays. It's not like it used to be. I remember when the swings were new, and families came here with their children at the weekends. It's the gangs, isn't it? People are afraid.'

'Which gangs?'

'Oh, don't ask me. I keep my head down and my eyes closed. I'm not stupid. Listen, can I go home now? I'm freezing.'

'Sure, go on. Give us a call if you think of anything else.' She handed over her card.

'I wouldn't work too hard on this one, love. If someone left him lying there in the rain, it's because he deserved it. Leave him in peace now, is my advice.'

5

The lawyer came out of the hospital room, pushing his client in a wheelchair. Slate clutched the red shoe in two hands. Mann seemed anxious.

'Any news?' Krush jumped up before they could get away. 'Did he remember anything?'

Slate gazed at her but showed no recognition.

'No,' Mann said. 'It's frightening. He just keeps asking where he is. I must have told him fifteen times. But I'm taking him away now. I spoke to Mr Slate's personal doctor at the clinic. They'll know what to do. They're getting everything prepared.'

'Which clinic?'

'It's called the Hexagon. It's–'

'I know where it is.'

'Well then, if you'll excuse me.' He started to push the wheelchair along the corridor, but Krush blocked his way.

'Let them go.' Carver, onto her second large coffee but still drowsy, called from a chair by the wall. 'Let them go, Krush. We can't detain him here.'

Krush ignored her. 'What about Mrs Slate? Have you been able to contact her?'

'I tried,' said Mann. 'There's no answer. But it's early. Iris'll be asleep. I'll keep trying.'

'Do you think the red shoe belongs to her?' Krush asked him.

'I have no idea.'

In the wheelchair, Slate squinted, he almost seemed to recognize her. 'Do I know you?'

'No,' Mann answered. 'This is just the detective. She's been helping you. But we don't need her help anymore. We're leaving.'

He pushed the wheelchair around Krush, but she kept pace as they moved along the corridor. In the background, an old man with a bandage over his eyes started singing *In My Liverpool Home*.

Krush raised her voice. 'How well do you know the Slate family?'

'I'm their lawyer, not their friend.'

On the other side of the waiting room, a group of women took up the refrain.

> *In my Liverpool home…*
> *We speak with an accent exceedingly rare…*

Krush leaned closer to speak over the racket. 'Really? The way you burst in here earlier, you seemed like a friend. How long have you known them?'

> *Meet under a statue exceedingly bare…*

'I went to school with Damon, but don't get the wrong idea. We weren't close in those days. It was later on, after I'd been practising law a while, that we met again. When I told Damon about my work, he said he was looking for a lawyer and, well, that was that. Iris, I didn't meet until recently. They only married a year and a half ago.'

Half the waiting room now joined in with the song.

> *And if you want a cathedral, we've got one to spare…*

Krush frowned over her shoulder. 'I'm going to arrest them in a minute if they don't shut up. What were Mr and Mrs Slate doing yesterday?'

'I haven't the foggiest. Now, please, the doctor's waiting for me at the Hexagon.'

Krush took out her card. 'Call me if he says anything. As soon as his memory comes back, I want to talk to him.'

Mann took the card but did not look at it. 'Is this really necessary? My client's had an accident, that's all.'

'I'll have to take the shoe.' She put on gloves.

'What?' Mann watched as she knelt by the wheelchair.

'I need to take this.' Krush prised the shoe from Slate's hands, while he watched, stupefied.

'This is hardly necessary,' the lawyer said.

'Have we met before?' Slate asked her.

'The thing's going to be covered in smudges and dirt by now,' Krush said. She put the shoe in an evidence bag and stood up, wincing, cradling her belly. 'What's your client's home address? I'll drive over and check everything's alright.'

'Number 15, Heron Lane. It's on the Wirral. I don't have time to write it down.'

'You don't have to. I'll remember.'

Mann shook his head and pushed the wheelchair away. Krush watched him pass between two whispering nurses and disappear around the corner. All the way, Slate kept looking back over his shoulder at the red shoe in the clear bag.

When they were gone, Krush returned to find Carver still sitting, sipping coffee.

'Does he seem suspicious to you?' she asked.

'He seems like a lawyer,' Carver said. 'You should go home, Detective, get some rest. You need it. I've been pregnant four times. I know what it's like.'

Krush pulled her jacket around her belly. 'What about the tunnel? Has anybody checked inside?'

'It's full of traffic at this time. Folks driving to work.'

'We need to look inside. What if the wife's in there?'

'She's not in the tunnel. There are CCTV cameras.'

'Still… it can't do any harm to take a look.'

'Are you listening to me? It's full of traffic.'

'So, shut it down.'

'I can't shut the tunnel, Krush. The city would grind to a halt. People have to get to work.'

'But–'

'Christ, you're stubborn. What do you expect to find underground?'

'We're missing a red shoe. The other one must be somewhere.'

'Listen,' said Carver. 'The tunnel closes at midnight for maintenance. You can check inside then, if you really want to. But you won't find anything. The operator told me there are cameras running all the way through. If a woman was wandering around, she'd have been spotted by now. Anyway, it won't be necessary. Iris Slate and her mysterious shoe will turn up at home watching TV. You'll see. Relax now, you've done enough.'

'No,' Krush said. 'I'm going to Slate's house. I'll check everything's alright. Then I'll go the Hexagon and see if he's recovered his memory. I'm going to find out what he was doing in that tunnel.'

'You realize, I only gave you this case because I wanted you to take it easy. Since you refuse to go on maternity leave, I wanted to keep you away from the frontlines.'

'I know you did.'

As she walked heavily away down the corridor, Carver called after her. 'Slow down, Detective. You're taking care of two people now. You were never good at taking care of one.'

6

A white van pulled up on the pavement by the park gate. Unmarked, with black windows, it rested under the branches of a cherry tree. Nobody came out.

Eleanor knocked on the driver's door. She tried the handle, but it was locked. She sensed somebody watching behind the tinted glass.

She knocked on the window. 'Open up. Police.'

The side door of the van slid open.

'Get in.' A man's voice. 'We need to talk.'

For a moment she hesitated. Through the door, she saw a bare, wood-lined interior. It might have been a small removals van. The man was seated on a wooden panel that folded down on the opposite side, partially hidden from view.

'Don't be shy.' He held up his ID to the open door. 'Chris Blaine. Detective Sergeant. Organised Crime Unit. We have things to discuss.'

'Oh. I'm Detective Rose–'

'I know who you are. Please, shut the door behind you.'

Eleanor climbed in, sat down on the rough panel and tried to feel comfortable.

'Tell me about your victim.' Blaine was tall and wiry in a dark suit. His white hair was styled in a quiff like the plume of a snowbird. He had deep wrinkles around his green eyes.

'He hasn't been identified,' Eleanor said. 'No wallet, no cards, just a slashed neck. We'll see what the autopsy turns up. What's this about?'

'I read your file. It's a hefty document.'

'I'm better in real life, honestly.'

Rain pattered on the metal roof just above her head.

'Don't be humble. You're an accomplished detective. But I dug deeper. I asked around. I can't go into details, and I won't name anyone but, well, there are some doubts about you.'

'Doubts…?'

'You left Liverpool five years ago without explanation. Cut everyone off, didn't even say goodbye. Then you turned up again out of the blue, as if nothing ever happened. They say you work in the same building as your sister, but you never talk to her. Even now, she's pregnant, but you don't talk. They also say, you solved a few big cases since you came back to Liverpool, but a lot of innocent people died along the way.'

'I–'

'They say you have no friends, no relationships. You don't socialise with other officers.'

'To be fair—'

'But you spend your time with homeless people. In fact, they say you've got a homeless drug addict living in your house right now.'

She waited to be certain he had finished. 'Anything else?'

He almost smiled. 'I don't care what you get up to with the homeless. That's your affair. What matters to me is: do you know the difference between right and wrong?'

'What's this about?'

He answered with another question. 'How well do you know the Marsh?' He gestured at the back of the van door, behind which the park and the surrounding terraced houses were concealed.

'I can't say I'm familiar with it.'

'Good. You're a blank slate.' He took out a notepad and tore off a page. 'I'll make it simple for you.'

As she watched, he drew a rough circle in the middle of the page. 'This is the Marsh. It's not really a circle, more like a trapezoid, but never mind. Now this is the border' — he drew a line through the centre of the circle — 'it runs right through the middle of the streets. To the west, that's Looney territory. To the east, it's the Gilchrists.'

He wrote an *L* in the left hemisphere, and a *G* in the right.

Eleanor took the paper and tried to match it to the dirty, petal-strewn streets she had walked through. 'And the park?'

'Bang in the middle, straddling the border. That's where your body was found.'

'So, you're saying it's a gang killing?'

'On the contrary.' Blaine sat up straight. His quiff brushed the ceiling. 'Your job is to make sure this whole business has nothing to do with Looneys and Gilchrists.'

Something about the way he said this, looking down at the metal floor of the van, a hint of regret in his voice; she sensed there was more to the story.

'I don't understand,' she said.

'You may not know it, but there's a war in this city. Invisible. Soldiers walk around just like ordinary people. There are borderlines and no man's lands in plain sight. You pass them every day without guessing.'

'OK.' She tried to make this description fit with the quiet park in the drizzle, the dog walkers, the rusted swings.

'There's a fragile peace right now. The gangs are trying to find a way to coexist, and we want to help them. Otherwise… you understand… we're talking about chaos, World War Three in Liverpool. My job is to make sure the peace holds.'

'And this body in the park?'

'…could ruin everything. Both sides swear they have nothing to do with it.'

'But, if that's true… Why was he dumped on the borderline?'

'That's what you have to find out – or not, as the case may be. One way or another, the murder will be written off as non-gang-related… Even if it's never solved.'

'You're telling me to cover things up?'

It was dry and airless in the back of the van. The ceiling was too low.

'Call it a favour,' he said. 'One we'll gladly repay. Name your price.'

Something banged in the front compartment of the van.

Eleanor flinched. 'What was that? Who's listening up there?'

'Nobody.'

'I'm sorry. I'm not qualified to deal with this.'

'You're the best qualified. You've been away from Liverpool; you've lost your accent; you have no connection with anyone here; you don't even have friends on the force. It makes you more acceptable to play the role of neutral. The gangs will be watching you. It's essential for them to believe you're not compromised; you won't take sides between them. We need you, Eleanor.'

'If I'm going to solve this case, I'll do it my way. That means finding the real culprit, whoever they are.' She got up from the panel.

'You're making a mistake,' Blaine said.

'Well, you know me. You've read my file.'

She jumped out of the van into the drizzle.

7

Driving into the Queensway Tunnel, the rainy outside world fell away. It was brightly lit inside, white and grey. The four lanes were busy with rush-hour traffic in a hypnotic stream. Overhead, a strip of phosphorescent lamps in the curved ceiling cast uniform light over the sterile walls. Krush was deep underground now. Trying not to think about that, she kept her eyes along the sides of the tunnel as they flashed past. There was no pavement and no hard shoulder. Red emergency phones appeared and vanished at intervals. There were doors in places, and occasionally a blocked-off side path branched away into darkness, but these details passed by too quickly to take in. It was absurd, of course, what she was looking for: a missing woman could not walk through the tunnel while it was filled with cars.

Krush saw a gap of daylight up ahead. The journey underground was already finished. She drove out into a fine mist of rain with a tinge of regret, certain she had missed something along the way. The dirty buildings of Birkenhead rose into the sky. The refrain of the old tunnel diggers' song passed through her mind. *We dug a hole, until we found another one.* They would be singing that by now in A&E.

Even in the open, the tunnel haunted her vision as she drove. Fifteen minutes later, she parked outside a large, detached house in New Brighton with a view of the pier. Seagulls perched along the roof called out a warning as she got out of the car. From outside the gate, the house looked asleep; curtains closed and no lights on inside. It was a beautiful building, in the old seafront style, pastel blue with large windows and a balcony. This was not a part of the city to which work often brought her. She usually found herself in the poorer, noisier areas.

As she surveyed the façade of the house, a curtain flickered in one of the upstairs windows. Somebody was watching.

She opened the gate and started up the path. A scream came from above, and a white bird swooped down from the roof.

'Jesus.'

The bird shrieked. She waved her arms over her head and ran. The tips of its wing grazed her hair.

The front door opened, and a girl called, 'Quick! Get inside!'

The bird screamed as she barrelled through the door. Wings beat in the air behind her. The door slammed shut.

'What the hell?' Krush dropped to her haunches.

'Sorry about that.' The girl wore a black onesie. She was scrawny, with bags under her eyes. 'We called the council, but the nests are protected by some environmental law. Dad says he's going to shoot them himself.'

'You're Mr Slate's daughter?'

The girl, around seventeen years old, eyed her suspiciously. 'Dad's not in at the moment. If you're here to see him—'

'I'm not here to see your dad.'

'Who are you?'

'Police. Detective Inspector Beth Krush. What's your name?'

'Claire. But… what's this about? Why?'

'Is your mum at home?'

Claire backed against the wall. 'Has something happened?'

'Your dad… erm, there's been an incident. He's in hospital, but they've done a brain scan, it's not too bad.'

The daughter froze.

In the shadow behind her, a voice called out. 'What did he do?'

A young man came part way down the stairs, but hung back, watching from above. His face was hidden in shadow, but his oversized, fluffy slippers occupied the middle of the staircase.

'Can you come down here, please? Police. I'm Detective Krush.'

'Why?' There was a shrill edge to his voice, the remainder of puberty. When he came into the light, his face was covered in acne, and a sparse moustache showed above his lips. He might have been fifteen years old. 'What did the fucker do now?'

'Please, Ian,' Claire said. 'Dad's in hospital.' She took out her mobile phone. 'I'll try and call him.'

'I don't think that's a good idea,' Krush said.

'Wait a minute.' Ian came down to the bottom step. 'Where's Mum?'

'Can we go in the living room and talk a minute?' Krush said.

'Where's Mum?' Ian shouted. 'Is she at the hospital too?'

'No. Actually, I was hoping she was here. Haven't you seen her this morning?'

'Oh God.' Claire dropped her phone.

* * *

In the living room, an overweight tabby cat lay on the window ledge watching the seagulls. Claire fell into the armchair next to it. Krush sat on an uncomfortable leather sofa opposite. Ian leaned in the doorway and stared at the floor, refusing to sit. In the light of the window, Claire looked even scrawnier. Her anxiety was adult, out of place in her underdeveloped frame.

On the wall, a kitsch portrait of Damon and Iris Slate hung over a fake fireplace. Iris wasn't smiling in the picture. She wore a dark dress and red shoes. Her husband, a foot and a half taller, was positioned behind her with both arms around her waist in an attitude of possession.

'Those shoes.' Krush pointed. 'Are they the same?'

'What?' Claire said.

'Those red shoes in the picture. Are they real?'

'What do you mean?' Claire was on the verge of tears.

'Of course they're real,' Ian shouted. 'Why would she be wearing unreal shoes?'

'Can someone please explain to me what's going on?' Claire said. She grabbed the cat and lifted it onto her knee.

'Calm down, both of you,' Krush said.

Their emotions were too raw, threatening to spill over. She looked for a way to pacify them, but she had never been gifted at dealing with young people.

'Your father seems to be suffering from amnesia. It's only his short-term memory, the doctor says. He remembers the past, but nothing from the last day or so.'

'And will it come back?' Claire's fingers dug into the cat's fur.

Krush got up and took a picture of the shoes on her phone. She studied the portrait from close up. Iris's eyes were so sad, so utterly out of place, it was as if her face had been grafted from a different painting onto this one. She took a few more pictures on her phone and backed away.

'We don't know,' she said. 'The doctors say it's possible. Apparently, it's not uncommon for people to lose their memory for a little while, and then afterwards they recover just fine.' She turned to Ian. 'Your father–'

'He's not my father. He doesn't even like me. He hates all of us. I bet his amnesia's not real.'

'What do you mean?' Krush said. 'Why wouldn't it be real?'

'He's a liar. He lies all the time.'

'But this–' Krush started to say.

'Ian,' Claire said. 'Please.'

Krush could not keep her eyes from straying to Iris's mournful face in the portrait. 'The important question now is where could your mother be?'

'I have no idea,' Ian said. 'If you want to know, you'd better ask that old prick.' He pointed at his stepfather in the frame. 'He knows, I'm sure. I don't believe in this amnesia story for a minute. He's done something to Mum and he's trying to cover it up.'

'But why?' Krush said.

Ian shook his head and ran out of the room. They heard him stomp up the stairs.

'We're not related,' Claire said.

It was obvious. Claire was pale and waifish, with fine black hair, big, round eyes, and thin lips. Ian was tall and lanky with a crooked jaw, reddish-blonde hair, and sunken eyes. While he had a strong Scouse accent, Claire's wispy accent was foreign. Krush tried to place it but couldn't.

'So, Iris is your stepmother?'

'Yes. But I don't hate her. I'm not like the others.'

'What do you mean?'

'Everyone in this house, all they do is argue. They can't bear living together. I don't know why nobody leaves.'

'When did you last see Iris?'

'Sometime yesterday, I guess. They went out last night, her and Dad. I don't know where they were going. We haven't been talking much recently, there was a big argument.'

'What about?' Krush said.

'Who knows? There are always arguments. Nobody remembers what started them, or why. The reasons don't matter. It's just that after a while, everyone starts to hate everyone else. Aren't all families like this?'

'I wouldn't know.' Krush got up.

'Can I go to see Dad now?'

'I'll drive you over there. But first, I need your help. I'd like to piece together last night's events, the best we can.'

'I was at home all night. I don't know what happened.'

'What time did your parents leave here?'

'I guess it was sixish.'

'They left together?'

'I think so… They didn't speak to me. I was up in my room. But when I came downstairs, they were both gone.'

'Did they take the car?'

'I don't know.'

Krush struggled to hide her frustration. 'Please, concentrate. Try and remember.'

Claire closed her eyes. 'Yes, I heard the car engine. They left in the car,' she said.

'Describe the car to me.'

'Dad has a lot of cars. He doesn't keep them all here. I couldn't tell you what they are, sorry. I don't drive, and I couldn't tell the difference between a Ferrari and a… and a Morris Minor. I don't even know what colour they are. I'm just… I'm not a car person. I don't notice them. I'm sorry. I'm no help at all.' She looked like she was about to cry.

'Don't apologise. They left around six in a car, that's something to start with. I need to check your parents' room now. Which is it?'

'They have separate rooms.'

'Separate?'

'The house is big, that's all. We've got more rooms than we can use. I shouldn't have said that, about everyone hating each other. It's normal for families to argue. My dad loves her. I really believe he loves Iris. He'd never hurt her.'

Krush noted that she never referred to Iris as "Mum", but that was understandable with stepparents. Still, there was something odd in this family. It didn't feel like a family at all.

8

Jeff was at the park gate smoking a cigarette, chatting to a woman in a slick raincoat.

'Hey,' Eleanor called. 'You were supposed to keep people away from the crime scene.'

'Oh.' He threw down his cigarette. 'Sorry, Detective. We were just talking.'

The woman in the raincoat turned and hurried across the street, before she could ask her anything.

'Did anyone else come by?' Eleanor said. 'Anybody acting suspicious?'

'Just the regular weirdoes. Everyone's mad around here, you know, but they do their best.'

'The victim was holding a woman's shoe,' Eleanor said. 'A red, high-heeled shoe. Does that mean anything to you?'

He stared with regret at the butt of his cigarette that fizzled on the concrete. 'This is more of a Nike place.'

The surrounding terraced houses appeared deserted behind the blossoming cherry trees.

'What happened here?' she said. 'It feels like it could have been a nice place, with the trees, and the park.'

'The trees… nobody takes care of them. The petals get everywhere. It's a mess. This time of year, it feels like it's snowing.'

'They're beautiful,' Eleanor said, looking around. 'But the park, it's all gone to rot. Half of these houses seem empty.'

'What can you do? The border runs right through here. It's a dead zone.'

'What do you mean?'

'In Looney territory, you can work with the Looneys to get things done. In Gilchrist territory, you can work with the Gilchrists. But here in the middle… well, if you have the chance, you just leave.'

'Do you think Looneys or Gilchrists had anything to do with this killing?'

'Oh, I couldn't say. Around here, we don't stick our necks out.'

'It's your job. You're police.'

Jeff avoided Eleanor's eyes. 'We don't meddle with the gangs,' he said. 'We just leave them alone.'

'Tell me the truth, do you know something?'

'Like what?' He grinned vacantly.

Was he hiding something, she wondered, or was he just stupid?

'Like, who killed that man,' she said.

'I don't know anything, that's what everyone around here says. "Don't think too hard, Jeff, you might hurt yourself," that's what they say.' He took a step back. 'I'd better get back to the office.'

'I need your help. You're the local expert. You're the guy who had sex under the tree.'

'Yeah, well, that was just a tree, and it was a long time ago.' He looked back over the park railings with something like nostalgia.

'Earlier on, you mentioned a gang of kids on bikes.'

'Did I?'

'There are bike tracks by where the body was dragged. Whose side are the kids on, Looneys or Gilchrists?'

He shrugged. 'They're just kids.'

Jeff seemed almost too casual, light-hearted, as if this was all just a joke. But it wasn't a joke.

'You said they carry knives,' she said. 'Our victim's throat was cut.'

'What can you do? It's bad parenting.'

Eleanor tried to make it fit with the story Blaine had told her in the van – invisible armies, Liverpool as a warzone. Somebody was lying.

'If the kids are out of control,' she said, 'why don't the Looneys or the Gilchrists stop them?'

'I guess… maybe they think it's funny.'

'Funny?'

He grinned in his nonchalant way but offered no explanation. Maybe he was telling the truth. She decided to put him on the spot.

'Tell me the truth.' She grabbed his arm, slowing him down. 'Do you think the kids could have killed our man?'

'Who can say? Nobody understands what goes through the heads of those kids. They're like aliens. You can't even talk to them.'

'Well, I'm good at talking.'

'Oh shite.'

* * *

They walked through the Marsh as the rain stopped and the day rose behind purple clouds. The paving slabs were uneven and cracked, damaged by the twisting roots of the cherry trees. Overgrown branches reached over the walls of the surrounding houses, touching windows, blocking out the light. A wash of petals covered the abandoned cars and skips, the scaffolding, and the council bins.

As they walked, Eleanor stopped to question passers-by, mostly dog walkers, but nobody wanted to talk. It was spring, the morning was bright, but it was freezing cold, a day to be indoors.

'It's the gangs, isn't it?' one woman said. 'What can you do? Have to keep yourself to yourself and stay out of trouble.'

'That's what I told her as well.' Jeff gave his gap-toothed grin.

'But which gang?' Eleanor said. 'There's more than one here.'

'It's none of my business.' The woman slipped away, and Eleanor let her go.

They continued walking until they had circled a long way around the park.

Suddenly, Jeff stopped. 'This is the border.'

'What?'

He looked down at the pavement under their feet, where a faded hopscotch grid with just visible.

'Gilchrist territory ends here,' he said. 'Can you feel it? There's a different world on one side.'

'What do you mean?' She looked up and down the street, but nothing had changed.

'That's Looney territory, on the other side.' He stepped away from the hopscotch grid. 'Depending who you are, one false step here could get you killed.'

She glanced around the surrounding homes, terraced houses with closed windows, half of them boarded up. A sleepy abandonment behind the trees. 'How do you know that?'

'I just know. Everyone around here does. It's one of those things you pick up.'

'And the gang of kids?'

He looked at the sky again. Maybe there was something he really expected to find there, something like a bird. 'They hang around the back alleys.'

'In the mornings too?'

'In the mornings, they sell drugs to students on the way to school.'

'Alright, so let's find one and talk to them.'

He looked around. 'Did you bring a bike?'

'A bike?'

'You won't catch them without a bike.'

They kept walking and crossed a mini roundabout. Most of the buildings were boarded up on both sides of the road.

'This used to be the centre,' Jeff said. 'There were shops and cafés and stuff. I was young then, but I remember. It was nice. Now it's all gone.'

'Why? What happened?'

'Economics, I guess. Maybe it was just bad luck.'

'What's that building?' She pointed out a largish, neo-Gothic block that was separated from the rest of the street by an overgrown garden behind railings.

'Oh, that was the library. One of them Carnegie libraries. God knows why they put it here. It's been closed for years, like everything else.'

'Huh.' Eleanor crossed the street to look through the railings, which were locked with a rusted chain. 'I always loved libraries, ever since I was a kid.'

'Aren't they boring?'

'They're a kind of sanctuary in the city,' she said.

Beyond an overgrowth of bushes and trees, the library windows were thick with dust. She could just make out the shelves inside, which were still lined with books. They sang to her. The library was flanked by a shuttered charity shop, and what had been a clothes store called Rumours.

'I don't get it,' she said. 'Why hasn't someone bought it and done it up? It's a nice building. They could've sold the books at least.'

'Legal dispute, I heard. There's a question of who owns the land and what they're allowed to do with it.'

'What a shame. A place like that—'

'Hey!' Jeff caught her arm with excitement. 'There's one! There's one of the kids!'

Eleanor spun around to see a lad in a tracksuit cycling along the opposite pavement. He took one glance, did a wheelie, and accelerated away.

'Stop!' She ran after him.

9

Damon and Iris Slate had adjoining bedrooms on the third floor. The room of "Liverpool's Richest Man", as the morning headlines were calling him, was mostly empty. There were no books on the shelves, and the bed showed no sign of having ever been slept in. Only a few suits in the wardrobe hinted that somebody lived here.

'Doesn't your dad have any belongings?' Krush said.

'He spends a lot of time in his other places,' Claire said. 'He has flats all over the city.'

'Where exactly?'

'I don't know the addresses, but he has one small place that's right by his office, close to the Liver Building. He sleeps there when he's too busy to come home.'

'Does that happen often?'

'All the time. People have no idea. They think because he's rich he spends his days relaxing, but it's not true. He works harder than anyone I know. He says he's addicted to it. He works all through the night without sleeping. That's why he's ill.'

'Ill?'

'He takes medication for stress or anxiety or something. All kinds of tablets. He doesn't like to talk about it. He's always with his private doctor at the clinic.'

'Alright. Let's check your stepmum's room.'

In Iris's room, wide windows opened onto a balcony facing the pier. To the left, the door of a walk-in wardrobe was open. Opposite, another door led to a private bathroom. It was immaculate and bare, like a hotel room set in order by the cleaners.

'Doesn't look like anyone slept here last night. Does Iris also sleep in other places?'

No answer. When Krush looked around, Claire had disappeared.

'Great.'

Krush stepped towards the balcony doors but stopped, seeing a seagull perched on the railing just outside. Beyond the bird, the city skyline shimmered in a haze of pollution and grey sky on the other side of the river. She was surprised to notice the windows of her own flat were visible from here, on the seventh floor of a tall, skinny block by the docks. The windows flashed silver in the watery light. It looked so lonely, so utterly unhomely, she could hardly believe she lived there.

On a dressing table with a mirror, she found a photograph of Iris and Damon on their wedding day. The wife looked two decades younger than the husband. Krush crossed the room and looked into the walk-in wardrobe. It was almost empty inside, just a few garments that looked like they had never been worn. Several rows of shoes were laid out neatly under the clothes racks. She knelt and checked but there was no red shoe.

The en-suite bathroom was clean. This house was so large, with so many rooms and landings, there might be other rooms that Iris used, other wardrobes and toilets. May as well start somewhere. She opened a chest of drawers by the bed and checked inside. Folded clothing and women's underwear, but nothing of interest.

She recrossed the room. Beneath a mirror on the opposite wall, a dresser was dotted with a few bottles of perfume and some jewellery. She pulled out a drawer containing several pairs of trashy earrings. The drawer was stuck; there was something inside at the back.

'What are you hiding?'

She turned it upside down, spilling jewellery and make-up onto the floor. She shook it. A small book dropped out from the back of the drawer and landed on the floor.

'Gotcha.'

A diary. She tilted the book to the light of the window. Most of the pages were empty but a few had been filled with cramped handwriting. Some of the words were difficult to read. Under March 12th, she read, "Shush! Quiet Please!" The rest of the page was blank. What did it mean?

March 13th contained a larger section of text, equally incomprehensible. She skimmed through until her eyes caught at one line in particular.

After you kill me… will I find you again?

'What the hell?' Breathless with desire to read more, she flicked through the pages. She was skimming too fast, seeking a keyword.

For April 2nd, she read:

> *Now that I know I'm going to die, it's strange, I don't feel sad. It's not happiness either. The feeling is too new and too different to have a name. It's life itself. All this time, I mistook life for something else, a kind of story, but now I see, it's not like that. It's not like that at all.*

It was as if Iris's safety depended on reading the text. An irrational feeling, but Krush did not resist it. She searched through for today's date, April 7th, but it was empty, of course. The day had hardly started. She flipped back to the previous day and found a few words circled in the middle of the page:

Heart of the City.

The day before that was missing; the page had been torn out. She looked inside the drawer and squeezed her hand into the back of the cabinet, but the lost page was not there.

'What's that?' a frightened voice called from the open door behind her.

Krush jumped. Claire came into the room. She frowned at the sight of the jewellery and make-up on the floor.

'Your stepmother's diary.' Trying to get up, Krush remembered she was pregnant. In the excitement of discovery, the weight in her body had fallen away, but it returned now redoubled.

Claire must have noticed her grimace. 'Here.' She offered her hands and pulled her up. 'Are you sure you should be–'

'I'm fine.'

'Can I see?' She reached for the diary.

Krush pulled it away. 'There's one line written for yesterday: Heart of the City. Do you know what that is?' She turned the page to let her read it.

Claire stared. 'I've no idea. Heart of the City. Is it a restaurant or something?'

'You tell me.'

Claire murmured. 'Heart of the City. What the hell?'

'Could it be a nightclub?' Krush said.

'I never heard of it.'

'Heart of the City…' Krush shook her head. 'No, it doesn't bring anything to mind. I'd better keep hold of this for now.' She longed to read the diary in private, but she would not look at it with Claire watching. She put the book in her pocket, with a sense of postponed pleasure.

'Can we go to the clinic now? I've packed a bag for Dad. Some spare clothes and stuff he might want.'

'Yeah, I guess it's time. Let's see if his memory came back.'

As they were crossing the hall, a door opened with a blast of rap music, and Ian poked his head out.

'You're going to see him?' he shouted over the racket.

'We're going to see Dad, yeah,' Claire said. 'Do you want to come?'

Ian laughed. He turned back inside but changed his mind. 'Don't believe a word he says, by the way.'

'Who?' Krush said.

'Damon Slate. Dad. Don't trust him. He's a game player. Everything's a game with him. Amnesia, that's exactly the kind of thing he'd come up with.'

'But… why would he?'

'I wouldn't know. I don't think the way he does. I don't understand anything with him. But he always has a reason, even if nobody else knows it.'

'That's not true,' Claire said.

Ian sneered at her. 'He hates my mum, you know. He screams at her all the time. You should have heard him a few days ago. "I'll kill you; I'll kill you, you cunt." Those were his exact words.'

'Is that true?' Krush asked Claire.

'I didn't hear it,' Claire said. 'And I don't believe it.'

'You didn't hear it because you didn't want to. Because you're afraid. We're living in hell here. You know what else that bastard said? He said, "I'll kill you secretly. Nobody will ever guess it was me. And after it's done, I'll laugh. I'll laugh until it hurts."'

'You're sick,' Claire said.

'No, *he* is.'

Krush raised her voice. 'Would you be willing to come down to the station and put the conversation you overheard on record?'

He shrugged. 'I don't care. I'll do whatever. Just find Mum.'

He ducked back inside and slammed the door shut. She heard a lock click on the other side.

10

The streets of the Marsh were now filled with groups of schoolkids in red uniforms who backed away from the police officers, laughing and whispering.

As they turned the corner of the street, Jeff stopped. 'There's another one.'

He pointed to a teenager in a black tracksuit seated on a bike at the entrance to an alleyway.

'Quick, before he sees us.' Eleanor started running.

'Wait!' Jeff scrambled after her.

The kid kicked off from the pavement.

'Stop!' Eleanor chased after him as the bike turned into an alley opening. 'I just want to talk to you!'

A crowd of schoolgirls broke out in screams and giggles as Eleanor ran between them.

'Stop!' she called. 'Police!'

Eleanor entered a narrow and twisting alley. Ahead of her, the bike made no sound over the stones. She looked back over her shoulder and could not see Jeff. She cursed under her breath and ran on.

The alley zigzagged between brick walls and leaning houses. She passed a few closed doors and trellises. Running around a corner, she almost collided with two schoolboys smoking.

'Excuse me.'

They were too stunned to react as she squeezed between them. Around the next corner, she reached an intersection where a narrower passage joined the first. Empty. The cyclist was gone.

'Shit.' She found a foothold in the nearest wall and hoisted herself up.

On the other side, a small backyard was deserted apart from a broken trampoline. There was nothing to see, just brick walls and dark windows. A door slammed shut somewhere nearby, echoing just around the corner along the side passage. She dropped down from the wall and followed the sound to a black, metal door set into a wall without a number or any sign. She peeped over the top. On the other side, a bike was propped against the wall of a yard filled with trodden cigarette butts. A back door into the terraced house was closed and the window next to it was dark behind dirty curtains.

'Are you sure you want to be climbing up there, love?' A voice in the alleyway gave her a shock.

'Whoa!' She slid down from the wall.

'Sorry, love.' A man walking a Rottweiler looked her up and down with amusement. 'It's just, you don't look like someone who'd want to go in that house.'

'Why? Who lives there?'

He frowned. 'Police, are you? Well, it's none of my business. I'll be on my way.'

'They're gangsters, aren't they?'

'I wouldn't know, honestly.' He turned and started in the opposite direction.

Eleanor followed him. 'Do you live around here?'

'Sort of.'

'Do you know anything about what happened in the park this morning?'

'Which park? No, I don't.'

'A man was found killed.'

'Well, there you go. That's why I don't walk Lilly in the park.'

'Can I show you a picture?'

'Persistent, aren't you?' The man glanced at the picture on her phone. 'I never saw him before in my life, and I'd like it to stay that way, thank you.' He hurried away, pulling the dog after him.

Eleanor let him go. Leaving the alley on the other side, she found Jeff hunched over, breathing deeply.

'What happened to you?' she said. 'I thought you were following.'

Between gulps of air, Jeff said, 'I… circled around… to catch them on the other side…'

'And did you see anyone come out?'

'No.'

'Alright, come on. I saw the backyard where that kid went. His bike was out there. Let's find the front of the house.'

They followed the row of terraced houses but each one looked identical, with the curtains drawn, the doors shut, and the narrow front yards filled with different coloured council bins. This was one of the poorest parts of Liverpool, invisible from the centre where giant towers glittered along the riverside. It might be nice, once in a while, to get a case in one of the posh areas, she thought.

'This could take a while,' Jeff said.

Eleanor rubbed her belly as they walked, feeling a twinge of pain that she failed to hide.

'Are you alright?' Jeff said.

'It's nothing.'

'Be careful. Could be appendicitis.'

'I don't have an appendix. They cut it out years ago.'

'Oh. Do they… can they grow back?'

'I'm fine, honestly. Maybe I should have more than just a vitamin tablet and black coffee for breakfast. Wait… I think it's this one.' She stopped outside the gate of number 11.

'Looks abandoned,' Jeff said.

He was not wrong. The windows were covered up on the inside with newspaper. The walls were coated in graffiti. The gutters had rotted and fallen inwards. And yet, snakes of overlaid bike tracks ran up and down the driveway.

'Look.' She kneeled to check the tracks. 'Some of these are recent. They go up to the front door.'

'How could anyone live in a dump like this?'

'I guess if they had nowhere else.' She went over to the front window and tried to see inside. With her nose against the glass, she peered through a gap between pages of newspaper and saw a teenager lying on a couch. At first, she thought he was asleep, but he raised one arm lazily and took a drag from a joint. 'There's a kid in there.'

'I don't like this.' Jeff hung back on the pavement.

'Come on. What are you afraid of?'

The doorbell had been torn out. She knocked on the door. No answer. She knocked again.

'Nobody's home, I guess.' Jeff still held back a few feet behind her.

Eleanor sensed a swish of movement and looked up to see the dirty curtain twitch in one of the bedroom windows.

'Somebody's watching.' She knocked again and ducked down to look through the letter box.

Inside, the hallway was filled with bikes. A staircase led upwards out of view.

'Hello!' She called through the letter box. 'Hello! Anybody home?'

Silence fell. The whole street seemed to tense, waiting for a response.

'Nothing?' Jeff said.

'They're in. They're listening, but they won't answer.' She banged again. 'Hello! Please, open up. I just want to talk.' She crossed back to the window and banged on it. 'Hello?'

When she looked through the gap between the curtains, the teenager had disappeared from the living room.

'They won't talk to us,' she said.

'That's just how it is. They don't like police.'

She took out her notepad and scribbled down a message.

> *Please call me. I'm with the police but I don't mean you any trouble. All I want is to communicate. I want to help. I think communication could benefit all of us.*

Jeff watched over her shoulder as she wrote. 'You may as well post it to Father Christmas.'

11

In silence, they entered the tunnel. It was like being swallowed. As she steered, Krush glanced at Claire, who was huddled against the window in the passenger seat, anxious and withdrawn.

'Tell me about your family.'

Claire did not lift her forehead from the windowpane. 'There's nothing to say.'

'When did your dad meet your stepmother?'

'He doesn't share his personal life with me. All I know is, they were married a year and a half ago. Before that, I had never heard of her. One day he just told me he was getting married. "Who is she?" I asked. He laughed. "Nobody like your mother." That's all he said.'

'What do you think he meant by that?'

'Nothing. He says weird things to throw people off. He thinks it makes him look smart.'

'What was your real mother like?'

'I don't remember. When I was little, Dad used to talk to me about her like she was a saint. Now he never mentions her. There are no pictures of her on the walls.'

'Do you get on with your stepmother?'

Claire kept her head turned to the window where the tunnel walls flashed past. 'I hardly know her. She's like a stranger who lives in our house.'

'Fair enough.'

In the silence, the tyres hummed over the tarmac; the tunnel vibrated around them. Slumped against the window, Claire might have been asleep.

Suddenly she looked up. 'Do you think Dad hurt her?'

Krush glanced at her. 'We have to wait for his memory to come back. Is it true what Ian said?'

'About their arguments? No. I mean, they argue a lot, but Iris is the one who starts most of them.'

'Did he really say he'd kill her?'

'You shouldn't listen to Ian. He hates everyone.'

'You and your stepbrother don't get along either?'

'I know it looks bad, we're supposed to be siblings, but it's different when you're not really related. You'd have to be a stepsister to understand.'

'My stepsister stabbed me once,' Krush said calmly. 'I could show you the scar.'

Claire gasped. 'And is she… is she in prison now?'

'She's a police detective, like me.'

'So, you're friends?'

'It's complicated.'

The tunnel walls flashed by, pale, unchanging, while Krush searched for a clue, with no idea what that might be; a woman-shaped hole; somebody's mother.

'Do you think…?' Claire let the sentence fall incomplete.

'Your stepmum hasn't been seen since yesterday. We have to consider the possibility something bad has happened. Where else could she be? Where does she work?'

'She doesn't have a job.'

'Family?'

'They're not on speaking terms. Her parents come from some dirt-poor part of the city. I don't know where. I've never met them. They weren't invited to the wedding.'

'What about friends? She must have someone.'

'I'm sure she does, but I've never met a friend of hers. I've never even heard a name of one.'

'So, what does Iris do all day? She doesn't have a job; she doesn't have friends; she doesn't speak to her family; and she doesn't spend time with you, apparently.'

'Ask the doctor. She's got mental health problems. I don't know what. I don't ask, and nobody tells. That's fine by me. I'm counting down the days until I leave home. I'm going to university next year, in Plymouth. As far away as I could get without leaving the country.'

12

Eleanor went over to forensics to check on their progress. She found Elliot in the morgue. The dead man lay on a tray beneath a sheet in the ghostly light.

'We've hardly started yet,' Elliot said. 'Dogface has nothing. No identifying marks.'

'*Dogface*?' she said with surprise.

'Sorry.' Elliot sounded embarrassed. 'That's what the guys started calling him. Don't look at me like that. It wasn't my idea. Anyway, I love dogs.'

'Can we stick to "the victim"?'

'Sure. Like I was saying, the *victim* is practically camouflaged. His clothes are as bland as you could ask for. There must be a million black tracksuits in Liverpool. We'll run the DNA and fingerprints, see if he turns up on any databases.'

'You don't sound optimistic,' Eleanor said.

'There's one thing.' He peeled back the sheet and lifted the dead man's arm by the wrist. 'See here.'

She leaned closer to see a small tattoo on the inside of the forearm. 'What is it?'

'What do you think?' There was almost a smile in the forensics chief's eye as he shone the overhanging lamp over the spot.

Eleanor saw it almost too clearly. 'It's a heart. A rough outline of a heart.'

'It's a patchy job, home-made. Could've been done in prison.'

'Odd. A heart is something for when you fall in love… not when you get jailed.'

Elliot let the dead man's arm drop. 'The harder thing to imagine is someone loving him in return. I know we're not supposed to, but, honestly, if evil had a face… I'm scared I'll see him in my dreams.'

'You'll be alright. You're a big boy.' She forced herself to look at the man's face with a feeling close to guilt. She had not called him "Dogface", but she had thought it. His contorted features were haunted. He had found no release, and no peace at the end.

She should have left then, but she hesitated.

Elliot saw her lingering by the door. 'Something else?'

'Have you heard anything about… well… about *me*?'

'What do you mean?'

'I heard there are "doubts" about me at the station.'

Elliot took a beat too long to respond. '*Doubts*? No. I haven't heard anything. Who told you that?'

'Chris Blaine from the Organised Crime Unit. He's been doing some research about me.'

'Why?'

'To find out if I'm suitable for this case, apparently.'

'What, to deal with a dead guy in a park?'

'There's more to it than that, he says.'

'Doubts about you?' A hint of some concealed emotion showed in Elliot's face as he turned away. Guilt. 'What kind of doubts?'

'I don't know. I guess they're gossiping about me in the canteen.'

He tried and did not quite manage to smile. 'Oh, I don't spend time in the canteen. I eat my pot noodles down here with the dead.'

* * *

Eleanor found herself carrying around a photograph of the nameless man. Nobody at the station was able to help. They turned away from the sight of him and shook their heads. Downstairs in the basement of HQ, Billy Walker, information officer and self-proclaimed Trotskyite, smiled ruefully.

'Looks like a dog,' he said.

'Don't you start.'

'That's all you've got, a headshot? It's not much, comrade.'

'There's also this.' She showed him a picture of the heart tattoo from the man's forearm.

'Weird.' He typed into his computer while she watched. 'Now, if it was a Liverpool FC tattoo, that would be another matter. I can also offer you a range of "Mum" tattoos. Say what you like, but criminals love their mums.'

'Let's try a different approach. Do you have anything on a gang of kids in the Marsh?'

'In the Marsh? That's Looney territory, isn't it?'

'There's a border, runs through the middle. Looneys on one side, Gilchrists on the other.'

'Alright, so which are the kids?'

'They're just teenagers on bikes, doing their own thing.'

'There's no scarcity of teens on bikes in Liverpool, God knows, but I don't know if the computer can help you.' He tutted to himself as he typed and clicked.

'Got anything?'

'In the Marsh, I've got Looneys and Gilchrists, that's all. There are no minors mentioned here for either side. But it gets complicated with kids, the law shields them from a lot of our systems.'

'So, there's nothing.'

'Don't look so glum. I'll dig. Sometimes things go missing in the databases. It's because officers get lazy, they don't fill in the boxes properly. I always tell them to be specific, but they don't listen. It's like looking for a needle in a haystack where each straw of hay is labelled differently.'

'I spoke to a local officer in the Marsh who seemed to know about them. A gang of kids, he said, riding bikes, carrying knives, selling drugs.'

'Well, you can tell your local officer he's welcome to come up here and update the database.'

'The dead man was found in King George V Park. Have you got anything on that?'

'King George V Park…' Walker clicked and grinned. 'Now we're talking. Four unsolved murders. A lovely place for a picnic.'

'Can you print those for me?'

'Are you sure you want to touch them?'

'What do you mean?'

'Four unsolved cases? Nobody needs that on their plate. I'd leave this park well alone, comrade.'

'Print everything you've got. And while you're at it, do you have anything for 11 Woodpecker Lane?'

'Pretty address. Sounds suspicious.' He typed into his computer. 'What happened there? Actually, don't tell me. I don't want to know. Let me imagine they're all happy and in love.'

'It's near the murder site. I think the gang of kids lives there, or at least they might use it as a base.'

Walker muttered to himself. 'It comes up as unoccupied. No owner listed. Nobody's paying any bills. Is it derelict?'

'There were people inside.'

'And what, you just walked up and knocked on the door?'

'I just walked up and knocked on the door. But nobody answered. Nobody answered at the neighbours' either.'

'Don't take it personally, but sounds like they don't want to talk to you. Was there anything else?'

'No. Well… maybe. Do you spend a lot of time talking to others in the canteen?'

'Erm, talking to people, not so much. I'm more of a computer guy.' He stared at the screen. Either he was avoiding eye contact with her, or he really was just a computer guy.

'Did you ever hear of any rumours about me?' she said.

'What kind of rumours?'

'I don't know. Dubious ones, I guess.'

'Office gossip? I don't get involved with that. Pointless chitchat at work, it only distracts the proletariat from gaining authentic class consciousness.'

'Right. Well, do me a favour… if you ever hear anything, let me know.'

'Will do.' He nodded. 'And if you hear anything about me, please, don't tell me. I'd rather not know.'

13

Slate's private clinic was just outside the city centre, housed in an old Catholic convent behind ivy-covered walls. A statue of the Virgin Mary still stood out front. Mann was seated in the waiting room with his eyes closed.

Claire ran towards him. 'Is Dad OK?'

'Oh, you're here?' The lawyer did not seem happy to see her. 'Yes, don't worry. He's having a heart scan now, but it's just a precaution. He'll be out in a minute. How did you…?' He stood up, seeing Krush. 'Detective. You brought my client's daughter. I'm not sure that was the wisest move.'

'Has Mr Slate's memory returned?'

'In part. He's stopped saying "Where am I?" every two minutes, thank God, but he's still shaky, and he can't remember anything from today or yesterday.'

'But is he alright?' Claire said. 'Can he come home?'

Mann patted her on the shoulder. 'Don't worry. The doctors here are the best.'

'Can we speak in private?' Krush said.

They left Claire in the waiting room and went out into a pretty smoking area, lined with saplings that had just broken into blossom. A statue of Jesus gazed heavenwards between two puddles.

'What did you find at Mr Slate's home?' Mann's voice was strained. His eyes fixed on the statue.

'Nothing. Well, something, maybe. Do you know what "Heart of the City" refers to?'

'Heart of the City? What is that?'

'I don't know. A restaurant maybe, or a bar.'

'I don't get out much. In this job, work never ends.'

'It was written in Iris's diary yesterday. My guess is, it's someplace she was going before she disappeared.'

'Her diary?' Something showed in the man's red face. 'I never knew…'

'Why should you?'

His eyes wandered over her jacket as if seeking the diary. 'What else is written in there?'

'I haven't had time to read it yet.'

Seeing him hesitate, she pushed. 'I need you to be totally honest with me. What's going on between your client and his wife?'

'I'm not a marriage counsellor.'

'They've been having difficulties, then?'

He tried to laugh, but the sound was strangled. 'All marriages are hard work.'

'I spoke to Mr Slate's stepson – Ian. He overhead his parents arguing recently. He said your client threatened to kill his wife.'

'Couples have arguments. Sometimes they say things they don't mean. Trust me, in my line of work, I've seen some big divorce cases. The things husbands and wives say to each other…'

'Still, he threatened to kill her, and now she's missing.'

'If my client said something stupid like that, it's because he lost his temper. He's been under a lot of stress. That's why his memory broke down. He's been negotiating a huge property deal lately. There's an amount of money on the table you wouldn't believe. It's a project that could transform the city. The mayor is involved. My client's a workaholic. He has a lot of weight on his shoulders.'

'I don't care about that. There's a missing woman. If your client can't explain where his wife is, I'm going to have to escalate this to a missing person case. Your client will be a prime suspect.'

'Hold on a minute,' Mann stammered. 'You're overreacting. You heard what your boss said. The mayor is keeping a close eye on things. Let's dampen down the rhetoric a little.'

'Give me one reason why Iris Slate would be lost from sight, and not answering her phone.'

Mann lowered his voice, even though they were alone. 'This is a secret, alright? My client is a very high-profile man. He has paparazzi following him around everywhere.'

'I'm a police detective, I don't have to make promises. You're obligated to tell me what you know.'

He sighed. 'Not very friendly, are you?'

'I'm not paid to be friendly. I'm paid to solve crimes.'

'But what crime has been committed?'

'That's what I'm going to find out and, believe me, I always find out everything.'

'I know you do. You forget, I know who you are, Detective Krush. It's my job to know.'

'Tell me then. Damon was arguing with his wife. Maybe one of them had an affair? Maybe both…?'

'You're not as smart as you think.' The lawyer grinned.

'Something else?' she said. 'What then?'

'My client's wife has psychological problems. You'd have to speak with the doctor here. She's got a personality disorder.'

'What kind?'

'Honestly, it's none of my business, and I don't care. The only reason I mention it, is she disappears sometimes. Nobody knows where she goes. Just takes off by herself. Won't answer the phone. She'll be gone for a week, but she always comes back. Afterwards, she never reveals where she's been.'

'And you never tried to find out?'

'I'm a busy man. I work so many hours in this job, I had to sign a contract to waive my human rights. I have so much responsibility, I can't sleep at night. You realize, if I make a mistake in my work, it can cost a client millions. That isn't a boast.'

'Alright. How did you find out about Iris's personality disorder?'

'Mr Slate told me, in confidence.'

'Why?'

'He wanted my opinion, from a legal point of view.' With a shake of the head, as if with regret, Mann tilted his face upwards into the air, where the rain had released tints of grass, leaves, and petals. 'My client wanted to know if he could divorce his wife on psychological grounds.'

'If he could divorce her for having a personality disorder?'

'Exactly. I told him, in my opinion, it probably was not sufficient legal grounds for a separation. But I promised to look into all the options.'

'Couldn't he just divorce her because he didn't like her anymore?'

'Of course, but then Iris would receive half his fortune and empire. Iris has no money of her own. She never did. She—' He stopped with a sound like a choke. He must have suddenly realized that, caught up in the legal details that preoccupied him, he had delivered a motive for murder.

Krush nodded. 'If what you're telling me is true, I hope for your client's sake his wife turns up.'

'Shit,' Mann said. His right hand searched fretfully in his jacket pocket but did not find anything. 'He couldn't have killed her. I'm certain of it.'

'How much money would he stand to lose in a divorce?'

'Oh… tens of millions. I'm not sure exactly.'

The words were absurd out here among the saplings, beneath a wall coated in ivy.

'But he didn't kill her,' Mann spat out. 'It doesn't make sense. I'd found a loophole in case of divorce. Mrs Slate and her family never told my client about her mental health problems before the marriage, even though they knew about them. They'd even consulted with doctors previously. That was a deliberate concealment. It makes the marriage contract null.'

'Really?'

'Should anyone present know of any reason that this couple should not be joined in holy matrimony, speak now or forever hold their peace,' Mann quoted with mock solemnity.

'But does that include a personality disorder? If you love somebody, doesn't love surpass mental health problems? If Damon really loved her, he would accept everything about her, wouldn't he? If not, he would be the one who broke the vow, because his love wasn't complete in the first place.'

'Well, that's the question, isn't it? How is love defined? It cuts two ways: if Iris really loved Damon, wouldn't she have made sure to explain her condition before the ceremony? It would be my job to win that argument.'

'You believe you would win such a divorce hearing?'

'You should know, Detective, I've never lost a case.'

A green trace in the breeze caught her. For a moment, she was thrown. In this ivy-covered space — a tiny sanctuary in the grey, relentless city — an attempt had been made to define love.

'Neither have I,' she said.

The door behind them opened, and a nurse looked out. 'The doctor asked for you. The patient is ready to go home.'

14

Eleanor read through the files. Four killings in the park over the last seven years, all following the same pattern. The victim was always a man, and in each case he was identified as a small-time drug dealer. Their throats were cut, and they were dumped on the edge of the park. No suspects had ever been arrested. Only one detail in her case was different to the others: the red shoe.

She took the lift up to the top floor at HQ, the Organised Crime Unit.

Detective Sergeant Blaine was studying a map of the city pinned to the wall behind his desk.

'Sorry to intrude,' she said from the doorway.

'Eleanor. I was wondering if I'd see you again.'

'It's about the guy in the park.'

'Of course.' He left the map and sat down on the other side of the desk. His snowy quiff had wilted since the morning. 'You've decided to cooperate with us?'

'I wanted to ask you a few questions.'

He smiled to reveal a set of gleaming, fake teeth. 'Fire away.'

'Our dead man has a heart tattoo on his wrist. Does that fit with any of the gang insignia you know of?'

'A heart. Can't say I ever heard of that. The Looneys usually have a naked woman tattooed somewhere on their bodies. The woman represents Liverpool, supposedly. They believe the city belongs to them. She's naked because they take whatever they want.'

'And the Gilchrists?'

'They're more old-fashioned. They have a tattoo of a crucifix with a snake. Because God loves the wicked.'

'Does he?'

'Some of these killers get spiritual in prison. The chaplains have an unfortunate tendency to point out certain lines in the Bible that, if twisted in the right way, might apply to them.'

'Like what?'

'Like the Parable of the Prodigal Son.'

'The Gilchrists see themselves as prodigal sons?'

'Or perhaps it's just because they have the word "Christ" in their name. It doesn't matter. The tattoos could be anything, it's just a way of showing membership in the group.'

'Our dead man doesn't have a naked woman or a crucifix.'

'That's good news for us. I've never heard of the heart tattoo with any of the gangs, but it could be a new thing. Trends change, and I'm getting old, as you can see.'

Eleanor flipped the pages of her notepad. 'I was told by a local officer in the Marsh, there's another gang. Not Looneys, and not Gilchrists. A group of kids. They ride around on bikes. They keep to themselves. Nobody even has a name for them.'

Blaine frowned. 'It seems unlikely.'

'Why?'

'The Looneys and the Gilchrists are powerful. They could easily deal with a gang of kids. It's not like that for us. The police would have difficulty, all the laws protecting minors from prosecution, but the Looneys, they wouldn't care about that.'

'Still, this local officer seemed to know what he was talking about. He grew up there, he knows everyone.'

'What's his name?'

'Derrick Jeffers, also known as Jeff, but he's low down in the pecking order, you wouldn't know him.'

'Indeed.' Blaine made a note.

'Do you think he might know something the Organised Crime Unit missed?'

'Maybe, or maybe not.' The detective sergeant stood up, as if to end the conversation.

'There's one more thing,' Eleanor said. 'The dead man was holding a red shoe in his hand. A woman's high-heeled shoe.'

Blaine sat back down. For a moment, he was silent. He stroked his quiff. 'A red shoe?'

'A single red shoe.'

'And has the other shoe been found?'

'Not yet.'

Blaine looked confused, almost frightened. He got up and went over to a filing cabinet. 'I've heard of sliced ears, cut eyebrows, pulled teeth, dog paws – all kinds of signatures. But… a woman's shoe?'

'A red, high-heeled shoe.'

He froze at the open filing cabinet. 'One thing you have to understand about the gangs is, they tend to leave women out of it. At least on a visible, public level. It's not that they're chivalrous, far from it, but the things that happen with women in that world are kept hidden. Don't ask me why. That's a question for psychologists. When they leave dead bodies out to be found, it's men. If a woman dies, they hide her, like they're ashamed.'

'So… maybe this isn't a gang killing?'

'The location fits, and the man's clothing.' He pulled out a few dossiers and carried them back to the table. 'Boundaries are shifting. The old ways of doing things are breaking down. God help us if…'

'If what?'

'If women aren't out of bounds… If innocent civilians are part of the game now.'

'You keep tabs underground, don't you? You're supposed to know what's going on.'

'The city is in flux. Jesus. A red shoe.'

'A red shoe.'

'Alright, Detective. I'll tell you what I'll do. I'll put you in touch with our top people on the ground. Lisa

Wainwright, she's the expert on the Looneys. She's been overseeing a long-term surveillance operation. Then there's Tommy Presley. He's our undercover agent in the Gilchrists. He's on sabbatical now. In fact, you should know, there are some fears about him. He may have got in over his head. Still, he knows more about that side of the border than anyone else, and he might just know something about your red shoe.'

'That's great.' She scribbled the names down.

'Don't thank me yet. Be careful, Detective. The city is on edge. Violence is ready to break out. Nobody knows what's going to happen.'

'You really don't know anything? You're the boss, aren't you?'

'The boss? I'm like the loveable grandad up here; the kids come to visit once a year. Other than that, they don't tell me anything. All I can tell you is, there are always alliances. That's how Liverpool works. Local politicians, criminals, construction deals, the police. It's how we get things done in this city.'

'All I want to do is to solve this case,' she said.

'Hold on to that. Your honesty might be what saves you in the end. Remember: stay out of the gangs' politics. Don't intervene. Don't get involved. Whatever you discover, whatever you see. *Never take sides.*'

15

Damon Slate was transformed. Seated next to his daughter in the waiting room, he smiled, with one leg crossed over the other, at ease in his suit that now fit him perfectly. His shirt was smoothed down and his tie had reappeared around his neck from somewhere.

'Are you cleared to go home?' Mann hurried towards them, followed by Krush.

'Yes, thank God,' Slate said. 'What a day.' In contrast to his lawyer, he seemed unconcerned.

'Has your memory returned?' Krush said.

'Have we met?'

It was almost funny, but he did not smile.

'That's Detective Krush,' Claire said. 'She's helping us. She's the one who drove me here.'

'Well then, you're in my gratitude.' He stood up and offered his hand.

When she shook it, it was firm, totally unlike the lost, tearful man of the morning.

'The doctors have given the all-clear?' Mann said.

'Yes, yes, don't worry. My blood pressure's too high, but what else is new? They checked my heart, my brain, everything. It's all OK. I just need to destress a little. Less work, more family time.' He put an arm around Claire and hugged her playfully.

'Well then, shall we go?' Mann picked up the bag Claire had brought. 'I'm parked outside.'

'Wait,' Krush said. 'Mr Slate, I need to have a chat with you before you leave. You seem much better now. Have you recovered your memory?'

He smiled and shrugged. 'It's the strangest feeling. Today and yesterday are like a black hole. Everything before that is fine, but... in between... nothing.'

'Nothing at all? Not even a sliver?'

He closed his eyes. 'I remember being in the dark.'

'You remember the tunnel?'

'Tunnel?' He opened his eyes. 'What tunnel?'

'Leave it,' Mann said. 'This isn't the time. We can figure out the past after my client has had a chance to rest.'

'I was in a tunnel...? I remember... what? Just a fragment, it might have been a dream. I remember reaching towards a web of light.'

'Anything else?' Krush scribbled the words down in her notepad.

'Please, Detective,' Mann intervened. 'My client has suffered a horrible experience. He needs to go home and rest. Can't these questions wait for another time?'

Ignoring him, she faced Slate. 'It's about your wife. Nobody knows where she is.'

'Iris?'

'You were holding her shoe when you came out of the tunnel.'

'I was?' His eyes phased out, looking into memory. 'Which shoe? Can you show me?'

'It's a red, high-heeled shoe.'

'Doesn't ring any bells. Are you sure it was hers? That's not her style.'

'She's wearing them in the portrait on your living room wall.'

'Oh. *Those* shoes.'

'Haven't you watched the video?' Krush said.

'What video?' Nervousness crept into his polished features.

'Haven't they shown you?'

'I didn't want to upset him,' Claire said.

'Not now,' Mann said. 'This isn't the right time. We don't want to risk a relapse.'

'But… hold on a moment.' Slate's face changed. 'Has something happened to Iris? Nobody told me anything. Where is she? Why isn't she here?'

'It's alright, don't panic.' Mann gave him an unconvincing pat on the shoulder. 'We're trying to find her. She's not at home and she's not answering the phone. But it's not been long. There's no reason to worry.'

Slate stared past him, his eyes fixing on Krush as if he was starting to recognize her. 'You said I was carrying a shoe. What about the other one?'

'We're looking for it.'

His panic appeared genuine. She had interviewed frightened relatives over the years, and they usually reacted in just this way, throwing out the first questions that came to mind. Hopeless, meaningless questions that they clung to, as if the answer was the most important thing in the world.

'You had an argument the other day with your wife,' she said.

'I did? I don't remember.'

Ian's warning about his stepdad flashed in her mind. She tried to read the truth in his face. Reading other people's emotions had never been her forte; that was more her half-sister's skillset. But Eleanor was not here.

'Mr Slate, what do you remember of last night? You were driving somewhere with your wife. Where were you going?'

'I'm sorry. It's all gone. It's like yesterday never existed.' He looked away. A sign of deception. She knew enough of body language to recognize that one.

'I found your wife's diary,' she said.

Silence. Perhaps he was trying to formulate a lie, or perhaps he was simply as confused as she was.

'I never knew she kept one.'

'It seems you don't know your wife very well. There's an entry for yesterday. It just says, "Heart of the City". Do you know what that means?'

Slate looked at Mann. Something was communicated wordlessly between them. What was it?

'I have no idea.' His voice faltered. 'Is it a restaurant?'

'Perhaps. I thought it might be where you were driving to last night. Do you remember anything about where you were going?'

He smiled thinly, his self-control returning. 'A restaurant. You're probably right. My wife liked to eat at fancy restaurants. I never know the names of any of them. I'm not a food person. She was always up to date with the newest places.'

Krush tensed. 'Why do you describe her in the past tense?'

'Pardon me?'

'You said, she *was* always up to date.'

'Did I?'

'Yes.'

'But… I thought you said… didn't you tell me she was…?'

'I didn't tell you anything. I only asked if you could remember where you were driving last night.'

'Last night? I was driving?'

'Your daughter says you left the house with your wife in the car.'

'Well then, it must be true. Why would Claire lie? I'm sorry, Detective, could these questions wait for another time? I'm feeling woozy.'

'Just one more. Which car did you leave in?'

He smiled sadly. 'I have lots of cars.'

'Alright, which car would you have driven yesterday, when you left home?'

'Probably the white Mercedes. It has tinted windows. I use it to get around town.'

'License plate?'

'DAZZ 79.' He looked embarrassed, or perhaps that was a trick he used to ingratiate himself, masking his vanity.

'Alright.' Mann stepped in between Krush and Slate. 'My patient is clearly confused. He's still suffering from the effects of whatever happened to him. I'm ending this conversation now. If you want to speak to us again, please schedule a meeting.'

Krush ignored him. Holding Slate's eye over the lawyer's shoulder, she said, 'There isn't time for legal niceties. Your wife is missing. We need to find her.'

'My wife is *missing?*'

'No, not officially,' Mann said. 'We haven't been able to track her down today, but that's normal. She's just taken off by herself somewhere, as she does from time to time.'

'That's all you have to say?' Krush persisted. 'Aren't you concerned about her?'

Slate smiled sadly. 'My wife, she, err, well… we've been estranged lately. She often takes off, and then I won't see her for a while. Sometimes days, sometimes weeks. She comes back when she runs out of money.'

'And where does she go?'

'I don't ask. I guess she spends time with her family, but I have no contact with them. They live on the other side of Liverpool, and they keep to themselves. I'm just "the rich bastard" to them. That's what they write when they send a Christmas card.'

'This conversation is over,' Mann said. 'I'm taking my client home now.'

'What about your car?' Krush said. 'Don't you want to find it?'

'What car?' Slate said.

Mann ushered him forward, in a rush to get out of there.

Krush followed them. 'The car you went out in last night. Where is it?'

'I don't know where I put it,' Slate said.

Mann kept on pushing him forwards. 'My client has many cars and many properties around the city. The car will turn up in one of his parking spaces.'

'Just wait a minute,' Krush said.

But Slate, his daughter, and his lawyer, walked away from her towards the exit. She followed with a sense of failure.

In the doorway, Slate stopped and turned back. He stared at her. 'We've met before, haven't we?'

'Yes, I interviewed you earlier, at the hospital.'

'No, before that. It was somewhere else we met. I recognize your face. Where was that?' His lazy eyes wandered over her body and stopped at the pregnant belly.

Yes. Now that he was self-possessed, his hair smoothed down, and his eyes sharpened with intelligence, she knew they had met before, but she could not think where it was either.

'Come on.' Mann grabbed his client's shoulder and pulled him away. 'Goodbye, Detective.'

'I'll see you again,' she called after them. 'This isn't finished.'

16

Dr David Chen's office was bright, with white walls and wide windows, one of those few places in Liverpool where she might allow herself to relax. The only catch was a tray of syringes set to one side. She hated syringes.

Chen examined her head to foot as she entered. He smiled. 'But, Detective… you're pregnant. Sit down, sit down. Hold on.' He rubbed the seat with a disinfectant wipe. 'Here, please.'

'Thank you.' Krush sat down with relief.

'What are you, five months along?'

'Something like that.'

'That's quite a bump.'

'The father was a tall, broad man. Genetics is a bitch.'

'Can't you take maternity leave?'

'Don't worry, they're taking care of me. This is just a nice, easy case. I'm looking after a celebrity.'

'I look after a few celebrities myself. Let me tell you, they're not easy. Can I?' He reached out a tentative hand over her belly.

'Err, OK.'

He gently felt the bump. 'Remarkable, yes, remarkable.'

She was glad when he sat back behind his desk.

'Doctor, I wanted to talk to you about your patient, Damon Slate.'

'Oh.' The smile disappeared from his face. In truth, it had never seemed entirely genuine.

'What can you tell me about Mr Slate's amnesia?'

'You mean, what caused it? Probably a shock. His blood pressure was very high. We've lowered it now. The pressure alone might have been enough to make the brain shut down.'

'What caused it to spike?'

'Probably an issue with his medication. He takes blood pressure tablets. He might have gotten mixed up and taken too many, or not enough. Or it's possible we've got the dosage wrong. It happens sometimes. I've told him to double the dose for a week and we'll see what happens.'

'Is it possible his symptoms could be faked?'

'You think he's pretending?'

Chen looked so upset, Krush almost regretted the question. 'I just need to make sure,' she said.

'But… why would he pretend?'

'Let's say, to cover up a crime.'

'What crime?'

'It's my job to ask the questions, Dr Chen. If you could please just answer them.'

The doctor leaned back in his chair and frowned. 'Could somebody fake amnesia symptoms? Maybe. But my client's blood pressure really was high. Under those conditions, it would be difficult to keep up the act.'

'Or… perhaps it would help. If he really was confused and spaced out, he just had to lean into the feeling – play dumb, stay quiet.'

Chen considered this. 'But why would he lie? Sorry. You told me not to ask questions, didn't you? Oh, there's another one.'

Krush flipped a page in her notebook. 'You also treat your patient's wife, Iris Slate?'

'That's correct.'

'What do you treat her for?'

He hesitated. 'I have a confidentiality agreement with the Slates. They don't want certain details to enter the public domain.'

'I won't keep a record of this conversation, and I won't divulge its content to anyone. I'm just to trying to find Iris, that's all. Currently, nobody knows where she is.'

'That happens. She takes off and disappears. It was why Damon brought her here in the first place. She'd been on antidepressants from the NHS for years, but he wanted me to take a deeper look at her.'

'And what did you find?'

'Nothing. I'm not a psychologist. But OK, Damon, I mean Mr Slate, he doesn't believe in psychologists. I agreed to help. We tested all Iris's organs and functions, her blood, brain, you name it. We couldn't find a single thing wrong. She believes she suffers from bipolar disorder. An NHS doctor diagnosed her years ago. But we're not in a position to verify that here. It's not a condition we treat.'

'Did Iris come here often?'

'Every month or so, but in the end, after we'd tested everything, she just came to chat. She found it peaceful here. I can understand that. With the trees and the statues of the Virgin. She's Catholic, you know. I'd measure her vitals and tell her they were all fine. She'd tell me about her difficulties. I told her she should speak to someone more experienced with mental health issues, but she didn't want to. She said she liked chatting to me.'

'Her "difficulties". What were those?'

'Her moods. Her depression. Her fears.'

'Fears of what?'

'That she might throw herself out of the window one afternoon.'

'Do you know about any marital issues between the Slates?'

'That's not my area. I just check their bodies, which are both excellent specimens, I can tell you. If Mr Slate would only work a little less and pay more attention to his health, he has the raw materials of an athlete.'

Krush took out Iris's diary. 'I found something. It seems Iris was keeping a journal. There are some strange things in here. I don't know what to make of it.'

'A diary.' Chen stared at the book in her hand. 'Ah, yes. That was actually my idea. I suggested she keep a diary to get her feelings down on paper. A way of coping, you know? Can I ask… what does it say?'

'I haven't had a chance to read it yet. I just glanced through. There are several passages that talk about killing.' She opened the diary and flicked through the pages. 'How about this one? Does this chime with anything she used to say when she came to talk to you?'

She watched his eyes move over the page behind his glasses as he read aloud:

> *Under the river. The only place I ever managed to just feel nothing at all.*

'Do you know what that means?'

'Yes, she did used to talk like that. "Under the river." I believe that's her way of describing a depressive episode.'

'A depressive episode… I guess that makes sense.'

The doctor took off his glasses and rubbed his eyes. He looked different without them, no longer calm and reassuring. 'Can I?' He flipped back through the pages. 'You see here. She writes, "Shush! Quiet please!" That's the obsessive thoughts. She was afraid to go near a window in case she might suddenly throw herself out. She couldn't get those images out of her mind. She wanted to silence them. You can imagine.'

Shush! Quiet please! Yes, Krush could imagine.

She took back the diary. 'Another thing she mentioned – this was on the day she disappeared – is "Heart of the City". Do you know what that means?'

'I fear the patient may have been talking about herself. Iris Slate was prone to narcissism.'

'*Was* prone?'

Chen hesitated. 'Excuse me. *Is* prone. You're right, we shouldn't assume the worst.'

'She saw herself as the heart of the city?'

'As I say, I'm not a psychologist. I wish I could be of more assistance, but, as you can see, I'm just a medical doctor.'

'She talks about a "grey hood". Does that ring any bells?'

'Not even one, but it sounds like depression again, doesn't it? That's how it is, they say. I've never been depressed myself, but I can imagine it's like a hood coming down over your head.'

'There's a page missing here. You can see where it was torn out. Did Iris ever mention anything about that?'

'No, and I doubt it would make any difference. It's impossible to interpret the meanderings of a depressed mind. All of that stuff is too personal to the patient. You'll lose yourself if you try to find her in there.'

17

Closeted in her office, Krush read through the diary again.

> *How far does it reach? They have people in the police, he says.*

She put the diary down with a sense of dread, as if she was being watched. Time to stop looking in its pages; she had to find Iris in the real world. But, searching in the databases and online, no traces could be found. No criminal record came up. A wider search failed to turn up a driver's licence or a National Insurance number. She seemed to have no bureaucratic presence at all. No tax records, no hospital reports, nothing. She did not even seem to have a social media account. It was as if Iris did not exist, and yet the portrait on the wall of her living room proved she did. Her rictus smile even hinted at a certain pain of existence.

Krush was tempted to let the case drop. It seemed nobody else was worried about Iris, and the missing woman herself had taken no trouble to be discovered.

She searched online again for "Heart of the City, Liverpool", but, just like before, this brought back nothing useful. The terms were too general. There did not appear to be a restaurant or a bar of that name. If there was, they did not have a website. Perhaps they had just opened.

* * *

Krush found the chief inspector in her office doing yoga on a mat. Carver had taken off her jacket and rolled up her shirtsleeves, and wore a sweatband over her hair.

'I see you're busy,' Krush said.

Carver did not get up from the mat, where she was sweating in a downward dog position. 'It's alright. I can talk while I stretch. Come in. Shut the door behind you. How are things with our celebrity amnesiac?'

'He's much better, although he claims he still doesn't remember what happened this morning.'

'What do you mean, "claims"? You don't believe him?'

'There's something off about it all.' She watched with amusement as the chief raised her arms heavenward and lowered them slowly.

For a moment, lost in internal meditation, or whatever was happening on the mat, the chief seemed to forget there was anybody else in the room. She closed her eyes, took a deep breath and slowly exhaled.

Krush cleared her throat and continued. 'While I was at Slate's house, his stepson told me not to trust him.'

'That's kids for you. I don't want to know what mine say about me.' Carver shifted upright on the mat. 'Anyway, thanks for helping out. The mayor will be glad to hear his friend is alright. Let's close the case on this one. Did you ever try yoga, Krush?'

'Yeah. I hated it.'

'Give it another chance. At the new gym I've joined, they offer special classes for pregnant women. It could be valuable. Even if you're not feeling spry, you can work on your breathing.'

It seemed the boss didn't want to talk about the Slate case except to shut it down.

But Krush was insistent. 'Listen, Slate's wife still hasn't shown up,' she said. 'She's not at home and she's not answering the phone.'

'Has she been reported missing?' Carver entered a new position. With her legs crossed, she twisted her back and head to the left until she was no longer looking at the detective.

'No,' Krush said. 'Her husband doesn't seem to care. He says she often takes off by herself for days at a time. I spoke to her doctor, and he confirmed it. She has mental health problems.'

'Well, there you go. Until she's reported missing, technically speaking, she isn't missing.'

'But… Slate was holding her shoe when he came out of the tunnel.'

'Do we even know it's her shoe?' Carver grunted as she twisted around to face the opposite direction.

'Not for certain.'

'Did you look for the other one while you were at the house?'

'Yeah. It's not there. But there's a portrait on the wall of the couple. She's wearing a shoe that looks just like it.'

'In a *painting*?'

'It's not an impressionist work.'

'Did Slate recognize it as his wife's shoe?'

'No, but he didn't say it wasn't hers either. He doesn't seem to know his wife terribly well.'

Carver untwisted. She sat facing forward, palms together, eyes closed. 'Here's a theory. Damon Slate went out last night and got involved in some hedonistic activity. Alcohol, drugs, I don't know. At some point in the early hours, he ended up with a prostitute. There was an argument, she threw him out. He wound up wandering around the city, wasted, with her shoe in his hand. It does sort of look like a whore's shoe, if you ask me.'

'I'm worried about Iris. If something's happened to her, we need to act now, before the trail goes cold.'

Carver did not open her eyes. 'What do you want from me?'

'I want to escalate this to a missing person case.'

'No, Krush. She's not missing until someone misses her.'

'Then let me look in the tunnel. We need to shut it down, get all the traffic out, and go through it carefully.'

Now Carver did open her eyes. Anger showed in her face, although she somehow kept her body motionless, hands still pressed together.

'No chance, Krush,' she said. 'I'm not shutting that tunnel down. The city would turn into one giant traffic jam.'

'But–'

'I told you already. If you want to check in the tunnel, wait until it closes at midnight. They already sent over the CCTV footage, didn't they?'

'Yeah.'

'And?'

'Nothing.'

'Like I said. If there was a woman lost in the tunnel, they would've spotted her by now.'

'Is it because of the mayor's phone call you're refusing to take this seriously?'

'Careful, Krush. Those words could be misconstrued. If you've nothing else to demand, please get on with your work.'

It was amazing how Carver stayed perfectly still on the mat while irritation tensed her face. There was no point arguing. Krush walked out and closed the door behind her. The boss had to be under Slate's influence. Could he really have such power?

* * *

Leaving HQ, Krush found three missed calls from her father. She swore under her breath and put the phone away, but before she could walk across the car park, it rang again. He would never leave her in peace. Since the pregnancy had developed, he was constantly hovering around, badgering her.

She accepted the call with a sigh. 'Yes?'

'Where are you?' Neil said.

'I'm just leaving work.'

'You were supposed to finish an hour ago.'

'Yeah, well, that's what this job is like.'

'I'm outside your flat.'

'Why?'

'I brought some food for you.'

'Dad, I don't need you to cook for me. I've got a top-of-the-range kitchen… and a microwave.'

'I know you don't want anyone's support, but you're pregnant, and you're alone. You have to learn to accept help. Where are you now, at the station? Wait there. I'll come and give you a lift home.'

'Don't bother. It's a short walk and I enjoy it.'

'I'm on my way now. Stay where you are.' He hung up.

Krush stared at the phone in her hand and felt an unexpected burst of anger towards Eleanor. Her half-sister was the one with all the problems, and yet Dad never bothered about Eleanor, he only hassled Krush, who had never needed help, and never wanted it.

Five minutes later, the car pulled up. Neil lowered the window. 'Get in.'

With a feeling of futility, she went around the other side of the car, while her father fiddled with the passenger seat, moving it backwards.

'Plenty of space,' he said.

'I would've had the abortion if I knew you were going to micromanage this whole process.' She climbed in beside him.

'I know, you don't like it when people care about you.'

'This isn't care, it's control.'

Neil pulled out from the kerb. 'If you would just move into the house, I wouldn't have to worry about you so much. You're on your own. Most people, when they're going to have a child, they have a support network. They have a partner at least.'

'I feel sorry for those people. They spend their lives surrounded by busybodies.'

'You don't have a husband. You don't even have a mother. Beth, If I don't help you, who will?'

'Nobody, with any luck.'

He scowled. 'You don't mean that. One of these days you're going to be stuck. You'll be alone, and you'll wish you had someone there who cared about you.' He shook his head. 'I'm worried about you. What would happen if the baby came early, and you were stuck on your own?'

'That's what phones are for.'

'What if your phone runs out of battery?'

'It won't.'

'Would it really be so unbearable to move into the house with me until the baby is born? I've done your old room up. Everything's taken care of. I know you like your solitude, but there's plenty of space, I wouldn't get in your way.'

'I like my flat, alright? I've got it set up the way I want it.'

They drove on in silence for a minute, and she hoped this conversation, which they had already argued to a truce several times before, was finally over, but as Neil pulled up outside the tower block where Krush lived, he cleared his throat again. 'It's because of Eleanor, isn't it?'

'What?'

'That's why you won't move back into your old room. It's because Eleanor is staying with me at the moment.'

'That's irrelevant.'

'I'll tell her to move out. She doesn't need it like you do. She's not pregnant. She can get her own place. When she first wanted to come home, I thought it would be just for a few days while she got back on her feet, but it's been months. I don't understand it. What's wrong with her?'

Krush laughed. 'Eleanor's just Eleanor, that's all. I gave up trying to make sense of her years ago.'

'Her friend the psychiatrist is staying with us now.'

'What?'

'Raymond. She says he's a psychiatrist, but I never saw any proof of it.'

'Raymond *Stray*? Raymond Stray is staying in your house?'

Stray, of course. A former psychiatrist who had been living rough and using heroin since his licence was revoked. The years on the streets had not diminished his abilities to manipulate others. Eleanor was the perfect target; she had always been emotionally weak.

'On the couch,' Neil said. 'It was only supposed to be for one night, Eleanor promised, but he's been there a week now. He's odd. It puts me on edge, having him around. He wears an eyepatch. It's unnerving. On the couch, Eleanor said, but he's living in the spare room already.'

Krush climbed out of the car. 'Don't worry. From what I know, Stray never stays anywhere very long. He's a wanderer on this planet.'

'He's *homeless*, you mean. What's Eleanor doing bringing homeless people to live with us? I know she means well, but it's my house. Maybe you could talk to her. You're her sister; she's always admired you.'

'Thanks for the lift.' Krush put the food parcel in her bag without looking at it. The thought of eating anything made her feel nauseous.

'Don't forget the pregnancy class tonight,' Neil called through the open door. 'I told Eileen you'll be there.'

'I can't. I'm working on a new case.'

'In your state?' He gestured towards her belly. 'What's wrong with this city? You should be taking it easy. Go to the class. Eileen will be waiting for you. I told her you'd be there.'

Krush groaned. Eileen was her father's neighbour, a New Age chatterbox and alternative medicine nutjob. Was that crazy woman fucking her dad? Some things were best not thought about.

'I might show my face,' she said.

18

In the living room, Eleanor lay on the couch with her eyes half closed. To one side, Raymond Stray hunched in the armchair with his fingertips joined together.

'These stomach pains of yours are interesting,' he said.

'I don't want to talk about that.'

'Why not?'

'I thought the purpose of these sessions was to work on psychology, not physiology.'

'It's all connected.'

'I've got the head of the Organised Crime Unit telling me there are doubts about me at the station, and you want to talk about stomach cramps.'

'OK. Why do you think your colleagues have these "doubts"?'

'I don't spend time with any of them outside work. How could I? They never invite me.'

'Maybe *you* should invite them?'

'Also, there's a formerly homeless psychiatrist living here, giving me therapy sessions instead of rent.'

'I don't see why that should matter to anyone.'

'It doesn't. I just… A new murder case landed on my desk. This dead guy, he's ugly. They're calling him Dogface in forensics. I don't know… It's like everyone's given up on him already. Nobody is bothered to even try and solve his murder. There's something so lonely about him.'

'And that resonated with you?'

'I don't know. Am I going crazy? Tell me, honestly.'

He paused. 'Last time, we agreed you needed to work on communication with your sister.'

'Yeah, well, it's not easy. She's hardly around the station. She keeps away. If she sees me, she heads in the opposite direction. If I approach, she runs off. If I try and say something, she puts her phone to her ear and pretends to be in the middle of a conversation. Or maybe it's a real conversation and I'm just being paranoid. The upshot is, she's too busy for me. She's too busy being the best mind on the force.'

'The "best mind", why?'

'You know this rich guy, Damon Slate; he was found wandering out of the tunnel? Apparently, the mayor rang the station in person to make sure our best detective was put on the job.'

'And they chose Krush.'

'Of course. She's the smartest. She always was.'

'Or perhaps it's because she's pregnant,' Stray said, 'and your boss wants to keep her out of harm's way.'

'Sure. We have to protect our best officer.'

Stray tutted. 'This need to compete with your sister, where does it come from?'

'It's not a competition. I've never tried to beat her, I only want her to recognize me, that's all.'

'She already does recognize you. You grew up together, you know each other better than anyone. It's just that, sometimes, those things we're too familiar with, we stop noticing them, we take them for granted.'

'I don't mean it like that,' Eleanor said. 'I just mean, I'm good at my job as well. Nobody sees that. They all think I'm crazy.'

'I suspect you're the only one who thinks that.'

'Why do you say that?' Eleanor sat up on the couch and looked at him. He had not moved an inch since the conversation – or "therapy" – began. He inclined forwards with his hands under his chin, sunk in reflection.

'I only mean that if our siblings have this effect on us, an entirely irrational effect, manifested in physical symptoms, then we shouldn't feel guilty.'

'What are you suggesting?'

At that moment, they heard the front door open. Neil sighed audibly in the vestibule as he took off his jacket and his shoes.

Eleanor shouted, 'Hi, Dad, we're in here.'

Neil poked his head in the door, saw Stray, and muttered something under his breath.

'Hello,' Stray said.

Neil shook his head and stomped away down the hall. They heard the kitchen door slam shut.

'Sorry,' Eleanor said. 'He's so rude sometimes.'

'It's reasonable. He's wondering why a strange, one-eyed man is staying in his house. I should leave here.' He stood up. 'I've abused your hospitality long enough.'

'And go where?'

'It doesn't matter. I've got by just fine up to now without a house.'

'You haven't been fine at all. Raymond, you can't go back to being homeless again. Once you have some money coming in, you can get your own flat. You've got your interview tomorrow at the police station. Everything will be fine, you'll see.'

'Yeah, that was a nice idea. I almost believed it. But nobody is hiring a washed-up weirdo like me. Nobody in psychiatry will touch me since my practice was closed down. I'm not qualified to do anything else. I've tried other things; I've been for job interviews. They take one look at me and that's enough. They wouldn't even employ me to wash dishes at the restaurant on the corner. No, after you've been homeless as long as I have, you can't shake it off. People see it in you right away. It doesn't matter if you take a shower and put clean clothes on. They know.'

'You'll get the job tomorrow,' Eleanor said. 'I spoke to my boss, and to Dr Shepherd. I've explained the situation. They understand. Your skills could really be useful at the station.'

'Eleanor, I'm sorry, I know you mean well, but I'm not going tomorrow.'

'What do you mean?'

'It's humiliating. They'll laugh me out of the place.'

'I told you – I spoke to them, I explained everything.'

'You're a nice person, Eleanor, you don't realize sometimes, other people aren't. I'm sure they nodded and smiled when you told them about me. They agreed to your face, but behind your back they shook their heads. This is the kind of thing that causes "doubts" about you. I'm not going in there just to be rejected. Christ, I've had a lifetime of humiliation. Back when I had to beg on street corners, I've been spat on, I've been kicked. I've had my fill.'

'Will you stop with the negativity? I feel like I should be the one giving you therapy. You'd be a great asset for the police. You're skilled in your field, much better than anything we have. You're way better than Dr Shepherd. He's useless.'

'The chances of a job like that for me ended years ago.'

'Just give it a chance. It's all set up. You'll embarrass me if you don't turn up now, after the efforts I made to get you the interview. They'll give you a fair hearing. My recommendation means something.'

'It won't anymore, once you've used it for my sake.'

'I don't care, Raymond. I just want to help you.'

'Please, don't get involved on my behalf. It never ends well for people who try to help me.'

'Talk to them tomorrow. That's all I ask. After that, I won't try to force you again.'

He sighed. 'I'll talk to them, but it'll end in failure. You'll see.'

'Whatever happens, just promise me, you won't disappear overnight like you did before. Don't abandon me. I'm as lost in this city as you are. Even though I grew up here, ever since I moved back, I feel like a stranger. I've got no friends. Things are tense at the station. My own sister won't talk to me. Dad's trying to kick me out. I've got demons, I know I have, but you've helped me. You're the only one who ever did. Promise you won't disappear.'

Stray looked tearful, which was unlike him. 'I've learned in life not to promise anything. We're not so in control as we imagine.'

Hearing these words, seeing him moved, Eleanor felt that he was already disappearing. He might be gone in the morning, and, why not? It was in his nature to slip away and take to the road.

'Next time,' she said, 'leave me a note at least.'

19

Beth Krush was alone. Back in this bare flat in the tower block overlooking the river. She had sworn to herself more than once she would leave it and find a nice, cosy bungalow somewhere. Too many memories here, and too little comfort. The windows were floor-to-ceiling, and the view outside was bleak, just grey sky and water. But she had not left. In the end, the flat had become her home, and a home was worth something. Besides, it suited her, it matched her personality.

Looking out of the window, she watched the river that seethed in the dark. She had never understood the way people talked about it. In Liverpool, the Mersey was supposed to represent home, but there was nothing homely about the sloshing brown water, the freezing currents. Living on the waterfront these years, she had grown used to the sound of it. The roar at night while she lay dreamless in bed had become a part of her consciousness, a form of tinnitus. Now when she had to stay in hotels for work, the silence was unfamiliar; she could not sleep without the white noise of the water.

The words "under the river" came to her from nowhere. Lying on the couch, she felt the baby kick in her belly. Funny. In a sense, it meant she was not alone after all, even though the isolation was overwhelming. But she could not quite bring herself to picture the thing inside her as a human, it felt more like a parasite consuming her. Really, she should have had it aborted while there was still time. Now it was too late. She had hesitated. In the confusion of the serious injury she had suffered, and the tangle of the past, with the exposure to the horrible violence of the serial killer case she had faced, the thought of killing the foetus had become unbearable. Or maybe it was something else, something she did not like to think about.

She was recovered now, back home from the hospital. Rationality was restored, it was only this being inside her that resisted in its mindlessness. She took out Iris's diary and started at the beginning. January 1st of that year, just three months ago. Not much to go on, but it was better than nothing. She read the first entry, from New Year's Day:

> *Does he love me? Sometimes I think he must, and then I'm afraid, and I wonder, is all this a mistake? They spoke about our marriage like it was a transaction. I was beautiful, they said, and he was rich. As if deals are made that way. I stared into the*

mirror and tried to see the woman from the wedding photographs, but she was gone. I walked around the house and told myself, 'You're rich now. This is what it feels like to be rich.' But I don't feel rich, and I don't feel beautiful either. The only thing I feel for certain is the transaction. Yes, something was bought and paid for and can never be refunded.

Useless. Krush flipped a few empty pages and came to another entry. This was one that Dr Chen had commented on.

Under the river. The only place I ever managed to just feel nothing at all.

According to Chen, "under the river" symbolised Iris's depression. Maybe he was right. The scary thought was, Krush felt that way herself. Was she depressed? Such questions were forbidden. She turned the page and kept reading.

D can never lose. He told me that once. He'd die before he let anybody beat him. That was the moment I knew I wanted to marry him. Not because I loved him. I stopped believing in fairytales long ago. He was the one human being I'd ever met who knew so clearly who he was. Not like me. Where I used to perceive separate personalities around me, now I only feel a blur of smeared identity, fragments of people.
But not him.

Iris's confused love life was boring and useless. It was all the same, a detached discussion of trivial emotional relationships, seen through a disturbed mind. Growing impatient, she skipped through the pages at random and read on.

O is the only one you could ever love. Why? because O is the ugliest. There's no falsehood in ugly, and no trick. Ugly is ugly. It bares its face to the world and

never hides it. Ugly has no money and no manners. It
stands naked and says, 'Look: I have nothing at all.
Who will love me?'

Could *O* stand for Iris herself? A nothing? Chen had called her a narcissist. In the end, this was impenetrable. She turned to the final entry, as if it might have changed since last time she checked. "Heart of the City" – was that really the last entry? No. She turned ahead and found, under April 10th, a single letter *X* marked in the middle of the page. Krush calculated… today was April 7th. *X* would take place in three days' time.

'What does it mean?'

It did not mean anything. It was even less intelligible than "Heart of the City". The diary became increasingly meaningless until there was only this single, resistant cipher. She stared at it. Whatever *X* was, she had two days left to find out. She flipped back to the previous month, and skimmed the few entries.

> *In fairytales, one side is good, and the other is evil. It*
> *makes sense in childhood. But the stories don't work*
> *if both sides are evil. Where is there to go? Only this*
> *tiny space in the middle, neither good nor evil, just a*
> *space.*

If Iris had been in the room with her, Krush might have grabbed her shoulders and shaken her. Talk of fairytales, enigmatic gibberish. She had learnt in this job that facts and logic solve cases. Everything else was just a form of illusion, it only existed to lead an unwary investigator off the path, until they were lost. That's how cases ended up stuck on a shelf, unsolved.

She turned back another page, with the odd sense of travelling backwards in time.

> *A "heart", he calls it. But is it a heart if it's an*
> *empty space? And if somebody fills that space, will it*

This was starting to sound too much like love, something Krush did not believe in. The words swam before her eyes and skipped randomly through the pages.

They'll never see the grey hood.

She closed the diary and let it fall. She only wanted to get out of this flat. She picked up the flyer Carver had given her.

Yoga for pregnancy.

The picture showed a woman with a giant belly seated cross-legged on a mat, with a tranquil expression on her face. She could almost smell the sweat in the gym and hear the hubbub of inane chatter. The pregnancy class with Eileen, her dad's neighbour, was even worse. No, the thought was unbearable.

The only way to fill the loneliness and boredom was to work. Unfortunately, she did not have much to work on. Carver was keeping her away from real jobs. The chief was presumably trying to help, but she did not understand; Krush loved the big cases, the difficult ones, the disturbing ones that nobody else wanted to touch. She thrived in complexity. Instead, all she had was this befuddled rich bastard and his missing wife, who might not be missing. There was not even a case file to spread out on the table, an activity that usually calmed her mind.

She had to stay awake until midnight when the tunnel closed for traffic. Well, staying awake had never been a problem. Filling the emptiness was life's task, and work was the only solution. She took a sheet of blank paper and wrote:

Iris's Diary: Theories
Under the river = Depression (Dr Chen)
D = Damon Slate

O = ?
Torn page = ?
Heart of the City = Iris? Narcissism (Dr Chen)
Grey hood = Suicide?

It was not much, but it was a start. She opened the diary again and began at page one.

> *The only thing I feel for certain is the transaction. Yes, something was bought and paid for and can never be refunded.*

20

Outside the tunnel, Krush was met by a traffic officer, Maureen Davies, who gave her a hard hat. The mouth of the tunnel curved above them like the entrance to a vast temple. A strip of lights along the centre of the roof cast ethereal light over the pale surfaces.

'It seems bigger on foot.' Krush took a step inside. 'I drove through here earlier today, but it was different in the car.'

'It's another world at night,' Davies said. 'It's spooky.'

The echoing passage receded downwards and curved out of view up ahead, haunted by a groaning wind.

'Come on.' Krush took a few steps inside. It was like being swallowed.

Behind her, Davies turned on her torch and cast a circle of light along the walls. 'Are you planning to walk through the whole thing?' she asked. 'It's two miles long. It's the longest road tunnel in the UK.'

'Of course it is. Everything in Liverpool is the best,' Krush said, and regretted it immediately – her sarcasm tended to alienate colleagues.

But Davies did not pick up on it. 'Oh, I know.'

Perhaps Krush was losing her edge; she risked becoming sincere.

'It shouldn't be necessary to check the whole tunnel,' Krush said. 'I watched the CCTV earlier. Our man came out of a maintenance door along this left-hand side, fifty yards inside.'

'And what are you expecting to find there?'

'I'd love to find a red shoe.'

'A red shoe?'

'Bright red. It's high-heeled, a size six.'

'Is it Cinderella you're looking for? She disappears after midnight.'

'What? Oh, no. It's a missing person case.'

'What am I talking about?' Davies asked the walls. 'Cinderella's shoe was made of glass, wasn't it? Well, don't get your hopes up. If there was a shoe like that down here, someone would've noticed.'

'I don't hope, I just investigate.'

Davies hummed to herself, a sound just hinting at disapproval.

There it was, the Krush alienation effect at work.

Krush tried to picture Slate as he stumbled forwards, but the tunnel was alien now she was on foot, and she struggled to match it to what she had seen on the cameras. She put on gloves and inspected the wall. A smooth covering reflected back the light, revealing nothing.

They probed deeper inside, and the walls remained the same, constantly repeating. It felt as though they were walking without moving as the view around them never changed, but when she glanced back, she saw the exit was lost from view behind a curve. The wind howled from further within, reaching her face with a freezing touch.

'I guess you don't suffer from claustrophobia, working here?' she heard herself say aloud.

Davies chuckled. 'The tunnel will cure you of that. Don't worry, lovie, it's perfectly safe. They have so many emergency measures nowadays. Even if both exits collapsed, we could still get out. And the air is fresh. There are vents and a pumping station. Honestly, this is the safest place in the city. If a bomb was dropped on Liverpool, you'd be sheltered down here.'

'I'm just glad there are no seagulls underground. This is the only part of the city that's safe from them.'

They continued along the tunnel without finding anything. Krush felt her concentration slacken as drowsiness swam in her blood. This goddamn baby sucked the energy from her body. She struggled to be sure she had not missed a red shoe, or a handprint, some vital clue in the emptiness.

'Here's the door,' Davies said.

They reached an opening in the wall protected by a thin metal barrier. On the other side, a short concrete ramp led upwards to a wooden door that was painted green. There was something comforting about that shade of green, a reminder of nature in the concrete abyss. Climbing the ramp, Krush stopped and grabbed her belly.

'Are you alright, lovie?' Davies said.

'Yeah, I just need a moment.'

'I can't believe they've got you out here exploring the tunnel in the middle of the night. In your condition, you should be in bed, getting your rest. They work us into the ground. It's crazy.'

'Actually, my colleagues would be delighted if I stayed at home. It was my idea to check the tunnel. My boss tried to talk me out of it. Unfortunately, it had to be after midnight. The only alternative would be to stop the traffic, but they won't do that for a woman who isn't technically missing.'

'Not "technically"?'

'Only theoretically.'

'I didn't know there were different types of missing. That's why little old Davies is on traffic duty, and you're a detective.'

'Come on.' Krush straightened and hurried up the ramp. On the other side of the green door, a sign said, "Do not return to your vehicles unless instructed it is safe to do so by emergency services."

There was nothing behind the door except a bare concrete space and another green door. A single bulb illuminated the grey surfaces and there was no sign of a red shoe. Down here, it was difficult to believe red shoes even existed. She looked around all four walls and knelt to check the floor and the corners.

'I'm sorry you came all this way for nothing,' Davies said.

'We haven't finished yet. Slate came through here. We know he did. The camera shows him coming out of the maintenance door into the tunnel. But how did he get in here?'

'There's only this way.' Davies opened the door in the opposite wall, revealing a metal staircase. 'But… if we go down there… we'll be here all night. It doesn't end.'

Krush went through the door and looked down. The steps circled around a concrete shaft. The walls were lined with cables and pipes. It was cold and dry.

'Alright,' she said. 'Let's go down.'

Davies hesitated at the top of the steps. 'Are you sure? I already came this way earlier. There's nothing to see. No Cinderella. No shoe.'

'There could be something tiny. Something you missed. I need to check.'

'I don't know, lovie, in your condition. There are passages on both sides of the car deck. That's miles and miles. We'd spend all night and still not check every little detail.'

'Well, we'll do our best. OK?' Krush started down the stairs.

She had tried to sound convincing but as she descended the metal steps around the thick concrete wall, she felt a tingling of panic mixed with exhaustion. The tunnel was already underground, and now they were going deeper. She had not anticipated another layer beneath the car deck. If she allowed herself to think about the profundity, the density of rock that cradled the tunnel, and the weight of the river above their heads, she might give way to dread.

'This is a mistake.' At the top of the stairs, Davies watched her go down, but did not follow.

'It's alright,' Krush called back up to her. 'You can leave me here. I'll find my way by myself.'

With a shake of the head, and a rueful look back towards the exit, Davies followed her down. 'No, you won't. You think the tunnel is simple, just a long hole with two ends, but it's much more than that. You'll see.'

The metal steps clanked as they climbed down in the glow of phosphorescent bulbs set in the concrete walls. Krush kept one hand on the railing.

'What's down here?' she said.

'The bore of the tunnel is circular. It's 13.4 metres in diameter. I'm not a maths person, but I think that's pretty big. The road section above, that's just one semi-circle. What you've seen is just the top half of the bore. Down here is the bottom.'

'It's bigger than I realized.'

'You have no idea.' Davies chuckled. 'It gives me the jitters, you know. Seventeen men were killed digging all this out.'

'I don't believe in ghosts,' said Krush.

'Neither do I, until I'm on my own.' At the bottom of the staircase Davies overtook her. 'Brace yourself,' she said.

'Why?'

Nearby, the wind roared. She followed the traffic officer left, around a wall of concrete, and was caught in a blast of air so strong it took her breath away.

Davies's hair blew crazily, covering her face, while she held onto her hard hat with one hand. She had to shout to be heard. 'This is the ventilation shaft!'

Krush pulled the whipping hair out of her eyes. 'I see!'

'Fresh air! It runs the length of the tunnel!'

'Is it like this the whole way?'

'I'm afraid so!'

'It's strong!' Krush tried to visualise Slate walking through the wind tunnel, but it was impossible to imagine anything with the gale in her face.

'You should see the fans!' Davies called. 'Twenty-six feet in diameter!'

Shielding her eyes from the wind, Krush peered along the shaft. It stretched away endlessly, a narrow passage with a sloping side. She stepped inside.

'What are you doing?' Davies shouted in her ear.

'I have to check it! He might have come through here! His wife…!'

'It's two miles long! You'll be here until the morning!'

'I don't sleep anyway!' Her throat was becoming hoarse from shouting into the wind.

'There's another tunnel like this one on the other side! That makes four miles! Are you going to walk through all of it?'

'If I have to!'

'Wait!' Davies grabbed her shoulder as she pushed forward into the gale.

'What?'

'There's a different passage I have to show you. If your man came through the tunnel… he didn't come this way. There's a better way. Less windy. It gets up to thirty-seven miles per hour down this section.'

At the words "less windy", Krush stopped. She looked again through the shield of her fingers into the dark passage of the wind and wondered if Slate could have wandered through here; if Iris might still be lost inside. 'Alright, show me the other passage.'

They retraced their steps back along the ventilation tunnel, and circled around the bottom of the staircase to another opening. It was a relief to be out of the screaming gale. Krush patted down her windblown hair beneath the hard hat. She followed Davies into a wide, empty tunnel some twenty feet in diameter.

'We're directly under the road deck now.' Davies pointed up at the bare concrete ceiling. 'The cars go overhead. On either side of these walls go the ventilation shafts.'

'What's this section for?' Krush shone her torch, and the beam was drowned in an expanse of darkness, picked out by small, intermittent lamps.

'It was intended for a tramline, but they never finished it. It wasn't needed. Everyone has a car now, anyway, don't they?'

Krush peered into the gloom. She felt queasy. 'I've lost my sense of direction. Which way is which?' With a hint of panic, she turned and looked in the opposite way, which only revealed an identical stretch of dull concrete and shadow.

'Don't worry, that's normal.' Davies grinned. She pointed her torch into the cavernous hollow. 'Liverpool is that way. Birkenhead's behind us. We're going this way, come on.' She headed in the direction of Liverpool.

Krush hurried to keep pace with her, afraid to be left alone. 'And all this underneath is just empty?' she said. 'It's just left unused?'

'They run cables and pipes through here.' Davies flashed her torch up into the corner of the ceiling that was thickly woven with wires. 'Everything's connected. If this tunnel was destroyed, the Wirral would be cut off from the world.'

They walked on some thirty yards. Krush's belly had never felt heavier. She waddled with both hands wrapped around it.

Davies looked back over her shoulder and frowned. 'Are you alright, lovie?'

'I'm fine.'

'I can't believe you would have gone through the wind shaft on your own.'

'It's my job.'

'Is it, though? I don't see any of your colleagues here. They're probably all in bed. Take my advice, don't go the extra mile. They'll only take advantage of you. I learnt that lesson a while ago.'

Yeah, Krush thought, that's why you've been a traffic officer for three decades.

'Come on, we're almost there.' Davies disappeared around a corner and Krush let go of her belly, determined not to give up.

The tunnels were vast. Between the car deck, the two ventilation shafts, and this ghostly tramline that had never been finished, not to mention countless side passages, it would take forever to go through it all and check every detail. The thought of it made her feel so weary, she might not make it to bed before she fell. She no longer had any idea what she wanted to find down here.

Around the other side of a gradual bend in the tunnel, a dim shape emerged up ahead. Coming closer, she saw a brick square that filled half of the passageway. Some kind of bunker. A green door was set beside a sign – "Refuge Point F" – and a red phone marked "SOS". She had never been so glad to find a doorway.

'Here we are.' Davies opened the door and hit a light switch. She stood aside for her. 'After you, Detective.'

Krush entered a space that was wider than she had expected. From outside, it appeared to be just a small cabin, but it led into a corridor through the tunnel wall. The walls were painted white, while the ceiling was covered with metal panels, and the floor was coral red. To one side, benches ran along the wall. Behind the green door, a screen was set into the wall above a phone. On the black screen, a simple message in white letters said, "This is a safe place. Remain here and stay calm."

It felt like returning to civilisation.

'Oh, we can sit down in here,' she said. 'I think I need to rest a moment.'

'Not only that,' Davies said. 'There's a toilet at the end of the corridor.'

Nobody could have sounded prouder to announce a toilet.

'Good to know.' Krush dropped onto the bench. It was peaceful in the faint buzz of the lights. She noticed a camera above the screen.

'Does that camera work?' she said.

'I assume so.' Davies sat down next to her. 'It's nice to rest a moment, isn't it?'

'I don't think I saw this room when the CCTV footage was sent through earlier. If Slate came this way, he must have passed the camera, right?'

'I suppose so.'

'What if he crawled? Could he have gone beneath the lens? It doesn't move, does it?'

'You'd have to ask in the control room.'

'Shut up a minute.' Krush dropped forward off the bench and fell to her knees.

'What are you doing?'

'What is that?' She crawled forwards.

'I don't understand.'

'There! What…?' She kneeled at the opposite wall in the space beneath the screen.

'Oh Lord.'

Krush put on her gloves. 'Somebody lost a button.'

21

'You'll be fine.' Eleanor pulled up in the car park at Merseyside Police HQ.

Fresh morning rain rattled over the metal roof as the engine died.

In the passenger seat, Stray contemplated the edifice of glass, a hundred windows looking down. 'I can't go in there.'

'What are you afraid of? You've been in worse places.' Eleanor gave him a smile that was presumably intended to be reassuring.

'Not dressed like this.'

He had on one of Neil's old suits, a brown jacket, and trousers that were too baggy. Everything he had tried on had been baggy. Stray was emaciated from a decade of homelessness. He would never put on weight again, even if he stuffed himself with food every day. That was not likely to happen anyway, he lost his appetite years ago and had grown used to scraps. Too much food now only made him nauseous.

'Look at the state of me. With this goddamn eyepatch, like a pirate who fell on hard times.'

'You look fine. You don't need two eyes. They won't hold it against you. All that matters is you're a talented psychiatrist.'

'You only think that because I'm your therapist.'

'No, you're my friend.'

'Patients often mistake their therapist for someone else. It's called "transference".'

'Just go upstairs and get it over with. They're waiting for you. If you don't get the job, it's no big deal. We'll find something else.'

Eleanor climbed out of the car, but Stray did not get out. He had not even removed his seat belt.

'Come on, get up.' Eleanor came around to the other side and opened his door.

'Please, don't make me do this,' he said. 'It's mortifying. They're going to laugh me out of the place. I'm not employable. I don't have an address, for God's sake.'

'You *do* have an address, I told you.'

'I can't accept your generosity, Eleanor.'

'You've helped me as well.'

'No, but… you think you know me. You don't. I'm a user. I exploit people's kindness. Do you think you're the first person who wanted to help me? Anyone who ever tried ended up hating me. Please, stop trying.'

'Yeah well, people have hated me as well. We'll cross that bridge when we come to it. I had to beg to arrange this interview. You're going to endure it. Come on, get up. You're going to be late. You–'

She broke off to clutch her stomach.

He saw her try to mask the pain with gritted teeth. 'Are you alright?'

'Yeah, yeah, I'm fine.'

'Your stomach again?'

'It comes out of nowhere, but it doesn't last long.'

'You should speak to a doctor. A real one, I mean.'

She straightened. 'It's gone now.'

Stray took off his seat belt and got out of the car. His legs were wobbling.

'How do you feel?' Eleanor said.

'Never better.'

22

Under the river. Krush woke with the diary in her hand. She must have fallen asleep reading it. Fragments of Iris's strange writings crisscrossed in her thoughts as she drove to the police station. She felt closer to the missing woman, and yet farther away; there was intimacy in reading these secret thoughts, but they were abstract, lacking recognizable names or places, they seemed to drift from the real world. Still, the more she read, the more she found patterns and codes. She recognized faces. Damon Slate, for example.

D always wins. Even when he seems to lose, he's already won. He sees farther into the future than the rest of us. He's always ten pages ahead. At the very moment you think he's beaten, he's already caught you in a net you don't see.

Krush found she could believe this. But then who was O?

O is the only one you could ever love. Why? because O is the ugliest.

Krush could imagine a woman staring in the mirror and viewing herself as O. *Look: I have nothing at all. Who will love me?* Yes, she could imagine it too easily.

Keeping her head down, wanting to avoid conversation, she waddled along the corridors of the station. In the canteen, Eleanor was making a coffee. Krush's heart almost stopped. She ducked out of sight before her sister might look up and catch her there, watching. She kept on walking.

Elliot was not in the forensics lab, but she found him in his office applying an electric massage pad to his neck.

'Stress?' she said.

'I don't know what it is. I can hardly turn my head left or right. Not good in my line of work.'

'I get it too. Sometimes it's like a spear going through the side of my neck and down my spine.'

'Jesus.' He held out the massage pad. 'Want to try this?'

'Those things don't work,' she said. 'The only solution to pain is to work it off.'

'Some might say work is the cause, not the cure.'

She tossed a clear evidence bag on his desk. 'What do you think that is?'

He held it up and considered the small, clear button inside. 'Are you serious?'

'I'm always serious. At university they used to say I lacked a sense of humour. People don't understand sarcasm.'

'The curious case of Benjamin Button.' He put on gloves and opened the evidence bag. 'Where did you find this?'

'Last night, after midnight, under the Queensway Tunnel. It was on the floor in an emergency shelter. Tell me what you see.'

'It's polyester, I guess. Looks like a button from a shirt. To be honest, it looks like a button from a standard police shirt. Want me to check it for DNA?'

'As a priority. See if it matches the shoe I dropped off.'

'A shoe?'

'I dropped it off with one of your helper elves yesterday.'

'Nobody mentioned it to me.'

'Does it matter? They'll have filed it and passed it along to another elf for processing.'

He put the button back in the bag and set it down. 'It's just…'

'What?'

'A shoe? There was something else about a shoe.' He got up and crossed the room to check in a pile of documents.

'Another shoe?'

'No, ignore me. I'm getting confused. It's just a shoe, and we have so much paperwork. Everything's backed up. It never ends. The "elves", as you call them, they keep changing. I don't even know their names anymore. And they put things in the strangest places. Honestly, if you want something done, make sure you hand it to me in person, don't drop it off with one of them.'

'Noted. Well, not wanting to put extra pressure on you, but if you could fast-track that shoe, and the button… I'd owe you one.'

'Do you know how many people in this building "owe me one"? Favours aren't worth shite. But I'll do it for you, Krush.'

'Because I ask nicely?'

He laughed. 'You don't ask nicely, but you solve cases, and that makes the paperwork worthwhile. Others here, they just send stuff around in circles.'

<h1 style="text-align:center">23</h1>

Eleanor walked the corridors of HQ with growing paranoia. *There are doubts about you.* Through each open door she glanced and tried to resist the impression that her colleagues had just stopped talking about her. She forced herself to enter the staff room. Spend some time with colleagues, fraternise a little, be part of the team. A group of officers fell silent. She almost did not notice Beth at the water fountain. A great balloon of water rose in the plastic canister on top of the machine as she filled her cup. Their eyes met for a moment, but she could not muster a sound. Beth's belly was even larger than the last time she saw it.

The officers turned away to hide their embarrassment as Krush hurried out, head down, without a word. Eleanor looked into the empty outline of the door where she had gone. She should say something to break the awkwardness, but her mind was empty. Instead, she crossed to the water fountain and filled a cup. The others resumed chatting but in hushed voices. Before she could approach them, they drifted out of the room without saying goodbye.

Were they whispering about her? Don't be paranoid, she told herself. They had witnessed her broken sibling relationship. They were right to have doubts. Not only that; she had just driven her heroin addict friend to the station for a job interview that she had set up herself. Maybe they were justified to tell stories behind her back.

Suddenly, she could not bear to be in the building. She knew she should stay and try to talk to someone, try to act normal, but she could not remember what normal looked like. She had to get out of here. She hurried out of the building only wanting to be alone.

* * *

Springtime in the city. Even though it was cold and damp, passers-by wore T-shirts, shorts, and flip-flops. These where the moments when Eleanor knew she did not belong. She put her hood up. She returned to the invisible borderline in the Marsh and entered the park. What remained of the crime scene tape lay in dirty puddles among litter and petals. Dog walkers and groups of kids loitered among the trees, scurrying away when she approached. She retraced her steps to the overgrown grass where the dead man was found. There was nothing left of the scene, not even an imprint in the grass. The rain had washed the blood away. There might have been no crime at all. So, what was she doing in this place?

She followed a narrow track through the bushes, wanting to explore the park farther. Beneath the branches of a tree weighed down with pink blossom, she found an old man smoking a bent cigarette. He was filthy.

'What are you doing down there?' Eleanor said.

He did not get up. 'Enjoying the cherry trees, Officer. Take a seat, join me.'

'You can't loiter here,' she said. 'This is a crime scene.'

He blew out smoke and smiled. 'Haven't you ever heard of *Hanami*? The Japanese festival of cherry blossom. It's easy. You sit under the trees and contemplate the transience of existence.'

'OK.'

'The cherry tree is *sakura* in Japanese. It only flowers for two weeks per year. Take the chance, enjoy it while you can.'

'I'm investigating a murder,' she said.

'Are you? Is that really what you're doing?'

'Yes.' For a moment, she almost doubted it. 'I'm interviewing people in the park to see if they witnessed anything.'

'You're looking for the wrong things in life. Sit down. Watch the petals. And, please, keep quiet, don't disturb me.'

She took out her phone and showed him the picture of the dead man. 'Recognize this guy?'

'Which side are you on?' he said, ignoring the image.

'I'm not on any side.'

'There are always sides.'

'I'm a police officer. I just want to solve this killing.'

'Well, good luck to you. I've never seen that man before, and I doubt anyone around here has.'

'Were you sitting under that tree yesterday as well?'

'Yesterday? Time is an illusion.'

'OK, this is becoming annoying.'

* * *

Eleanor called in at the local police station, but Jeff was not there. His colleagues could not say where he had gone, but they shared a knowing glance with each other. It seemed Jeff was a subject of amusement, perhaps of suspicion. Another officer offered to accompany her, but there was something off-putting in his smile, in the way he raised his eyebrows when she asked about Jeff. She decided to carry on alone.

Schools, she had learned over the years, often knew a lot more than the police about what was really going on in a local area. St Vitus's, with their red uniforms, was just a few blocks from the park. It was surrounded by barbed wire and flowering trees. Seagulls circled overhead. Eleanor crossed the car park, ignoring a few students who watched her with curiosity and malice, and entered the building.

She made some enquiries and soon she was seated opposite the headmaster, Mr Drysdale, in his office overlooking the yard.

'A visit from the police,' he said. 'This is an unexpected pleasure. We ring the police all the time, you know, but they never show up. They're embarrassed to show their faces here.'

'I want to talk to you about the kids on bikes.'

'Why bother? We both know nothing ever gets fixed.' Drysdale had a bristly moustache and protruding teeth, giving him a rattish appearance.

'I'm different to other police,' Eleanor said. 'I want to help.'

'And how do you propose to do that?'

'By talking to this gang of kids. Nobody seems to know who they are, where they live, what they do.'

'Indeed,' he said. 'I think it's because, in a certain way, they're not really a gang.'

'What do you mean?'

'It's a question of definitions. A real gang is like an army. It has a structure, organisation, chain of command. There's a boss at the top, like a general, and authority works its way down via lieutenants to the foot soldiers at the bottom.'

'Sounds like you know a lot about gangs.'

'In this job, you have to. In Garston, at one of the schools I worked in previously, there was a local gang causing chaos. They used to come onto the school grounds to deal drugs in broad daylight, bullying students, intimidating members of staff. The police wouldn't lift a finger. We had hard evidence of what was going on. These scumbags were caught on our security cameras. Their faces were there, clear as day. But the police just apologised and said there was nothing they could do. It would never get through the courts, the laws won't let them interfere, et cetera, et cetera.'

'I'm sorry about that.'

'Don't be. So, finally I decided to take action myself. I set up a meeting with the gang's leader, or one of the leaders anyway. A guy called Skinny – must have been somebody's idea of a joke, this guy was obese.'

'You set up a meeting, on your own?'

'It was simple. We arranged a time and a place, and we met, just the two of us.'

'And what happened?'

'I asked him nicely to stop his foot soldiers coming on the school grounds. I told him they could do whatever they liked outside the grounds. There was a covered lane behind the school where they could carry out their deals safe from view. We'd leave them in peace to do what they wanted there, so long as they didn't enter the grounds.'

'And what did he say?'

'He said, "Fair enough."'

'And?'

'And that stopped it. No more dealers on school grounds.'

'He agreed to your demands, simple as that?'

Drysdale smiled and looked even more rattish than before. 'I should explain, our friend Skinny had two kids attending the school. One of them had some quite serious special needs. We had gone to efforts to accommodate him.'

'I never knew gangsters to be so amenable.'

'Maybe you need to change your tactics. I've heard of police who managed to work with the gangsters; not for good purposes, mind you.'

'If you're talking about corruption… I'm not corrupt.'

'Everybody's corrupt in one way or another.'

She decided to ignore that. 'And the gang around here, the kids?'

'They're different. They don't go to school. If they don't go to school, there's really nothing I can do as headmaster. Like I said, I'm not sure they're a gang at all. They don't seem to have that top-down structure. It's looser than that. They're more informal. Kids come and go. They cooperate with each other, but there's no hierarchy. Nobody seems to be in charge. Unless…'

'Unless what?'

'Unless their boss is smarter than other bosses. Whoever they are, they keep out of sight. Their name is secret. *If* they really exist.'

Eleanor took out her phone. 'Do you recognize this man?'

Drysdale shook his head. 'He's the one killed in the park? All the kids are chatting about it. You'd think a celebrity came to the school, they're so excited.'

'And do they know anything? Have you heard anything – rumours, gossip?'

'Nothing. Nobody saw or heard anything. The gangs are smart. There are never any witnesses when they kill some poor bastard.'

'You think it was a gang killing then?'

'I have no thoughts.' He slid the phone back across the table. 'I've never seen that man before in my life. I don't believe he's from the Marsh. In this job, you get to know a lot of people, not just students. We're at the heart of the community. That guy, not wanting to speak ill of the dead, but that's a face I'd remember.'

'How about this?' She showed him a picture of the red shoe. 'Any idea what this means?'

'It doesn't belong to anyone in this school, if that's what you mean. We have a uniform policy.' The headmaster sat back in his chair and chuckled. 'A red shoe? Doesn't it seem a bit artificial? A bit staged? Detective, someone is playing games with you.'

24

Dr John Shepherd's office was surprisingly messy for a police psychologist. His desk was covered in files, and the bin in the corner was overflowing with crumpled paper. When Stray came through the door, he found himself presented with two empty seats on the nearside of the desk. He chose the one on the left. The police psychologist sat in silence and skimmed through one of the documents in front of him, as if there was nobody else in the room.

'The silence technique,' Stray said. 'Sit and say nothing, and wait for the subject to speak first. They reveal themselves in that way.'

Shepherd glanced up. 'You may have used such tricks in your time, but I don't.'

'Is that right? So why are you using the old two-seat option? Throw the subject off by confronting them with a random choice.'

'Sometimes I have two people in here at the same time, that's all.'

'Fine.' Stray sat back in the chair. 'Let's do it your way, then.'

'Indeed. I'm a busy man. As you know, a mutual acquaintance of ours, Eleanor Rose, has put you forward as a candidate for psychological consultant to the Merseyside Police. This is a role in which you would offer services such as profiling criminal suspects and evaluating the mental state of prisoners. I'm not sure what you told Detective Rose, but–'

'I didn't tell her anything. All this was her idea. She came up with it by herself.'

'Quite. Well, I've had a look at the documents you submitted. You certainly are the most unusual applicant.'

'Thanks… I suppose.'

'There's a nurse outside. We'll need to take blood and urine samples. If we find any trace of narcotics in your system–'

'You won't find anything.'

Stray tried to sound assertive, but a hint of doubt sounded in his voice. It had been months since he last used. He had been careful to avoid drugs while he was staying with Eleanor and her stepfather. His desire to go straight was genuine. Still, the tests might pick up some lingering traces. He had consumed so much stuff over the years – half of which he couldn't even be sure what it was, or what it was cut with – that now he had no idea what substances might still be floating around in his body.

He tried to smile. 'I'm a clean-living man,' he said.

Shepherd made no comment, and turned a page in the file in front of him. 'I see the address you've put down here is the same as Rose's. Are you living with her permanently?'

'No, it's just a temporary arrangement. She's helping me out while I get back on my feet.'

'Can I ask… What exactly is the relationship between yourself and Detective Rose?'

He was tempted to reply, "therapist and patient", but he only said, 'Friends.'

'An interesting "friendship".' Shepherd looked puzzled, but he let it drop and turned a page. 'Your criminal record check came back clean, although we have some apprehension about the wrongdoings that took place at your former practice.'

'That was all carried out by my associate. I had nothing to do with it.'

'Indeed. I've read up on the case. You were granted immunity from prosecution in return for serving as the key witness. Immunity is not quite the same as innocence. I'm aware of the deals that get made in court.'

'Then you know I have nothing to prove.'

Shepherd did not respond to that. He adjusted his glasses and picked up another file. 'Moving on to your more recent activities… I understand you've been homeless, off and on, for several years.'

'My goal is to stop living rough, but I need a job first, so I can make money to pay rent. I can't get a job however, since I have no home. It's like the old question – how do you call the phone company if you don't have a phone?'

'There are government schemes to help people get back into work.'

Stray stifled a laugh.

'The position with us is a different matter,' Shepherd continued. 'Working with the police entails responsibility. You understand, if we brought you in on an investigation, and the defence team found out about your background, they could bring it up in court as a means to get the case thrown out. Or if the media found out, they could spin your involvement as police incompetence. There are already enough hit pieces against us in the media. We don't need any more.'

'In other words, you won't consider me for this position. You haven't asked me anything about all my years of research and practice, my extensive experience, the papers I've written, the awards I've won, all the things I could positively contribute to psychological matters in law enforcement. You're not interested in any of this because you already made your mind up, before I set foot in the door, that you would never consider me for a role.'

'I'm sorry,' Shepherd said. 'As a peer in the psychology community, I have sympathy, but you can appreciate my position.'

'What I can't appreciate is why you allowed this so-called interview to go ahead. This is a waste of my time and yours. Why am I even sitting here?'

Shepherd turned away as if these words were painful to him.

'I know why.' Stray jumped up. Suddenly, he was furious. 'It's because Eleanor pressured you. You felt embarrassed to say no to her. That's weak behaviour for "a peer in the psychology community".'

'Sit down,' Shepherd said.

'Fuck you.' Stray walked towards the door. 'And you can fuck your urine test as well. What was the purpose of that in a fake interview? Just to humiliate me?'

'Sit down,' Shepherd shouted. 'And lower your voice. This is a place of law and order.'

'What's the point in sitting down?'

'There's something else I want to talk to you about.'

Stray hesitated. If he had any dignity left, he would have run out and slammed the door behind him, but the years of degradation had eaten away his self-esteem. All he had left of his former personality was curiosity.

'Talk to me about what?' he said.

'It's a secret. I'm not going to shout it across the room while you're standing over there. Sit down if you want to listen... or be my guest if you want to storm out of here. I'll tell Eleanor I tried to interview you but you swore at me and slammed the door on your way out.'

'A secret?'

25

Eleanor crossed the border from the Looney side to the Gilchrist side, and tried to sense the difference. Everything was identical: the same terraced houses, boarded-up windows, abandoned cars with no wheels, and trees in blossom.

She found the address she had been given for Tommy Presley, an undercover officer who had infiltrated the Gilchrists. She knocked, but Presley did not answer. The door gave way slightly beneath her hand. She pushed and it opened inwards. She noticed the door keys were in the lock.

She called through the gap. 'Anybody home?'

The street was quiet, but her view of the overlooking houses was blocked by an enormous tree outside the gate. She knew it was dangerous to hang around out front, drawing attention to herself, even though she was dressed in plain clothes. If anybody spotted her as a police officer, Presley's cover would be compromised. That was why she was carrying a bible, and some religious pamphlets. She took the keys out of the lock and went inside, closing the door behind her.

'Hello?'

The shadowy hall smelled of – what? she wondered. Something wrong. A sharp, acid stench. She flicked the light switch and saw dirty footprints in the carpet, leading towards a closed door.

'Hello?' she called out in the hallway. 'I found your keys in the lock. I hope you don't mind?'

The first door opened onto a messy living room, shrouded in dull red light through the closed curtains. The bad smell issued from in here. Cigarette smoke, alcohol, sweat, decaying food, blood. As her eyes adjusted, she saw a chaos of piled plates, mouldy leftovers, empty vodka bottles. On the rug, a dark bloodstain had soaked through the fibres. A huge TV set in the corner was broken, the screen shattered. It watched over the room like a wrecked eye. In front it, a low table was coated in dust. Among the old food and bottles, several ashtrays had overflowed. A grey hoodie lay crumpled on the back of an armchair. Looking closer, she saw that one sleeve was stained with what might have been blood.

On the back wall, facing the broken TV, an outline of a human being drawn in red marker pen was covered in gashes. A knife stuck out of the plasterwork at the spot where its heart would have been.

A cat's litter tray by the door was filled with dried cat shit. Well, that explained the smell.

'Jesus.' She found herself clutching the bible tightly as she backed into the hall.

The dirty footprints led up to a kitchen. It was just as dirty in here as in the living room. A man was slumped in a plastic chair at a table where a line of cocaine had been neatly arranged but not snorted. A Beretta 9000s pistol lay pointing towards her.

Her first thought was that he was dead, and he deserved it. Wearing just a pair of underpants, his bare chest revealed several tattoo designs, including the crucifix and snake that symbolised the Gilchrists, and a long centipede that circled around his left arm coming all the way down to his hand, where its antennae reached across his palm. In that hand, a crumpled joint had gone out between his forefinger and index. His other hand rested on the table beside an empty bottle of vodka. A long trail of drool hung from his lip. His wiry moustache was rimmed with cocaine. Stubble was growing back on his head among the scabs where he had shaved it down to the skin. An ugly-looking scar crossed his chest over his heart. To judge from the lumpy, gnarled tissue, it had been stitched up by an amateur. For all that, his deathly face, blanched white with vivid purple weals around his eyes, was oddly beautiful.

She inched closer. 'Tommy?'

'Oh God.' He jerked awake, shook his head, and jumped out of the chair.

'Stay back. Police.' Eleanor grabbed the pistol from the table.

'Oh God. Oh God. Oh God.' He clawed at his face, stumbled to the wall, and held onto to it.

'Are you Tommy Presley?'

'This is hell, isn't it? I'm in hell.' He crossed to the sink, opened the tap, and stuck his head under the stream of cold water.

'Are you… alright?'

'I need coffee.' He staggered away from the sink and turned on the kettle, almost capsizing it.

He opened a cupboard and knocked down a few mugs that smashed on the floor, before he found a jar of instant coffee.

'Can I do that?' Eleanor watched as his shaking hands struggled to open the lid.

'Jesus and Mary, please help me.' Finally, the lid came loose, and he threw it over his shoulder. He tipped out a big, dried clump of coffee granules into a cup.

'Can I…?'

'There's no time.' He poured cold water into the cup and stirred it with his forefinger.

'I don't think it works that way.'

He swigged back the cold coffee in a few gulps, dropped the empty mug to the tiles where it shattered, and stood, kneading his eyes, while brown liquid dripped from his moustache.

'Oh God.' He dropped down and slid back against the cabinet doors until he was on the floor, with his head in his hands.

'What happened to you?' Eleanor said.

'They warned me, don't go too far, Tommy, but I never listened. I never do. When I was a little kid, I used to throw myself down the stairs. Mam said, "You've got a death wish," but I never knew what she meant. I didn't believe in death.'

'There's a bloodstain on the rug in your living room,' Eleanor said.

He lifted his head and studied her with one agonised pupil. 'Who are you again?'

'Eleanor Rose, Detective Inspector.'

'Oh shit. Have you come to pull me out? I told them, I can't come out now, not now. This isn't the moment.'

'I haven't come to do anything to you. I'm investigating a murder. I want your help, that's all.'

'I can't help anyone. Whatever I touch turns to shit. That bloodstain on the rug, that was my cat. Ron Gilchrist butchered it. He's a sadist, you know? I mean, an actual sadist. He can't help himself. He understands it's wrong, but it's the only thing that brings him pleasure nowadays. He needs to hurt things.'

'The leader of the Gilchrist gang was in your house?' Seeing him calm down, she laid the pistol back on the table.

'Oh, Ronny's been here often,' he said. 'We go to the Liverpool game together. I'm godfather to one of his kids. Only a bastard kid – I'm not boasting – but still, a kid of his.'

'You're friends?'

'I don't know if people like Ron have friends. I used to think it was me who was playing a role – the world's most daring undercover cop – sitting in a sauna with the chief of the villains… He has a sauna in his house, you know? It's not all bad, being evil. But nowadays, I feel like it's him. It's been him all along. He's the one who's acting, and I'm the naïve prick. He's never really been my friend. But me, I guess I needed friendship more than I realized. I actually started to like him.'

'He killed your cat.'

'You can't imagine – what's your name, Eleanor? – Eleanor, you can't imagine what it's like, to force yourself to smile, to try to laugh, while they cut your cat up in front of you, like it's a joke.'

'It doesn't sound like a joke.'

Presley clutched his face as if he was trying to hold it in one piece. 'That's the problem. Ron's got the idea in his head he's funny. These bosses, they're surrounded by yes-men. Idiots who pretend to laugh at his jokes. It's got so bad, he actually thinks he's some kind of comedian, but Ron Gilchrist is the most humourless man I ever met in my life.'

'You *do* need to get out.'

He groaned. 'It's too late. They'd never let me leave. They'd kill me first, and not nicely. I'd be the subject of one of Ron's stand-up routines.'

'We can get you out. We can move people across the country, give them new identities.'

'That's the problem. Look at me.' He held up his arm to show the long centipede tattoo. As his muscles tensed, it seemed to crawl. 'This is my identity. I really am this. I can't go back. I wouldn't want to, even if you could wave a magic wand and make it happen.'

'You're just hungover, you'll be alright after a good night's sleep.'

Presley laughed, a desolate sound. 'Eleanor Rose, God bless you, maybe you're my guardian angel, but I don't think you understand. A hangover like this, this is the kind that never goes away. Speaking of which… I can't feel my legs. Could you bring me over that cocaine? I'll be better after a line.'

'No. I need your help. I'm investigating a killing in the Marsh.' She took out her phone and held out the image of the victim to his bloodshot eyes. 'Do you recognize this man?'

Presley pulled a face. 'He's not one of ours, not a Gilchrist.'

'Could he be a Looney?'

'If he is, it wasn't us who killed him. I would've known. I'm in the loop with Ron and his comedians.'

'I'm working on a theory that it might have been a gang of kids. There are bike tracks next to where the body was found.'

'Kids? What are you raving about? It was the Looneys who killed your ugly friend.'

'But why would they?'

'It's just what they do. There are no reasons.'

'I was told there was a truce. The Organised Crime Unit–'

Presley laughed. 'Oh Christ.'

'What's so funny? I met with Chris Blaine.'

He laughed until he coughed and doubled up in pain. 'Shit. I need help.'

'I don't get the joke. The Unit–'

'The Unit *is* the joke. Organised Crime are on the side of the Looneys.'

'That's not possible. Sergeant Blaine said the policy was neutrality. Don't intervene. Don't get involved. That's what I was told yesterday. Never take sides.'

'The sergeant is an old fogey who's afraid to leave his office. He's a weak man who lets his underlings run the show while he sits upstairs and plays online poker.'

'But–'

'No. This isn't the kind of war where you can stay neutral. The Merseyside Police aren't Switzerland. They're on the Looneys' side.'

'Why would they favour the Looneys?'

'Isn't it obvious? The Looneys are the strongest, the most ruthless, the most dangerous. Everyone's terrified of them. If the war comes out in the open, they're most likely to win. They outnumber us, they have greater resources, and they have the support of the police, even if the police don't admit it.'

It was disturbing the way he said "us". He really had crossed the line. He had become a Gilchrist.

'That's absurd,' she said, but her voice faltered.

Presley rubbed his bloodshot eyes. 'If you were betting on a horse race, would you bet on the fastest horse or the slowest? In a war, you want to position yourself to be on the winning side. It's common sense.'

'If it's so obvious, then why do you stick to the losing side?'

He grinned. 'I'm a romantic, it's just the way I was born. Besides, we're not as bad as they are. I mean, the Gilchrists are bad in an old-fashioned way, but the Looneys are different. They're like the KGB. I'm not exaggerating. Everyone knows, Wayne Looney's personal hero is Joseph

Stalin. He literally has a portrait of Stalin in his master bedroom. Not that I've seen it. They say he has a shelf of Comrade Stalin's writings in his library. I doubt anyone's ever read a page of it, but still. Believe me, if the Looneys gain total control over this city, it'll be a catastrophe. With police support, they become unstoppable. They become the real power behind the scenes.'

'The police *don't* support them.'

'I like you, Eleanor Rose; you're a romantic as well. You should join our side. We'll watch the city burn down together. A beautiful, lost cause.'

<h1 style="text-align:center">26</h1>

'It's about Eleanor Rose,' Shepherd said. He cleared the files away to make a space on the desk between them.

Stray watched, trying to anticipate. 'You brought me here to talk about Eleanor. I should've guessed.'

Shepherd got up and walked across his office. He glanced out into the corridor then locked the door from the inside. When he was seated, he leaned across the desk. 'There have been some concerns.'

'What concerns?'

'About her mental health.'

'I don't like where this conversation is going.'

'I imagine you don't. After all, if Detective Rose is suffering from emotional issues, that suits you quite well, doesn't it? You're not above using your psychological insights to take advantage of people. I've heard about what happened with your sister.'

'What are you implying?'

'Come on. I know it's been years since you worked in a clinic, but you haven't lost your touch. You know it's odd for a woman to take a homeless man into her house. A man she hardly knows, a drug addict.'

'OK, you've made your point. I'm an exploiter of human goodness. I accept the criticism. It's not like I don't feel guilty. I'll tell Eleanor tonight I'm going to move out. I'll apologise for taking advantage of her kindness.'

Shepherd laughed. 'Christ, Stray, stop with the self-flagellation. It's not you I'm worried about, it's Eleanor. I'm only citing your living with her as an example. But it's not the only example.'

'Things happen,' Stray said. 'Life is complex. We're all making it up as we go along.'

'I think you know more than you let on.' Shepherd stared into his one eye, and Stray let him.

'Maybe.'

In truth, Stray knew very well why Eleanor had left Liverpool and why she came back. These things were secret, and he would not share them. Even at his lowest moments, he had never betrayed a patient's confidentiality.

Shepherd shrugged. 'And then there are the two major cases she's been involved in since she came back to Liverpool.'

'Both of those cases were solved,' Stray said. 'You should feel grateful for her work.'

'Oh, we do. There's just the little issue that both cases ended up with dead bodies all over the place, and Detective Rose has never been able to explain what happened.'

'Are you suggesting it was her fault?'

Shepherd dismissed this with a wave of the hand. 'You can evade the question all you like, but we both know something is up with Detective Rose. That's how you ended up so close with her, isn't it? She needed psychological help, and you were able to provide it. That's how you weaselled your way into her life.'

'I didn't weasel! She invited me.'

'It's alright, Stray, we're not here to criticise. All I want is to get to the truth about our subject's condition. That's where you come in.'

'You want me to betray her trust.'

'Not at all. We want you to help her. Anything you can tell us about her state of mind, her symptoms, her behaviour, emotions… it's all useful. You know more than anyone. I bet you've done therapy sessions, haven't you? With a couch, as if you were Sigmund Freud. I know more about you than you realize. I contacted some of your ex-colleagues and spoke with them. Your work was never really about therapy; it was about exploration. You didn't want to help patients; you wanted to learn about their delusions. You love to delve into manias and psychoses. You're "an explorer of the extremes of the human mind". Don't try to deny it. One of your former colleagues said that was a quote of yours, and you said it often.'

'I said a lot of dumb things in the past. It doesn't mean I believe them now.'

'I'm not judging you, Stray. I just want your assistance. It's a simple deal. If you provide information about your patient, I'll pull a few strings and throw you some unofficial work for us at the station. I can't make promises, but I should be able to put something your way that would at least help to get you on your feet.'

'And in return, I'd spy on Eleanor for you, and spill her secrets behind her back.'

'In strict confidence. She'd never find out you talked to us. It's all for her own benefit.'

Stray stood up. 'Thank you for your time. I'll be going now. Please, don't contact me again.'

'You think you're helping her,' Shepherd said, as he watched him walk to the door, 'but you're not. Even you can see, she's falling apart. She's on the brink of disaster.'

Stray managed to say nothing else. He closed the door behind him and heard no more in the empty corridor. A small victory in the chess match of psychologists.

27

Krush drove over to the Marsh, where Iris's family lived. Her surname had been Bottle before she married. At the local police station in the Marsh, she discovered that the Bottles were a notorious family of petty criminals, and troublemakers. Accompanied by the local officer, Derrick "Jeff" Jeffers, she drove over to the Bottles' house and parked at the side of the road beside an apple tree. White blossom shivered on the breeze along its antlered branches. She climbed out of the car into the cold. Jeff did not get out.

She opened her door and leaned inside. 'What are you doing? Come on. The sooner we get this over with, the sooner you can get back to whatever you had to do today.'

Jeff stared through the windscreen at number 19, the Bottles' house. There were no lights on inside. 'If it's alright with you, boss, I'll hang back here.'

'Why?'

'The thing is… I'm from round here, you know. I grew up just a few streets over. People know me. I actually lost my virginity in a skip down this road. It's easier for you. You'll go back to the centre afterwards and never show your face in this street again. Me, I have to live here.'

'It's just a job,' Krush said. 'It's not personal. A police officer is a role you play, it's not who you are. Come on, get out of the car. The Bottles are not going to be angry. We're here to help them.'

'If you say so.' He climbed out, but he looked down the driveway towards the house with undisguised fear.

'What are you afraid of?'

'Hopefully they won't be home anyway.'

'You'd better hope they are, or we'll be coming back later.'

The paved front yard was untidy with children's toys lying among the petals in dirty puddles and some large piles of dog shit. Krush rang the doorbell. Someone shouted inside. A dog barked viciously. Jeff looked nervous. She took a step back from the door. Just on the other side, a man yelled at the dog.

The door opened and a teenage boy looked out. 'What do you want?'

Somewhere in the hall behind him, the dog was barking like crazy. It was big, like a Rottweiler.

'I'm looking for Iris,' Krush said.

The boy squinted as if the daylight hurt his eyes. 'Iris who?'

'Iris Slate. She used to be a Bottle, but she's married now.'

'Oh. No, Iris doesn't come round here since she got married. She's rich now. She's too fancy.'

Inside the house, a man shouted, 'Who's that, Jedd?'

'Nobody!' Jedd yelled back across the hall that was hidden behind the half-closed door.

The dog kept barking.

'What?' the voice inside shouted, louder this time.

'I said, nobody!'

A door slammed somewhere off the unseen hall.

The boy looked from Krush to Jeff and back to Krush again. 'Can I go now?'

'When did you last see Iris?' Krush said.

'I don't know. Who cares?'

'Is there an adult inside I could speak to?' she said.

He scratched his head. 'What for?'

'We're looking for Iris,' Krush said. 'Is she your sister?'

'I told you, she's not here.'

Krush glanced at Jeff, hoping he might know how to communicate with this teenager, but Jeff was staring at the floor.

'We're worried about Iris,' she said. 'She's gone missing.'

'That's what she does,' Jedd said. 'She's an attention seeker. Things got better when she moved out. Dad stopped going nuts, and Mum stopped crying all the time.'

Somebody whispered behind the door. Jedd looked back inside. 'Get lost, Lucy.'

A little girl, maybe five years old, peeked out around the edge of the door.

'I said, get lost!' Jedd shouted.

The little girl stuck her thumb in her mouth and stared at Jeff. She raised her other hand, which was holding a chewed rabbit teddy, and pointed at him. The police officer blushed and looked away.

'Get back inside, Lucy!' Jedd shrieked.

Heavy footsteps sounded in the hall. 'Who the hell is out there?'

The door swung open and a middle-aged man with a bare chest looked out. 'What do you want?' he snapped at Jeff.

Jeff did not reply. He twiddled with the collar of his high-vis jacket.

'We're looking for Iris,' Krush said.

'What are you, police?' He stared at Jeff. 'I know you, don't I?'

Jeff shook his head.

'Detective Inspector Beth Krush.' She took out her badge, but the man ignored it.

'We've got nothing to say to police. You'll only twist the words around anyway.' His belly was fat, hairy, and tattooed with a lion's head.

'We only want to help,' Krush said.

'Tell that to our Johnny, he's been inside two years now, and he's never done nothing.'

While the man recounted these facts, Jedd, who came up to the height of the man's chest, nodded in agreement, with an angry expression.

'I don't know anything about that,' Krush said.

'And our Petey got beat up in prison last year,' the man shouted. 'Almost lost his eye. Not that you care.'

Jedd nodded vociferously.

The man's face was flushed. 'And our cousin, Benny–'

'You care about your family, evidently.' Krush raised her voice. 'Iris has gone missing. We're worried about her.'

'That one. What's she done now?'

'When did you last see her?'

He looked around the filthy front yard without finding an answer. 'Dunno.'

'Don't you ever exchange text messages?'

'Nah. She got a new phone a while ago. Never told any of us the number.'

'I take it you're her brother.'

'We've got a different dad.'

'What's your name?'

'What is it to you?'

'A common courtesy. I told you my name. What's yours?'

'Geod.'

'I thought *he* was Jedd?' She pointed to Jedd, who glowered back at her from Geod's side.

'I'm Geod with a *G*, the little shit is spelled with a *J*.'

'I'm not a little shit!'

'Shut up, shitbag.'

'Shitbag!' Lucy said, from around the edge of the door.

'Stay inside, Lucy!' Geod pushed the little girl back.

The dog, farther back inside the house, did not stop barking.

Krush rubbed her belly. 'Listen, Mr Bottle. I'm concerned about your sister. I don't know where she is. If you can't tell me anything about her, is there anyone else in the house who can?'

'No.'

'What about Iris's parents?'

'Her dad's not around anymore. Mam's upstairs, but she's asleep.'

Krush checked her watch. 'Isn't it time she got up?'

'Mam's sick. I'm not going to disturb her for no good reason.'

'Isn't your sister's disappearance a good reason?'

'How do you know she's disappeared, if you don't know where she is?'

Krush tried to make sense of this. 'Come again?'

'Look, maybe nobody told you. Iris has issues. She was always that way, even when she was little. Sometimes she runs away. It's her way of dealing with it. She always comes back.'

'What if something bad happened to her?'

'That's her husband's job now, not ours. It doesn't sound like he's worried. If you're up here wasting our time, it's because he doesn't care.'

'Mr Bottle, I have reason to believe something seriously wrong may have happened to Iris. I can't explain the details to you now, but I can tell you that there are some mysterious circumstances.'

'That's not my problem.'

'You want to help your sister, don't you?'

'Nobody can help her.'

'I can. You don't know me, but I promise, whatever she's mixed up in, I can help. I need somebody – a family member or a friend – to declare her missing. Then I'll be able to set up a proper investigation with police resources. But so long as she's not missing, technically speaking, my hands are tied.'

'You came over here because you thought I'd be stupid enough to sign a form. Once I signed one, I'd have to sign ten. I'd have to go up to your station and be interviewed twenty times. I'd be constantly called up and driven around. No, thanks. Iris left our lives long ago, and she did it gladly. She never looked back.'

'Well, if that's how you feel.'

'It is how I feel.'

Krush looked at Jeff, one last chance for him to contribute, but Jeff was examining the paving slabs.

She took out her card. 'That's that then. If you hear anything about Iris…'

'You can keep your card. I'm not having any police shit in the house. Fuck, one of the neighbours might see it. They'd think we'd turned snitch. We'd wake up one morning and find "Grass" spraypainted over the front window.'

Geod ducked inside and slammed the door shut.

Krush stared at it for a moment, waiting for her anger to relent.

'Told you,' Jeff said.

28

Eleanor had always hated the Queen Elizabeth II Law Courts. The building was baffling, vast, brutalist, formed from ribbed concrete panels in a dull reddish tone. The city was full of these ugly behemoths, construction projects that are often blamed on corruption in local government. But not everything was corrupt, Eleanor told herself; sometimes, city planners just had bad taste. She pushed through the glass doors and entered the building.

Detective Sergeant Lisa Wainwright was sitting in a back room drinking coffee from a plastic cup. Behind a pair of dark sunglasses, she seemed to be praying to herself.

'Is it that bad?' Eleanor said.

'You're the one Grandad sent over.'

'If you mean Chris Blaine, then yes.'

'We have a few names for him. Grandad is the kindest.'

'Eleanor Rose.'

They shook hands.

'Excuse the sunglasses,' Wainwright said. 'The light gives me migraines. This goddamn job. Doctor says I need a long holiday, but it's impossible to take a day off right now.'

'The gang situation is tense?' Eleanor sat down next to her.

'You know I envy you murder cops. You solve killings after the victim's already dead. Over here, we're trying to solve the ones that haven't happen yet.'

'It's a murder I needed your help with, if you have time to talk.'

'I've got all day. We're waiting for a case to start but the defendant hasn't turned up. The taxpayer covers the costs. All these people, the judges, prosecutors, police, everyone sitting around twiddling their thumbs... their time isn't free.'

'A man was found dead on the border yesterday.' Eleanor took out her phone.

'I figured that's what this was about.' Wainwright glanced at the picture. 'Well, he wasn't killed for his looks.'

Eleanor flicked to the next picture. 'How about this? He was found holding a red shoe.'

'Christ. Weird things happen along that border, but I've never heard of a red shoe.'

'And this... this is a picture of a tattoo on the victim's forearm.'

'Never seen it before. It's not anything to do with the Looneys. You'd have to ask someone else about the Gilchrists.'

'I already did.' Eleanor put her phone away. 'So, you don't think this killing is connected to the gang situation?'

'He was found on the border. It can't be a coincidence.'

'Do you think the Looneys–'

'It wasn't Looneys, I can assure you. When the Looneys kill a man, he disappears. Going to Narnia, we call it. He's in a different reality now. And they don't cut a man's throat either, that's too soft. If they kill you, they make sure you know about it.'

Wainwright's lips curved upwards slightly, as if with pleasure.

'So–' Eleanor started.

'So, it was the Gilchrists.'

'I spoke to Tommy Presley. He's certain it wasn't them.'

'Tommy?' Wainwright laughed. 'Yeah, well, Tommy isn't police at this point. He crossed the line long ago. He's just another gangster, not even a competent one.'

'You're saying he's been corrupted?'

Wainwright's laugh had a cruel edge. 'You talk like a nun. Listen, I'll make it simple for you. Looneys are methodical, professional. They're neat and tidy. Gilchrists are messy, disorganised. This was a sloppy business. It's got Gilchrist written all over it.'

'You almost sound like you admire the Looneys.'

A strange look crossed Wainwright's face. 'It's not my job to judge them. I'm more like a primatologist studying orangutangs in the wild. I observe, that's all.'

'Is it possible it could have been someone else? A local officer in the Marsh told me there's a gang of kids running amok.'

'Perhaps. But if so, you don't have to concern yourself with that. The Looneys will deliver justice.'

'Are you talking about… vigilante justice?'

'I'm talking about orangutangs, remember.'

'No,' Eleanor said. 'This is my case. I have to solve it. I'm going to solve it right.'

Wainwright laughed. 'Is it because of the heart tattoo? You've connected to this ugly bastard, haven't you? Take my advice: don't.'

'I just want to do my job.'

'You know, I've heard about you.' Wainwright adjusted her sunglasses. Though the eyes behind the black lenses were concealed, Eleanor felt herself being scrutinised.

'Heard what?'

'There are things going on you don't understand,' Wainwright said. 'Things you wouldn't want to know. In the Unit, we're struggling to hold things together. God knows, we're underfunded, understaffed, but we do our best. If we fail… I'm talking about open warfare in the streets. Don't get involved. Don't intervene.'

'But–'

The door opened and a man looked in. 'Sergeant? They're starting to fill the courtroom now. You ready?'

'At last.' She scrunched up the empty cup and dropped it into a bin in the corner.

29

They sat at the back of the courtroom. Wood panelling on the walls gave a feeling of security – the orderliness and legitimacy of the law – but Eleanor had learned these things could be illusory. The accused, pointed out to her by Wainwright, was a smirking youth. Unlike most of the people in the room, who were dressed smartly, the accused wore a tracksuit. He lounged back in his seat as if this space was his living room.

'He looks so young,' Eleanor whispered.

'They all do,' Wainwright said. 'They've found the fountain of youth, I'm certain, somewhere in Liverpool.'

'He's not frightened at all. You'd never guess he was up for murder.'

'Oh, I think he's frightened. I don't buy the nonchalant act. We all have our own ways of showing fear.'

Eleanor winced as a sharp pain flared again in her stomach. 'Goddammit.' She grimaced, rubbing her belly.

'Are you alright?'

'Yeah, it's nothing. Stomach cramps. I don't know. Maybe I should have more than just black coffee for lunch.'

'Do you need…?' Wainwright fished in her bag.

'No. I'm fine, honestly.' Eleanor straightened, looking around the courtroom self-consciously, but nobody paid any attention to them on the back row. 'Which gang is the accused connected to?'

'The Looneys.'

'The Looneys and the Gilchrists really hate each other?'

'Of course. They've always despised each other, but something happened a year or so ago that set things on fire.'

'What was that?'

'According to one version of events, it happened at a wedding. Something as stupid as a snub, an argument about seating arrangements. God knows. How it started doesn't matter; it's how it's going to end that worries me.'

'And your informers?'

'Nobody breathes a word. They're waiting to see how this plays out, who wins. The Gilchrists are strong contenders. There are other groups as well. But the Looneys are different. It's a more systematic violence with them. They're waging a campaign of terror.'

Eleanor chose her words carefully. 'What if I wanted to go into that world myself? I mean, what if I reached out to some gangsters?'

'You want to find your own informants? Don't even think about it.'

'But—'

'Listen, it's just not worth it… not for some ugly bastard like your dead man. Nobody's going to mourn him.'

'You don't even know who he is.'

'I've been in this job a while; I can tell a piece of shit when I see one.'

'But the red shoe… I can't help feeling, this case is more than just a dead drug dealer.'

'Are you sure you're alright?' Wainwright's tone had changed.

'What do you mean?'

'No offence, but I heard a rumour. They say you've got issues. Mental health stuff. Now you're in here talking about red shoes.'

'I'm fine. I've got a therapist. I'm working through things like anyone else.'

'Sure.' Wainwright fell silent, watching as a man in a green suit hurried into the courtroom and sat next to the suspect. He cupped his hand over the kid's ear and muttered some secret words to him.

'Who's that?' Eleanor whispered.

'The lawyer. Mann's his name. He's the best, and he's expensive. Whoever paid this kid to kill, it was someone with a lot of money.'

30

After the police station, Stray only wanted to get as far away as possible. The humiliation stung. Of course, he could never be employed by the police. It was insane of Eleanor to come up with such an idea, and just as crazy that he had allowed her to talk him into it. Worst of all was Shepherd's smug face, sitting there on the other side of the desk, in judgement. A so-called psychologist, an inferior talent, a charlatan who could never imagine some of the recesses of the mind Stray had explored during his long years living rough. And Shepherd actually thought he could use Stray against Eleanor, turn him into a spy. He felt the rage rising in his throat as he stumbled through puddles, ignoring the faceless pedestrians as he pushed past them.

He had crossed half the city centre before he stopped to wonder where he was going. Eleanor's house was in the opposite direction, but he no longer wanted to go back. Neil hated him, and justifiably so. Eleanor would be disappointed to hear about the failure of the interview, but it would not stop her. She would keep looking for new ways to help him no matter how many times he failed. She was not the kind of person who could accept the simple truth: there was no possibility of help for Raymond Stray.

He put his hand into his jacket pocket to reassure himself the cash was still there. Ten crisp banknotes Eleanor had taken out of a machine and forced him to accept, despite his best efforts. 'Just to get you started. Pay me back when you're earning money again,' she'd said. He had not touched this money, and he lived in constant paranoia about losing it. He did not even own a wallet. The cash was loose in his jacket pocket – Neil's jacket, technically – beside a key to the house Eleanor had had cut for him. He could hardly believe it was real, but the cash was still there. He would have taken it out of his pocket to make sure, but he feared the greedy eyes of passing strangers.

It was time to face the truth: the real reason he had not spent this money was to keep it in reserve in case the desire for drugs became unbearable. And if he had kept it for this reason, then it was a simple step of logic to see it was always going to be spent on drugs. He was, after all, incurable. There was guilty consolation in this thought, and he almost managed to laugh at the memory of Shepherd and his judgemental smile from the other side of the desk, the side that was forever closed to him. Shepherd had never tasted heroin.

Half an hour later, he found Barn Owl in his shed in the scrapyard among the abandoned dock buildings north of the city. Barn Owl wore a tracksuit and appeared to have a tea cosy on his head. He was drinking from a mug with no handle. His hair and eyebrows were white, even though he could not have been more than thirty years old. His teeth, however, were black.

'Doctor! I thought I'd never see you again. I was offended you never came to say goodbye.'

'I never went anywhere.'

'People said you'd gone straight, got off the streets. They said you shacked up with some dumb rich piece who let you live in her house and spend her money.'

'This is a mistake.' Stray looked back at the open door, but there was no freedom out there, just piles of scrap metal.

'Don't take it badly, mate. Don't be like that. Come on, sit down. We haven't had a chat in a while.'

Stray back-pedalled. 'I've just remembered. I need to be somewhere.'

'You can't! I've got a dream to tell you, and a problem. God, I'm glad you turned up. There isn't anyone who gives advice like you do.' He grabbed a stool and set it in front of Stray. 'Did you ever hear of something called "Heart of the City"? I've seen it. It's real. It's a secret of course, but people like us, well, we're invisible. Nobody cares what we see. Still, I'm scared. What if…?'

'I'm sorry, I can't help anyone. I'm not in the right state. Tell me another time.'

'Don't be like that. Here.' He pulled out a bag of powder from his tracksuit. 'This is what you came for, isn't it?'

'No,' Stray said, staring at the bag. He could not take his eye off it.

'Come on, I'll give you a little hit for free, if you'll listen to my dream. Just a little one, a palette cleanser. You'll be able to carry on with whatever is so important. Got to take care of your rich woman, haven't you?' Barn Owl snickered in his nasty way.

'I can't,' Stray said, but he found himself sitting down.

'That's better. You just sit there and take the weight off. You know you're always welcome here. I'm glad you never left the streets. I knew it wasn't true what they said. "He'll be back," I told them. "The Doc is one of us. You can rely on him."'

'It's not like that,' Stray said. 'I really am trying to get clean. I haven't touched drugs in a few months.'

'Don't be daft. You can't leave the drugs now, mate. They're part of you. We both know there's no going back.' He set a small stove between them and lit it.

'No, I really am going clean. It's just, it's hard. I tried to get a job, but no one will give me a chance.'

Barn Owl gave a sad smile. 'That's how it is, mate. They don't want us. They hate us.'

Stray stared into the water as it started to bubble. 'There must be a way back into the world. It can't just be impossible.'

'It *is* impossible, and you know it. Ask any of the lads. Once you come this far, you never go back. Once or twice, you might fool yourself, or you might fool them, but in the end, you'll be back here, sitting on that stool, with the pan heating up. Be honest, mate, you don't want to go back, do you? Not really. That world's fake. All those ignorant cunts who walk past every day and won't throw a quid to a starving man. They don't see us, you know. We're part of the city background to them, like pigeons and dog shit.'

'There are good people. I've met them.'

'Ah, of course, your woman. You're a sly one, Doc. You're one of the best. I bet you snaked your way right into her life. She'll believe anything you say. She'll do anything for you now. Give you money. Let you stay in her house as long as you like. You're smarter than all those bigwigs who think they run the city. Rich bastards in their towers, arrogant pricks. Nah, you're the one who sees deeper. You see everything. That's why you're so sad.'

'No, it's not like that. I'm not using Eleanor… I wanted to help her. She needs help. She has some complexes, childhood issues, unresolved family conflict. There's something there, a puzzle, beneath the surface. I need to find out what it is.'

Barn Owl grinned. 'You see? You took one look at her, and you saw all her weaknesses. It was easy for you to control her. I bet she thinks she's the one in control. She has no idea about you. I bet she's a looker as well, isn't she? Who else could pull it off, Doc? Only you.'

'It's not like that.'

'Whatever you say.' Barn Owl laughed with that ugly, sniggering sound.

'I have to leave.' Stray stood up too quickly, knocking his stool over.

'What are you doing? Where are you going?'

He had no answer to that.

'Come back!' Barn Owl shouted after him as he stumbled to the door. 'You'll be back here, Doctor. Don't kid yourself. The world won't take you back. You'll be here again, and you'll listen to my dream.'

31

At the Pier Head, several groups of tourists were taking photographs in front of the Royal Liver Building. They tried to smile into the camera's eye as the endless wind off the river blew their hair sideways. Krush found it odd that a pile of concrete could inspire such devotion. She had always felt the Liver Building to be ugly. The gigantic seabirds on top were menacing, like pterodactyls. Or perhaps it was just that she was a born contrarian, as her dad said. In any case, of these towering blocks on the waterfront, she preferred the neighbouring George's Dock Building. Its utility appealed to her, and its simple design. A cuboid air shaft rising out of a square engine room, all in pale stone. It had to be one of the most attractive buildings ever constructed to house ventilation machinery.

Inside, the Mersey Tunnels Police employed fifty-one officers to oversee the sprawl of tunnels beneath the city. She was taken up to the control room, where Sergeant Lee Shipley was seated at a wide desk in front of a wall covered in screens.

He greeted her with a sheepish grin. 'It's not every day we get murder police in here.'

'Must be nice,' Krush said.

Shipley introduced her to two colleagues, Constables Erica Jones and Roy Ogden. Sagging in swivel chairs, they hardly took their eyes off the screens. Young, perhaps mid-twenties, they were out of place in this dark room. Shipley on the other hand was in his fifties and wore thick glasses. Long years of staring into the silver light of these screens had imparted a permanent squint to his eyelids.

Krush let her eyes wander over the array of camera views that were all identical and yet constantly changing: each showed a short stretch of grey tunnel with a car flying through.

'You know, you didn't have to come all the way over here,' Shipley said. 'We can send video footage to you.'

'I like to see what I'm working with. Anyway, I always wanted to visit this building.'

She crossed to a map of the tunnels on the wall. 'Slate came out here.' She pointed to the city centre exit. 'I went inside last night and tried to follow his path. Based on what the cameras show, he came along this way.' She traced the direction with her finger and tapped on the spot where a maintenance door was marked. 'He came out of this door. It's around fifty feet inside.'

It was strange to see the tunnel mapped out, utterly different to the experience of walking through it at night.

'The cameras don't show the rest of his journey,' she said. 'I believe he may have wandered through the ventilation shafts, but it still doesn't explain how he got inside the tunnel in the first place.'

The others stared where she pointed with nervous expressions. Murder police have that effect.

'We checked all the cameras,' Shipley said. 'There's no sign of him entering.'

'And yet, he did enter.' Krush left the map and peered into the wall of screens. In the rolling motion of the cars, she could not imagine a man walking among them in his Armani suit, carrying a red shoe.

'We checked every last camera,' Shipley said. 'There's no sign.'

'Are there any blind spots the cameras don't show? Anywhere he might have snuck in?'

'Here and there. But not at the entrances.'

'What about in the side tunnels? Are they all covered as well?'

'Not entirely.' Shipley clicked a button and one of the screens changed to show an array of eight camera views, empty passageways, corners of tunnel. 'But the main areas are covered. He would have to pass through one of them.'

Krush recognized a section of the ventilation shaft in one of the boxes, but it was different, seen like this, without the wind blowing in her face.

'Anyway,' Ogden added, 'there's no access to the passageways from outside the tunnels.'

'I found a button below the car deck,' Krush said.

The officers exchanged odd glances.

'Slate's button?' Ogden said.

'We're checking it.'

'Could he have come down in the lift?' Jones said.

Ogden did not take his eyes away from the screen. 'The lift is closed at night.'

'You have a lift?' Krush said.

'Sure,' Shipley said. 'For maintenance work. It's just below our feet. We sit on top of the tunnel here. Anyway, I suppose you want to see the car now?'

He brought up a video on the screen of a car entering the tunnel. A white Mercedes with tinted windows, registration DAZZ 79, Slate's car.

Slate's car entered the tunnel in Birkenhead at 18.30. Krush stared at the frozen image on the screen, but it was impossible to perceive anything through the tinted windows. She hunched closer. The other officers leaned over her shoulders.

'Alright.' She sat down into an adjustable swivel chair with wheels. Comfortable, it bore the weight of her belly with ease, and the wheels glided smoothly as she shifted forwards. They often wondered, back at HQ, where the Merseyside Police budget disappeared to. Now she knew.

'We need to track the car's journey,' she said. 'Through the whole of the tunnel. One camera at a time.'

'The whole journey?' Jones said. 'It's just a car driving through a tunnel.'

'So, we'll watch it drive.'

Jones shared a glance with Ogden. He clicked. The frozen image came to life. The car glided quickly forwards and out of view.

'Can you slow it down?' Krush checked Ogden's shirt from the side as he operated the computer, but no buttons were missing. 'Can I?' she lifted his tie and inspected the buttons. They were just like the one she had found in the passage beneath the car deck.

It made sense – most likely the button belonged to someone who worked here.

'Is that a standard tunnel police shirt?' she said.

'Yeah. We all wear them.'

'Are you missing a button?'

'I don't understand.' He checked under the tie and shook his head. 'Why would a button be missing?'

'What about the spare button in the lining?'

Almost smiling with bemusement, he reached inside the bottom of the shirt. 'Yeah, the spare button's there.'

The others followed suit, showing all the buttons on their shirts. None were missing. They looked at her like she was crazy. Maybe she was.

'OK, let's get back to this.' Krush pointed at the screen.

'Sure.'

They watched the clip again in slow motion. The car crept forwards, pixel by pixel, to disappear off the top of the screen.

'This is the next camera.' Jones clicked and brought up a new box. It was identical to the first. The car appeared at the bottom of the screen and crawled slowly forwards, disappearing at the top.

Krush stared until it no longer seemed to be a car in a tunnel, it was only geometry. A dark oblong that floated upwards through a fuzzy emptiness.

'Alright,' she said, 'next camera.'

The next clip came up and it might as well have been the same one as before. The car, the tunnel, the slow floating upwards, it was all the same. Lulled by the repetitive images, she lost track of time and was surprised when she glanced at her watch to see that she had been in this room for almost an hour.

'Are there places between the cameras where we might miss something?' she said.

'Only short gaps,' Ogden said. 'But we'd know if anything happened in between because the car would slow down. There's a minimum speed limit in the tunnel. You can see there are cars in front and behind your Mercedes. There would be a collision if it stopped.'

She tried to think but her mind was numbed by the screen that had left an oblong after-image floating behind her eyes. She blinked and shook her head.

'We call that "screen eye".' Shipley chuckled. 'There are painkillers in the drawer for headaches.'

'I'm fine.'

'Suit yourself.'

'Alright, next camera.' Krush wiped sweat from her brow. 'It's hot in here. Or is it just me?'

Nobody replied. They continued working through the cameras, and the car kept up its slow crawl from one screen to the next without slowing or speeding up. As she got used to the task, she noticed that the tunnel was not as straight as it had seemed. In some of the clips, it could be seen to bend. Doorways and hidden exits occasionally flashed along the side of the car.

Nobody spoke. The only sound was the clicking of the mouse as Jones worked through the cameras. Krush was too hot. She was starting to feel drowsy. She forced herself to stare at the screen, but her eyes could not find purchase. Finally, the car left the tunnel at the other end and disappeared. Only five minutes had elapsed between entering and exiting. There was no sign of Iris or anybody through the tinted windows.

32

There was nobody home when Stray returned, thank God. In Neil's kitchen, he made a drink with the fancy coffee machine. This had become one of Stray's greatest pleasures since he'd started living here. He drank it strong and bitter, no sugar, no milk; and scalding hot. His pleasure sensors were all used up from years of excess, and he required intensity to feel anything. He drank two cups quickly, wanting to make them last, almost tearful when the second one ended.

It was clear now, there was no way to break the cycle he was trapped in, except to take advantage of Eleanor. If that was the case, then the logical conclusion was unavoidable: he would have to exploit her generosity and gullibility to the maximum in order to gain his independence. Only in that way would he be free, he would no longer have to rely on others. He would never use anybody again.

Upstairs, he found a few sheets of paper and a pen in Eleanor's room, snuck back to his bed in the spare room, and closed the door. He had never betrayed a patient before. If he was going to do it, he would have to do it the right way. There was no way to save himself other than to find a job; and to get the job, he would have to take Shepherd's deal. If he could twist this logic around all the way, he might even be able to trick himself into believing that he was really doing it for Eleanor's benefit.

He took a moment to compose his thoughts, but – who was he kidding? – his thoughts crawled like cockroaches. He wrote:

Eleanor Rose: Psychological Evaluation

Observations:
Patient displays anxiety, confusion, traces of paranoia. Has no friendships or relationships. Cannot communicate with sister. Struggles to engage with other colleagues. Has returned to live in parent's house, unable to live independently. Does not eat properly. Psychosomatic symptoms including stomach pains.

Provisional Diagnosis:
Hysterical neurosis caused by bereavement and/or underlying family trauma. Patient lost both parents at an early age. Only surviving guardian is stepfather. The loss and death of former fiancé has not been processed.

Recommendations:
Therapy. Medication. Sabbatical from work. Career change.

A sound downstairs made him jump up in fright. The front door slammed shut.

Eleanor called from the vestibule. 'Hello? Anybody home?'

In horror, he stuffed the sheet of paper under his pillow. Beneath the fear, he felt a layer almost of pleasure. Working again, he had managed to forget about drugs for a brief while. His hand had stopped trembling.

Eleanor was coming up the stairs. 'Stray! Are you there?'

He tried to control his voice. 'Oh, hello!'

Christ, he sounded guilty.

She knocked on his door. 'Everything alright? How was the interview?'

'Erm…' He looked around the room for proof of his treachery, and spotted the pen lying in the middle of the mattress. He snatched it up and stuck it in his pocket. 'It was… I don't know.'

'Well, what did Shepherd say?'

'He said he'd get back to me.'

'Ah ha! There you go.' She smiled. 'He didn't say no. I told you it was worth it.'

To see her smile was the worst. He was a liar, and he was good at it. He did not want to speak at all for the lies that would tumble out of his mouth.

'What are you doing in here?' She looked around the spare room, his meagre, gifted possessions.

Was the treacherous page visible, sticking out beneath the pillow? He tried to block her view in the doorway. 'I was just… having a nap. But, Eleanor, where have you… You're soaking wet.'

She looked down and seemed to notice suddenly she was dripping water onto the carpet. 'Oh. It started raining. I didn't have my umbrella.'

'Are you OK?'

'I need your help.'

'A therapy session? Sure, just, let's go downstairs and put the kettle on.'

'Not a therapy session.'

'What then?'

'You have contacts in the underworld, don't you? You know drug dealers and users.'

'Eleanor, I'm trying to leave that world behind.'

'I'm not asking you to go back, I'm just looking for a way in. I'm trying to solve a murder connected to some gangland problem, but nobody will talk to me. The Organised Crime Unit are blocking me on every side.'

'I really don't think I can help you with this. I'm sorry.'

'Well, just come with me. You don't have to do anything.'

'Come with you… where?'

'To the border.'

33

Eleanor drove through the intensifying rain. Watching the windscreen wipers, Stray tried and failed to resist a growing dread. She was making a mistake, and he was helping her.

'There's one main pub in the Marsh,' Eleanor said. 'The Tin Whistle.'

'Pubs with musical names are always rough. This is not a good idea.'

'Relax. We'll just go in, have a drink, ask around, and leave.'

'You are aware they don't like police in these places?'

'You're not police. And me, well, that's why I'm wearing this.'

Stray examined her outfit: a red-and-black checked jacket over jeans and a black sweater.

He almost laughed. 'It's not a lumberjack convention. If you want to fit in around here, you wear a tracksuit or a football shirt. Just make sure you check which team first. The pubs are red or blue, they're not ecumenical churches.'

'It's a red pub. I'm not a total idiot, you know. This is the only red jacket I had.'

He shook his head. 'Oh boy.'

'Will you stop worrying? I thought you were tough. You've lived on the streets. What's a lime and soda in a pub compared to that?'

'When I was on the street, I was alone. I wasn't responsible for anyone except myself, and I didn't care about myself. But helping you, that's a different matter.'

'I'm a police officer. In the worst-case scenario, I'll show my badge. If it comes to it, I got my black belt in karate while I was living in London.'

'You should've worn that,' Stray said.

'You know what I think? I think you're just embarrassed. You're ashamed to be seen with me in public. You think it'll damage your street cred. Is that it?'

'You could have a career in psychology if you ever quit the police.'

'Shut up.'

'I have no shame left.' He tried to smile but failed. 'Something's going wrong with you, Eleanor. You should be investigating with another police officer, not with a washed-up junky.'

'I told you already, the police won't help. The Organised Crime Unit has basically forbidden me to investigate the gangs. But it seems obvious my victim was killed by one of them. I spoke to the Gilchrist expert, and to the Looney expert, and they both refused to help. It's worse than that, they're blocking me.'

'With good reason, I imagine. Let this case go. It's not worth it.'

Eleanor stared through the tracks of rain as she drove. 'I'm going to solve this case. I've made my mind up. This man, whoever he was, has been abandoned. Nobody cares. They call him "Dogface" at the station. But he has a tattoo of a heart. He must have loved somebody.'

'You're scaring me now, Eleanor. This isn't how detectives are supposed to talk. It's a job, not a fairytale.'

'Why are you being like that?' She turned from the wheel and her expression was hostile. 'I thought you were on my side,' she said.

'I *am* on your side. I want to help you. But you're mixing the lines. You're investigating outside the rules. You're trying to cheat the game.'

'So what, if my intentions are good?'

'If you cross to the other side, you won't stay good. It doesn't work that way. Take it from me, I've been to the bottom.'

'But you *are* good, Raymond, you are good. I see it in you.'

34

The wall of Krush's bedroom was turning into a kind of shrine. Among photographs of Iris and Damon Slate, she added quotations from the diary, maps and diagrams of the tunnel, and a picture of the red shoe beside a sketch of the button. She had to make sure her case was solid, indisputable. Clearly, the mayor had the ear of the police chief. Damon Slate, their only suspect, showed no fear. He believed himself to be untouchable, and perhaps he was right. How far did his influence reach?

She scanned the wall of evidence again and felt a nagging lack. The button might belong to one of the tunnel police. The shoe could be anybody's. She was still waiting on DNA results, but Elliot was backed up at work and distracted. Perhaps Carver had told him to slow down the Slate investigation as well. How compromised was the chief?

Krush needed more. Another day was almost over. The chances of finding Iris alive receded. The detective was alone, exhausted, and out of ideas. She had never known herself to be so depleted. The pregnancy really was draining her, despite her efforts to ignore it. She found herself staring at the picture she had taken of Iris's sad face in the portrait on the Slates' wall. The dark eyes glittered with – what? – anger, sorrow, madness? She turned away in revulsion.

If she could just drop in at the casino… She had not been there in months, not since she found out she was pregnant. The casino had been one of her guilty pleasures for years, although detectives were not supposed to go there. But she did not go to gamble or to drink, she went to count the cards. It was a mental exercise that kept her sharp. If she made a little money out of it, so much the better, but the enjoyment was in beating the game, nothing more. She did not need money. She was well paid for her work, and she hardly spent any of her salary. There was nothing she wanted.

A quick visit to the casino, just a ten-minute walk away along the docks, might clear her mind. The calming presence of the numbers would settle her thoughts. Logic would return.

Krush found peace in mathematics. After Mum died, Dad was so consumed in grief he neglected his only child and let a layer of dust cover every surface of their home. Little Beth used to sit in her room and play with a deck of cards. With no idea about the rules of any games, she invented her own. These were strange games with no winning or losing, that only stretched out in a peaceful endlessness. The idea was to guess what card was on top, but the game became complicated as she learnt the ratios of numbers and types. She began to calculate probabilities, without knowing what that meant; and she pushed her memory to breaking point, until she could memorise the entire random order of a shuffled deck. Occasionally, she managed to forget that Mum was dead.

She should not go to the casino, of course. So why was she walking through the rain beneath her umbrella? Just a moment ago she had been warm, dry, and safe in her flat. Now she was wandering between crowds in the dark, while cars flashed past spraying water in the streetlight.

Frightening impulses swam beneath the tight grip of her consciousness. A grip that was slipping. Reading the diary had intoxicated her. Iris had almost become a friend, the only person she could confide in.

Carver was probably right – Iris would turn up safe and sound tomorrow, and all of these anxieties would look foolish. But the doubt persisted. It was not too late to turn around and go back home, but she had already come this far. Just one game of cards in the casino, and everything would be alright. It was bright and warm in there, a kind of sanctuary, a place to forget that the world spun out of control, and Krush was just one woman trying to make it all hold together.

35

The Tin Whistle was crowded even on a rainy night. A drooping Ireland flag hung from the ceiling over the corner table where Eleanor sat down with her pint of Guinness, and Stray with his lime and soda. The walls were adorned with Liverpool FC shirts and faded photographs of players in red kits. Glancing around the other tables, she saw mostly middle-aged and older men, some of them wearing worker overalls. Behind the bar, an obese woman stole a glance over at their corner table.

Eleanor caught Stray staring at somebody across the room. 'Do you know that man?'

'What? No. Who?'

'You were looking at him, and he looked back. I thought–'

'If anybody looks at me, it's only because of this.' He pointed to his eyepatch.

But a moment later the man across the room got up from his table and shuffled towards them.

'Shit,' Stray muttered.

'Doctor, is that you?' He smiled, revealing just a few solitary teeth. He might have looked like a baby except the teeth were stained brown.

Stray looked confused. 'Eh…'

'Don't you know me? It's Elroy. Remember?'

'Ah, of course. You've had a haircut.'

Elroy fingered his bald scalp that was blotchy and covered in scabs. 'You're funny. Haven't seen you in ages. I heard you were off the streets.' He glanced at Eleanor. 'Is she yours?'

'Hi,' Eleanor said.

Stray blushed. 'No. This is my friend. I'm just helping her.'

'You're working with police, now?' Elroy stepped backwards. His smile collapsed.

'No, it's not like that. It's just, someone died.'

'Who died?'

'Do you know this man?' Eleanor brought up the photograph of the dead man on her phone. 'He was found in the park.'

Elroy looked at the screen but did not touch it. He shook his head. 'Never saw him in my life.'

'How about this?' She brought up the image of the heart tattoo. 'Ever seen that before?'

Elroy squinted. 'A heart? It was on your dead guy? He doesn't look the romantic type. I'll be going now.' He stepped away. 'Be seeing you, Doctor.'

'Who was he?' Eleanor watched Elroy shuffle away and disappear into a group at the bar.

'Nobody.'

'He knew you.'

'Elroy's one of those guys, lives on and off the streets. Sometimes he has money, but he spends it all on drink and then he's broke again.'

'You do know him then.'

'It's a common story. There are lots like him. We cross paths, but it doesn't mean they know me. They always think they do, but they don't. They have no idea about me, really.'

'He was willing to talk to you at least. That's a start. Nobody wants to talk to me, but with you… Do you recognize anyone else in here?'

'No, and I don't like this. I want to go home. Being seen working with police, it's not good for me. When I end up homeless again, people like Elroy will turn their backs on me. I'll be lost.'

'You're not going to end up homeless again.'

'Easy for you to say.'

'Come on,' she said, 'let's just ask a few people. What harm can it do?'

* * *

Stray was not used to drinking lime and soda. He ducked into the pub toilet and stood at the long, rusted latrine. The door opened behind his back, letting in a blast of Irish music. He glanced around and saw a man wearing a paper mask of King Charles III. It might have been left over from a coronation party, but the royals were not popular around here. Somebody had drawn a moustache and a pair of glasses on the monarch's face. The masked man stood too close beside Stray at the latrine. Stray shuffled aside to make space, but the man shuffled closer, his elbow pressing into this side. He reeked of cigarette smoke.

'You need to leave here now,' the king said.

'What?' Stray glanced and saw the side of his head behind the mask. A bald scalp, flushed red and beaded with perspiration.

'Leave. Get out of this pub and don't come back.' He pissed in a powerful stream that sprayed noisily in the latrine.

'I was just leaving anyway.'

'No. I mean leave *forever*. Stop working with that police bitch. She's too curious. She's sticking her nose in. Nobody would pay her any mind except you're helping her. They're good people here, good at heart. They'll talk to you. They trust you.'

'You've got it wrong. I'm a homeless loser. Nobody cares about me.'

'It's because you're a homeless loser they trust you. They feel sorry for you. Me, I see through you. I know you're a game player. You're up to something. I don't know what you're using this dumb woman for, and I don't care, but you can't do it in here.'

'Why?'

'She's looking for something she's not supposed to find.'

The man kept pissing. There was no let-up in the stream of urine. He must have been drinking lager all day, Stray thought.

'Well then, leave her in peace,' Stray said. 'She'll never find it.'

'That's my idea. The problem is, with you around, she might just stumble on it. Then she'll be sad. Believe me, she'll regret it for the rest of her life.'

'What are you talking about?'

The man stopped pissing with a sigh and buttoned himself up. He took out a roll of cash. 'Take this. It's a gift. Free of charge.'

'There are no free gifts. I'm a psychologist. I've seen it before. Gifts are about control. The white elephant—'

'Shut up.' King Charles stuffed the roll of notes into Stray's pocket. 'You take that to tide you over. Get back on the road. It's where you belong. Get out of Liverpool, find a nice street corner or an abandoned house, and be free. It's what you want. You know it is. You're used to the road now; you'll never be able to live in society again.'

'She won't let me. I already tried to leave more than once.'

'Sneak out. Wait till she's asleep and creep out of the house. Hit the road. You'll be well gone by the time she wakes up. Leave a note. Beg her not to look for you. It's for the best, for her and for you.'

'And if I don't?'

'She'll die. The blame will fall on you, the weird homeless guy who wormed his way into her life. We'll make sure it does.'

Stray stood paralysed at the urinal while the man washed his hands, whistling to himself, and walked out.

36

Mo's Casino was inconspicuous from the outside, a white building at the edge of the Queens Dock, facing the water. Only the tinted windows on the street side gave a hint of sin. A doorman eyed her belly as Krush approached the entrance. Evidently, her attempt to conceal the baby bump under a baggy coat had been in vain. But the man made no comment as he pulled the thick glass door open for her. As soon as she felt the deep, red carpet under her feet, the rush was like coming home. It had been too long.

The games room was quiet, just a few groups dotted around, but it was still early in this vampiric world. Many punters would not arrive until after midnight. She liked it better when it was quiet. With a glass of mineral water in hand, she wandered between the tables, watching the croupiers at work, and studying the players. They were all amateurish, betting when they should fold, and folding when they should bet. They were blind to numbers.

Tonight, she did not even want to play, she only wanted to watch the croupier's hands as he shuffled and cut. She had just found a solitary place to sit, when she noticed a noisy group enter the room from a private door at the far side – a few men in suits and several young women in trashy dresses, drinking cocktails. But, who was that? While the others giggled, one man gazed back at her a beat too long. It was Damon Slate.

And then she knew, this was why they had recognized each other at the hospital. She had not made the connection earlier, because the setting was so absurdly different, and in his confusion he had looked like a different man. Too late. She had just grabbed her purse and stood up to leave, when the lawyer, Mann, started taking quick steps towards her. Behind him, Slate sipped a cocktail and watched.

'What are you doing, Detective?' Mann said. 'You can't spy on my client.'

'I'm not spying.'

'Do you expect me to believe you came out to the casino tonight just to have a flutter? A police officer, and heavily pregnant at that.'

'I don't expect you to believe anything. I enjoy the casino. I've been a member for years. Ask anyone who works here.'

'Considering my client owns this establishment, that won't be difficult to verify.'

Failure. A stupid mistake. It burned in her chest; she had been caught out. She should have known Slate was the owner. Furious at herself, she set her jaw and tried to keep her face neutral.

'What do you want?' Mann said.

'To unwind. To spend a few hours winning money out of your boss's pocket.'

'You don't seem the type to throw their money away.'

'I don't lose.'

Behind Mann's back, across the room, Slate was watching, stroking his chin, curious.

'I'm going back over there now,' Mann said. 'I would advise you to leave, if you don't want a complaint filed at police HQ tomorrow morning. You have no reason to be here. There's no criminal case to investigate. The mayor asked for your assistance because my client had an accident. You were kind enough to help out. It's all resolved now. That's the end of the story.'

'Did Iris come home yet?' Krush said.

'What? No. I mean, not that I'm aware of. But I'm trying not to upset Damon. He's had a very difficult couple of days. I'm steering clear of those conversations, and I'd appreciate it if you would too.'

Over the lawyer's shoulder, Krush watched Slate for a sign of guilt. He was staring into space, not paying any attention to the gambling tables, or to the drink in his hand.

'Is Mr Slate's memory back completely now?' Krush said.

'No. Dr Chen said the missing day will probably never come back. He also said we have to avoid stress. That includes you.'

'Sure, I get it. I'm just a bit surprised your client would be in the mood to go out drinking and gambling while his wife is missing. Isn't he concerned about her?'

'You were informed already. Iris has mental health problems. She takes off by herself. She likes it that way. She doesn't want to be followed and observed. That's how their marriage works. She likes to be left in peace, and he's happy to let her do that.'

'From what you told me previously, their marriage is not working very well.'

'Marriages are complex.' He glanced at her left hand. 'Perhaps you wouldn't know.'

She glanced at his hand, also ringless. 'Would *you?* Excuse me.'

She was about to walk away when, to her astonishment, Damon Slate approached.

He patted his lawyer on the shoulder. 'Leave us alone a minute, Mann.' He held out his hand to Krush. 'I understand it's you I have to thank after my little incident.'

'You don't have to thank me for anything.' She ignored his hand, which trembled slightly. 'I was doing my job. I still am.'

'I take it we spoke at the hospital?'

'You don't remember?'

'Everything's a blur. Things are coming back slowly. I'm sorry if I was a nuisance. Please, let me introduce myself, properly this time. I'm Damon Slate. This is my casino. It's not the only building I own.'

There was something in the way he said that. Was it a threat or just vanity?

She grabbed his outstretched hand and shook it. 'Beth Krush. This is my city.'

He smiled. 'You're my guest tonight. What would you like to drink? It's on the house.'

'Nothing.'

He glanced at her baby bump and smiled. 'Of course. In that case, some free poker chips, courtesy of the house.'

'I can't accept gifts,' she said. 'I'm a police officer.'

'You're off the clock now, aren't you? And besides, in a casino, there are no gifts. The chips we give out are always recouped. For every free credit we extend, the gambler pays us back double in the end.'

Before she could refuse, he had signalled to the croupier at the next table. She found herself sitting next to him. A small stack of chips was beside her, and a couple of face-down cards in front of her. It happened quickly, the way mistakes do.

'Madame?' the croupier said.

She glanced at the cards. 'I stand.'

Slate twisted, and lost. Krush found her small pile of chips enlarged.

They played a few hands, and she watched him carefully as he continued to lose. He showed no sign of dismay as his chips were drawn in by the croupier. He was wealthy, of course, and these sums were trivial to him. Perhaps that was why he played so clumsily. It was almost as if he lost on purpose. Keeping count of the cards, Krush tried to understand his absurd decisions. He twisted when he should stick, and he stuck when he should twist.

'Looks like I lose again.' He smiled.

'The money in here's all yours in the end, isn't it?'

He pushed another few chips forwards. 'For me, it's not about money. It's not for you either, I can tell. You're the kind who likes a system. You enjoy figuring out the numbers.'

'Sure.'

'I'm the opposite,' he said. 'That's why I play poker. Poker is the truest game.'

'You can count cards in poker too.'

'You can try, but it's not about the cards; it's about the players. You can never eliminate the bluff. It's impossible to factor in all the psychology of the others. You have to play a different way. I'm good at poker.' He grinned, not afraid to boast. 'Do you know why? I can read people, but people can't read me. I learnt that long ago. It's how I've thrived.'

'Do you really believe that?'

'Check my bank balance. I didn't start out rich, you know. I was poor as shit like everyone else in Liverpool. But I can make deals, I can sell anything. When you're poor and you have nothing to sell, you'd better be good at bluffing. I know how to read a buyer. I know which mask to put on.'

'Are you wearing a mask now?'

'Truth be told, it's all masks. I have no face of my own. But, among friends–'

'We're not friends,' Krush said.

'And yet, you helped me. I was in a bad situation, and you came, you went the extra mile.'

'That's my job.'

'I don't think other police officers are like you.'

It felt like a poker game already, and her opponent knew how to bluff. It was her greatest fear. She could solve any kind of puzzle that was logical, but she feared the irrational. Was he bluffing now?

She looked for a lever and found one. 'I've been reading Iris's diary. Can I ask–'

'Iris's diary?' His eyes skipped to the cards on the table. 'I wasn't aware she had one.'

'Really? It was Dr Chen who suggested she keep it, as a way to process her emotions.'

'Is that right? Dr Chen. He never mentioned it to me.'

'Can I ask you something?'

'Fire away.'

'What is "Heart of the City"?'

He did not flinch, but he hesitated a moment too long. 'I have no idea. It's in the diary?'

'It was the only thing written on the day you had your little incident in the tunnel. I assume it's where you were driving to when you left the house with your wife.'

'I'm afraid I don't remember any of that.'

'What about the grey hood?'

His self-composure was impressive. Just a tremor showed in his eyelid. Or perhaps he really was innocent. 'A grey hood?' he said. 'Would it be facetious of me to suggest it might be a piece of Iris's clothing?'

'Does she have something with a grey hood?'

'Alas, I've never paid much attention to clothes. Don't laugh. I have a personal stylist who dresses me.'

Krush did not laugh. 'Mr Slate, at what point are you going to start worrying about your wife?'

'I always worry about her. She has issues, you know? She's not a happy person.'

'If you declared her missing, it would help us to find her.'

'When she goes away, she doesn't want to be found. She'd be angry if I went looking for her. She'd be furious if I authorised a police search.'

'You won't help then?'

'Detective, whatever you might think, I really do love my wife. She may not love me, but I do love her. She's the only woman I've ever loved, and the only one I ever will.'

The baby kicked hard in Krush's stomach, and she gritted her teeth.

Slate saw the pain she wanted to conceal. 'Are you alright?'

She had never been comfortable with discussions of love. It was an illogical subject, a dangerous emotion that humans played at recklessly. She had no idea what time it was. There were no clocks in the casino.

'It's late.' She jumped up. 'I shouldn't be here.' She backed away from the table.

'But your chips…'

'Give them to the croupier. He's earned them.'

37

As soon as he came back from the toilets, trying not to shake, Stray put on his jacket. 'I think we should go now.'

'Why?' Eleanor looked up from her second Guinness.

'It's just… we're making things worse,' he said, 'not better.'

'You look flustered. Did something happen? Sit down. I can't talk to you while you're standing up.'

Drinkers at the other tables watched as Stray sat back down, without removing his jacket.

He leaned forward to speak over the Irish music playing on the speakers. 'They're not stupid in here. They see what's happening. They realize you're police, and I'm helping you. They're only going to put up walls. If you want to communicate, you'll have to find a different way.'

She looked about and did not see anything. The other tables were immersed in their own conversations, oblivious to the world. But, of course, it made sense for Stray to feel out of place in the pub, she thought. After his years of homelessness, he would not be used to such noisy, sociable places.

'You call *me* paranoid?' Eleanor tried to smile. 'It's just a pub. Give it ten minutes. We'll chat to a few more locals, then we can go home. People like going to pubs, you know. If you're not careful, you might actually enjoy yourself.'

Stray relented, but he shook his head as he followed her. They approached a circular table of middle-aged men and showed the pictures on Eleanor's phone. The men grumbled and shook their heads, and looked at her with naked suspicion. Their answers were addressed to Stray rather than to her, but Stray kept his eyes down on the stained floor. Eleanor left a few of her cards at the table, but nobody picked them up. It was sad to leave them there, where they would only soak up spilled beer.

'What about him in the corner with the dog?' She pointed to a man with a long white beard who was seated beside a mongrel with matted fur. 'He looks homeless. Do you know him?'

'I'm not friends with every homeless soul, you know.'

'Come on.' She approached the man and pulled out an empty stool from beneath his table. 'Can I sit here a minute?'

'Which side are you on?' the man said.

'I'm not on any side.'

'Maybe that's where you're going wrong.' The man's glassy eyes fixed on Stray. 'Do I know you?'

'No.'

'I'd just like to ask you a few questions,' Eleanor said. 'It won't take long.'

'Ask what you want, but I won't answer.'

The dog lifted its head and sniffed. It looked ancient. Wearily, it raised itself on its filthy front paws.

'Stay down, Barney,' the old man said.

'Cute name.' Eleanor scratched the dog's head and it nuzzled against her.

The man kicked the dog. 'Stay down, I said.'

'He's alright. I don't mind.' She smelled Barney's dirty fur as he let his head slump in her lap.

'The stupid animal likes you,' the old man said. 'Most people in here, he growls if they come close.'

'I love dogs.'

'It shows. Well, if you're a dog person, you can ask me three questions, but buy me a drink first.'

'I'll get it,' Stray said. He shuffled away towards the bar.

Eleanor took out her phone. 'Do you recognize this individual?'

'That's an easy one. No.'

'Next question: have you ever seen this heart tattoo before?'

'You're wasting your questions, love. I wouldn't know anything like that.'

'Last question: do you know anything about a gang of kids that ride bikes around here?'

'All I know is to keep my distance. Barney hates bikes.'

The dog let out a mournful whine.

'Well then, I'll leave you in peace.' She looked about and could not see Stray in the crowd at the bar.

'Wait,' the man said.

'I'm fresh out of questions.'

'It's been a long time since I spoke to a woman. Sit a little longer,' he said. 'Anyway, Barney likes you.'

'I can't. I have to talk to everyone in here, and I don't have all night.'

Where was Stray?

'I get it,' the man said. 'It's my fault for being revolting. I wasn't always like this, like a rotting sheep. Listen, is it gangs you're interested in?'

'Why do you say that?'

'That dead man you're bothering people about, he must have been a gangster.'

'That's what we assume.'

'Well, don't let on that I told you, but in the side room, where the pool table is, you'll find a gang member. He wears a cap. Pogo, they call him. God knows why.'

He pointed and she saw the edge of a pool table just visible through an open door across the other side of the bar.

'Which gang does Pogo belong to?' she said.

'I have no idea. None of that business is anything to do with me. People whisper is all. Not to me, of course, nobody talks to me, but I overhear things. I sit here in my corner, and I listen. They say he's a big spender. He's got his own tab in this place. Half the people who come in here charge their drinks to it. He parks outside in a flashy car. He's always got young girls around him.'

'Thank you,' Eleanor said, 'that's useful information.'

'Don't you dare tell anyone where you got it from.'

'Don't worry, I won't.'

As she got up to leave, the man pulled Barney away from her. 'Tell your friend over there, he should get his own.' He gestured towards Stray who was walking back to the table carrying some drinks.

'Tell him what?' Eleanor said.

'His own dog, I mean. A homeless man should have a dog. Without a dog, he's lost.'

* * *

As soon as Eleanor entered the pool room, followed by a reluctant Stray, silence fell. A man at the table, who was just leaning to take a shot, froze in mid action. He was wearing a cap, Pogo. To his left, another man holding a pool cue stared. Two teenage girls wearing too much make-up perched uncomfortably on bar stools. They appeared to be completely drunk. It was smoky in the room, and dark. She noticed a full ashtray on the edge of the pool table. There were no windows.

She tried to smile. 'Don't mind me. Please, carry on with your game.'

Nobody responded. She looked for Stray to say something, but he cowered behind her.

'I don't mean any trouble.' She tried to sound natural, but the smoke was so thick she could not help coughing. 'I guess this bar doesn't have a licence for smoking indoors, but, hey ho, I don't care.'

'This is a private room.' The voice came from the corner of the room.

There was another man there, whom she had not noticed at first, sunk low on a stool in the shadow behind a haze of smoke. He wore a cardboard mask of King Charles III.

'Sorry, I wasn't aware.'

Nobody moved or spoke.

'Listen. I'll be open with you. I'm police. I'm not here to cause you any trouble. Whatever you may think, I'm not your enemy.'

The paralysed bodies in the smoke could not remain tensed any longer. Pogo took the shot and pocketed the red ball in the corner of the table.

Eleanor took out her card and held it to the weak light. 'My details are here. You can call me anytime. All I want is communication. I know relations with police haven't always been ideal. I'd like to change that. I'd like to build connections. We can help each other. Quid pro quo. We all want the same thing, don't we? We want this city to flourish. We love this city. That's what unites us.'

Pogo stared past her shoulder at Stray, with a puzzled expression. The man in the mask leaned back in the shadow.

'We should leave now,' Stray said.

'I'm just going to put this down here.' Eleanor laid her card on the edge of the pool table and backed away.

<h1 align="center">38</h1>

Krush dreamt of poker. She counted the cards, but the numbers did not add up. The harder she tried to concentrate, the worse she failed. Impossible combinations slipped out of the deck. She was falling behind. She was losing the game. It was already lost. 'This is my casino,' a voice said. 'It's not the only building I own.'

She woke in a pool of sweat with the duvet twisted around her, and pain like a knife in her belly. The words "under the river" caught on her dry tongue. It was still dark outside. She fumbled for the switch on the bedside lamp and almost fell out of the bed.

'Oh, fuck my life.'

The light came on. She hardly recognized what it showed. The whole wall facing the bed was covered with sheets of paper, diagrams, question marks. In the centre, Iris Slate looked out of a picture from her wedding day, and gazed at the world as if through the end of a long tunnel. Another twenty-four hours had passed and, with it, the chances of finding her alive were halved. One day closer to April 10th, marked in Iris's diary with an X. Time was running out.

She reached for the diary on the bedside table and could not find it. She looked in the drawer, under the pillow, and on the floor, but the diary was not there. She could not remember what she had done with it. She felt her anxiety rise as she climbed out of the bed into the cold, with one hand on her belly. A quick check of the morning headlines usually helped to settle her nerves, but she could not find her laptop either. Now she felt sick. She was an organised person. Everything in her life had its set place. She could usually find her belongings with her eyes closed

– her mobile phone, her keys, her laptop… but this morning she could not find anything. Pregnancy was scrambling her brain.

'Shut up,' she said, at a kick from the baby.

She wandered through the flat and found the front door ajar. Impossible. She never left the door open. She had a ritual, before she went to bed each night, of checking every door, every window, every switch in the flat. She closed the door now and opened it. It clicked into place just like always. She checked the lock and the handle, the frame, but there was no sign of any break-in.

She no longer tried to control her fear. It flowed freely. She raced from room to room. Her laptop was gone. Her mobile phone was gone. Her keys were gone. Iris's diary was gone.

She picked up the receiver on the landline. There was only one phone number that she could remember: her childhood home. She dialled it and heard the tone ring and ring.

Neil answered, sleepy and irritated. 'What is it?'

'Your daughter.'

'Beth? What… why are you calling the landline? It's six o'clock.'

She stared into the empty grey windows. 'I don't know.'

'Are you… are you alright? Is it the baby?'

'There's been a break-in. They took my laptop, my phone, my car keys. I don't know what else. I need to check everything. But… how? How did they get in? They must have walked around me while I was sleeping. It's not possible.'

'I'll come round right away,' Neil said.

'No, don't. Sorry. I don't know why I rang you. I'm in a daze.'

'Have you rung the police?'

'I *am* the police.'

'Ring the station. What, are you too proud to admit you got burgled?'

'No. It's just… I can't.'

The truth grew and twisted in her mind: if Carver found out what had happened, she would take Krush off the case and force her into maternity leave.

'I'm coming now,' Neil said. 'Don't go anywhere.'

'Dad, no–'

Damon Slate was behind this. Who else? She had told him about Iris's diary, and he had sent someone to steal it. The laptop, the phone, the car keys, they were just camouflage, to make this look like a regular break-in. Nobody else cared about the diary, only Slate and Krush. No other thief would have taken it.

He owned half the city, everyone said. He must have had a key to the door. They had walked right in. They might have leaned over her and listened to her breathing in her sleep. They might have touched her skin. Revolting.

These people were aware of her address, of course. 'I know exactly who you are, Beth Krush,' the lawyer had said at the hospital. She should have taken him more seriously. She should not have underestimated these people. She had been guilty of a kind of snobbery, assuming they were stupid, that she could easily outwit them. They had been one step ahead of her from the first moment. And now she had lost her only weapon against them.

39

It was early, still dark. With sinking futility, Eleanor crossed the border again. She made her way back to the house where the kids lived, 11 Woodpecker Lane. Her colleagues had blocked her in every direction. If Gilchrists or Looneys were responsible for the killing, she had no way of finding out. The loose end was this supposed gang of kids that maybe was no gang at all. If nobody else would talk to her, they might.

She walked over the bike tyre tracks that led up to the front door. Pale petals blew past her gaze, turning on the wind. She banged three times on the door and stepped back. Nothing stirred in the house. She crouched and peeked through the letter box, but the hallway inside was deserted. She knocked again. No response. In the gap between sheets of newspaper covering the living room window, she looked again for the kid on the couch, but the room was empty and dark.

She went back to the front door and banged as hard as she could. Nothing moved. She shouted through the letter box. 'Open up! I know somebody's in there. Open up!' She banged again. 'I'm going to stay out here all day. I won't leave until somebody talks to me.'

Nothing.

She banged and shouted louder. 'I just want to talk! I don't care what you're up to!'

Nothing.

'Goddammit.'

She sat down on the front step with her back against the shut door. She had said she would wait all day, and she would. Surely, they would have to come out eventually, or somebody would arrive from the street. She waited. It was almost peaceful watching the quiet street from her vantage point. Pale petals caught against corners of the walls, on the tyres of parked cars, the gate posts. It seemed like a waste, this excess dumped into the streets. What was the point? Her mind was drifting.

After five minutes sitting there, it started to rain in fat, gentle drops.

'Perfect.'

She banged on the door and shouted through the letter box. 'I'm still here! I'm not going anywhere! You'll have to talk to me!'

But her voice was growing hoarse, and her knocking was weaker. Maybe she really was losing it.

The rain fell heavier, and she put up her collar. The weather would not stop her. But nothing moved inside. For a moment, she was filled with doubt. Was this even the right house? She heard a car approaching and jumped up from the front step. The car moved slowly, a grey BMW, it stopped in the middle of the road outside the front gate.

Eleanor walked towards it, trying to look calm. She looked for the driver's face in the side window, but it was obscured by reflections, the terraced houses that blocked the light, and the looming, alien trees.

The door opened. 'Get in, Detective.'

She crouched to look inside. Sergeant Lisa Wainwright was seated behind the wheel. She was still wearing her sunglasses.

'What are you doing here?' Eleanor said.

'Just get in. We have to talk.'

* * *

Wainwright drove around the block. 'I told you; the situation is delicate. You can't just go barging into places. We're maintaining a wait-and-see approach.'

'That's what I was doing on the doorstep. I was waiting to see.'

'No, you were sticking your nose into things.'

'Tell me the truth about that house.'

'I can't. Not now. Look, this is the critical moment. You wouldn't guess, from the outside. It's all quiet, but it's too quiet. Whether people know, or whether they just feel it somehow, the city is waiting to see what happens. People feel the blood in the air.'

'What blood?'

'The blood waiting to run.'

'You lied to me before,' Eleanor said. 'You said you didn't know anything about a gang of kids, but now you pick me up from outside their house.'

'I didn't lie,' said Wainwright. 'I got a phone call, that's all.'

'A phone call from who?'

'Just a phone call. "One of your officers is making a noise. Come and collect her." So I did.'

'I don't believe you.'

'That's your affair.'

'Who lives in that house? Who was listening in there?'

'Nobody. It's deserted.'

'The kids' bike tracks run up and down the drive.'

'Kids go where they want. We couldn't stop them, even if we wanted to. You know this. The courts have got our hands tied when it comes to minors.'

Wainwright's phone on the dashboard buzzed. She glanced at it and stopped the car. 'I have to drop you off here. I've got things to do.'

'I could come with you.'

'I don't think so.' Wainwright leaned across her to open the passenger door. 'I'm sorry we had to get to know each other like this. You seem like a nice person. Maybe in different circumstances, we could've been friends.'

Eleanor climbed out of the car into the rain, a downpour now. 'What do you mean by that?'

'It's just...' Wainwright hesitated.

'Tell me.'

'Does it occur to you that if you were given this case, it's because nobody wants it solved?'

Eleanor shivered in the deluge. 'Who told you that?'

'Just...' Wainwright looked pained. 'I don't know you, alright? I have no idea what's going on in your life. Maybe you've got some issues you need to deal with. I think people higher up have got suspicions about you.'

'You *think*, or you *know*?'

'You seem like a nice person.'

'You already said that.'

'It's just… sometimes, nice people don't make the best police officers. You have to be tough in this business.'

'I see. You think I don't have what it takes. Or someone you spoke to thinks it.'

'Don't get mad at me. If we're having this conversation at all, it's only because I wanted to help.'

'I'm going to find out the name of that dead man in the park,' Eleanor said. 'And I'm going to find out why he was killed.'

'Goodbye, Eleanor Rose. Good luck.'

The door closed, and the car pulled quickly away.

40

'You won't believe this!' Elliot shouted across the morgue.

'What?' Crossing the tiles, Eleanor saw his plastic gloves were covered in blood.

He put down a pair of tweezers in a dish by the side of the body which was partially exposed beneath a plastic sheet.

'Dogface didn't die from the wound in his throat.'

'Are we still calling him that?' Eleanor stopped in the circle of light beneath a hanging lamp and forced herself to look. The snarl on the dead man's mottled face was uglier than she had remembered. Beneath his ripped throat, the chest cavity was empty. The organs had been removed.

'Sorry,' Elliot said. 'Have you found a name for him yet?'

'No. Nobody recognizes him. Nobody cares he's dead. I feel like I've failed him.'

'It's not your fault, Eleanor. Some jobs are just like that. You have to be able to put them aside and move on. No use beating yourself up.'

'What did you find out?'

Behind his surgeon's mask, speckled with blood, Elliot's eyes smiled. 'Look at this.'

The victim's heart lay in a metal bowl to one side. A dark, fleshly lump, it was hard to believe it ever belonged to a human with a name.

'He died of a heart attack,' Elliot said.

'But… his throat…?'

'He was already dead when they cut his throat. It makes sense, actually. It explains why we didn't find a lot of blood at the crime scene.'

'Why would they cut his throat if his heart had stopped?'

'Your guess is as good as mine.'

'To make sure he was dead?' She leaned to examine the wound in his neck, a deep, wide gash. 'Perhaps to deface the corpse because… well, because they hated him.'

'I don't envy your job,' Elliot said. 'Here, I just have to cut the bodies up. What I do is like science. What you do… it's more a guessing game.'

'And the heart attack, what caused it? Did you find drugs in his system?'

'Negative. His blood came back clean. There's no obvious cause. Could've been congenital. That happens sometimes. Or…'

'Fear,' Eleanor said. 'He was terrified.'

'And with reason. Look at this.' Elliot pulled away the bottom part of the sheet to show lesions around the dead man's ankles.'

'He was tied up,' she said. 'Signs of torture?'

'He took some blows to the head and side,' Elliot said. 'He's got some bruised ribs. Someone must've punched or kicked him pretty hard.'

'So' – she closed her eyes – 'they tied him up, beat him. Perhaps they threatened something worse. They had a knife, after all.' She opened her eyes, and turned to Elliot. 'Do you have any idea about the blade?'

'It was probably a pocketknife. Something small but sharp.'

'So, they had a knife, they might have threatened to cut his balls off…'

'…and his heart packed in,' Elliot supplied. 'He might have had a weak heart. He couldn't take it.'

'It's a working theory. But it still doesn't explain why they cut his throat after he was already dead.'

'That's for you to puzzle out, Detective. Or don't bother. Bury this poor bastard and let him rest in peace.' Elliot pulled the plastic sheet over the desecrated body, hiding it from view. 'Cheer up.' He took off his bloodied gloves and dropped them in the bin. 'I've got a surprise for you.'

'What?'

'You're not going to believe it.'

'Just tell me.'

'Prepare yourself to be shocked.' He took off his mask to reveal a wide grin.

Still smiling, he crossed the room and sat down at a metal desk. She could not imagine what he was so pleased about, and felt disturbed at the misplaced emotion.

'I believe this belongs to your investigation.' He rummaged in a box and pulled out the red high-heeled shoe in a clear evidence bag.

'The shoe?'

'There's no blood on it, but there are prints and there's DNA. At least three different people touched it. One of them was Dogface. The other two don't match with anybody in our databases.'

'OK.' She tried to hide her disappointment. Elliot's smile had hinted at something more decisive.

'There's also this.' He reached into the box and pulled out another shoe, red, high-heeled, in its own evidence bag.

'What?' Amazed, she grabbed it from his hand. 'The matching partner? But… where did you find it?'

'That's the funny thing…'

41

The two red shoes lay side by side in the middle of Carver's desk. In separate labelled, transparent bags they were reunited and yet apart. From the other side of the desk, the police chief shook her head dismally. The sisters eyed the two shoes in silence. Krush had not looked at or spoken a word to her sister since entering the room.

'The shoes match,' Carver said. 'Forensics compared the DNA. They were worn by the same person.'

'Iris Slate.' Krush reached for the nearest shoe, but Carver pulled it out of reach.

'That's our working theory, but it's not so simple. DNA shows several people touched these shoes. One has three sets of prints, the other has five.'

Krush sat back. 'Naturally. The medics will have touched the shoe Damon was holding when they took him to hospital.'

'How did the shoes end up miles apart?' Eleanor said.

Carver regarded the sisters. 'That's what I need the two of you to tell me.'

'The two of us?' Krush adjusted her chair but did not look at her half-sister. 'This is my case. I found the first shoe.'

'Well, Detective Rose found the other one. You'll have to work together. Can you manage that?'

Eleanor waited for her sister to say something, but she stayed silent.

'If you two can't cooperate,' Carver said, 'I'll find someone else to take over. I'm serious. I need to know. Can you two work as a team to solve this case?'

'Yes,' Eleanor said.

Krush tensed. 'I suppose so.'

They had not been in such close proximity in years. Eleanor could smell her sister, a shocking intimacy. She felt the weight of her oversized belly as if it were her own.

'That's not good enough.' Carver raised her voice. 'Listen, I don't know what's going on between you two, and I don't care. Families are weird, I get it. I've got a brother I haven't spoken to in a decade. Didn't even invite me to his wedding. But this is work and it's important. You're police officers. Be professional. Can you work together?'

'Yes,' Eleanor said. 'We can work together.'

'Yes,' Krush said. 'I'll work with anybody. I don't care. But let's make something clear. This is my case. I'm in charge.'

'But–' Eleanor gave up. There was no point arguing. She had forgotten the intensity in her sister's dark eyes. Eyes that saw past the surface-level comforts of the world, only searching for the truth, a painful truth that left its scar in her gaze, though she never blinked.

'My case is more important,' Krush said. 'I'm investigating a missing woman and a well-known businessman – a man who owns half the properties in this city and has high-up connections. He's best pals with the mayor. My partner meanwhile is investigating a dead gangster in a park.'

The way she said "my partner" sounded as if there was no relationship between them and never had been.

'About that,' Carver said. 'With your pregnancy, I don't want you working the gang angle. I don't want you to set foot in the Marsh, or near the border. Got it? Let Eleanor deal with that stuff. You focus on Damon Slate.'

Krush nodded. 'Fine by me. *She* can do what she wants in the Marsh. We won't need to spend much time together, but we'll touch base and share information.'

Carver looked from one sister to the other. 'What the hell happened between you two?'

'Nothing,' Krush said.

Eleanor found no words. Raw pain flared in her belly, and she tried not to let it show.

'Alright.' Carver picked up the first shoe, checked the attached label, and placed it in front of Eleanor. The other one, she placed in front of Krush. 'Do it your way. You're both excellent detectives and I see no reason why this shouldn't work. But I'm going to be keeping a close eye on things. If you can't work together, I'll break this partnership up and find someone else.'

'You don't have anything to worry about,' Eleanor said, but her new partner still refused to look at her.

'Good.' Carver stood up. 'Use the empty office next door as a shared investigation room. I want to be able to keep tabs. Hopefully, we can solve this quickly and without fuss. Remember, the media is watching us. Damon Slate is a big name in this city, and his lawyers will pounce if we make one mistake. Now, is there anything else?'

Krush did not stand. 'Yes. We need to declare Iris Slate missing immediately. We should have done it yesterday. There's no time left to waste.'

'We already spoke about that,' Carver said. 'Nobody in her family believes she's missing. They all agree, she goes off by herself.'

Krush stared her down. 'How far are you willing to go to cover for the mayor's friend?'

'Be very careful with your words, Krush. You're on a tightrope now. You think you're too accomplished around here to fall, but nobody is. If you want to interview Damon Slate about this – the shoes, the diary, your theories – go ahead and speak to him. But don't push it. Don't even think about dragging him in here in handcuffs. Damon Slate is important, and he's popular. The man's suffering from some kind of head injury, or God knows what, and there's no evidence at all he's done anything wrong. There'd be an outcry against us.'

Krush nodded. 'I'll speak to him, and I'll prove to you, he knows where his wife is.' She got up to leave, and Eleanor followed suit.

'Can I talk to you for a moment, Detective Rose?' Carver said.

'Just me?' Eleanor felt her sister's suspicious glance.

'Just you. Don't look sheepish. It's an unconnected matter – bureaucracy.'

'I'll leave you alone then.' Krush walked out and shut the door behind her.

As soon as they were alone, Carver let out a sigh. 'It's about your half-sister.'

'Oh.' Eleanor rubbed her stomach.

'She's five months pregnant but she won't stop.'

'That's Beth.'

'I put her on the Slate case because I thought it would be nice and easy. A rich bastard who had an accident. I thought she might even get some perks, a ride in a limousine, a fancy dinner. But Krush has a way of sniffing out violent crime even where there is none.'

'You don't believe her theory about the missing wife?'

'I don't know what to believe. No crime has been committed, at least not "officially". A man had an accident and lost his memory. His wife has gone camping for all we know. As things stand, there's nothing to investigate.'

'If Beth thinks there's foul play…'

'…then there's probably foul play. Indeed. I'm going to need you to watch her. Keep her out of trouble. If this case escalates, even in the slightest way, you let me know. I'll have her taken off it and sent on maternity leave, whether she likes it or not.'

'I'll do my best… but I've never been able to change Beth's mind, truth be told.'

'Who could? Still, you must have learnt over the years how to manage her. You're still alive, after all. I don't know how long I'll last at this job the way things are going.

Nobody warned me about Beth Krush when I accepted the position.'

'*Manage* her? I wouldn't say I ever tried to do that.'

Eleanor tried to keep the growing sense of guilt from showing in her face. It felt like betrayal to talk about her sister behind her back. She knew her sister disliked her, and now this conversation seemed to justify the dislike.

'She's a brilliant detective,' Eleanor blurted. The best she could come up with.

'Nobody denies that. But when you've been in the job as long as I have, you come to learn, brilliance is dangerous. The best police officer is hard-working and solid, reliable, gets the job done. But brilliance... that's something else – that's for poets, saxophonists, tortured geniuses, and the like. I don't need it at the station.'

'I'll do my best.'

'Don't look so glum.' Carver got up and walked over to the door. 'Think of this as a second chance to patch things up. It's uncomfortable for the whole station the way you two ignore each other. If this partnership goes well, maybe you'll be friends again.'

42

Trying to keep the guilt from showing in her face, Eleanor found her sister in the office next door, setting up an evidence board. 'Great,' she said, 'you got started. Shall I–'

'What did the boss want to talk to you about?'

'Erm, nothing.'

'Don't play stupid,' Krush said. 'She told you to keep an eye on me, didn't she? On account of this.' She stuck out her baby bump in a gesture that was almost obscene.

'She's concerned about you. You're five months pregnant.'

'Give me a break.' With her back turned, Krush wrote something on the whiteboard with a marker.

Eleanor studied her handiwork. Three boards were pushed together against the back wall, a mishmash of bits of paper, pictures, and scribbles in different-coloured marker pen. Despite her oversized belly, Krush looked too small beneath the array of information.

'You're the best detective we've got,' Eleanor said. 'It's understandable. We have to take care of you.'

'It's too late to play nice. Listen, the mayor has been in Carver's ear. They're all watching out for their man, Slate. He's the money pot. He's bankrolled half the investment in the city, as well as the mayor's election campaign. Nobody wants their darling to be investigated, and that includes Carver.'

'You're talking about corruption?'

'Iris wrote in the diary that Slate has power over the police. Look.' She pointed at a clipping on the evidence board.

'All this was in the diary?' She studied the rest of the board.

In the middle, a sheet of paper was headed, "Iris's Diary: Theories". She read:

> *Under the river = Depression (Dr Chen)*
> *D = Damon Slate*
> *O = ?*
> *Heart of the City = Iris? Narcissism. (Dr Chen)*
> *Grey hood = ?*

Her eye caught at the bottom of the page. 'Grey hood… what's that?'

'I don't know. The diary doesn't explain. Why, does it mean something to you?'

'A grey hood? I feel like… maybe… did I see something? No. It's nothing. Ignore me.'

'Carver has already sabotaged the investigation. You just heard it with your own ears. Iris Slate is missing. We need to set up a full-scale search. It should've started days ago. But here we are.'

'Why would Carver stop that?' Eleanor said.

'Imagine the headlines for Slate. He can't have that. Neither can the mayor; he's too close to the flame.'

'But… are you sure she's missing? Isn't it possible Slate is telling the truth? Maybe she really has just gone off somewhere by herself.'

'You sound like them. Slate… the lawyer… Iris's family, they all agree, she runs off from time to time. They think she's just crazy.'

'Maybe it's not crazy to run away from these people,' Eleanor said.

Krush scoffed. 'You would say that. You're the one who ran away from here, from everyone, and never said goodbye.'

'Hey, I'm just trying to help.'

When Krush turned from the board, her eyes were hostile. 'You want to help? My flat was broken into last night while I was asleep. They took Iris's diary. It was the most important piece of evidence I had.'

'What? Why didn't you say so earlier? Does Carver know?'

'Nobody knows except you and me. If Carver finds out I was burgled, she'll take me off the case and put me on maternity leave.'

'But… Jesus Christ… are you alright?'

Krush seemed thrown by the question. She rubbed her belly. 'Yeah, I'm fine, I guess. It was a shock, that's all. It's disturbing to think of a stranger in your room while you're asleep.'

'Of course it is. Beth, you need to take a break.'

'Don't start with that. I'm warning you. If we're going to work together, I need to know you're on my side. If you're just Carver's spy… well, there won't be any family reunions in future.'

'You know I'm on your side. I always have been.'

'That's not true. Don't kid yourself.'

Eleanor sat down and tried not to feel hurt. The evidence board swam in front of her eyes, a complex of coloured lines like a map of the underground.

'Let's just focus on the case, alright?' Krush said. 'Neither of us wants to deal with family stuff. Our first priority is to bring Slate in for questioning.'

'You know we can't. Between his lawyers and our boss, the media…'

'He ordered a break-in at my flat. That's good enough. I checked the documentation. Slate owns the whole goddamn building I live in. He owns, or part-owns, all the towers along the waterfront. His construction firm have their fingers everywhere.'

'Maybe you're right,' Eleanor said, 'but it's not enough to arrest him. You know it isn't. So, now what?'

'Fine. We can't arrest Slate. So, let's have a civilised conversation with him.'

* * *

They drove through the city. Krush looked out of the window and kept silent.

Eleanor would have turned the radio on, but she knew it would only annoy her sister. 'You know Dad really wants you to move back in while you're pregnant,' she said.

'Yeah, he only tells me every day.'

'He thinks it's my fault. He says if I moved out, you'd agree to move in.'

Krush did not reply.

This attempt at conversation had been a false start.

Still, she tried. 'I'd do that, if you wanted me to. I'd move out today. I need to get a place of my own anyway. Moving back into my old room was only supposed to be temporary. Somehow, I got stuck.'

'I have no intention of moving back in with Dad,' Krush said. 'It makes no difference if you're there or not.'

'Oh.'

'Let's make a pact: no conversations about family while we're in the car, hey?'

Eleanor sighed. 'Fine.'

She looked for a way in again. 'What else does it say in Iris's diary?'

'A lot of bizarre stuff. I spent the morning trying to write it down from memory. It's written in a strange style, sort of symbolic. I spoke to Iris's doctor. He said it's about her depression. He suggested she write her feelings down. She uses metaphors like "under the river" to describe how she feels. There's nothing literal in it. It's like a poem. I hate poetry.'

'Under the river. That could be the tunnel?' Eleanor said.

'Sure, but what about the tunnel? It's too vague. There are other details like that. The grey hood's another one. And "Heart of the City". She wrote that on the day she disappeared.'

'Is it a restaurant?'

'If it is, they have terrible marketing. I've searched everywhere. There's no trace of a Heart of the City.'

'I guess you're right. It's poetic, not literal. But, if it's just poetry, why did her husband want to steal it?'

'That's what's bugging me. There must be something incriminating, something I missed.'

'What about Slate's amnesia. How do you explain that?'

Krush shook her head. 'I bet he's faking it.'

'Faking it? Why?'

'Isn't it a bit convenient? His wife disappears at the same time as his memory? Then, while I'm at his house, Slate's stepson tells me his dad is a liar, a manipulator. He warns me not to believe a word he says.'

'But...' Eleanor looked for a way to argue that wouldn't antagonise her sister. 'The doctors checked Slate, didn't they? How could he fake it?'

'I don't know.' Krush sounded defeated.

They drove in silence for a few moments while the rain streaked down the windows.

'Stray could talk to him,' Eleanor said. 'I'm certain, Stray would know if the amnesia was real. He might be able to bring back the missing memories. He has gifts, you know.'

'Jeez, Eleanor. Come on. Get a grip. Don't you know they laugh behind your back about this stuff? You tried to get your homeless addict friend a consultant job at HQ.'

'They laugh? Really? Who laughs?'

'People are worried about you. You're the only one who doesn't see it: Stray is a user. Look what happened to his sister for God's sake. He's snaked his way into your life. He lives rent-free in the house. Now you're running around doing errands for him. You give him money, don't you? You give him clothes, food, what else? Open your eyes.'

'He's a good man, and a talented psychiatrist. If you let him talk to Slate, he'll find the answers you're seeking.'

'Sure, and we can both be laughing stocks at the station.'

43

In the living room of Slate's house, the detectives sat on the sofa opposite Ian and Claire.

'No news from Iris?' Krush said.

The two step-siblings exchanged sullen glances.

'No,' Claire said. 'But that's normal. She often stays out and doesn't tell anyone.'

'Do you know where your dad is?' Krush said.

'No.' Ian stared at the floor.

'He never came home last night,' Claire said. She looked nervous.

'We've been told that your mother often goes away by herself. Is that true?' Eleanor looked from one sibling to the other, but neither of them returned her gaze.

Ian ground his teeth. He watched the cat as it dropped down from the window ledge and looked around the room at all the people. It meowed reproachfully.

'Keep that thing away from me,' Krush said.

'It's alright, she doesn't approach strangers.' Claire moved to pick up the cat, but it slunk away from her and skipped across the room. The others watched as it jumped up on Eleanor's knee.

'I have a thing with animals,' she said, apologetically.

The cat found a comfortable position in her lap and settled.

'Stupid creature.' Krush leaned further away against the far side of the sofa. 'The situation is this,' she began. 'Nobody's seen Iris for three days, but, officially speaking, she isn't considered a missing person. Somebody needs to declare her as missing. Until then, we're limited in what we can do in looking for her. Your father doesn't appear to be concerned about her whereabouts. Her actual family don't care either – I spoke to them yesterday. Are you two willing to declare her missing?'

'But… what would that mean?' Claire stared at the cat. 'I don't want to get my dad in trouble.'

'It's nothing,' Krush said. 'Just a formality, paperwork.'

'So… we'd have to go down to the station?' Claire looked frightened.

'I'll do it,' Ian said. 'I'll do it right now.' His face tensed with what might have been hatred.

Eleanor was about to ask him why he was so keen to cooperate, but Krush jumped up from the couch.

'Good.' She headed towards the door. While we're here, we need to take some items that belong to your parents,' Krush said. 'For DNA checks. We found a few items during the investigation, but they don't match any DNA in the database.' She set off up the staircase.

The two kids had not moved. They seemed sunken in shock.

'Wait for me.' Eleanor ran up the stairs after her.

Up ahead, Krush went through a door. 'This is Iris's room.'

'They have separate rooms?' Eleanor entered the room and found her sister putting on a pair of plastic gloves.

'What should we take? A strand of hair would be perfect,' Krush said. The sound of seagulls squawking came through the window as she leaned over the bed with a magnifying glass. 'There must be one here somewhere.'

Eleanor knelt to check the floor. 'I don't know. It's so tidy in here, it feels like nobody has ever lived here.'

The screams of the seagulls were so loud they seemed to be inside the house.

'Hold on.' Krush froze.

'What is it?'

Krush stared at the window. 'The birds… The seagulls are screaming. There's somebody outside.' She ran to the window and pressed her face against the glass. 'Oh shit.'

Eleanor looked over her shoulder and saw a man climbing over the gate in the back garden. With one arm, he shielded himself from a swooping gull.

'That's him,' Krush said. 'That's Slate.'

'What?'

'He's sneaking out the back. He was in the house this whole time. Shit!' She set off running.

'No.' Eleanor overtook her and squeezed through the door ahead of her. 'Let me. You shouldn't be racing down the stairs in your condition.'

She sprinted away before Krush could argue. The staircase rattled as she charged down to the ground floor and jumped the final few steps.

Claire put her head out of the living door in amazement. 'What is it?'

'Your dad's outside,' said Eleanor.

'What?'

'Stay here. Don't let my partner come after me.'

She kept running through the hall into a wide kitchen with marble worktops. At the end of the room, a glass door hung open onto the garden. She burst outside onto a beautiful patio and the air was filled with seagulls' wings.

'Get away from me!' she shouted.

With both arms over her head, she ran to the end of the patio into a neatly mown lawn. Wings beat the air. The smell of cut grass was raw and gorgeous.

Eleanor came to the back fence Slate had climbed over. Somebody else's garden was on the other side, dense with overgrown grass and sagging apple trees in blossom. Peering over the edge, she saw him seated in the grass in his suit.

'What are you doing down there?' she said.

'I landed on my ankle. I think it's sprained. Shit.' Slate grabbed a tuft of grass and threw it aside.

'Police. I'm Detective Inspector Eleanor Rose. Can you walk? I'm going to need you to come back to the house.'

* * *

Back at the house, Slate pulled out a chair at the kitchen table and fell into it. 'Christ, my ankle.' He looked in pain.

Eleanor and Krush stared at him in silence.

Claire appeared at the door. 'Are you alright?' she asked.

'Yeah, I just landed awkwardly. It's going to be swollen. This is all I need.'

'Can you leave us a moment?' Krush asked Claire.

The girl turned and ran out sobbing.

Krush closed the door. 'Mr Slate, you're going to have to accompany us to the station.'

'What, why?'

'Resisting the police is a crime.'

'I didn't resist anyone. I came in here voluntarily.' He turned to Eleanor. 'Didn't I?'

Eleanor pulled a feather out of her hair. 'Why did you run out the back door?'

'I didn't know it was police. I thought it must be friends and family wanting to see me. After what happened with that goddamn video going viral, everyone wants to drop in and talk. I couldn't face it. I heard the doorbell, so I went and hid in the kitchen. I waited until I heard you go upstairs then I ran out the back.'

'That's preposterous,' Krush said.

'Why would I run away?' He appealed again to Eleanor. Evidently, she came across as the more friendly.

'Don't look at me,' Eleanor said. 'Answer the question.'

'I've nothing to hide. No crime has been committed, has it?'

'I've been trying to contact you all morning,' Krush said. 'If you really cared about your wife, you'd be desperate for updates about her; you'd pick up the phone.'

'I've got my phone turned off. I don't want to be disturbed. The doctor told me to avoid stress.'

Eleanor folded her arms, attempting to look unamenable. 'I don't buy it,' she said. 'Have you had any contact with your wife today?'

'No, but I told you, that's normal. She does her own thing, and I let her. Ours is quite a modern marriage.'

'You really don't care where she is?' Eleanor said.

'But… what do you want me to say? She's not missing, is she? Not officially, I mean.'

'Actually, she is,' Krush said. 'Your son agreed to file a missing person report.'

'Ian? I'll kill him.'

'What did you say?' Krush's eyes flashed.

'Oh, come on. I don't mean it literally. It's just what you say when you have kids.' He glanced at her baby bump. 'You'll find out.' He turned to Eleanor again with his dumb appeal. 'You have to understand, Ian is Iris's son, not mine. He hates me, even though I give him everything. I paid for all of this, everything he has. But that's normal, it's just family. I don't resent it.'

'Come on.' Krush held out her hand. 'Can you stand up? Let's get this over with. We'll drive you and Ian to the station and write up the paperwork.'

'But, really? Am I a suspect?'

'You're a witness in what is now a missing person case,' Krush said. 'You were the last person we know of to see Iris.'

44

In the interview room, Slate smiled to himself. He looked around the dull, windowless walls, the two-way mirror, the closed door, and seemed delighted.

'Who's behind the mirror?' he said.

Krush ignored this. 'I want to talk about Iris.'

Seated beside her, Eleanor watched the suspect. She tried to work out if his blasé attitude was natural or just an act. Everything seemed like a game to him. From the moment they had entered the police station and led him through the corridors, he had shown no fear, only curiosity about his new surroundings.

'Mr Slate,' Krush said. 'Your wife has been declared missing. Her son signed the paperwork.'

'Ah well, if she's been *declared*…'

'She was last seen three nights ago with you. You left the house together in your car around six, according to your daughter. Since then, Iris hasn't been seen, and you were found lost in the tunnel, holding her shoe,' Krush said.

'It is hard to believe, isn't it?' he retorted, then fell silent.

For a moment, Krush and Slate held each other's eyes. Slate tilted his head as he examined her. It was as if he were the interviewer.

Eleanor sensed a strangely personal tension between them.

'It gets harder,' Krush said. 'The other shoe was found at a murder scene in the park.'

Slate's smile disappeared. He sat forward but did not answer.

'How do you explain that?' Eleanor pressed him.

'I… I don't know. A murder scene. Which… Who was…'

Eleanor was fascinated. She waited to see what he would say next, but Krush pushed ahead. 'Mr Slate–'

She was interrupted by the door opening. Carver's glare swept over the room, settling on Eleanor's face for some reason. 'What's going on in here?'

'We're just having a chat.' Slate grinned. 'Nice to see you again, Chief Inspector.'

'Alright, you two.' Carver pointed at the detectives in turn. 'In my office. Now.'

* * *

'I told you both, very clearly.' Carver stood behind her desk. 'That man is important. You can't just harass him. He's not some street corner scally. He has the best lawyers, he has allies, he has influence. They'll come after us.'

'If I could–' Krush started but Carver silenced her with a glare.

'Just listen for once, Detective. Do you have any idea how thin the ice is under our feet? There are already multiple cases against Merseyside Police in court. We've got an internal investigation for corruption. The local newspapers are making fun at our expense. Every new allegation makes the front pages. The national media has started paying attention. Downing Street's breathing down our necks. One more false step and I'll be gone. So will you. Don't think you're too precious to be touched. They'll reassign you to some hole in the middle of nowhere. You'll spend the rest of your career looking for missing cats.'

'Iris Slate has been gone now for over forty-eight hours.' Krush's tone was cold and precise. 'We've passed the critical threshold. The chances of finding her alive shrink with every hour that passes.'

'She's not missing,' Carver said. 'Not until someone declares it.'

'We just filed the paperwork,' Krush said. 'It's official now.'

Carver froze. 'Who declared it?'

'Iris's son.' Krush stood up. 'Now, if that's all, I need to get back to interviewing my suspect. As I said—'

'Sit down, Detective!' Carver shouted.

Krush dropped back heavily into the seat.

'If I could—' Eleanor started.

'No,' Carver said. 'You be quiet as well. I should've known better than to let two siblings work together. You're in conspiracy against me. I should've been informed immediately when the missing person report was filed. Now I look ridiculous. What's going on here? Why are you working behind my back?'

'We're not working behind your back,' Krush said. 'We only just filed the form. We were going to call you at the first opportunity, but we didn't want to waste time. Like you say, the suspect is important. We couldn't just leave him sitting around.'

'The "suspect"? Slate is an official suspect now?'

'Can you suggest anybody else?' Krush sounded just a touch sarcastic.

'You should have consulted with me before you brought him in. There will be consequences. Once the media gets wind, the station will be surrounded by cameras.'

'And if he's guilty?' Krush said.

'And if he's innocent? What'll the media say, if it turns out he's been falsely accused?'

'That's not my concern,' Krush said. 'He was the last person to see his wife. When we visited his house to speak to him, he tried to run away from us.'

Carver pointed at Eleanor. 'Is that true? I need to know exactly what happened.'

'Well…' Eleanor looked for an answer that would satisfy both her sister and the boss. 'It was his daughter who opened the front door to us. We spoke to his kids in the living room while he was hiding in the kitchen. He claims he didn't know it was police. He says he was trying to avoid visitors. When we went upstairs, he tried to sneak out the back.'

'For Christ's sake.' Carver covered her face with her hands. 'This is going to cost me my job.'

Krush was impassive. 'It won't. Not if you let me get on with what I have to do.'

'If I could just say something,' Eleanor interjected. 'Nobody's saying Damon Slate killed his wife. Something happened to him in that tunnel. There might have been an accident before he entered, or something else. Something violent. Something so bad, it caused a mental breakdown. Whatever it was, it must have been serious for him to have lost his memory.'

'I don't buy the amnesia,' Krush said. 'It's an act. He knows what happened to his wife and he's trying to cover it up.'

Carver removed her hands from her face to look at Eleanor. 'Keep talking.'

'I'd like to bring in a psychiatrist to look at Slate. I'm thinking, perhaps under therapy, we could bring back the memories he's lost.'

Krush groaned. 'You're playing into his hands. This is what he wants. Can't you see? It's all a distraction. The longer we play along, the more time gets wasted, the smaller the chances of his wife ever being found.'

Carver rubbed her temples. 'I'll speak to Dr Shepherd. I don't know if there's any use. Psychology is all mumbo jumbo to me, but Shepherd might be able to help.'

'It *is* mumbo jumbo,' Krush said.

Eleanor took a breath. 'I know neither of you wants to hear this, but Raymond Stray would be the best person. He's much more qualified than Shepherd. In one session with Slate, he'd get to the bottom of what's really happened, I'm sure of it.'

Carver threw her arms up. 'I don't know who's the crazier out of you two sisters.'

Krush, for once, was silent.

'I'll talk to Shepherd,' Carver said. 'Don't even think about bringing Raymond Stray, or any other homeless person you may know, in on this. In the meantime, our official line is Slate isn't a suspect. He's working with the police to locate his wife, who may be missing. Eleanor, you'll have to deal with the media.'

'Me?'

'They'll be crawling all over us. This is your mess, clean it up. Write a missing person bulletin for the evening news reports. Find a picture of Iris Slate that looks nice. Remember, the police are working *constructively* with Damon Slate. He isn't a suspect.'

Krush got up, cradling her belly. 'Can we all get on with our jobs now?' she said.

Eleanor felt a twinge in her own stomach.

Carver nodded. 'Notify the public about the missing woman. We want posters, media adverts, the works. Somebody must have seen her. With any luck, she'll turn up fine. All of this will go away.'

'It won't,' Krush said, and walked out of the room.

45

When they returned to the interview room, they found Slate chatting with his lawyer, laughing about something. Eleanor paused in the doorway. She recognized him from somewhere. Yes, it was him, unmistakable in his green suit, the lawyer Wainwright had pointed out to her at the courts, representing the underage killer.

She glanced at Krush. 'Maybe we should–'

Krush sat down. 'This is a missing person case now. It's serious. You two need to stop messing around.'

'Oh, we don't mess around,' Mann said. 'I'll have a report for wrongful arrest drawn up before the end of today.'

'Your client has been unable to explain how one of his wife's shoes ended up in a murder scene while he was holding the other.'

Mann did not flinch. 'Can you prove who those shoes belong to?'

'You're talking about proof?' Krush almost shouted. 'We've got a tangible connection between your client and a murder.'

'For all we know, whoever killed your victim could have assaulted my client as well. It's your job to figure that out. You're the detectives, remember,' said the lawyer.

'Let's all just start over.' Eleanor would have sat but Mann had taken her chair and there were no others in the room. She would have to bring one in, but she was afraid to leave the room and miss anything.

'Your client is not under arrest,' she said. 'We want to work together with you to find Iris, that's all. We appreciate your cooperation, and we intend to do everything within our power to bring Mrs Slate home safely.'

'I'm glad to see you've changed your tone.' Mann set his closed briefcase on the table. 'I've heard about your missing person report. You pressured a minor to sign that document. You realize we could sue? The headlines wouldn't look good. My client's son is only fifteen years old.'

'Nobody pressured anyone,' Krush said. 'The kid's concerned about his mum, and it's understandable. She hasn't been seen in days. My only question is why you two don't care.'

'Iris always takes off by herself,' Slate said. 'Two days is nothing.'

Mann patted him on the knee. 'It's alright,' he said, 'don't let them provoke you. Don't say anything. I'll deal with this.'

'I bet that briefcase is empty,' Krush said. 'Don't think you can intimidate me with vague legal threats. I'm not afraid.'

Eleanor, leaning against the wall, cleared her throat. 'We're putting out a missing person call for Mrs Slate. We'll appeal to the public. There'll be bulletins in the evening news. If what you say is true, if she's just gone off somewhere by herself, she should report herself as safe when she sees the news.'

'I'm not sure you fully understand.' Slate smiled sadly.

Mann turned to him, but his employer waved him off. 'It's alright, let me speak. I've nothing to hide. I'm happy to cooperate with the detectives.'

He held Krush's eye. He had been watching her this whole time, and hardly seemed to notice Eleanor.

'Honestly, I'm touched by your concern,' he said. 'But you should know, my wife… when she disappears, it's like she's vanished off the face of the planet. She won't answer the phone, and she won't see anybody. She certainly won't be reading newspapers or watching the news. She won't know we're looking for her, and nobody will see her. I fear your efforts will be wasted.'

'She must have somebody she goes to?' Krush said. 'I checked with her family and none of them have had any contact.'

'Iris's family is, regrettably, an advert for contraceptive education at state schools,' Slate said.

'What about friends?' Krush said.

'I assume she must have some, but she keeps them secret from me. Let's all put our cards on the table–'

'Damon.' Mann flashed a warning look at his client.

'It's alright, I trust the detectives,' Slate said. Again, he only focused on Krush. Eleanor felt invisible.

'It's no secret, really,' he continued. 'My wife doesn't love me.'

'And do *you* love her?' Eleanor said.

'Depends what you mean by love.'

Krush scoffed. 'This is absurd. We're not here to discuss the semantics of love. Do you understand how a case like this works? After forty-eight hours, the chances of finding a missing person are cut in half. Every hour that passes after that makes it exponentially less likely she'll ever be found.'

'I agree,' Mann said. 'There's no need to discuss my client's marital life. It's irrelevant.'

'Not to me.' Eleanor detached herself from the wall and leaned on the table. 'I want to know. Do you love her?'

Slate grinned weakly and looked away. A crack showed in his composure. For the first time, a response did not come smoothly to him.

'Don't answer,' Mann said.

'But I want to answer. I want to cooperate. If these detectives believe for some reason that Iris is in danger, I'll gladly answer any question, no matter how irrelevant.'

Mann sighed. Krush tutted.

Now Slate held Eleanor's eye. 'I guess *we're* the romantics in this equation.' He grinned.

'Just tell us,' she said.

'I'm a possessive man. When I see something valuable, I have to have it. It's an obsession. The harder it is to gain, the more I desire it. If I have to fight for it, even better. I love the fight. Now, my wife, she's an extremely beautiful woman. She's precious. Every man wants her. As soon as I saw her, I knew, I had to have her.'

'We were talking about love,' Eleanor said. 'Not possession.'

He shrugged. 'I wanted her. Now she's mine. Do I love her? That depends. There are days when I can't stand the sight of her. I know she despises me, and I wonder why she ever married me. It's not easy to live with somebody who holds you in contempt. I've tried everything to make her happy. She lives in total luxury. I allow her son to live with us, and I give him everything he wants. He loathes me as well. I don't complain.'

'Why do they hate you so much?' Krush said.

'I've often pondered that. In the end, I've come to the conclusion that some people are just born that way. They overflow with hatred.'

'Why don't you leave her?' Eleanor said.

Mann tensed. 'Who's talking about divorce? Nobody said anything about divorce.'

'*You* did,' Krush said.

Slate patted him on the shoulder. 'Forgive my lawyer. He's a good man, but he's so consumed by his job, he sees the world in terms of litigation. I promise you; I have no intention of divorcing my wife.'

'Even though, as you claim, she hates you?' Eleanor studied his face for a hint of pain at these words, but he was blandly urbane.

'I told you already, Detective. I'm possessive. The things I possess, I don't give them away. I've got cars worth more than most people's mortgages. I never even drive them. What use are they to me? Why don't I just sell them? It's the possession that counts, not the use. But perhaps you'd need to be rich to understand that.'

'Enough.' Krush turned to Eleanor. 'He's playing with you. That's what he does. He's a game player. We need to stick to the facts.'

'I quite agree,' Mann said. 'That's why I'm submitting a request for my client to be released from here immediately.'

'He's free to leave,' Eleanor said. 'We told you already, your client isn't in trouble. We only want to cooperate with him to find his wife.'

'In that case…' Mann stood up. 'We'll be leaving.'

But Damon Slate did not stand up. He peered into the two-way mirror. 'Do you really think something bad happened to Iris?'

'Yes,' Krush said.

'They don't know anything,' Mann said. 'They're just guessing. If they really thought Iris was in danger, they'd be out searching for her, instead of harassing you. No, this is a classic case of police going after a celebrity figure. They're fishing for headlines to distract the public from the truth.'

'Which truth?' Eleanor said, and regretted the question.

'Everyone knows it,' Mann said. 'There's a crisis with policing in this city. You're being sued and investigated from all sides. Come on. We're leaving.'

Slate stood up. 'If you hear anything about Iris. Anything at all… please call me right away.'

46

Putting together a bulletin on Iris was not so straightforward. There was little to no information about her online or in any of their databases. In the end, Eleanor used a picture taken from the Slates' wedding. Iris's face was tense with concealed emotion among cheering guests.

Gripping her husband's hand, she gazed through a drift of confetti.

'Who are you?' Eleanor held the picture to the light.

Most people smile when their pictures are taken. They have no idea that one day, their face might end up on a poster beneath the word "MISSING". But Iris did not smile. She stared fiercely out of the monochrome square into the normal world from which she had been torn. To judge from the total absence of information about her, she was already missing, long before anyone noticed.

Bulletins were sent out to local news outlets, and the posters were distributed.

Krush watched sullenly. 'None of this will bring her back.'

'We have to try at least,' said Eleanor.

'We've hit a dead end. Slate has all the power; we have none. The boss won't let us do anything.'

'It's the same with the other shoe,' Eleanor said. 'The shoe from the park. Organised Crime don't want anyone digging around in the Marsh. Every step I take, they block me.'

'The *Marsh*. Iris's family live there. I tried to talk to them, but that was hopeless as well. This is all connected, somehow.'

'There's a gang war taking place,' Eleanor said. 'Looneys and Gilchrists. The border runs right through the park. But our dead man didn't belong to either gang, or so it seems.'

'I don't think this is about gangs,' Krush said. 'My guess is, Slate killed his wife and tried to cover it up as a gang killing. That's why your man was found in the park with the shoe. That's why they cut his throat after he was already dead; to make it look like she was implicated a gangland killing.'

'But, in that case, where is Iris's body?'

'That's what I'm going to discover.'

'And why was Slate in the tunnel? If he covered the crime up as a gang killing, he wouldn't need the defence of amnesia.'

'There is a reason... we just haven't figured it out yet.'

'I think he's innocent,' Eleanor said.

'Why?'

'It's just a feeling. Watching him, listening to the way he speaks, he doesn't seem like a guilty man.'

Krush scoffed. 'Oh, well, if you have a *feeling.*'

'That's your weakness, Beth. You were never good at reading people. You have all the logical reasoning skills, but the problem is, human beings aren't rational. You need empathy to read them.'

'All of that – emotions, feelings – it's a kind of distortion. Our job is to see through the distortion to the facts. But you, Eleanor, you lose your way in the irrational. In the end, you'll wander too far.'

Stung, Eleanor raised her voice. 'Damon Slate is innocent, I'm certain of it.'

'And I'm certain he's guilty.'

'I...' Eleanor let it drop.

This partnership was a chance to rebuild their relationship, but it was already going wrong. Eleanor had antagonised her sister, and she had done it on purpose. She knew where her weaknesses and insecurities lay. Perhaps the truth was, she did not want to fix things between them at all.

'I don't want to argue with you,' Eleanor said. 'We need to work together. There's no other way to solve the case. Between Carver and the mayor protecting Slate, and the Organised Crime Unit in the Marsh, there's only me and you.'

Krush pulled out a chair and fell into it. Rubbing her belly, she looked exhausted. The crowded evidence board loomed over her like a wave about to crash. Eleanor could not bear it. Ever since childhood, she had lived half in awe of her sister as a relentless, tireless force. Now she looked tired and demoralised. The wrinkles at the corner of her eyes were accentuated. The grey streak in her hair looked lifeless.

'Are you alright?' she said.

'I'm fine. It's just been a long day. The break-in at my place was a scare.'

'You know Dad would love for you to move back in with us.'

'Forget it.'

Krush had closed over again.

'What are you going to do now?' Eleanor said.

'I have to piece together everything I can remember from the stolen diary. That should take all night. I'm convinced, that's where the clue is. It must be. That's why they stole it.'

'Can I help?'

'No. If you want to be useful, the best thing you can do is keep out of the way. Stop talking about psychology, for God's sake. Carver will bring in Shepherd now, and the whole case will get bogged down. You're playing into their hands with this nonsense. Stop encouraging them. You let Slate play you like a fool in that interview room.'

Eleanor tried to not take offence. 'I have my way of dealing with suspects; you have yours.'

'You don't know who you're dealing with. These guys aren't simple crooks. Slate is a poker player. He likes to bluff.'

'You make it sound like you've actually played cards with him.'

'Maybe I have.'

'What do you mean?' She stared at her sister, and did not quite recognize her. 'You've met Slate somewhere else, haven't you?'

'I met him in the casino. He owns the place, as it turns out. I didn't know that beforehand.'

'What were you doing in the casino?'

'If you must know, I go there sometimes to unwind.'

'You never went to the casino before…' Eleanor trailed off.

'…before you walked out of our lives without saying goodbye?' Krush supplied. 'A lot changed after you left. The casino is a harmless habit. It keeps my brain sharp, and it helps me relax.'

'And you met Slate there?'

'I watched how he plays. He's reckless. He's too rich to give a damn. He plays for something else. I'm not sure what, maybe he's just bored. Maybe he enjoys bluffing for the sake of it. Some people say it's an adrenaline rush, but I've never understood that. Adrenaline is addictive, they say.'

'Be careful, Beth, you're getting sucked in with this. It's not like you.'

'How would you know what I'm like?'

'It's become personal between you and Slate. I saw the looks on both of your faces. It's a kind of war between you. You both want to win.'

'You're imagining things. But even if you were right… don't worry. I don't lose.'

'Neither does he.'

'That's what makes him vulnerable. He's too sure of himself.'

'And yet…' Eleanor gazed at the photograph of Slate on the evidence board, powerful and immaculate in his wedding suit. 'I believe in the amnesia,' she said. 'Something happened to him. He really is concerned about his wife, I can tell. He doesn't know where she is.'

'That's the game,' Krush said. 'We won't find Iris until we beat him.'

But, hunched in the chair, grimacing as she cradled her belly, Krush did not look ready to beat anyone.

47

Stray had cooked dinner and set the table. The kitchen was filled with steam and a rich, savoury aroma when Eleanor walked in.

'Sit down.' He waved a spatula. 'It's ready. I was just waiting for you to get home.'

She almost laughed at the apron he was wearing. 'Where did you find that thing?'

'This? It was at the bottom of a drawer.'

'I didn't even realize we had one.'

'Aprons are a pillar of civilisation. You don't want to walk around with food all over your clothes, do you?'

'It must have belonged to Mum, but I don't remember her ever wearing it.'

'Could you call Neil? He's watching TV.'

At that moment, Neil shuffled into the room in his slippers. 'What's all this?' He gestured towards Stray with a rolled-up newspaper. 'He's cooking now, is he?'

'I wanted to treat you guys,' Stray said. 'I really appreciate everything you've done for me, and I wanted to do something in return.'

Neil sniffed the air and frowned. 'What is that?'

'Mushroom stroganoff. I hope it's alright. I couldn't get any meat.'

'Mushroom *what?*' Neil looked appalled.

'Stroganoff. It's a Russian dish. My grandma showed me how to make it, in another lifetime.'

Seeing Neil hesitate, Eleanor pulled out a chair for him. 'Let's just sit down.'

Neil was a fussy eater who mainly lived off tinned food, ready meals, and takeaways. When they were growing up, it was always their mum who cooked, and later it was Eleanor, after, well, just after.

'I see.' Neil sat and fingered the empty white dish that was set in front of him. 'I don't recognize these plates.'

'I found them at the back of a cupboard,' Stray said. 'There's all kinds of stuff in this kitchen, hidden away.'

'They must have been a wedding gift.' Neil picked the plate up and turned it over. 'A lot of the household things got boxed and never used. Your mum liked to keep them for special occasions. But there were no special occasions.'

'Well, we'll use them today.' Eleanor sat beside her dad and looked at the plate, trying to remember if she had used them before. She would have loved to discover a remnant of her mother and a trace of whatever happiness she must have known with Neil once. But it was just a plate, like any other.

'I hope you're hungry.' Stray carried two pans over and set them on the table. He served out a dollop of rice and the stroganoff for each of them.

'It smells amazing.' Eleanor nudged Neil, who eyed the plate of food in front of him with suspicion.

'I suppose it can't hurt to try something new.' He poked about in the sauce with his fork, which he held in the wrong hand, as always, and dug out a small piece of mushroom. He brought it to his mouth, sniffed, and nibbled it.

Stray tensed.

Neil chewed slowly and swallowed. 'Not bad,' he said.

Stray beamed. 'I'm glad it's tolerable. I haven't made stroganoff in years.'

Eleanor ate a forkful. With her mouth full, she said, 'It's great! I never knew you could cook.'

'I'm a dilettante in the kitchen, really, but I've always loved food. Sometimes, when I had to beg in the city centre, the worst thing was watching how people ate sandwiches without even taking the trouble to savour the experience. They'd rip it out of the packet and stuff it down and throw the plastic away. That was torture.'

'We don't know what we have, do we?' Neil ate with gusto now.

Eleanor could not help but smile. It was almost like a family dinner, except that none of them were actually related.

'Oh, by the way,' she said. 'I wanted to ask both of you, have you ever heard of "Heart of the City"?'

'Heart of the City?' Stray looked thoughtful. 'What is it, the name of a place?'

'Perhaps. It might be a restaurant or a nightclub, or a shop.'

'Never heard of it,' Neil said.

'It rings a bell,' Stray said. 'But I'm not sure where I heard it.'

'You've heard it before?' Eleanor asked.

'Maybe, or maybe I'm imagining things.'

'Heart of the City,' Neil said. 'What's at the centre of Liverpool? Where would that be? You'd have to look at a map. It might be the Anglican cathedral.'

'Or... what if it refers to the most precious part?' Stray said. 'What would that be? The Liver Building?'

'The football club,' Neil said.

'What about the river?' Stray said.

'Or the docks?' Neil stood up. 'Well, that dinner was surprisingly edible.'

'I'm glad you enjoyed it,' Stray said.

'Where did you get the ingredients? Not at the corner store, I imagine.'

Stray swallowed the last of his stroganoff. 'There's an area around the back of the big supermarket where they keep all the bins. It's well guarded nowadays. In the old days, the supermarkets just left the expired stuff out where anyone could take it, but now there's barbed wire. I found a back alley where you can climb over safely.'

Neil gasped. 'You got it out of a bin?'

'Oh, don't worry.' Stray smiled. 'It's all perfectly healthy. I've lived off supermarket refuse for years. They throw away things that still have plenty of shelf life. Honestly, with the preservatives they put in stuff now, some of it will never go off.'

'You *stole* it?' Eleanor set down her fork. 'You realize, they have security cameras outside the supermarkets. If they saw you climbing the wall… I'm trying to get you a job at the station.'

'Why should they care?' Stray stammered. 'This stuff was all thrown away. It was never going to be eaten. The trucks come after midnight and take it. It gets dumped in a pit.'

Eleanor looked down at her plate that was almost empty. 'I can't believe you could be so reckless. If anyone found out–'

'I want him out of my house.' Neil pointed, standing up. 'I want him gone, understood?' He stormed out of the kitchen and slammed the door behind him.

48

Just like that, Raymond Stray was gone. Eleanor searched through the house in mounting panic and could not find him.

In the living room, Neil was watching the news. 'Damon Slate's wife has been reported missing,' he said. 'Imagine that. All that money, and just as fucked up as the rest of us.'

On the TV, she watched the images of Iris's face play in a reel, snapshots that Eleanor herself had picked out and sent to the media outlets. Seeing the missing woman like that, lonely in the glowing screen, her withdrawal from the world was absolute. She knew then, they would never recover her.

'What are you looking for?' Neil said.

'Raymond. He was in the kitchen a moment ago. Have you seen him?'

'I heard the front door shut before.'

'And, what, he just walked out into the rain, in the dark?'

Neil shrugged. His eyes did not leave the television screen. 'I guess so.'

'He didn't even say goodbye. No. This can't be right. Did he even take a bag? Did he take any food… Anything?' She sprinted across the hall and up the stairs.

The door to the spare room was open. Inside, the bed and Stray's things remained just like before. His bag, technically *her* bag – everything he now owned, they had given him – lay on the floor. She ran to the window and opened the curtains. Outside, in the beating rain, the street was empty.

'No!'

She picked up the bag and pulled out a few items of clothes and some papers. She skimmed through the first page.

Eleanor Rose: Psychological Evaluation
Observations:
Patient displays anxiety, confusion, traces of paranoia. Has no friendships or relationships. Cannot communicate with sister.

She read through the whole document in a daze, and let it fall to the floor. *Hysterical neurosis… Recommendations… Medication… career change.*

The paper dropped from her hand.

He had betrayed her. Was it for Dr Shepherd he wrote this? That would explain why he was so reluctant to talk about the interview. It also explained why Shepherd had agreed to interview Stray in the first place. *There are doubts about you.* Everyone thought she was crazy. Even Stray thought it. And if they all thought it… it must be true. She was out of her mind. This must be insanity right now, even if it felt like cold, hard reality. She felt nothing but the need to run for her life. But she did not run, she stood frozen in the middle of the room.

How long was she motionless?

The ringtone of her phone across the hall broke the enchantment. She darted out of the room and grabbed it. An unknown number. She accepted the call before it could ring out.

'Hello?'

No response. She strained to hear over the static and caught a trace of somebody breathing.

'Who is this?' she said. 'I can hear you. Say something.'

The voice was a whisper. 'Eleanor Rose?'

'Yeah, this is Detective Rose. What do you want?'

'I… I got your card. You left it somewhere you shouldn't have.' The man's voice was rough and broken with fright. It sounded like he was by a highway somewhere; she heard cars screaming past him.

'Oh, yeah. I gave it out in the pub. Did we speak there?'

'Listen… I… I *know*.' His voice cut out as a car's horn blasted through the speaker from whatever roadside he cowered at.

'What did you say? I can't hear you.'

'I know,' he said. 'I know who that man is. The dead man.'

She reached blindly for the notepad on the dresser. 'The man in the park? Alright, that's good. Tell me what you know.'

'How much will you pay?'

'What?'

'I want…' He hesitated. 'Two hundred quid.'

This number was lower than she had expected. Without stopping to reflect, she said, 'Fine. Tell me the name.'

'Two hundred. You'll pay? In cash.'

'Yes.' No sooner had she said it, she regretted accepting the bargain. There were protocols for this kind of thing, and forms to fill in. A police officer was not supposed to simply hand over cash to criminals. 'Listen, I'm not sure–'

'Send your friend with the money,' the voice said.

'What are you talking about?'

'The doctor. I trust him. I don't know you. If he brings the money, I'll tell him the name of the dead man, but I won't speak to anyone else.'

'Who, Stray? That's not possible, I'm afraid.'

'The doctor or nobody. He has to come alone. If I see somebody with him, the deal's off, and you'll never find out what you want to know.'

She wondered if she could accept this deal.

'I'll text you the spot,' the man said. 'Remember, he comes alone, or the deal's off. Two hundred quid in notes. Don't try to mess me around.'

'I need to–'

The man hung up.

49

Eleanor drove through the downpour, looking for Stray in the car headlights that swept the road. He was not difficult to find. Sitting on the floor at the corner of the street, with his eyes closed, he let the rain soak through his jacket.

She opened the side door. 'Get in.'

'What's the point?'

'I need your help.'

'The therapy's finished.'

'Not that kind of help. Come on, you're drenched. Are you going to sit out there all night in the rain?'

She reached her hand out into the cold. Stray stared at it.

He got up gingerly. 'I never could resist a cry for help.'

In the passenger seat, he dripped water into the upholstery, while Eleanor drove.

'Did you really run away without even taking a bag?'

'I don't know. Neil told me I should leave. I couldn't argue. I guess I just freaked out. I had to get out of there right away. There wasn't time to pack. Anyway, my rucksack belongs to you. My clothes belong to Neil. There was nothing to take that was really mine.'

'But… you weren't even going to say goodbye?'

'Goodbyes are painful. I needed to think. I needed to get outside in the fresh air and be alone.'

'In the rain, you mean.'

'I'm old friends with the rain. I've lived with all my clothes so soaked through, the world was saturated. When you reach that point, there's nothing left to try and keep dry. You just sit and let the water run over you.'

'Promise me, you won't do that again. You'll catch pneumonia and die.'

'How about you just tell me where we're going?'

'A man called me. He must have picked up one of the cards I left in the pub. He said he'll tell me the name of the victim in the park. But he'll only talk to you.'

'Alright, stop the car,' Stray said. 'Turn around. This is a mistake.'

'Too late now. I already accepted the deal. We're almost there.'

'I'm not police. I'm not qualified to do this.'

'You're better than qualified. People actually talk to you. They trust you. Somehow, on the force, we lost the trust of these communities a long time ago.'

'You're blurring the lines. If criminals trust me, it's because they think I'm one of them. But you're not. You belong on the other side of the law. Why don't you call Krush? You're supposed to be partners now, aren't you? Never mind family.'

'I have to do this by myself. I want to prove to her I can do it. First thing tomorrow, when I speak to her, I'll have a new lead in the case, and she'll have nothing. She'll realize then, that she does need me.'

'You could still call her. Just to talk to her.'

'That would only scare her away. Believe me, I've learnt my lesson over the years. Beth's like a cat; you have to let her come to you. You can't force it. This investigation is the best chance we've had in years to patch things up. I have to be careful.' Eleanor glanced across at her passenger. 'Stop doing that.'

'What? I didn't do anything.'

'You're psychoanalysing me in your head.'

'Maybe just a little,' he said.

'If you'd grown up with Beth, you'd feel the same way. Listen,' Eleanor said, 'this isn't the only thing I need your help with.'

'I should've stayed sitting in the rain. It was peaceful.'

'Did you ever hear of a condition called transient global amnesia?'

'TGA, sure. I've come across it.'

'Damon Slate supposedly lost his short-term memory the night he was found in the tunnel, the night his wife went missing. His memory has come back now, but he still can't remember anything from that day.'

'Sounds like TGA.'

'Beth thinks he's faking it. She thinks he killed his wife and is now faking amnesia to cover up.'

'This is becoming interesting.'

'Would you be able to tell if a patient was faking amnesia?'

'I've never tried, but yes, I can usually tell if somebody's telling the truth. However, in this case, even without speaking to him, my assumption is the amnesia is real. To fake it seems like an unnecessary risk when there are other ways to cover up a crime.'

'I agree. But, if you spoke to him, could you tell if he was faking it?'

'Yes.'

'And if the amnesia was real, could you help him recover his memories?'

Stray sighed. He stared blankly through the window. 'Long ago, in a different reality where I was a successful person, I did help patients recover memories. But I never tried it with TGA. The condition is not well understood in general, and I'm not up to date with the latest research.'

'But you could try? You might be able to glean something from his memory, even just a fragment.'

'We both know it's not feasible. I don't have a licence anymore to practise. Your bosses would never agree to it, and Slate's lawyers would call foul. As soon as they found out a homeless junky was being asked to treat their client, your case would be ruined.'

'Stop being a pessimist,' Eleanor said. 'I'll to talk to Shepherd about bringing you in for an informal session with Slate.'

Stray laughed. 'Do yourself a favour, Eleanor, don't bring up ideas like this at work. It only damages your status in the eyes of your colleagues. They already think you're crazy for spending time with me at all.'

'I don't care what they think. If we can't find a way to crack this Slate case, then I'll bring you in. If I have to bend the rules, I'll bend them. That's one thing I've learnt. The law, in order to operate, needs to be able to bend. Everyone else does it; why can't I?'

'It's a dangerous path you're headed down, Eleanor. You're trying to bridge two worlds that have to be kept separate.'

'They've never been separate. I used to believe that, when I was naïve and idealistic. Since then, I've found out, it's all connected. The police and the government are hand in hand with criminal elements. It's always worked that way, and it always will.'

'So, what? You want to change sides? You want to become a corrupt officer?'

'No, I want to be a good officer who is able to communicate with the other side of the law. It's the only way. I see that now. To police the underworld, we have to maintain communication among the criminals.'

'I can't help you there.'

'You're the only one who can. If I could convince Beth, she'd make Shepherd and Carver listen. Nobody's ever been able to resist her.'

'Good luck with that.'

'There's something not right with Beth. It's this case. She's obsessed. She's locked in the evidence room trying to rewrite Iris's diary from memory. She thinks the answer is hidden in there somewhere, but, based on what I've seen, it's just gibberish. She's looking for symbols, I don't know what exactly. "Heart of the City" is one of them. What does it mean? Probably nothing. Just the imagination of a mentally disturbed individual.'

'You can tell Beth Krush from me, if there's a hidden meaning in the diary, it's on the surface. The mistake people make in interpretation is they dig for something buried deep down. But the truth isn't like that. Any decent psychotherapist knows: the truth hides in plain sight.'

50

'Are you sure you want me to do this?' Stray said.

Eleanor looked out through the windshield into the dark. 'No.'

The meeting place was on the other side of the street, through a back alley among crowded, downtrodden houses. With a leaden feeling of knowingly making a mistake, she had taken out two hundred pounds from a cash machine. It was in Stray's pocket now.

'You'll be alright,' she said, and did not believe it. 'This guy, whoever he is, he knows you from somewhere. He called you "the doctor". He said he trusted you. I don't think he's going to hurt you. He didn't sound violent on the phone, he was just… scared.'

'It's not myself I'm worried about,' Stray said. 'This isn't going to end well.'

'It'll be OK. Just get the info and hurry back here.'

'As your therapist, I really think–'

'You're not my therapist anymore, Raymond.'

'You're firing me?'

'I'm just… changing our relationship. We're friends, alright? We don't need to be therapist and patient. Friends help each other.'

'If I was really your friend, Eleanor, I wouldn't be here now with your money in my pocket. I would've told you this is wrong, and I would have refused to help.'

'And as a therapist, would you do it?'

'I would have asked you what you think this journey really means. I would have asked you: what do you really want? Is it really about finding this dead gangster, or is it something else? But… I'm not your therapist anymore.'

'No, you're not, and this conversation is taking too long.' She checked the clock on the dashboard. 'You'll be late to meet our guy.'

Stray sighed. 'Last chance: are you sure?'

'You really don't want to?'

'No.'

'Are you refusing?'

'I'm sorry, Eleanor, but I can't do this.'

'You can and you will. Do you know why? You owe me this. I found your report to Dr Shepherd.'

Stray groaned. 'That was… I can explain…'

'I don't want to talk about it. It's too painful.'

'I just…' he stuttered. 'Shepherd forced me… it was the only way they'd give me a chance. I thought, if I did this, maybe I could get back on my feet and then I wouldn't have to take advantage of your kindness anymore.'

Eleanor's face was impassive. She would not look at him. 'I said, I don't want to talk about it. Will you do this favour for me?'

'Yes.'

'Good.' Still not looking at him, she leaned across and opened his door. 'Don't hand over the money until he gives you the information.'

'And if he demands the money first?'

'Of course he'll demand the money first. But you tell him "no". He'll agree to the deal on our terms. The information is worthless to him, but the cash isn't. He's not going to refuse once he sees the money.'

Stray climbed out into the cold. 'I was never going to deliver that report, you know. I wrote it just in case, but I'd decided to throw it away.'

Eleanor pulled the door shut and was alone.

* * *

At first, he could not see the man. It was dark in the alley. There was no streetlamp, which was why this spot was chosen, naturally. Stray stopped and listened, but the only sound was the feint rumble of cars from the main road a block away. He took a step forward and sank into a puddle. Freezing water seeped through his socks, but he was already soaked through. He had been born that way.

'Don't come any closer.'

A torch flashed on, dazzling him, and he covered his eyes.

'Who are you?' Stray said.

'Yes.' Beyond the light, a hidden man breathed hoarsely. 'It is you. You came.'

Stray did not recognize his voice. 'Have we met before?'

'It doesn't matter. You're alone?' He sounded nervous. The torch flashed along the empty alleyway behind him, but quickly returned to shine in Stray's face.

'Yes, I'm alone.'

'You're working with police now? A rat. You never seemed the type.'

'I'm not a rat. I'm just helping a friend.'

The man wheezed in the dark. 'A friend, right. A pretty one. How did you bag her? Is that what they teach you at those fancy universities?'

'Do you have information to share or not?'

'Did you bring the money?'

'Yes.' Stray tried to make him out behind the torch, but the light was too bright.

The man did not sound dangerous; he seemed more afraid than Stray was. But then, fear made people crazy. He had seen fear close up over the years. Fear was unpredictable.

'Show me,' the man said.

With one hand shielding his eyes from the torch, Stray reached slowly into his pocket and pulled out the cash. 'It's all here.'

'Alright. Hand it over.'

'Give me the info first.'

'No. The money first.' A quiver of desperation in his voice.

Stray knew that quiver, it was the need of an addict, a barely restrained violence. Instantly, it was as if they had switched places in the dark, and now he was the one who quivered. He was the one whose being was reduced to a tissue in a gale of pure need. He could only think of Eleanor's instructions, the warmth of sitting in the car, and her humane presence.

He heard himself echo her instructions. 'Give me the information first. Then you can have the money.'

The beam of light in his face trembled. 'Half the money first.'

Stray longed to hand it over, like giving the money to himself. He only wanted to silence the other man's desire before it overwhelmed his own. But he thought of what Eleanor would say if he gave away the money and got nothing back.

'The information first. Tell me and you can have the money. This can all be over in a moment. Tell me.'

'That murder,' the man stammered. 'The murder in the park. His name was Baxter. I never heard his first name. He wasn't from Liverpool. Some kind of drifter.'

'Who was he?'

'A piece of shit. Did odd jobs. Nobody liked him. Nobody will miss him. Let him go. Give me the money now.'

'Isn't there anything else you can tell me? Where did you meet him?'

'Give it to me!' The torch dropped and splashed in a puddle as the man jumped forwards in the dark.

Stray felt hands tearing and fumbling at his clothes. 'Get off!'

'Give it to me! Give it to me!'

'Here.' He pulled out the wad of notes. 'Take it.'

The money was ripped from his hand. A few loose notes fluttered in the air. Darkness. He stood in the dark with his empty palm held out. The sound of running feet vanished through the puddles.

51

It was late when Stray left the house. The hours had passed interminably while he waited for the others to fall asleep. Neil, as usual, had stayed up late, dozing in front of the television. It was after one when Stray heard him turn the TV set off and wearily climb the stairs. The house fell silent. Stray crept out into the hall and listened. There was no sound from Eleanor's room or from Neil's. It was time to leave. He hoisted the bag on his shoulder, wincing as it rattled. He checked one more time that he had not forgotten anything.

The letter lay on top of the made bed that he had not slept in, a white square in the dark. He knew the text by heart, having spent all day playing the sentences over in his mind.

> *Eleanor,*
> *Thank you for everything. I know you tried your best to help me, but just like everyone else who ever tried, it's time now for you to give up. Please accept me for who I am, a wreck who lost his last chance long ago. Let me leave. Don't try to come after me. Don't try to find me or to bring me back. This is the best thing for all of us. I'm alone now as I should be. I can't hurt anybody this way.*
> *You are a person with a very generous heart. It's not easy for you to give up on somebody. As your former therapist, if there is one last lesson I can offer you, let it be that in life, sometimes, self-preservation means being hard. You have to be tough, or others will only take advantage of your kindness. I wish you all the best with your journey.*
> *Your friend,*
> *Raymond Stray*

With gritted teeth he snuck down the stairs. He could not bear to look back up over his shoulder into the warm space where human beings were dreaming. He would never sleep in such a comfortable bed again. The front door was the hardest part, grinding against the vestibule tiles, horribly loud in the silence. The wind blew into the house with a sudden rush, fluttering the junk mail piled to one side.

Stray closed his eyes and entered that wind. He had left the key upstairs. Once the door was closed, he would never be able to go back inside again. It felt like the final door of his life. He was surprised to feel tears welling at the corners of his eyes as he hesitated outside. He had not guessed that he was still capable of such foolish emotions. Sensitivity doesn't survive on the streets. He pulled the door shut and hurried away, blinded as the wind broke the tears in his eyes.

52

Eleanor dressed quickly in the dark. She crept through the hall not wanting to wake Neil or Stray. Stray's door was partially ajar. He always slept that way, accustomed to the open road. She hurried down the stairs, but she was not quick enough. She heard her stepfather's bedroom door creak open.

'Psst. Eleanor, are you going to see Beth?'

'Shush. You'll wake Stray.'

'He'll be fine. He's used to sleeping on concrete. Nothing can wake him now.' Neil came into the landing with his dressing gown flapping behind him. 'Have you had breakfast? Shall I make toast?'

'There's no time. Something big came up in the case. I have to get Beth on the way to work.'

'Why don't you bring her here and we'll all have some toast and a cup of tea together? Like a family.'

'You know she'd never agree to that.' Eleanor grabbed an umbrella. She opened the front door, letting in a blast of cold wind.

'Wait a second.' Neil followed her along the path, waddling in his slippers.

She climbed into the car, and he stooped through the open door.

'Eleanor, you know, you have to take care of your sister. That's what family's for. She's pregnant. She's living alone. Tell her, she needs to slow down.'

'Do you imagine Beth listens to me?'

'Just give her this message from me: sometimes in life, you have to stop and just take care of yourself.'

'I'll tell her, if you promise to be nice to Stray. He almost ran away last night.'

Neil stepped back from the car, a worried look on his face. 'I don't understand how you can put a stranger above your own family.'

There was nothing to say to that. She closed the door and pulled away, leaving her stepfather by the side of the road, his dressing gown ballooning in the wind.

As she drove onto the main road, her phone started ringing. She thought it must be her sister calling to say impatiently, "Where are you?" But the number was unknown. She set it to speaker.

'Is that Detective Rose?' A woman's voice. Young, tremulous, and tearful.

'Yeah, this is Eleanor Rose. Who am I speaking with?'

'It's Claire Slate.'

'Oh.' She gripped the wheel more tightly. 'Is there any news? Any response to the missing posters?'

'No. Nothing. It's not that. It's… Dad. He didn't come home last night. I've tried calling him. I've texted him saying "Please respond", but… nothing. I'm worried something's happened to him.'

'OK. It's good you called. Your dad often stays out with work, right? Probably he's busy with something.'

'Yeah, he often stays away. It's just, last night, before he went out, he was upset.'

Claire's voice was so mouse-like, Eleanor could hardly hear it over the sound of the windscreen wipers. 'Can you speak up, please? I'm driving. What did you say?'

'I said, he was upset last night. I heard him sobbing. When I came in the room, he tried to hide it, but I saw him wipe away tears.'

'And did he say anything? Did he say why he was upset?'

'He wouldn't tell me anything. But he was afraid. I could tell,' Claire said. 'I've never seen him like that before.'

'Afraid of what?'

'I don't know. And now he's gone. What if… what if he's disappeared as well? What if, whoever… whatever happened to Iris… it's happened to him too?'

'It's too early to start worrying. Let's not jump to conclusions. Nothing in our investigation so far suggests your dad's in danger.'

'What do you mean?' Claire shouted through the phone. 'He was in the tunnel, lost. His memory was gone. Of course something happened.'

'OK, calm down. Let's talk through this slowly. I'm driving at the moment. I have to concentrate on the road.'

'You think he's guilty, don't you? You're no better than that partner of yours. You made your minds up from the start. You think he's evil, because he's rich.'

'That's not true. We're just trying to find Iris, that's all.'

'I know my dad seems like a villain. Everybody hates him. Maybe they're right to. But what you don't see is how stressed he is. He has panic attacks all the time. His doctor warned him he has to take a break, just take a holiday, go to a beach somewhere and forget about the business. But Dad can't stop. He's addicted. Sometimes I catch him crying. I walk in the kitchen, and he's just on his own in the dark sobbing. There's a bottle of whisky beside him on the table. I ask him what's wrong, but he can't even talk he's crying so hard.'

'Doesn't your dad tell you anything about his life?'

'Not if he can avoid it,' Claire said. 'All I know is, there's some big deal they're working on. He never talks to me about business. He says he'd rather keep me out of it.'

'Why? Do you think there could be some illegal practices in what he's doing?'

Claire hesitated. 'Maybe. He told me once that the construction business is all crooked. He said he was "an honest man trying to work in a corrupt world".'

'That's what corrupt people always say. Listen, I have to go now. But I'll see what I can find out. I'll call you right away if anything turns up. In the meantime, keep trying to contact your dad. Let me know if you manage to track him down.'

'Whatever.' Claire hung up.

53

Krush was seated on the step outside her hotel. With her head sunk as if asleep, and her face hidden beneath a hood in the drizzle, Eleanor did not recognize her at first.

Pulling up at the kerb, she lowered the window. 'Is that you?'

Krush raised her head. 'What took you so long?'

'I have a message from Dad: you have to take care of yourself. Something like that. I don't remember the exact wording.'

'Message received' – Krush climbed into the passenger seat – 'and deleted.'

'He wants us both to go back home and have toast and a cup of tea with him before we start work.'

'Dad's tea is undrinkable. His toast is burnt.'

Eleanor pulled out from the kerb into the empty street. The tarmac glistened beneath a patina of rain. 'There was another message as well, now I think of it, from Raymond Stray.'

'A message to me?'

'About Iris's diary. He says, the truth is always in plain sight, not hidden below the surface.'

'With a few more gems like this, I could write a self-help book. It doesn't matter anyway. The diary is lost, and we're out of time.'

'That's not like you, Beth. You never give up on a case.'

'It just feels like… this is one the city doesn't want solved. Every way I turn is a dead end. I rang the station already. There are no responses to our bulletin on Iris. Nobody's been in touch about the missing posters.'

'It's still early. I just got a phone call from Claire Slate. She said her dad never came home last night. He's not responding to calls or messages. She said he was upset before he went out. She found him sobbing. She said he seemed afraid.'

Krush stared through the distortion of the rain on the passenger seat window. 'It's too late then. We missed our chance.'

'What makes you say that?'

'Today was marked in Iris's diary with an X. If something is going to happen, it will happen today before midnight, I'm certain.'

'An X? It might just be someone's birthday she wanted to remember. Or a trip to have her eyes tested.'

'With an X? No. That's not Iris's style. She didn't use the diary to record trivial events. There are no dentist appointments or lunch dates in there. Like Dr Chen suggested, she used it to process her emotions. Everything in there is personal.'

Eleanor veered into the left-hand lane, approaching a junction at the traffic lights.

'Where are you going?' Krush said. 'This isn't the way to the station.'

'We're not going to the station.'

'Why not?'

'There's a new development in the case. Something I didn't tell you yet.'

'What?' Krush sat up in the passenger seat.

It was a sweet moment for Eleanor, and she let it last a second too long. Just to let it sink in that Eleanor had been the one to make a breakthrough, while Krush, the brilliant detective, was stuck.

'I got a name for my dead man in the park. His surname was Baxter.'

'How did you find that out?'

'Detective work.'

'Don't get cocky, Eleanor. Just a surname? What about a first name? Who was your source? How do you know they're reliable?'

'My source only knew the surname, but I did some digging. There's a Johnny Baxter who works for Damon Slate. He's a foreman in his construction firm. I tried to track him down, but he's unavailable. I got an address though. We're going to pay him a call.'

'But… when did you find this out?'

'Last night.'

'Why didn't you call me straight away?'

'I focus on the park angle; you're on the Slate angle. That's what we agreed, isn't it?'

Eleanor had not expected her sister to say "well done" or "great work". The only satisfaction was to see the surprise and confusion that she could not hide. But there was something else, something worse – a creeping unease in her worn face. It was frightening. Liverpool needed Beth Krush.

What had the city done to her?

54

Johnny Baxter lived on the second floor of a housing estate on the northern periphery of the city, close to the tunnel entrance. The detectives followed a covered walkway around a courtyard where the rain poured down. Nobody answered the door. The window beside it was covered over with cardboard.

'Looks like there's been a break-in,' Krush said.

'We'll have to get a permit and come back.'

'We don't need a permit. He's dead. He's not going to complain.'

'*If* he's the same Baxter as our dead man.' Eleanor looked up and down the walkway but there was nobody around. The building was lifeless.

'…which he is,' Krush said.

Eleanor tried the handle. 'Alright, but how do you intend to open it? I don't think we can break it down between us.'

'We'll go in the same way the last person did. That carboard is on the *outside* of the window. Why would they cover it from outside? Somebody broke the window, climbed into the flat, then sealed it up from outside after they left.'

'Why would they?'

'Let's find out.' Krush tore down the flimsy covering that was only held in place by masking tape.

A small opening was revealed, lined with jagged bits of glass in the frame.

'There's no way you'll be able to climb through with, with your…' Eleanor struggled to finish her sentence.

'With this baby bump the size of a small horse?' Krush supplied. 'I know. That's why you have to do it.'

'Ah jeez.' Eleanor leaned through the window and pushed aside a pair of tattered curtains that smelled of smoke. On the other side, there was nothing to see except an empty room in the dark. 'Haven't climbed through a window in years.'

She put on gloves and fastened her coat to protect herself from the glass. She checked along the lifeless walkway. Krush gave her a leg-up and she clambered through the window. Fragments of glass ground against her as she squeezed through the frame and tumbled down on the other side. 'Ouch!'

'What do you see?' Krush said.

'Oh, I'm fine, thanks.' She got up and brushed the bits of glass and plaster from her coat. 'This room is empty. Seems like a spare bedroom.'

She opened the door on the opposite wall.

'Be careful.' Krush's catlike eyes watched her through the window.

'Lights aren't working.' Eleanor flicked the switch a few times, then took out her torch.

She went out through the door into a hallway.

'What's out there?' Krush shouted after her.

'Nothing. The hall's empty. It smells funny though.'

'Smells of what?'

'Cigarettes and depression, I guess. Hold on, I'll see if I can open the front door from inside.' She stepped through a pile of junk mail and tried the door. On the other side, Krush's outline was visible through a small pane of frosted glass.

'Any luck?' Krush called through the pane.

'It's locked with a key. I'll see if there's a spare hanging anywhere.'

Eleanor flashed her torch along the hall. There was a jacket hanging on a hook by the door. It stunk of smoke. She turned the pockets inside out but there was only a pack of chewing gum.

'No key,' she shouted through the front door. 'I'll try the other rooms.'

'Be careful,' Krush said. 'If anyone's in there, you'll be trapped.'

'There's nobody. It feels dead.'

'I wish I could get in. Maybe I could try the window…'

'Don't even think about it.'

Eleanor entered a small kitchen. In the roaming light of her torch, it was almost bare. She opened the curtains, letting in cold light and a view over a car park. The curtains smelled of smoke, but there was a whiff of bleach in here too. A mop and bucket were set against the wall. Somebody had cleaned up. The worktops and the sink were clear. Checking the cupboards, she found just a few plates, bowls and cups arranged neatly.

'Found anything?' Krush shouted from back along the corridor.

'No!' she yelled back.

She crouched over the bucket and found the mophead had dried into a hard crust stuck to the bottom. It must have stood there several days.

'Eleanor!' her sister's voice was distant, back along the walkway.

'Just a minute!' she shouted back, unsure if she would hear her.

She left the kitchen and looked inside a cramped bathroom with a shower cabinet in the corner. The green tiles gleamed in milky light coming through a frosted-glass window. Cleaning products were set out on the floor alongside a few packs of sponges and flannels. By the sink, a single toothbrush stuck out of a chipped mug. There was something melancholic about it. She looked in the mirror. That ugly man might have considered his own face in this glass, and wondered why he was born that way, while others are born beautiful. *Dogface*. Perhaps he had a handsome brother somewhere, with two toothbrushes in the mug by the sink. They shared the same DNA, so why were they so different?

'Eleanor!' Krush shouted and banged on the front door. 'Did you fall asleep in there?'

'I'm almost done.'

She entered a small bedroom and opened the curtains to let in dismal, grey light over a mess of clothes strewn over the floor. The sheets and duvet on the mattress had been left in a sweaty pile. A full ashtray lay by the pillow. The drawers were full of cheap clothes and the same pervasive odour of old smoke hung over it all. She checked under the bed and found a pair of binoculars and a scrap of paper with two words written on it:

Grey hood.

The wardrobe contained only a few shirts on hangers. One of these was sticking out as if it had been stuffed there in a hurry. She pulled it out. A white, short-sleeve shirt with a black tie loosely fastened beneath the collar. It looked like part of a police uniform. There were gashes on the shoulders where epaulettes had been roughly cut out. It *was* part of a police uniform. A button was missing below the collar.

Something was wrong. This did not belong here.

'Eleanor!' Krush's voice from outside was edged with panic. 'Eleanor!'

Footsteps clattered.

'Beth?' She ran through the flat and saw no silhouette through the frosted glass in the front door. Heavy footsteps echoed in the building. She rattled the door handle, knowing it was locked.

'Beth!' she cried.

The footsteps receded down the stairwell. Eleanor clambered through the fragments of glass in the small window and dropped down into the walkway.

'Beth! Where are you?'

<h1 style="text-align:center">55</h1>

Eleanor found her sister by the front exit downstairs, leaning against the wall, gasping for breath.

'Are you alright?'

'I don't know.' Half doubled-over, eyes closed, jaws clenched, Krush held onto the wall with one hand.

'What happened?' Eleanor reached out in concern, but drew back, afraid to touch her.

'My phone...' Krush gestured at the broken pieces where her mobile had smashed against the floor.

'It'll be alright. These things are indestructible.' Eleanor scooped up the main section. 'Well, your screen's shattered, but they can fix that.'

'Shit. This is what Dad said would happen.' Her words came out slowly between panting breaths. 'He said I'd be on my own one day, unable to stand up, with no phone to call for help. Promise you won't tell him about this.'

'You're not on your own.' Eleanor sat down next to her sister.

Their shoulders touched against the wall. For once, Krush did not pull away. She let her head drop onto Eleanor's shoulder, as her panicked breathing slowed. Her hair brushed Eleanor's neck. The feeling was like a jolt of electricity.

'I'm going to drive you to the doctor,' Eleanor said. 'You need to get checked out.'

'No. I'll be alright in a moment. I'm already feeling better.'

'If you say so.' Eleanor would have sat there like that all day. They were together at last. 'What happened?' she asked.

'I just… I don't know… it was like my whole insides squeezed together and I couldn't breathe. I was scared, scared of the baby, like it was going to come out too soon, or I don't know what.'

'Let's just rest here for as long as you need.'

'God. I fucked up. There was a kid in a tracksuit. He came up the stairs, took one look at me and ran. I chased, but he was too fast. By the time I got down here, he was already gone.'

'You didn't fuck up.'

'I did. If I hadn't been like this' – she cradled her belly – 'I would've caught him.'

'But why do you suppose this kid was important?'

'Why did he run?'

'Kids run from police. It's what they do.'

Krush straightened, still breathing heavily. 'If he's part of the gang, and the gang killed Baxter… they might have sent him to check, or, I don't know, maybe they forgot something.'

'There's no trace of a struggle inside. No sign of Baxter. But there's a police uniform. A shirt at least. The epaulettes have been cut off, but I think it may be from the tunnel police. There's a button missing.'

'You found it?'

'And this.' She pulled out the piece of paper.

'They'll never see the grey hood…' Krush said, and her weakness vanished. She pulled herself up. 'Come on. We're making progress. Let's keep going.'

It was beautiful, the way she said "we", thought Eleanor.

'We're close,' Krush said. 'We're right on the edge.'

'How can you tell?'

'Because we have to be. It has to be today. Tomorrow's too late.' Krush stepped away from the wall but immediately doubled over in pain.

'Jesus, Beth, will you stop a minute. Just rest for a moment.' Eleanor put her hand on her sister's shoulder.

Krush pushed her away. 'I'm fine. Don't worry about me.'

'You're clearly in pain.' In fact, Eleanor felt the same pain in her stomach, a weeping gash. 'You have to slow down a moment.'

'There isn't time. It feels like with this case, it's slipping away. It's almost ruined. We'll never find Iris if we don't hurry. It's going to haunt me forever. I know it will.'

* * *

They drove over to the construction site where Baxter worked. In the passenger seat, Krush turned over the shirt with the missing button.

'Looks like the epaulettes were cut off with a pair of scissors. But it's from the Mersey Tunnels Police, I'm certain. Baxter was in the tunnel. This proves it. You did it, Eleanor. This is the breakthrough. We have to arrest Slate now. Show him the evidence. Force him to talk.'

You did it, Eleanor. The words were sweet, almost inconceivable.

Three decades ago, they first met. They were shy to begin with. Eleanor, just a teen, was convinced her new sibling hated her. That summer, Krush discovered Sherlock Holmes. The two new sisters sat up late at night reading the stories aloud to one another. Through the long, warm afternoons, they played at detectives, investigating relatives and neighbours, the park, the corner shop. Krush was always Sherlock, and Eleanor was Watson. It worked that way. For the first time, she had felt a sense of kinship. It seemed like that summer would never end. One day, she wanted to be Sherlock. It was only fair; she had played Watson this whole time. Krush refused, but Eleanor would not back down. They never played the game again. Summer ended.

Somehow, despite her desire to win back her friendship, Eleanor still could not bring herself to accept the role of Watson.

'I don't think Slate killed Baxter,' she said.

'What?' Krush looked up at her from the shirt. 'He was in the same place as the victim, at some point, on the night of the killing. And they were both holding a shoe. It hangs together.'

'What's the motive?'

'Obvious. Iris was in love with Baxter. There are passages in her diary about another man. In one place, she talks about how ugly he is. She writes, "O is the only one you could ever love. Why? because O is the ugliest."'

'That doesn't prove anything.' Or did it? Eleanor was not sure of anything anymore. 'They call him Dogface at the station. He is ugly, I guess. But that's not sufficient.'

'It's good enough to bring Slate in for interrogation,' Krush said. 'Iris was having an affair. Slate found out. He killed both of them… it's a motive.'

'But, still, it doesn't fit. Slate was in the tunnel; Baxter was found on the other side of town.'

'There's a reason. There must be. We just haven't figured it out yet.'

Eleanor shook her head. 'I don't see it. I'm certain he's innocent. Really, I am.'

'Based on what – a feeling?'

'A feeling, yes. The way he speaks about Iris. His face when he says her name. He didn't kill her.'

'A feeling isn't good enough, Eleanor. The facts add up. We have to arrest Slate now, before it's too late.'

'His daughter said he was sobbing last night.'

'Yeah, sobbing with guilt. He killed his wife.'

'We need more. If we arrest him now, our case won't hang together. Mann will get him released, and Carver will shut the investigation down.'

'Goddammit.' Krush fell silent. Defeated. It was not like her.

Eleanor would have preferred to let her win, but she could not.

'Alright, what do you suggest?' Krush said.

'We'll ask around at the construction site. See if anyone there can tell us anything about Baxter.'

Krush turned to stare out of the window 'Where is the site, exactly?'

'The Marsh. Where else?'

56

They drove through the spring rain, a tunnel of trees acned with pink petals, back to the border.

The building site was on the edge of the Marsh, in Looney territory. A billboard outside declared, "HOMES FOR THE FUTURE". Partially smeared with mud, the picture showed a futuristic block of flats, shiny, silver and glass, with vines growing over balconies. On the other side of the sign, however, was only a wide foundation pit filled with rainwater, and a skeleton of scaffolding behind tarpaulin. Workers moved in the drizzle, carrying equipment, shouting into the wind.

A grey BMW was parked just outside the site.

'Is that...' Eleanor took a step, but before she could approach, the car pulled out from the kerb and raced away. She watched it disappear around the corner. 'Was that...'

'What?' Krush said.

'I think that was Lisa Wainwright's car. What's the Organised Crime Unit doing here?'

'Let's find out.'

They collected hard hats at the entrance and followed directions to where the boss was to be found on the other side of the pit. They saw him talking to a group of figures in billowing raincoats.

'Wait,' Eleanor said. 'Is that the mayor?'

Krush wiped rain from her eyelashes. 'Yes. And that's Mann, Slate's lawyer. Who are the other guys?'

'I think that's Wayne Looney. I checked out pictures of him and the other gang members in the database. Yeah, that's him, I'm sure of it. The other guy, I don't know. It's suspicious.' Eleanor took out her phone and snapped a few pictures. 'Looks like the whole gang's here.'

'Not everyone. Where's Slate? Come on.' Krush started towards the group.

They saw her coming. The mayor frowned, turned, and hurried away, followed by Looney.

Mann tried to smile as the detectives approached. 'What a pleasant surprise. How is your investigation going?'

'We're closing in.' Krush watched over his shoulder as the mayor and Looney slipped away. 'What are you doing here?'

'I was just having a chat with the foreman, and our architects.' Mann gestured to a man and a woman to one side who wore suits beneath yellow vests. 'This is an ambitious construction project.'

'What about the mayor?' Eleanor said.

For a moment, Mann had seemed caught off guard, but now he recovered his composure. 'The development of this wasteland is part of the council's long-term urban regeneration plan. We're rebuilding Liverpool.'

'Is that why Wayne Looney is involved?' Krush said. 'The famous philanthropist.'

Mann hesitated. 'Erm, that's just a potential investor in the project. I don't know him. He was here by coincidence.'

'But the Looneys—' Eleanor started to say.

'And where is your client?' Krush spoke over her.

'Damon?' Mann's face was inscrutable. 'I'm not his keeper.'

'You know he never came home last night?' Eleanor said. 'Claire called me. She's worried about him. She hasn't been able to get hold of him. He won't answer the phone. He's not responding to messages.'

'He's a busy man.' Mann's eye twitched with some concealed reaction.

'When did you last speak to him?' she said.

'I'm not sure. Yesterday, I guess.'

'You guess?' Krush said.

'Alright, let me see. It was last night, around ten o'clock. I spoke to him on the phone about some business matter. He seemed fine to me. He was laughing and joking.'

'It's today, you know.' Krush stared him down. 'Today was marked with an X in Iris's diary.'

'And what's that supposed to mean?'

'You'll find out before midnight.'

'Well then, we won't have long to wait.' He removed his hard hat and smoothed his thinning hair.

Krush suddenly grunted with pain.

'Are you alright?' he asked.

'No.' She grabbed Eleanor's shoulder and shoved her face into her chest with a grunt of pain. The intimacy was shocking.

Speechless, Eleanor did not know whether to embrace her in return, and only gently patted her. 'Should we?'

'I'm fine,' Krush said, but did not lift her head.

Just the hint of a grin showed on Mann's lips. 'I think your partner is sick. You should take care of her. You're sisters, after all.'

'I said, I'm fine.' Krush straightened. 'We're looking for a foreman who works here, a Johnny Baxter.'

Mann gestured to the site chief beside him, who had stayed quiet up to now. 'This is Clive. He'll answer any questions. If you'll excuse me, I have somewhere I need to be.'

He stalked away through a crowd of workers. Eleanor's eyes followed him through the muddy space where the homes of the future belonged.

57

'It's Baxter you wanted to talk about?' Clive said.

The site chief was short and overweight, with a wide face and thick, white stubble.

'Where is he?' Eleanor said.

'Hasn't turned up the last few days. Not answering phone calls either.'

'Is this him?' She took out her phone and showed the picture of the dead man from the park.

'Oh, Jesus. What happened? He's…'

'That's Baxter?' She kept the phone held up before his eyes. 'Please, look again. Be certain. Are you sure?'

'Think anybody could mistake him? Put that thing away, for God's sake. I just ate.'

'How well did you know him?' Krush said.

'I didn't. He was new on the job. He only just turned up in Liverpool. I think he was Irish or Scottish. His accent was strange.'

Eleanor scribbled down a note. 'And you employed him as a foreman, just like that, a complete stranger?'

'Truth be told, it was an order from above.'

'From whom, Damon Slate?'

Clive fingered the stubble on his chin. 'The order came from above, that's all I know.'

Krush considered this. 'So… you got a message one day "from above", telling you to employ Johnny Baxter as a foreman?'

'Yup.'

'When was this?' Eleanor said.

He shrugged. 'I dunno. Three months ago, I guess.'

'Three months ago?' Eleanor looked at Krush, but her sister did not return the glance. 'You took on a new foreman, someone you never heard of before, while the job was already in progress. Is that normal?'

'Nothing about this job has been normal,' Clive said. 'We've been plagued with delays. Recently, stuff has been going missing from the site. Not just a few bolts and screws, I mean, big pieces of equipment. And workers have been acting up, threatening to strike, quitting in the middle of the job. New guys are coming in all the time. I've never known a site like this one.'

Eleanor looked about the rainy pit, the flaps of tarpaulin, the sullen workers, and found she could believe him.

'How do you explain these disappearances?' Krush said.

'Theft. Plain and simple. Bastards nicking our stuff to work on their own side projects.'

'Didn't you report any of this to the police?' Krush asked.

'Sure, they sent an officer from the local station. He took a few photographs and never came back.'

'What was his name?' Eleanor said.

'I don't know. Jeff, something like that.'

Eleanor jumped at the name. 'Jeff? Derrick Jeffers? Talks too much?'

'Could be. He was useless anyway. It doesn't matter. In this world, we solve our own problems. We'll find out who stole that stuff. Once a man has a reputation in Liverpool, he'll never work on another construction site. Not a decent one like ours.'

'Is there anything you can tell me about Baxter?' Eleanor said.

'Not a bean,' Clive said. 'He came in on time, and he left on time. He never spoke to anybody. If I'm being honest, I never trusted him. He seemed sort of secretive. The rest of the guys kept away from him. They resent it when a guy gets a job for free from upstairs. It doesn't feel fair. Baxter knew it too. He could tell he wasn't liked. He kept to himself.'

Krush stared into the rain. Her face was blank.

Eleanor had never seen her so bewildered. It was frightening. 'Are you OK?' she asked.

'I'm a bit faint. I need to sit down for a moment.'

'Not wanting to stick my nose in other people's business,' Clive said, 'but I think your partner needs to go to hospital.'

Eleanor waited for Krush to rebut this with a sarcastic comment, but she only groaned.

* * *

In the waiting room at the doctor's, Krush found a seat in the corner and sat down. It was crowded, stuffy and hot.

Eleanor filled two cups of water at the fountain and carried them over. 'Here. Drink.'

Krush was fanning herself with a magazine. 'I hate this place.'

'When did you last get a check-up?'

'Truth be told, I've been lax. I cancelled the last appointment. I was too busy.'

'I don't want to nag you, Beth–'

'Good. Don't.'

'…but you have to start taking this pregnancy more seriously. You're going to hurt yourself, and the baby.'

'Don't worry about the baby, he's an ox. He's strong and he's happy. I can feel him laughing sometimes.'

'I thought you didn't believe in feelings.'

Krush sat up, looking around the room of bored faces. 'This is going to take all day. We could be waiting hours to see a doctor. In the meantime, the case is slipping through our fingers.'

'Forget about the case. Your health is more important. The city needs you, Beth.'

'The city doesn't need anything. It's not alive. Liverpool's just a pile of concrete, tarmac, bricks, and glass. I never understood how anyone could love a city the way they do around here.'

Eleanor sensed the other women in the waiting room prick up their ears. It was not done to question Liverpool or to doubt that it was the greatest place in the world.

Eleanor lowered her voice. 'And yet, you never left,' she said. 'You could've taken a job anywhere.'

'Like you did?' Krush almost cracked a smile. 'How did London work out for you?'

'It would've been fine, if you'd been there as well.'

'Yeah, well. We're not Sherlock and Watson anymore. Let's not kid ourselves.' Krush looked up as the nurse came in to call the next patient, but it was somebody else. 'Alright. Enough wasting time. If you want to leave me here, go ahead. I'll be fine. You go to the tunnel police with the jacket and see what they can tell you.'

Eleanor was stunned at that. 'You'd stay here by yourself?'

'Yeah. I'll talk to the doctor. They can scan the baby and tell me how gigantic it is, the usual chitchat. When I'm done, I'll call, and you can pick me up.'

'You're sure?'

'Of course. Come on, Eleanor, you're a detective. You can handle this without me for half an hour. Check with the tunnel police and call right away if you find anything out.'

'Right,' said Eleanor, but it did not feel right. Her sister was changed.

58

At the George's Dock Building, Eleanor met Constable Roy Ogden. She showed him the shirt with the missing button.

'Where did you find this?' He laid the shirt on a desk and smoothed it out.

'It's connected to a case I'm working on. Do you think it could belong to a tunnel police officer?'

'It looks like a police officer's shirt, but with the epaulettes removed, it could be any kind of police.'

'We found a loose button in the tunnel. We think it belongs on this shirt.'

'I see.' He rubbed at the loose thread where the button was missing. 'Are you a colleague of Detective Krush? She was over here the other day looking at video footage.'

'I'm her partner.' It felt good to say that.

It was odd, she realized suddenly, she did not want to solve this case. It had brought her and her sister together. When it ended, they might go back to how it was before, avoiding each other in the canteen, sneaking away down the stairways of the station. If the case could only last forever...

Ogden glanced at the closed door of the office. 'You think someone from the tunnel police could be involved with... with what happened with Damon Slate?'

'We're not ruling out anything at the moment.'

He lowered his voice. 'And... his wife... Iris Slate. I saw the bulletins. Is she dead?'

'We don't know. We haven't given up hope of finding her alive.' Eleanor took out her phone and showed him the picture of Baxter. 'Do you recognize this man?'

Ogden glanced and pulled a face. 'Jesus, no. Was he the one–'

'We found the shirt in his wardrobe.'

'He's never worked here, not in the four years I've been at the tunnel.'

'The shirt was in his wardrobe, but that doesn't mean it belonged to him.'

'If someone from the tunnel police was involved…' Ogden let the sentence fall away.

'Yes?'

'It's not possible.' He looked around the empty room. 'I know everyone here. They're good people.'

'Is there something you're not telling me?'

He lowered his eyes, and she sensed the depths of the tunnel beneath their feet. It must be eerie working in this place.

'What is it?' she said.

'It's just… it's nothing… really. I shouldn't.'

'Just tell me.'

He hesitated. 'Do you believe in solidarity?'

'It depends what you mean. If you're talking about police corruption, then no.'

'Something odd happened that night.'

'Which night?'

'When Slate was lost in the tunnel.'

'Go on.'

'The tunnel closed at midnight for maintenance. There was an electrical fault with the lights. Part of the tunnel was in complete darkness for a stretch.'

'So…'

'So, the cameras don't show everything that happened.'

'When my partner was looking at the camera footage, was she made aware of this?'

'Not exactly. The boss, Sergeant Shipley, told us to leave this information out of it unless we were specifically asked.'

'You lied to her.'

'Not a lie. We just didn't volunteer information. We would've answered if asked specifically.'

'I need to speak to Sergeant Shipley.'

'He's away on holiday.'

'Whereabouts?'

'I dunno. It was a last-minute thing. I didn't even know he was gone, until Erica told me.'

'Alright, you'll have to explain it yourself then. Why the cover-up?'

'It wasn't a cover-up, honestly. We didn't know at the time that Iris Slate was missing. We thought it was just about Damon Slate in the tunnel. We were afraid of awkward questions from the media, or enquiries from higher up. It was sort of embarrassing for us, you know? We lost a celebrity in one of our tunnels. But now… this police uniform turns up, and I start to wonder… what if the lights going out wasn't an accident?'

59

As soon as Eleanor was gone, Krush had called a taxi. On the way out, she informed the receptionist she did not need to see the doctor anymore.

'But… are you sure?' The woman looked at her belly with a kind of superstitious awe. 'You're here now. You may as well speak to the doctor. He'll be with you soon.'

'There's no time. I have to go.' She rushed out before anyone else could argue with her.

The taxi driver was only moderately irritating, eyeing her belly in the rear-view mirror and telling stories about when his wife gave birth during the middle of *EastEnders*. Krush blanked out the noise. She needed to concentrate. Her phone started to ring. Eleanor. She rejected the call.

This was not the moment to have to explain or justify what she was doing.

The taxi driver wittered on, something about gynaecologists.

She interrupted. 'Can you go any faster?'

'I'm following the speed limit. You're police, aren't you? I don't want to get arrested.'

'I'm not a traffic cop. I'm only interested in murder.'

'Righto.'

He stayed silent after that. Finally, they arrived at the casino. As they were pulling up outside, she saw Mann approaching the front entrance.

'Shit. I have to go.' She jumped out and set off running after him.

'Hey!' the driver called through the open door. 'You forgot to pay.'

'Send a bill to police HQ, it's Beth Krush.'

'But...?'

She kept running.

Mann, in the entrance, saw her. His shoulders drooped, and his face showed something like despair. His wispy hair was windblown, and his green suit was creased.

'Are you following me, Detective?' he said.

Krush stopped, out of breath, in the door that he held open. 'I'm looking for your client. Have you heard anything from him?'

'I'm looking for him as well. He's not responding to messages. I'm starting to worry.'

'You think he's here?'

'Sometimes he has a late session at the casino. This is his sanctuary. When he plays, he turns off his phone. This is the one place where he manages to cut off the outside world.'

At that moment, Slate came running down the stairs carrying a briefcase. He did not notice them until he was halfway across the foyer, at which point he stopped dead.

'Damon.' His lawyer looked furious. 'What the hell? Where were you?'

'What's she doing here?' Slate looked a mess: unshaven, hair sticking up, his shirt crumpled and half undone, his eyes red.

'I was looking for you.' Krush brushed past Mann. 'What's in here?'

Slate did not resist as she took the briefcase from his hand.

'Are you drunk?' Mann asked his client.

'I don't know anymore.'

'You were supposed to sign the lease today.'

'Oh, that. What does it matter?'

Krush meanwhile had set the briefcase down on the floor. It was stuffed with cash. 'What's this?'

Mann gasped. 'You raided the casino coffers?'

'You weren't planning to leave the city, were you?' Krush said.

'Why would I?' Slate said.

'I'm going to need you to come back down to the station. We found your foreman.'

'What's that to me?' Slate said.

'He was holding your wife's shoe.'

60

The call was from an unknown number, but Eleanor did not hesitate. The time left to find Iris was shrinking. She put the call through the car's speakers while she drove.

'Eleanor Rose?' A man's voice with a strong Scouse accent came through. It was too loud, surrounding her in the car.

She lowered the volume. 'Who is this?'

'I found your card in a puddle of beer.' There was a leer in his tone.

'What do you want? I'm going to hang up now.'

'Suit yourself. I thought you'd want to talk, that's all.'

'To talk about what? Tell me your name, please.'

He chuckled. 'I don't think so. It's Daz you're after, isn't it?'

'What?'

'Damon Slate. That rich cunt. You're chasing him, aren't you?'

'I never said that.'

'Ah well. I must have misunderstood. I'll hang up then.'

'No. Wait. What did you want to say?'

'You are chasing him?'

'In a manner of speaking.'

'How much would you pay to know the truth?'

She tried to think of the right answer, but the questions came too fast, and the voice was insidious. She knew she was being played with.

'Listen, I can't discuss this on the phone,' she said. 'Can we meet?'

'That depends.'

'On what?'

'On what you're willing to give up.'

'I'll give up my time, how about that?'

The man laughed. 'Not generous enough.'

'I'm starting to think this is a prank call. I'm going to hang up.' But she did not hang up. She waited to hear what would come next.

'There are rumours about you, you know,' the man said.

'What rumours?'

'They say you're trying to go over to the other side. Talking to gangsters. Trying to connect with the underworld.'

'This is some kind of a joke, isn't it?'

'You want to sell yourself, but you can't figure out how. You've pimped yourself around the bars, looking for a buyer that might be interested in a corrupt cop. But nobody's biting.'

Now, Eleanor was just angry. 'You want to bite, is that it?'

'Let's say, I'm tempted.'

'You're a gangster?'

'We don't use that word around here. I'm a businessman, just like Damon Slate.'

'And you need help.'

'I don't need anything. But Slate is a competitor. It wouldn't harm me if his stock took a stumble.'

'Perhaps we can assist each other, but not on the phone. Let's meet.'

'I'll think about it.'

The phone line went dead.

61

On the other side of the two-way mirror, Damon Slate sat in the interview room. He leaned back in his chair, apparently at ease, although his eyes were red, and his suit was stained with alcohol and cigarette ash. It was an utterly different man to the one who had sat in this same room the day before. Beside him, Mann whispered in his ear through cupped hands. Whatever he said caused Slate to shake his head.

Krush watched through the glass. 'We'll nail him this time,' she said.

'I don't believe it,' Eleanor said.

Behind them, Carver swore under her breath. 'This is a goddamn mess. If you're wrong, Krush…'

'I'm not wrong. I caught him with a bag of cash about to flee the city. We've identified his foreman now. He can't keep lying.'

'And if he's not lying?' Eleanor said.

'Alright, you two,' Carver said. 'Stop bickering. Go in and get the whole story out of him. Get his statement written up and then we'll decide how to proceed.'

'There's only one way to proceed,' Krush said, 'put him in a cell. This is the moment. Look at him: he's falling apart. He's a wreck. He knows the game is up. If we put pressure on him now, he'll finally crack. He'll tell us where his wife is.'

'*If* he knows,' Eleanor said.

'He knows.'

'We need to put him in front of a psychiatrist,' Eleanor said. 'Somebody who can deal with the amnesia.'

'Please,' Krush said, 'not this again.'

'Let her finish,' Carver said.

'I don't know if Slate is guilty or not,' Eleanor said, 'but I believe his amnesia was real. If he would agree to undergo hypnosis with a psychiatrist–'

'Unbelievable,' Krush said. 'Can't you see he's stalling for time? We're playing into his hands.'

'I tend to agree with Rose,' the chief said. 'I spoke to Dr Shepherd, and he said it's worth a shot. He's ready to conduct a psychological evaluation, if the suspect is willing.'

'It won't work with Dr Shepherd,' Eleanor said. 'It has to be Raymond Stray.'

'Impossible.' Carver crossed her arms.

'Can we stop with this now?' Krush said. 'Come on. Slate's been sweating in there long enough.' She walked out.

A moment later, they saw her enter the interview room on the other side of the glass.

Slate tried to smile as she sat down.

'I'd better get in there too.' Eleanor hurried after her sister.

As she was entering the interview room, Mann came out. He was flustered, angry.

'Everything alright?' Eleanor said.

'I have some things to take care of. My client will talk to you without my presence.' He scowled. 'But you have my number. Please, call if anything comes up.'

62

'Mr Slate,' Krush said. 'What do you know about a man by the name of Johnny Baxter?'

'Never heard of him. Is he a gambler?'

'He was a foreman on one of your construction sites,' Krush said.

'Why should I care about a foreman?'

'Because he was murdered. The same night you found your way into the tunnel. Funnily enough, he was holding Iris's other shoe.'

Slate looked nauseous. He loosened his collar. 'Ah… well. I don't fraternise with the workers. I have to maintain some distance. I'm sorry he's dead. I'll make sure the company sends condolences to his family.'

'You really don't know him?' Krush said. 'That's interesting. He was given the job, despite a lack of experience, on your specific orders.'

'This is the first I've heard about it.' Slate looked around but his lawyer was gone.

'Three months ago,' Krush said, 'the order came down from above to give him the job.'

'Says who?'

'Your site chief. I just spoke to him.'

Slate massaged his face. 'Oh God.'

'What? Is there something you're not telling me?'

'I swear it wasn't me who gave the order to employ your dead guy, whatever his name was.'

'Who else then?'

Slate slumped forwards with his head in his hands. 'Could it have been Iris? Sometimes my wife asks me for favours. Yes. I remember now, it must have been three or four months ago, she asked me to find a job for an old friend of hers. I gave the order to keep her happy, but I never met the man. I didn't even know his name. I'd forgotten about it until now.'

Eleanor and Krush looked at each other. Was it enough to keep him in custody?

Slate had regained his composure. 'I'll make a bet with you right now. I bet you Iris is back home safe and sound in a few days,' he said.

Krush hesitated. 'The odds are not in your favour.'

'That's how I like it. I'll pay you a million pounds if she doesn't turn up alive and well. A million pounds in cash. I'm not joking. But if *I* win… all I want off you is a smile, and a game of cards.'

'That's not how this works,' Krush said. 'I don't need to make a bet with you. I can put you in prison right now.'

'You're bluffing.'

'You knew Johnny Baxter, and he knew Iris. Now he's dead, and she's missing. He was in the tunnel. He lost a button there. You were in the tunnel as well, with Iris's shoe. It fits together. It's enough to remand you in custody. You'll spend tonight in jail.'

'Don't be ridiculous, Detective. We both know I'll be back out in the street before nightfall. I have the best lawyer in the business, and besides, I'm innocent.'

Eleanor spoke up. 'Mr Slate, would you be willing to do a session with one of our psychologists? We can try hypnosis to bring back your missing memories.'

'Hypnosis.' Slate coughed. He rubbed his eyes. 'Does that… does that really work?'

'No,' Krush said.

'Yes,' Eleanor said.

'And I… do I have to do it, or can I refuse?'

'You can refuse, of course.' Eleanor tried to decipher his confused expression. Was he afraid?

He adjusted his collar. 'Well then, if you think it might help to find Iris. I agree, of course. When can we do it?'

'Dr Shepherd said he'd be available,' Eleanor said. 'I'll see if we can do it now.'

'You can do this without me.' Krush got up scowling and walked to the door.

'Wait–' Eleanor called after her.

In the doorway, Krush turned back and pointed at Slate. 'You're not leaving this place until you give us something.'

He could not quite smile. 'I'll leave whenever I want to, but right now, I choose to stay and help. If you really think something bad has happened to Iris… I'll do the hypnosis, and anything else you want.'

'You'd better hope it works, or you're not going home.' Krush slammed the door behind her.

Slate raised his eyebrows at Eleanor. 'Growing up in your family must've been intense, hey?'

63

Slate smiled when they brought him into the spare office. 'Dr Shepherd, how are you?'

Shepherd blushed.

'Do you know each other?' Eleanor said.

'No.' The doctor motioned to the door. 'Nobody else can be in the room during the hypnosis. It's essential that nobody enters while the procedure is taking place. Understood?'

Eleanor went outside with the guard. As soon as the door closed, she felt certain this was a mistake. There was a chair against the wall, but she was too agitated to sit down. The guard opened a newspaper. The sound of the page-turning was too loud as Eleanor strained to pick up a hint from the other side of the door, where Shepherd and his subject were locked in together. Tiny sounds came to life. She heard the ticking of the clock on the wall in the corridor; a door banging somewhere around the corner; footsteps clattered in the stairway. Five minutes passed in tense silence. The guard had almost finished his newspaper.

Somebody groaned on the other side of the door, or perhaps it was just an illusion created by her brain to fill the emptiness.

'Did you hear that?' the guard said. 'What was that?'

Eleanor put a finger to her lips. Behind the door, another groan, longer this time, like somebody with toothache.

The guard stood up. 'Should we go inside?'

She reached for the handle but stopped. 'No,' she whispered. 'Dr Shepherd said we mustn't break the hypnosis.'

The guard shook his head and sat back down. He was looking for his place in the newspaper when a shout broke through the door. Not a word, but a guttural syllable, almost like an orgasm.

The guard jumped up. 'I think we should go in.'

'No. Dr Shepherd would call for help if he needed us.'

'But what if… what if something happened to the doctor?' The guard came closer.

They listened at the door but, the room on the other side was hushed. Eleanor closed her eyes and tried to hear. There was just a small, repetitive sound, like sobbing. Finally, there was nothing.

The guard went back to his chair. 'I guess you were right.'

The door opened and Dr Shepherd looked out. 'You can take your suspect away now.'

'What happened, how did it go?' Eleanor scanned the doctor's face, which was pale, shocked.

'You'll receive my full report as soon as it's written up.' He tried to sound authoritative, but his voice was shaky.

'We heard groans through the door,' she said.

'The subject had a nightmare while he was under hypnosis.'

'Is that all you can tell me?'

'What else do you want me to say?'

The guard entered the room. 'Come on, pal, let's go.'

Slate stretched and rubbed his eyes. 'Wow. That was the best sleep I've had in years. I don't know how you did it, Doctor. Everyone should try hypnosis.'

'Yeah well.' Shepherd collected his papers together into a briefcase. His hands trembled.

'What's the matter?' Slate said. 'Did I say something weird? Did I… did I talk about Iris? Did I say where she is?'

'No,' Shepherd said. 'No, you didn't talk about your wife. You don't know where she is.'

'That's a relief.' Slate followed the guard out of the room. Passing Eleanor in the doorway, he held her eye. 'Have you ever been hypnotised? It's the strangest feeling.'

'Yes,' she said. 'I was hypnotised once.'

'Ah, so then, you know.' There was something about the way he said this, almost mocking.

Perhaps he knew about what had happened to her in the past. The disturbing thought occurred to her that he might know a lot about her. He was a wealthy man, well-connected; he might know everything.

'I don't remember it at all,' she said.

'They say some people are more open to it than others. I guess we're alike, Detective.'

'Come on.' The guard pushed him in the back. 'Shut up now.'

Eleanor watched them move away down the corridor. When they were out of sight, she went into the spare office, where Shepherd had closed his briefcase and was about to leave.

'I heard weird noises through the door,' she said.

'That's normal.'

'Those weren't normal noises.'

Shepherd took off his glasses and polished them. 'Sometimes patients have vivid dreams.'

'What about?'

'I don't know.'

'He really didn't say anything about his wife?'

'No.'

'Did he remember what happened that night?'

'He remembered being in a tunnel, that's all.'

'Whom was he with, in the tunnel?'

'He was alone.'

'How did he get in there?'

'I don't know.' Shepherd put on his glasses and walked out of the room. 'You'll receive my report.'

'But, isn't there anything you can tell me now? We're looking for a missing woman. It's urgent. We're concerned about her.'

'Psychology can't bring back missing people. That's your job, not mine.' He walked away.

Shaken, Eleanor was heading back in search of her sister when Carver called her name down the corridor.

'Rose! My office. Now. It's urgent.'

64

When Eleanor entered Carver's office, she found Krush already seated, waiting for her. The lawyer, Mann, looking more composed now, was on the other side of the desk, beside the chief inspector, as if he was in charge.

'What's he doing here?' Eleanor pointed at him.

'Just sit down,' Carver said. 'You need to listen to what he has to say.'

She sat beside her sister and watched as Mann set his briefcase in the middle of the desk. 'I have something you should listen to.'

He placed a small speaker between them and turned it on.

'What is this?' Eleanor said.

'You'll see.' He smiled icily.

Static sounded out of the device, and a grainy voice came out. Eleanor recognized it with trickling horror.

> *You want to sell yourself, but you can't figure out how. You've pimped yourself around the bars, looking for an underworld that might be interested in a corrupt cop. But nobody's biting.*

'Turn this off,' she said, as her own voice came out of the speaker.

> *You want to bite, is that it?*

'Eleanor!' Krush grabbed her arm. 'What the hell is this?'

> *Let's say, I'm tempted.*

But Eleanor was frozen. She could not speak but only listened, with her sister's fingers digging into her arm.

> *You're a gangster?*

> *We don't use that word around here. I'm a businessman, just like Damon Slate.*

> *And you need help.*

> *I don't need anything. But Slate is a competitor. It wouldn't harm me if his stock took a stumble.*

The speaker went silent.

Krush released her arm. 'Oh God.'

Mann leaned back with his fingers laced together. 'I have the document drawn up already. We intend to press charges against the police for conspiracy with criminal figures to try and bring down my client.'

'But… that's ridiculous. That's…' Eleanor looked for the words. 'This is a set-up.' She turned to Krush, but her sister would not look at her. 'I received that call earlier from an unknown number. I don't even know who that man was.'

'How convenient,' Mann said.

'How did you come by that recording?' Krush asked him. Her voice betrayed no anger, just calculation.

'I don't need to disclose my sources. If you're not convinced about the extent to which Detective Rose here is compromised, perhaps this will sway you.' He reached into the briefcase.

Eleanor felt nauseous, but she could not look away as he pulled out a sheaf of photographs and arranged them on the desk. She already knew without having to glance.

'You'll recognize your colleague in these pictures. Here you might also recognize a local gangster known as Pogo, a known member of the Looneys. These pictures were taken in a pub called the Tin Whistle.'

Krush picked up one of the photographs. 'Eleanor… what did you do?'

'You'll notice as well,' Mann continued, 'this man, Raymond Stray. A drug addict who is apparently living with the detective at this time.'

'This is a set-up.' Eleanor looked at Krush and Carver, but they were staring at the pictures. 'You must see this is a set-up.'

Mann closed his briefcase and stood up. 'You can keep the photographs. I'll have the legal paperwork in front of you by the morning.'

'There's no need for paperwork.' Carver's hands were balled into fists. 'We'll release your client immediately. He was never an official suspect. Our intention is only to cooperate with you as best we can to find Iris Slate.'

Mann nodded. 'Very well. In that case, I look forward to our future working together.'

His eyes caught Krush's with defiance as he walked out. The room fell into silence. Eleanor looked at Carver, but Carver only shook her head.

'I…' Eleanor stammered. 'You have to believe me. This is a set-up. Slate's sabotaging our investigation.'

'He's succeeded,' Carver said. 'I'm shutting it down now.'

'No!' Krush jumped up. 'Take Eleanor off the case; it was her dumb mistake. Let me finish it. Assign me a new partner if you want. We can't stop now. We're so close.'

'Sit down, Detective.'

Krush remained standing. 'Give me until midnight. I'm certain, whatever is happening, it's today. Today was marked in Iris's diary with an *X*.'

'I fear you've read too much into that diary,' the chief said. 'Will you sit down? You're impossible.'

Krush banged on the desk. 'Give me until midnight.'

'You're relentless. Fine. You have until midnight, Krush. But not *you*, Eleanor. You need to keep a mile away from this investigation. Merseyside Police can't afford another lawsuit.'

'You're letting him win.' Biting back tears, Eleanor appealed to Krush. 'Come on. We made a good team. We were making progress on the case. We were close.'

Krush would not look at her. 'I'm sorry. I just think, maybe this job isn't for you.'

'I can't…' She looked for an argument but could only find a pool of anger inside.

'You need help. You know you do. That's why you're hanging around with Raymond Stray, as if he could help you. But that's part of your problem, you can't tell the difference between the poison and the cure. You can't see he's a charlatan who's using you. Take a break, Eleanor. Take time and seek real help, not Stray's kind.'

'You don't know anything about me,' Eleanor managed to say.

'I know you better than anyone,' Krush said.

Carver looked on while they argued, astonished, seemingly powerless to intervene even though she was in charge.

'I'm not saying this to hurt your feelings,' Krush said. 'Just, it would be better for you, better for us, better for the police, if you transferred away from murder to something else. I don't know what. Honestly, I think you'd make a great primary school teacher.'

Krush's words were stupefying. Eleanor opened her mouth but could not make a sound.

'I'm sorry, Eleanor, honestly,' Krush said.

Carver raised a hand to speak. 'If I could…'

Suddenly Eleanor's anger broke free. She turned to her sister and almost grabbed hold of her. 'You think you're smarter than the whole world, but you're wrong. You can't read other people. You can't tell if someone's lying to you. I bet someone lied right to your face in this investigation and you never knew. That's why it's stalled. That's why you're stuck. You'll never solve it without me.'

Krush did not respond.

Carver slumped in her seat, her head between her hands, exhausted. 'I don't know what's wrong between you two, but putting you together was a mistake. I won't make it again. Eleanor, I'm temporarily relieving you of duties.'

'But–'

'No buts. I'm sending you for a full psychological evaluation. You're not going back into the field until it's all checked out.'

'Can I…' Eleanor started to argue but the chief had already moved on.

'As for you, Krush, you have until midnight. Tomorrow, you're going on maternity leave.'

'There won't be a case tomorrow.' Krush walked out.

65

Eleanor ran out of the station. She drove home in a daze. In a single mistake, everything had been lost. The case was ruined. Worse than that, the partnership with Beth was gone. She could almost howl to think of the conversations they had shared in this car, in which, somehow, they had never really talked. They had never been Sherlock Holmes and Watson; her sister was just Sherlock alone, and she always would be.

"A primary school teacher". The words jangled in her skull. She knew what her sister thought about primary school teachers.

Humiliation burned in an empty space in her mind where she tried to think what to do, but no thoughts emerged. She longed for a sanctuary, but there were no sanctuaries in the adult world, and childhood was long gone. The parks were overgrown, swings and slides left to rust; and the libraries were derelict, locked, and boarded up. The closest she had found to sanctuary in recent years was therapy with Raymond Stray. There was a kind of peace there, lying on the couch, describing her dreams, while Stray sat with his eyes closed and his fingers joined together like he was praying. He listened and hardly spoke a word.

She needed to get her head straight before she did something crazy like quit the police force. And maybe that was not such a crazy idea. She no longer felt any belonging in that world. All of her ideas were rejected, all of her ventures had failed. Her colleagues in the corridors and common areas at the station, always seemed to share a glance and turn away from her… it wasn't just paranoia, she knew it now. Dr Shepherd was scheming against her. Lisa Wainwright thought she was "too nice". Her own sister thought she was an idiot. Even the criminal world rejected her. Her efforts to reach out in that direction had ended in disaster. There was something wrong with her, and even they could see it. They had used her. They would be laughing at her now.

There was something broken, some cloud of mistakes and failure that hung about her, invisible to herself, but transparent to everybody else. She saw it in their eyes. Dr Shepherd had a way of smiling to himself when he spoke to her, a hint of amusement that he just failed to conceal. Stray's psychological evaluation form confirmed it. *Hysterical neurosis.*

She parked outside the house and ran inside.

'What's up with you?' Neil came into the hall in his dressing gown. 'You look like you ran over someone's cat.'

'Where's Stray? I need to talk to him.'

'Oh, he's gone.'

'Gone? What do you mean?'

'He left a letter on the bed in the spare room. He decided it was time to move on, and I can't say I disagree with him.'

'But…' She ran up the stairs so fast she almost tripped.

'Be careful!' Neil called after her.

Stray's few belongings were missing. She snatched up a folded slip of paper that was lying on top of the duvet cover.

'This can't be happening.'

But it was. Eleanor read through the note three times and screwed it into a ball. He had left no address, no phone number, no indication of his plans. It was obvious: he had no desire to see her again. Even Stray had washed his hands of her. Her abandonment was complete.

Back downstairs, Neil was watching television in the living room.

'How long ago did he leave?' she said.

Neil did not move his eyes away from the quiz show he was watching. 'Beats me. Must have been sometime in the middle of the night. I've been here all day. I haven't moved.'

'I need to find him.'

'Why?' With undisguised irritation, Neil lowered the volume. 'What are you doing home at this time? Where's Beth? I thought you were supposed to be working together?'

'I'm on my own now.'

'But…'

'I'll solve this case by myself. I'll find Iris Slate before Beth does, before anyone else. I'll prove them all wrong. They can burn their psychological evaluation forms, Shepherd and his stupid smile.'

Neil stared fearfully. 'Are you sure you don't want a cup of tea and some toast?'

'I have to go.' She walked out into the downpour.

66

When Stray woke up, there was a moment, just before he opened his eyes, when he almost believed he was lying in the spare bedroom in Neil's house. Only, what was that smell? The house was peaceful, submerged in rest. Soon he would hear one of the doors on the landing open and Neil would shuffle out in his slippers, or Eleanor would knock gently and call his name. But the voice that cried out in the dark was not Eleanor's.

'Help me!' a woman screamed.

Stray opened his eyes. The smell was rot. From where he lay on a bit of tattered rug, he saw the ceiling overhead was green with mould. The walls bulged with damp plasterwork, speckled with mushrooms and mildew. Rain beat against the broken windows and formed puddles on the floor.

'No!' the woman screamed. 'No! Please! Help me!'

Stray tried to lift himself, but his body was so heavy, his limbs felt broken.

A man next to him laughed, a sound papery and cruel. 'Leave it, Doc. She's having a nightmare. Susie always has the same nightmare, every time she falls asleep.'

Stray tried to turn his head to see who was behind him, but he could not. The man's voice rattled. He sounded too old.

Stray tried to speak but his tongue stuck to his palate. He groaned and managed to bring out a word. 'Where?'

The man laughed again. 'That must've been some rat poison, wasn't it? Cunts trying to poison us. As soon as it swirled in my blood, I knew we were fucked. "You've done it this time," I told myself. "See you in the morning, you bastard. If you wake up." That's the last thing I remember.'

'Help me!' the woman screamed. 'No!'

Stray tried to see her, but she was turned away. Her hair was white, her shoulders emaciated. She shook in her sleep.

'There she goes again,' the man said. 'My theory is, something awful happened when she was a kid. But she won't say. Everyone's tried to ask her. Even when she's dead drunk, she won't tell what it was.'

Stray opened his mouth but all that came out was a sob.

'That's alright,' the man said. 'You're safe here. We're all safe. This old house is about to fall into the river. Nobody but us has been inside in years. Even the kids and the rabid dogs don't dare. It's too wretched.'

Stray tried to understand the weeping that drew itself from him so softly, but he gave up.

'Aye,' the man said. 'Today's a bloody day in Liverpool. Anyone with a head on their shoulders should hide away and wait for it to pass.'

'What do you mean?' Stray tried to sit up. Broken with tears, he sounded to himself like a child.

'You were wise to get away. You always knew best, Doc. That police bitch you were leeching off. She's in trouble. She's sniffing where she doesn't belong. You were smart to abandon her. You got out at the right moment.'

The tears stopped. Stray managed to lift his head and look around. Lying close behind him was a man with no hair and no teeth. His eyes were glassy with glaucoma.

'I didn't abandon her,' Stray said. 'I only wanted to help. But I failed. She's better off without me. Eleanor will be OK. Her instincts are just. She can take care of herself.'

'Oh, no.' The cloudy eyes gleamed. 'No. They say she's looking for "Heart of the City". She's been asking all around the city, leaving her card, talking to the wrong people. People might have spared her on your account. But you dumped her, and smartly.'

'What are you talking about?'

'If she finds "Heart of the City", if her instincts are right…'

Stray could move now. He pulled himself into a sitting position. 'Have you been there, to Heart of the City?'

'Who, *me*? Are you crazy?'

'But you know where it is?'

'I heard things, that's all. How's a man like me supposed to find it? I can't even see you, and you're close enough to touch. But your police friend, she'll find it, with all those smart computers they've got.'

'What is "Heart of the City"?'

'Do you imagine anyone shares secrets with me? All I know is, it's a killing place. Everyone dies.'

'How do you know that? Who told you?'

'Open your ears. The rumours are like flies. In the pubs, the alleyways, the squats, every Scouser knows. There's a buzz in the air. Can't you feel it? Everyone knows, even if they can't explain it, there's something vile about to happen in Liverpool. That's why they're getting out of the city, or bunkering down like us and hiding. I'm surprised at you. You must've got too comfortable in their posh house.

Living with a woman. You've gone soft, Doc.' The man giggled. A long thread of drool hung from his chapped lips.

'Rumours,' Stray said. 'Is that all it is? A "buzz" in the air? Do you know anything factual about "Heart of the City"?'

The man laughed like a child.

Stray's limbs came to life. He grabbed the man by the shoulders. 'What is it? Tell me!'

'Oh, you really care about that woman.' He laughed and did not try to fight him off. 'Careful, Doc. You know we can't have feelings in this world. Not in a room like this one.' His eyes reflected the mouldy surfaces.

'Just tell me what you know.'

'There was a guy in a squat a few days ago. He said he'd been to "Heart of the City".'

'Who was he?'

'I have no idea, and it doesn't matter anyway; he'll be long gone by now. He did odd jobs and dirty work. He'd been paid by a fella to help out there. But that was before. Now, he said, all he wanted to do was get far away from Liverpool before it all explodes.'

'Explodes? What are you talking about?'

'You've lost your touch, Raymond Stray. How could you not know? It's today it happens. It's the killing day.'

67

An *X* on a page. The day was halfway through. Krush's chances of solving the riddle were cut in half.

She drove over to Slate's house, but nobody was home. Even his kids had gone somewhere. The curtains were closed. The seagulls had flown away.

The station was empty. She went all the way up to the top floor, but Sergeant Blaine was not in his office. She asked around where Lisa Wainwright might be found, but nobody knew. Top members of the Organised Crime Unit were not responding to calls or messages. It seemed they were busy. HQ was quiet, eerie. Everybody seemed to be on holiday. The public shied away; the reception area was peaceful for once. She was starting to suspect this might be one of those dreams where she wandered endless corridors in search of something that could not be named.

She tried calling Mann, then Slate without success. She took a spare squad car and drove over to Slate Tower, but it was closed. The front entrance was locked, and a sign outside said, "CLOSED FOR BUSINESS". No explanation was offered. She tried Mann's office nearby, but it was also closed. They had escaped her.

Feeling desperate, she drove over to the casino but that was closed as well. There was not even a cleaner or a guard. Nobody answered at the back door. A sense of dead ends caught in her throat. There was no worse moment in a case than when all momentum faded, the threads came to nothing, and the enquiry was over. She hated to give up, and she hated to fail. Colleagues had commented over the years that she never knew when to stop. She would keep on pushing a case even when everyone else called it quits. They did not understand, failure was like death to Beth Krush.

When her phone vibrated in her pocket, need lurched in her exhausted chest. She pulled it out too fast, it slipped out of her hand and fell to the ground.

'Shit.' She grabbed it up and turned the screen.

It was only her father calling. Despair. She rejected the call.

She drank a coffee from the vending machine, but it did not help to clear the fog of weariness and depression. Just for something to do, she drove over to the construction site where they had spotted Mann and the mayor, but the site was shut. The rain fell gently into an empty foundation pit while the closed fences shivered in the breeze. There was nobody to ask, not even the foreman or a guard at the gate. The work had been abandoned. Some of their tools and equipment had been left out as drizzle filled the bottom of the pit.

The case lay there in the mud as well, exposed, and unwanted. There was nothing left to investigate. No suspects, no trails, and no desire. Something had gone wrong, and she could not shake off the feeling it was her own fault. They had made progress while Eleanor was alongside her in the car, but now she had pushed her away again. Why did she do that? It was shameful. Eleanor's defeated eyes haunted her. She would not be able to think clearly until she shed the guilt. She took a breath and rang her sister.

No response. Of course. Not even Eleanor was answering the phone now.

All she had left was Iris's diary, and what was that? A fragmentary reproduction, pieced together from failing memory. An X on a blank space.

As the rain tinkled on the roof of the car, she turned the pages of her notepad and looked for the clue she had missed somewhere between the lines.

68

Eleanor crossed the border. She was in Gilchrist territory now. 'Don't take sides,' Blaine had warned her. 'Don't intervene.' Well, she had tried it that way and failed. All this time, she had been unable to make a breakthrough in the Marsh because she had stuck to the rule of 'Don't take sides.' But this had only ended in failure. The Organised Crime Unit were not neutral, they had to be involved in whatever was going on. There was only one option left for her: to take a side. Now was the time to choose, and she chose the Gilchrists. Or at least, she was walking up the driveway of Tommy Presley's terraced house. Before she had a chance to knock, the door opened and he stared out wildly at the day.

'Tommy, I–'

'What are you doing here?'

'I need to talk to you.'

'Not now.'

'What are those for?' She pointed at a pair of binoculars on a string around his neck.

'Nothing. You have to leave here now, it's not safe.' He was about to close the door but she wedged her foot inside.

'Listen to me.' She let the words out uncontrolled. 'I need your help. You need mine.'

Perhaps it was the frenzy in her face made him stop. 'What is it? What happened?'

'They're against you,' she shouted. 'The police. The mayor. Damon Slate. Everyone, the whole city's working with the Looneys. It's not a cold war anymore. They're making their move. They're taking you down.'

Presley fingered the binoculars. 'Will you stop shouting?' He looked around in terror. 'Jesus. You'll get us both killed.'

'Let's go inside.'

'Now?' He glanced at the Rolex on his wrist over the centipede's neck. 'I can't. I have to go. You don't understand what's happening today. It's–'

'Fine. I'll stand out here and shout it so the whole street can hear.'

'You're crazy! Standing out in the rain. Can't you see you're soaking wet?'

'I'll stand and shout all day and let anybody hear.'

'Fuck my life. Alright, inside. But only five minutes. Shit, I'm already late as it is.'

In the kitchen, Presley threw a dirty towel at her, and she patted down her damp hair.

'Look at this.' She took out her phone and pulled up the picture of Wayne Looney, the mayor, and Slate's lawyer at the construction site. 'Know where this is?'

He took the phone and zoomed in the image. 'Shit. It doesn't prove anything.'

'They're working together, it's obvious.'

'Everyone knows the mayor's dirty. Slate as well. But they always kept out of the war. Have they taken sides?' He stared at the image. 'They wouldn't dare…'

'You know who else was at the construction site? Lisa Wainwright. I didn't get a chance to take a picture, but she was parked outside. As soon as we approached, she pulled away and sped off.'

'The Organised Crime Unit is everywhere. They spy on every deal that goes down. Construction is a dirty business, lot of money, and it's at the heart of what's going on in Liverpool. All the rebuilding, the redevelopment.'

'You know who else was there? Derrick Jeffers. You know Jeff?'

'Everyone in the Marsh knows Jeff.'

'He was investigating thefts on the site, supposedly. My guess is, he was covering them up.'

Presley sighed. 'What do you want?'

'Tell me the truth about the Marsh.' She took her phone back and pocketed it.

'What truth? That it's a shithole?'

'Why is there a gang of kids running things? Why don't you or the Looneys stop them?'

He glanced at his watch again and sighed. 'The Marsh is a buffer zone. The war has been going on forever now. Long before I got involved. A generation ago, there was a big sit-down, after things got real nasty. The police brokered the talks, but that was secret. The public never found out. In the end it was agreed, the Marsh would be a buffer zone between the two sides. Neither one would try to move in there. It gave us space, breathing room, and it allowed for negotiation.'

'Negotiation, how?'

'We'd meet in the middle. The Marsh is like Switzerland. We can have our meetings here. The kids run it and both sides let them. It's useful for us because they serve as couriers, mediators.'

'Did the kids kill my dead guy in the park?'

'All I know is, it wasn't the Gilchrists.'

'No. It was the Looneys.' She saw it clearly now. 'They cut his throat with a pocketknife to make it look like the kids did it. They dumped him on the border to pin it on them.'

'Why would the Looneys do that?' Presley said.

'They're going to take the Marsh. The kids need to go. The Gilchrists too. The mayor's on their side. It's part of his re-election campaign. He's hitched his wagon to urban redevelopment. He wants to rebuild this area, and Slate's going to do it for him, but he needs the cold war to end first. The police are on board. I found a police uniform in the flat of our dead guy from the park. There's corruption involved. I don't know how far it goes but it's there. They've chosen sides. They've chosen the Looneys.'

'I need a drink.' He got up and opened a cupboard. 'I'm all out of polite stuff. Want vodka?'

'No, thanks.' She watched him take a long slug from the bottle.

He swallowed, wiped his lips and closed his eyes. 'Christ.'

'Alright, give me some.' She took the bottle and swallowed a mouthful.

It burned in her throat, and the pain was good.

'What now?' Presley said.

'Tell me about Heart of the City.' She set the bottle down and watched his wasted face for a reaction.

His green eyes were beautiful. His voice was desolate. 'I can't do that.'

'It's here, isn't it? It's the buffer zone. It's Switzerland, but where exactly?'

'You're pushing too hard now, Eleanor. If you take one more step, you'll cross all the way over.'

'I've already made the step. I've chosen sides. I'm with the Gilchrists now. I'm with you. Lisa Wainwright and the rest of the Organised Crime Unit are with the Looneys. You understand what that means? They have to make sure the Looneys win. Once they join the war, they have to be on the right side of it. They have to make sure their choice was right.'

'So, we're fucked.' He grabbed the bottle and swallowed another mouthful.

'I'm going to help you.'

'How?'

'Take me to Heart of the City.'

'I can't do that.'

'You can. You have to. You have no choice.'

'They'd kill me.'

'They won't. Call your boss. Tell him what I've just told you. Explain everything. Then take me there.'

Presley sank to the floor with his head in his hands. 'Have you not stopped to think, not even once, that maybe we're supposed to lose? If the Unit has chosen sides, really, it's because that's the right side. The Looneys are the best choice. Me and you, we're on the wrong side.'

'You don't believe that.'

He lifted his face to show tears in his eyes. 'The Unit left me here to die.'

'No. There's still time to change everything.'

To her amazement, he laughed. He laughed until he choked, trying to bring out words. 'Oh God, Eleanor, you're funny. You have no idea how funny you are. You came all the way over here and stood in the rain and banged on my door. But you don't even know what's happening.'

'Tell me then. For once in my miserable life, I wish someone would just tell me.'

His laughter died. 'I'll call someone. If they agree, I'll take you where you want to go. But if they say no…'

'Then pity for me.'

'Then pity for you. A cop on the wrong side who knows too much. Organised Crime won't lift a finger to save you. And the Unit will make damn well sure no one ever finds out the truth about what happened.'

'Make the call.'

69

'The city's dead today,' the taxi driver said.

In the back seat, Stray shivered and tried to hide his nausea. This journey would cost him the last of the cash that the gangster had stuffed in his pocket in the pub toilets. It was almost a relief to spend it and be free of the guilty association. They had paid him to abandon Eleanor, and he had taken the money. The last crumpled notes had been hidden in his sock last night, the little left over after the drugs were paid for. It was almost a miracle, after he was able to walk again, to find the bit of money still there, pressed against his clammy foot.

'There's something in the air,' the driver continued, untroubled by his passenger's silence. 'Can you feel it? It's eerie.'

'We're in the zodiac of Aries,' Stray said. 'Violence hangs over us.'

They coasted along empty streets, past shuttered buildings and closed curtains.

'I picked up a fella this morning,' the driver said. 'Going to the airport. You never saw a man so nervous. He kept looking at his watch like he was going to be late. "Can you go any faster?" he said. I told him, "Relax.

Nobody's going to die." But, what's the use? Some people are just like that. They never stop.'

'Yeah.' Stray clutched himself tightly trying not to vomit as the taxi rolled over a speed bump.

The driver eyed him in the rear-view mirror. 'What do you do, pal?'

'I'm a psychiatrist.'

'Psychiatrist? I don't drive many of those around. Not going to analyse me, are you?'

'Not likely. My fees are extortionate.'

'You don't treat a lot of taxi drivers, then?'

'I've always been fascinated by taxi drivers. They tap into the collective unconscious. You can learn a lot by listening to them.'

'Oh, well. I'll tell that to the wife. She says I talk a load of rubbish.'

* * *

Stray ran up the driveway with a guilty feeling of returning home. This had never been his home. He knew it as soon as the door opened, and Neil looked out with pure anguish in his face.

'Neil, I'm sorry. I–'

'You?'

'I need to speak to Eleanor. It's urgent.'

'You're too late.' Something had changed in Neil. He seemed a stranger in his own doorway, holding back out of sight while the flap of his dressing gown fluttered in the wind.

'Why?' Stray said. 'Has something happened?'

Neil poked his head out to look up and down the street. 'Did you come alone?'

'You know I don't have friends.'

'Did anyone follow you?'

Stray looked about but the street was deserted. The taxi had already pulled away and driven off. 'I don't understand. What are you afraid of?'

'You'd better come in,' Neil said.

'OK.'

Neil grabbed his sleeve and pulled Stray through into the vestibule, slamming the door behind him. Even inside, he seemed agitated and afraid.

'Are you alright?' Stray said.

'I've tried ringing Eleanor. Her phone's switched off. Beth's not answering either. Not that that's unusual.'

'But… what is it?'

'I have to show you something.'

They crossed the hall and entered the kitchen. The curtains were closed but the lights were turned on. Seated at the kitchen table was Damon Slate.

70

The pact was made. They would take her to Heart of the City, but only if she agreed to be blindfolded; only if she agreed to leave her mobile phone behind; only if she agreed to stay silent and to not ask any questions. It was insane, of course, but here she was. That was the nice thing about having the psychological evaluation form filled out on your behalf; you did not have to resist it anymore. A hysterical neurotic. Accept the diagnosis and enjoy it. Be yourself. She was alone now, but she was free. The funny thing was, the pains in her belly had disappeared. Stray was right all along; it was only her sister's pregnancy that caused it.

The car rolled over a pothole, and she rocked against the locked door. Blindfolded in the back seat, she had tried to map the journey of the vehicle in her mind, tracing the turns and stops, but the way quickly became tangled. She figured they must be deliberately circling and backtracking to throw off her sense of direction. She was lost already, and she knew it.

The three men smoked constantly. The air in the car was thick, and she struggled not to cough. The driver's window was open, but hers was not. Every now and then a spray of rainwater reached her in the back seat, and she tried to catch it on her tongue. No longer a police officer, she had no badge or uniform or ranking. She had given up everything.

The three men in the car smoked and laughed, but their laughter was bleak. The Gilchrist beside her was large. She could not see him, but her arm brushed against his sometimes when the car turned a corner too quickly, and their knees touched. She could hear him breathing, a wheeze that might have indicated asthma but more likely obesity. Presley was sitting in the passenger seat; she could hear him whisper from time to time to the driver.

The man beside her grumbled to himself. 'This is a mistake.'

'What choice do we have?' Presley said.

The driver grunted. 'We could kill her now and bury her.'

She almost shouted out at that, but she had promised to say nothing, and Presley had insisted; her life depended on it.

'It's going to be fine,' Presley said. 'Everything's going to go sweetly, just like planned.'

'But she–' the driver started.

'She's one of us,' Presley said. 'She's chosen her side. We need her. The others have chosen sides as well, and they're against us.'

'We only have her word for that,' the man beside her said.

She heard him unscrew the lid from a bottle and take a gulp from it. She tried to smell the liquid – whisky? – but the smoke was overpowering.

'You saw the photograph,' Presley said. 'And besides, we've known for a while the game is up. Let's not kid ourselves any longer.'

The others did not respond to this.

'When we get there,' the man beside her said, 'you just keep quiet.'

It took a moment to realize he was talking to her. 'OK,' she said.

'Whatever they want, you just nod and do it. Don't ask questions. Don't refuse anything. If you're not sure what to answer to a question, just say you're a birdwatcher.'

'A birdwatcher? So, I just–'

'You'll have our protection. But… if it goes wrong for us…'

'…it goes wrong for me as well.'

'You understand.'

'It's too late to change my mind now, anyway, isn't it?'

'I like her,' the driver said. 'She's not afraid.'

In fact, she had never been so afraid in her whole life.

71

'Where am I?' Slate said.

His daughter Claire stroked his arm. 'I told you two minutes ago, remember? You're in a safe place. It's OK.'

He looked around the room with the astonishment of a baby. 'Why are we here?'

Claire turned to Stray. 'He's been like this for the last hour. Can you help him? You're a doctor, aren't you?'

Stray stared at this man in his tailored, silver-grey suit. His face was red. 'Loosen his collar,' he said. 'Take his tie off. He's hot. It looks like his blood pressure is too high.'

Slate did not resist when his daughter lifted his collar. His wandering eyes stopped at Stray's face. 'Who are you?'

'I'm Raymond Stray. I'm a psychiatrist. I'm going to try to help you.'

'But… why? Is something wrong with me?'

'What's the last thing you can remember?'

Slate blinked. 'I… I don't know.'

'Do you remember coming to this house?'

He looked around the room. 'But… where is this? I've never been here before. Is this… Do I live here?'

'No, Dad.' Claire removed the tie and set it aside. 'This is the detective's house. Eleanor Rose. You wanted to come here. It was your idea.'

'But… why?'

'I don't know. You told me to pack a bag and get ready. You were terrified. I ran upstairs. When I came back down, you were like this. You couldn't remember anything. But you had the piece of paper in your hand, with the detective's address.'

'I… I did? In my hand? Which detective? Are they here?'

'Try to think,' Stray said. 'Do you remember how you arrived at this house?'

Slate rubbed his red face. 'I don't remember anything.' Tears welled in his eyes. 'Is… is Iris here?'

'No,' Claire said.

'Where is she?'

The daughter looked at Stray for help, but Stray was lost.

'Your wife is on her way,' he improvised. 'We've called her. Just relax, please, sir. Just try to relax.'

Slate's eyes were wild. 'Who are you? Do you know me?'

'He's a doctor,' Claire said. 'Don't worry. He's a doctor. He's going to help us.'

Stray stood up. He signalled to Claire. 'Can I have a word with you in the hall?'

She stroked her father's shoulder. 'Alright. Just sit there, Dad. Stay calm. I'm going to have a word with the doctor for a moment. I'll be back right away.'

In the hall, Stray closed the door behind them. On the other side, the sound of the TV played in the living room. Neil was watching one of his beloved quiz shows.

'Can you do something?' Claire said. 'Can you help him?'

'It's not a job for a psychiatrist. You have to take him to hospital.'

'I can't. He told me he was afraid. They're after him, he said. They'd find him at the hospital.'

'Who is "they"?'

'I don't know. Before his memory failed, he said we had to pack bags and get away.'

'What else did he say?'

'He was panicking about something. I came down the stairs at home and he was in the kitchen. He was crying. His sobs were so loud I could hear them through the door. I didn't know what to do. I asked if he was alright, and he… he just hugged me and cried into my shoulder. He's never done that before. We never had that kind of relationship. We're not touchy-feely in our family.'

'And then, what happened?'

'I asked what was wrong and he said everything was wrong. "We're all going to die," he said.'

'Who's going to die?'

'I don't know. I said we should call Mann. That's his lawyer, his best friend, but he almost shouted at me. You should've seen the look in his eyes. He said Mann's a part of it, whatever "it" is. He said they're all against him. All his friends. Dr Chen as well. He was so upset I couldn't bear it. I told him he must be delirious. He said there was something happening today, bigger than anyone could imagine.'

'What thing?'

'I don't know. I said to call the police, but he said the police are part of it too. "That's the worst of it," he said. Then he said, "Detective Rose. She's the only one we can trust." But it had to be now. He had to leave right away. He kept looking at his watch. "Is it already too late?" he said. "Too late for what?" I said. Then he went crazy. He ran to the front door and looked outside. He said, "They're coming here. They're coming here to get me. I have to get out." That was when I ran upstairs to grab my stuff.'

'Did he say why Detective Rose could help?'

'No. A moment later, his memory was gone. Suddenly he was quiet. "What's happening?" he said. And it all started, like you see it now. He can't remember anything for half a minute. He just asks the same questions again. "Where am I? Why am I here?"'

'So, you brought him to us… That's good. You did the right thing.'

'But when I got here, Detective Rose was gone.'

'I don't like this,' Stray said. 'There's something horrible taking place in Liverpool.'

'Can you hypnotise him? Eleanor said you could. If you bring his memory back… maybe… it's not too late to stop what's going to happen.'

The kitchen door opened, and Slate stumbled out into the hall. 'Where am I?' he shouted. 'Where am I?'

'We need to get his blood pressure down now,' Stray said. 'It's serious.'

'But how?' Claire said.

'Call an ambulance.'

'We can't go to hospital. They'll find him there.'

'Who is "they"?'

'I don't know.' She was on the verge of tears. 'The police will find out where he is. The only safe place is here.'

'Where am I?' Slate said. 'Please, tell me. Please.'

Stray held his wrist and counted the pulse that thundered in his arteries. 'We have to take him to hospital. It's urgent. We have to get his pressure down now.'

'No!' Claire shouted. 'Not the hospital. He's in danger, I know he is. Whoever took Iris, they'll take him too.'

Stray tried to think. 'There's one possibility, but it's crazy. Could we…? No, it's impossible. It'll never work.'

'What is it?' Claire said. 'Just do it. We have to try something.'

'We'll do it ourselves. We need to take blood out of his arm. That'll bring the pressure down.'

'Blood?' Claire looked horrified.

'Where am I?' Slate staggered and fell against the wall. He slid down to the floor. 'What am I doing here?'

<h1 style="text-align:center">72</h1>

When Eleanor climbed out of the car, her feet were unsteady on the pavement. A tiny patch of light broke through the corner of her blindfold, but not enough to see anything. A strong wind blew the rain in her face, and she sucked it up, relieved to be out of the smoke-filled car. She smelled leaves and petals and exhaust fumes.

'Can't I take this off now?' she reached for the blindfold, but her hand was pulled away.

'If you take that off, you die.'

'Sorry.'

'It's just me and you now,' Presley said. 'Come on.' He shoved her in the back, and she stumbled forward over uneven paving stones.

She could feel his fear as he smoked and coughed beside her.

'They're watching us,' he muttered.

The blindfold had worked its way loose, revealing a hint of grey. A metal gate creaked open.

'Stop here,' he said.

Footsteps approached. 'What's this?' A kid's voice, with a touch of adolescent rawness.

'You seen the bird?' Presley said.

'Not even a pigeon. Been looking all day. Who's she?'

'A birdwatcher. She needs to go down.'

'She's with you?'

'I'm standing next to her, aren't I?'

'Nobody said nothing to me about this. Why does she need to go down?'

'She just does. You know who I am, don't you? We agreed to play this game. It was never our idea. If it has to be like this, fair fucks, but she's going down there as well.'

The kid grunted. 'And if she can't?'

'Then it's off. Everything's off.'

'Mate, I don't like this. I need to call someone.'

'No, you don't.' Presley's voice was hard, commanding. Eleanor understood how he had survived in this world.

'It'll be my neck,' the kid said.

'No, it'll be mine,' Presley said. 'What harm can she do? She's got nothing. No weapon. No phone. Search her.'

'Wait here.' The kid scampered away.

'Stay calm now,' Presley whispered. 'We're almost there.'

She heard two more kids come running out. 'Search her,' the first one said.

She was grabbed roughly. 'You carrying anything, girl?'

How young were they? Fifteen, maybe sixteen? she wondered.

'I asked you a question?'

Old enough to enjoy cruelty.

'No.' She hardly recognized her own voice.

'No phone on you?'

'No.'

'No kind of weapon?' His hand reached into her pockets and felt all over her.

'No,' she said. There was nothing she could do but stand in the horrible blindness while he squeezed and patted her front and back.

'She's clean,' he said. 'But I don't like it.'

'There's no time,' Presley said. 'Decide now, or we walk away.'

'She can go down,' the first kid said, 'but she can't come back up.'

'That's all we wanted.'

'Let's do it now then. It's getting late.'

Eleanor was shoved in the back and allowed herself to be dragged forwards.

'Alright.' Presley's voice remained behind. 'I'll see you when it starts.'

But he was not talking to her; he was talking to the kids. Already his voice grew distant. She was really on her own now.

'This way.' The kid dragged her. 'Fucking Tommy,' he muttered to himself.

Somebody knocked on a door. It opened heavily, grinding on its hinges.

A reedy voice spoke from inside. 'What's this? Another one?'

'She has to go down. I've checked her. She's clean.'

'What the fuck? She's not supposed to be here.'

'That's what I said.'

'Something's wrong.'

'Everything's wrong. But she's not dangerous. Look, she's light as a feather.'

It was shocking to hear herself discussed so openly, as if she was not real, as if she was not standing next to them.

'Is it a trick?' the reedy voice said.

'Tommy said it was OK. He said he'll take the blame if it turns to shit. It's too late now anyway, he's already gone. I can't go back after him.'

'Tommy brought her himself? This is serious.'

'It's nothing. Everything's fine. Will you keep calm?'

'What are you doing here, girl?' the reedy voice said.

Suddenly, she was present in the conversation.

'I'm just watching for the bird.' She tried to control her voice, but it came out desperate. 'Has anyone spotted it?'

For a moment nobody spoke. She must have made a mistake.

'Jesus Christ,' the reedy voice said. 'I don't like this. Not a bit. Take her down now, but you remember, when this all fucks up, it was me who told you so.'

The door creaked, and she was pulled into darkness. The corner of her blindfold no longer let in light. This was the moment to pay close attention. She had to focus on every detail. The musty smell, the sound of rain dripping through from above.

'Keep moving.' The kid pushed her forwards.

This place was large. They crossed what had to be a kind of foyer or large entrance hall. Her right hand reached out, brushing a dusty surface where the wallpaper flaked away.

'Careful,' he said. 'There's a staircase here.'

He grasped her around the waist to position her at the top step, and placed her hand onto a banister leading downwards.

'Alright, go on down.' He gave her a push.

She descended. One wooden step at a time, she went down, gripping the banister, while he followed. At the bottom, her hands found a door.

'Wait a second.' The kid banged on the door. 'All clear in there?' he shouted. 'Step away! I'm going to open now!'

She heard him pull aside a bolt and turn a key. He was breathing heavily. The door opened.

'Go on, quickly.' He shoved her roughly and she fell with a scream onto a cold stone floor.

The door slammed shut behind her, and the bolt clicked into place on the other side. The key turned in the lock.

She took off her blindfold.

73

Neil, bewildered, searched the utility room, and found a needle and thread.

'Thank you.' Stray took the needle between his thumb and forefinger. 'We don't need the thread.'

'What kind of a doctor are you, really?' Neil said.

'Any luck contacting Eleanor or Beth?'

'Neither of them will pick up. I'm getting worried. It's like when they were sixteen all over again.'

'It'll be alright.' Stray tried to find his once reliable voice that used to soothe nervous patients, but it came out like a raven's caw. 'Everything will be fine, you'll see.'

Neil nodded. 'Thanks, Raymond.'

It seemed the magic voice still worked. Perhaps there was hope. 'Don't thank me,' he said. 'I have no idea what I'm doing.'

'I'm sorry about… well, I'm sorry about everything.'

'If I were you, I'd go back in the living room and watch TV. Turn the volume up. You won't want to see what's happening in the kitchen.'

'Just try not to make a mess.' Neil shuffled back along the hall.

Stray was relieved to watch him disappear and close the door behind him.

Back in the kitchen, Claire had boiled water and prepared some clean towels. She looked up fearfully when Stray came back in and stared at the needle he held between thumb and forefinger.

'Are you sure this is safe?' she said.

'No. If there's dirt on the needle, it could cause sepsis. But we'll clean it thoroughly, and we'll use boiled water.'

'Where am I?' Slate, who lay on the tiles with his head propped up on a cushion, tried to get up, but could not. 'What's happening to me? I feel… Where am I?'

'He's getting worse,' Claire said.

'OK, just try to keep him calm. If you stay calm yourself, Claire, that will help. You're all he recognizes in the world right now. You're his rock. Just be relaxed, and he'll feel that.'

Slate groaned. 'Where am I?'

'Don't worry, I'm with you.' Claire stroked his forehead with a cold flannel. 'Don't be scared.'

Stray doused the needle with boiling water, dried it on a clean towel, and poured antibacterial hand gel over it. 'Alright, here goes.'

Slate watched with horror as Stray squatted down beside him. 'Who are you?'

'I'm a doctor, sort of. I want to help you.' He tried to hide the needle from view.

Slate's eyes were almost popping out of his livid face. 'What is that?'

'This is just, well… we need to lower your blood pressure. It's too high. You could have a heart attack or a stroke.'

'But, why?' he panted, almost hyperventilating. 'Where am I?'

Claire stroked his forehead. 'It's alright. The doctor's going to help. There's nothing to be afraid of.'

If only that was true.

Stray tried to remember what was supposed to happen, but he had never done this in a medical capacity. It was a different kind of needle he was used to.

'Roll his sleeve up for me, please. You need to wrap the shirt around his bicep as hard as you can.'

He watched as she rolled the sleeve up.

'What are you doing?' Slate was too weakened and dazed to resist.

'Don't worry.' Claire fastened the shirt around his arm, but in truth, it was hardly necessary.

Stray saw how the vein bulged out of his arm in the crook of his elbow, blood surging through. Yup, that was a lively one. He had come to love veins over the years.

'Alright.' He held up the needle and watched his hand to see if it was steady. It shivered hopelessly in the air. Focus, he told himself. *Focus*.

He brought it down gradually. 'Hold his arm steady now, tightly.'

'What's happening?' Slate said. 'Where am I?'

The point of the needle trembled. With his left hand, he gripped Slate's forearm and stared at the fat throb of the vein. He told himself, that's life, that's life itself, and lowered the tip.

'You may feel a little prick.'

The needle caught in the skin and held. Just a little push was all it needed to break the surface, but something restrained him, fear, revulsion, or doubt.

'What are you doing?' Slate shouted.

'Stick it in!' Claire said. 'Stick it in!'

He pushed. Blood spurted up and splashed his face. It was hot, stunning, intoxicating, but he held his grip and watched it flow. Life's pulse, the deep source under the river.

'Is it working?' Claire almost shrieked.

'It's working. It's working. Hold on tight. Don't let go.'

Slate moaned and writhed, but they gripped his arm while the blood sprayed out.

He remembered then he was supposed to set down a bowl. Blood spattered the tiles and their clothes, Slate's beautiful shirt. No matter. Let it run freely.

'A good, old-fashioned bloodletting,' he heard himself say. 'I can tick that off my bucket list.'

74

Krush read over the words, again and again, until there was only Iris's voice in her head, and the sound of the rain on the car roof. She had read her notes from the diary through again, certain she had missed something. Most of the entries were so cryptic yet banal, it was impossible to interpret them.

> *The princesses of L, G, and R. They hate me of course. At the wedding, they couldn't hide their contempt. R isn't as bad, she's just young and stupid. She only hates me because she copies what the others do. My only company. How can I live with them?*

Did it mean anything? Surely not. All of this was worthless, but there was no other way forward. She tried to clear her mind, and kept reading.

> *Does D really believe what he says? If I go underground, I'll come back up, he says. But he can't hold eye contact anymore. We both know, if I go underground, I'll never come back. Still, he'd let me go down. I really do believe he loves me. Is that why? Is this what love is?*

Dr Chen said it was about depression. Under the river, going underground. Heart of the City. Thus far, she had allowed herself to be influenced by that view. But what if…

'You can't read other people,' Eleanor had shouted at her in that horrible meeting. The words still lashed her. 'You can't tell if someone's lying to you. I bet someone lied right to your face in this investigation and you never knew. That's why it's stalled.'

The words were hurtful and true. What if Dr Chen was the one who had lied to her face? She took out her phone and rang the clinic. Nobody picked up, naturally. An automated message informed patients that the Hexagon was closed today for building repairs.

If Dr Chen had lied, then the diary was not about depression, it was describing reality. Yes, she saw it now, these were not descriptions of internal emotional states. They described something real, something in the external world that frightened Iris. Still, the meaning eluded her.

What if the diary could be read literally? There was a place Iris had to go, but she was afraid. Heart of the City. It was somewhere in the middle, the Marsh, surely, the middle of the border. But where exactly in the Marsh, and why?

Yes, Krush discerned the cloudy outline of a story. The diary was literal, not symbolic. Chen had thrown her off the scent on purpose.

Mann had been on the building site with the mayor and a notorious gang leader. The police were watching as well. Shit. Was all this about land? The construction site? No, Slate already owned that. Heart of the City had to be somewhere else, somewhere in-between.

Her phone vibrated on the empty seat where Eleanor should have been. She snatched it up hungrily, but it was only Neil again. She rejected the call.

Everything led back to the Marsh, the place where Iris grew up. The borderland. Krush looked out of the windows of her car, as if she might be able to see it now. All of this came back to these streets, the giant trees whose roots twisted up, breaking the paving stones. The garbage of petals like snowfall, caught in gutters, smeared on dirty windscreens, clustered in alleyway openings.

But where exactly? She opened up a map of Liverpool on her phone and zoomed in. She slowly scrolled along the green outlines of roads, as if walking them. And there it was, so obvious, and yet she had somehow missed it from the beginning…

Shush! Quiet please!

75

Slate lay on his back on the sofa in the reddish gloom. The scarlet curtains were closed, and the lights turned off. In the crook of his elbow, a spot of blood seeped through the improvised bandage.

Stray hunched over his patient and whispered. 'You're in a dream now. Rest. Sink. Keep sinking lower until you reach the deepest place. Float there. Don't try to think, only listen to my voice. Let everything else fall away. Float, float, sink lower.'

Slate's breathing slowed but his forehead still burned when Stray held his palm over it.

'Sink, keep on sinking. The deeper you sink, the more softly you float. Float now.'

Slate's breath slackened.

'That's good,' Stray said. 'You're doing good. Just float. Now, when you're ready… don't rush it… I want you to tell me… where are you?'

'In a tunnel.' Slate's voice was innocent.

'A tunnel, where?'

'Under the river.' It was uncanny how childlike this proud, wealthy man became.

'Describe it to me.'

'I'm a long way under the river. It's dark in here. I feel afraid. I'm scared. I'm terrified.'

Stray shushed him. 'Don't be afraid. You're safe here. Just keep floating. Keep on sinking. Any moment, if you feel the fear rise, just focus on sinking deeper. As you sink, you float. Alright. Good. Very good. Tell me… who's there with you in the tunnel?'

'It's… I'm alone. I've never been so alone. It's dark. Where is everybody? Where is the world?'

'Sink. Sink lower. Remember to float. You're not alone.'

'Where's Iris? I thought… maybe… I thought she was just here, just out of sight… but she's gone. I'm alone.'

'You're not alone. There's someone there with you. Who is it? Can you see them?'

Slate screamed. He spasmed on the sofa, and his hands tore at Stray while he shrieked. They fell together onto the floor as the door opened and feet came running in.

'Dad!' Claire pulled him away. 'Dad! What's wrong? What's wrong?'

Panting, soaked in sweat, Slate let himself be embraced. 'Where am I?' he said. 'What is this place?'

'It didn't work,' Claire moaned.

Stray tried to hide his shaking hands from the others. 'It partially worked,' he said. 'He remembered being in the tunnel. Whatever's going on with his memory, that's where it started. The first time this happened, he was in the tunnel. He never lost his memory before that, did he?'

'Not that I know of,' Claire said.

Slate pointed at him. 'Who are you?' he said. 'Why am I here?'

'We need to take him to the tunnel,' Stray said. 'Maybe there his memories will come back, and he'll remember everything.'

'But… we can't,' she said.

'There's no alternative.'

76

Three women were seated around a little table eating crumpets off paper plates. They looked at Eleanor in amazement.

One of them pointed with a plastic knife. 'Who the hell is she?'

In the light of a single bulb overhead, she looked to be around forty years old. She had blonde hair and wore a tracksuit that clashed with the showy jewellery around her wrists and neck. Her companions were similarly attired and also blonde. One of them was maybe a decade younger, the other might have been older. They all had suntans so artificial they bordered on tangerine.

'I'm Eleanor Rose.'

It was a wide, windowless basement, piled with crates of books and fitted out with table and chairs, a sofa, and a television with a DVD player. At the other end of the cellar, a curtain had been hung from the ceiling to serve as a divider. Behind that, shadow leaked out.

'You're not supposed to be down here,' the older of the three said. 'I don't know where it happened, darling, but somewhere in life you took a bad wrong turn.'

The youngest tittered. 'Well, she's here now. May as will sit down.' She kicked an empty chair towards her. 'We're eating crumpets. There's a toaster in the corner.'

'Hold on a minute, Liz.' The first woman waved the plastic knife at her. 'You can't just give away crumpets to any old sod who walks in. There's hardly any left.'

'Shut up, Marge. There's a whole box of them. You'll be sick of crumpets by the time you get out of here. If you ever get out.'

'I'm not hungry.' Eleanor sat down. She stared at their faces in turn, trying to place them. She had seen them before somewhere, and recently, but she could not think of where.

'Who are you?' Liz said. 'What are you doing down here?'

'I'm police.'

'Jesus Christ.' Liz pushed her plate away.

The others drew back from the table.

'I don't understand,' Marge said. 'How did you get in? Why did they let you?'

'I'm with the Gilchrists,' Eleanor said.

The two other women turned on Marge.

'Is that true?' Liz said.

'I never saw the bitch before in my life,' Marge said. 'She's definitely not one of ours. We don't talk to police. You know we don't.'

Eleanor repressed the urge to reach out and take the plastic knife out of her hand.

'Well, she says she's with you, and they let her in here. So, somebody's lying,' Liz said.

Marge turned to Eleanor again. 'Tell the truth. Why are you down here?'

She took a breath and by the time she exhaled, she knew, truth was the only card she had left. 'I'm looking for Iris Slate.'

Silence fell around the table. The women's eyes shifted from glance to glance, wondering who lied, who told the truth. Eleanor realized then where she recognized them from: they were all in the background of the wedding photographs for Damon and Iris Slate. She pictured them on the evidence board in the spare office. Marge Gilchrist, wife of Ron; and Dawn Looney, wife of Wayne. The youngest, Liz, was presumably married to the leader of the gang of kids. She looked barely seventeen.

Liz fell back in her chair. 'Well, if that's what you're after, knock yourself out.' She pointed over her shoulder to the dividing curtain. 'She's back there.'

'Iris is sick,' Liz said.

'What's wrong with her?'

The women shrugged.

'Iris is some kind of crazy,' Marge said. 'She's always been that way. Sometimes she's fine, sometimes she's not. As soon as she got down here, she had one of her episodes.'

'What do you mean, "episode"?'

'She just lies on her back and stares at the ceiling. She's awake, but she won't speak, and she won't get up,' Marge said.

'You can get her to move if you grab her,' Liz said. 'She'll let you sit her up or shift her aside, but other than that… it's like, she can move, she just doesn't want to. She swallows food when we feed it to her. She drinks if you lift her head and hold a cup to her lips. But if you don't do it, I guess she'd just starve to death.'

'It's obvious, isn't it?' Marge said. 'Iris wants to die.'

'Wait, how long have you all been down here?' asked Eleanor.

'Four days now,' Marge said. 'But you should know that already, if you're one of us.'

'And how long will you stay?' Eleanor said.

'As long as it takes, of course.' Liz almost laughed at her ignorance.

'I need to see Iris.' Eleanor got up and crossed the cellar.

She ducked under the curtain. The others did not follow. It was darker back here on the other side of the partition, where the light was blotted out. It smelled of sleep. Four mattresses were laid out on the floor with duvets and pillows. On the farthest, Iris was curled up facing the wall.

'Are you alright?' Eleanor squatted down next to her. 'I'm Eleanor Rose. I'm a police officer. I'm… I'm a friend. I'm here to help.'

The woman in the bed did not reply, but Eleanor noticed her eyes were open, staring at the wall.

'It's alright,' she whispered. 'I'm not one of those others in there. I'm different. I'm police. I've been looking for you all over the city.'

'Is it over then?' Iris's voice was toneless, inhuman, dead.

Taken by surprise, Eleanor did not know how to answer. She leaned closer, not wanting the others to hear.

'No, it's not over. But I'm going to get you out. You need to go home and lie in your own bed.'

Iris did not reply. She closed her eyes. Her face showed no emotion.

Eleanor looked for a way to break through to her. 'We found Johnny Baxter.'

Iris's eyes opened, gleaming with horror. 'He's…'

'He's dead. We found him in the park holding your shoe.'

'Dead.' Iris rolled away in the dark and let out a painful sob.

'But I can help you.'

Iris's laughter was like sorrow. 'We knew all along it was a trap.'

'A trap?'

'But we had to play along.'

'Why?'

'It was the only way. So that they'd all die. Damon and his cronies. And then I could be free. I could never escape him while he was alive. He'd never divorce me; he'd chase me anywhere in the world I ran. He has unlimited money. He can do anything he pleases, but he'd never let me go. Johnny was sure he could get me out in time, but I knew all along he was wrong. I don't care. It was supposed to be this way. Me and Damon… we were supposed to die in the same place, at the same time.'

'You're not going to die. I'm going to get you out.'

Iris laughed again. 'Nobody's going to leave here alive. Least of all you.'

'They won't hurt me. I'm police. I can protect you.'

'Do you have a phone? Do you have a weapon?' Iris's voice was toneless.

'No. They wouldn't let me bring anything. I had to be blindfolded.'

'Does anybody know where you are?'

'No.'

'Well, then. You're dead as well.'

'But what do you mean? Why? What is this place? Why are you down here?'

'The others haven't realized yet. They're too dumb.'

'Haven't realized what?'

'That woman back there at the table. That's not Dawn Looney. It looks like her, she's almost identical, but it's not the same woman. I don't know where they found her. I don't know what they paid her. But that's not Dawn Looney.'

'Wait there.' Eleanor jumped up. She ran back across the cellar to the metal door and banged on it. 'Hey! Let me out! I'm ready to come out now!' She banged and kicked against the door. 'Hey! Can you hear me? Let me out!'

Behind her, at the table, the three women watched with a mixture of amusement and confusion.

'Save your energy, love,' Marge said. 'You can come down here, but nobody can come out. That's the rule. They'll never let you out.'

77

Krush drove to the Marsh. At the local police station, she asked for Jeff, but nobody was sure where he was. His colleagues looked at each other in amusement. Evidently, Jeff was the butt of jokes around here. Krush looked around the canteen and staff areas, without finding him. She was about to give up when she heard a sound and entered a dark storeroom. She turned the light on. Somebody was crying.

'Hello? Is anyone in here?' She followed the sound around the shelves and found Jeff in the far corner, huddled against the wall. 'What are you doing in here?'

He did not look up at her. She saw that he was shivering.

'I need you to come with me,' she said.

Jeff flinched. 'I can't. I'm sick.'

He looked it. Deathly pale, his forehead was beaded with sweat and his eyes were red with insomnia.

'You're not sick,' Krush said. 'You're just afraid. You know you fucked up.'

'What are you talking about?' His voice was weak. He lacked the will to argue.

'I need you to come with me now to Heart of the City,' Krush said.

He went rigid in his seat. 'What? I... I...' He stuttered but could not find anything to say.

'I know you've been working for the Looneys. You're a stooge for them here in the Marsh. You've been taking care of Damon Slate's big building site project, covering up all the illegal goings-on.'

'You can't... you don't...'

'It's alright. I'm not here about that. I want you to help me. I want to go to Heart of the City, and I want to be let inside. I want the Looneys to believe I'm one of them. You'll tell them I'm a corrupt officer, that you trust me, and we'll go inside together.'

For a moment, Jeff's face was blank, caught between lies. Finally, he realized there was no point in trying to deny it.

When he spoke, his voice was dry. 'It's too dangerous.'

'That's why you're hiding away in here. You know what's going on, even if the rest of your colleagues have no idea.'

'It'll be alright,' he whispered. 'They promised me, nobody would get hurt.'

'Who promised?'

He did not reply or look up.

'How long have you worked for the Looneys?' she said.

Still he did not respond.

'Come on, get up. We're leaving now, before it's too late.' She grabbed at his arms.

'It's already too late.' He allowed himself to be pulled up.

'We're going to Heart of the City now. Don't try to argue or I'll tell your colleagues out there the truth about you.'

'But… why are you doing this?'

'I'm not your enemy. I'm taking sides. I need to find Iris. The Looneys know where she is, don't they? She's at Heart of the City. You'll take me there, and you'll tell the Looneys I'm on your side.'

'But… honestly… I can't tell you where it is. They'd kill me and you as well.'

'Don't worry. I already know where it is. I only need you to come with me and vouch for me.'

'But… how did you–'

'It was written in Iris's diary.'

* * *

Krush surveyed what should have been a main road of little shops but was a wasteland of derelict buildings behind overgrown trees. The rain had stopped, and the air was fresh with wet leaves and petals on the glistening tarmac. Two empty cars were parked outside the library – black, off-road vehicles, more suited to the countryside than this abandoned town centre. Four other vehicles were parked on the opposite pavement – two black 4x4s, one white VW with fancy hubcaps and, farther along, a grey BMW.

'Keen readers around here?' She approached the first car and peered through the tinted windows. 'Nobody home.'

The second car was empty as well.

'Where is everybody?'

'I don't know,' Jeff said. 'Honestly, I don't know anything.'

'So you keep telling me. Let's try and get inside.'

But the gate outside the library was locked. 'Of course.' She looked around, and sensed herself being watched from the vehicles across the street. 'Let's check the other cars.'

In the first, a black 4x4, a man behind the steering wheel was watching through a pair of binoculars.

He flinched when she knocked on the window.

'Police. Open up.' She held her badge up.

Behind her, Jeff hung back, nervously glancing around.

The window lowered. The driver was wearing a red cap. 'Jeff,' he said. He did not smile. 'What do you want?'

'Pogo, it's you.' Jeff looked at the floor. 'I just–'

'You're not supposed to be here now.'

'We're here to help,' Krush said. 'I'm with him. We're on your side. You need our help.'

'You've got the wrong idea, love. I don't need anyone's help.'

'What are you doing out here then?' Krush said.

Pogo turned to Jeff. 'She's really with you?'

Jeff nodded fearfully, more like a hostage than an accomplice.

'What are the binoculars for?' Krush said.

'I'm a birdwatcher.'

'You look like a bouncer.'

'Don't stereotype me.'

'What would a birdwatcher be doing here?' She peered over his shoulder at three other men inside the car, who were all looking out of the windows through binoculars.

'You wouldn't believe it, but there's a rare bird passing through this part of the country today. On its migration path. You only get one chance all year to spot it.'

Now she understood. All this, it was like a weird joke. 'It's the grey hood you're looking for?'

He frowned. 'How did you…'

'I know a few things about birds. Did you spot it yet?'

In the back seat, two young men in tracksuits, smoking cigarettes, had binoculars around their necks, waiting for the grey hood. She almost laughed.

'No,' the man said. 'It only passes through the UK one week in a year. It stops off in this part of Liverpool for one day only.'

'How oddly specific,' she said.

'Was there anything else, Officer?'

She knocked on the bonnet above his head. 'I'll be keeping an eye on you.' She turned to Jeff. 'Come on.'

She walked over to the second car, parked five yards away, with the creepy sense of eyes in binoculars behind her.

The window lowered before she had a chance to knock. The man inside smiled. He wore a hoodie and had a pair of binoculars around his neck. The head of a centipede tattoo showed on his hand. His smile was not aimed at Krush.

'Is that you, Jeff?' he said.

Jeff did not return the smile. 'Tommy. What are you doing here?'

'Waiting for the bird. Same as everyone. Have you ever heard its call? Sounds like this.' He made a high-pitched peeping sound.

Three other men with binoculars were seated in the car.

'I never realized there were so many birdwatchers in Liverpool,' Krush said.

He grinned and she knew that smile from somewhere. 'Liverpool's on the flight path of many migratory birds. Didn't you know, there's a lay line that runs right through the city? It's on account of that, Liverpool's a spiritual place.'

She stared at his face, that was oddly beautiful beneath the cuts and bruises. 'I know you, don't I?'

'No. But I know you. You took sides, Beth Krush. You're with the Looneys now.'

'And you?' she asked.

'I'm on the opposite side.' He rolled his window back up.

Ten yards farther along, in a white VW, four kids in tracksuits were smoking. They looked about sixteen years old. They lowered their binoculars and stared with hostility as Krush approached.

'Forget it.' She stopped. 'No point talking to them. It'll just be the same story. Birds, migrations. No. We have to get inside the library.'

'We can't,' Jeff said.

'We can try at least.' She set off towards the library, but he did not follow.

'I don't think…'

'Don't try too hard,' she said. 'It's not your strong suit.'

Peering through the railings of the gate, the library was covered in graffiti. The windows were cracked. A broken pram with no wheels stuck out among the bin bags, bits of paper, rusted bike parts, a burnt car chassis.

'It's like a public dump,' she said.

Through the windows, rows of bookshelves could be seen, still filled with dusty books. She crouched to examine a series of boot prints in the mud.

'This gate's been opened recently. There's a track through the dirt.' She shook the railings that were chained together. 'There's no way of getting in without a key. Help me climb over.'

'I don't think that's a good idea,' Jeff said.

She placed one foot in a rivet and tested it. 'I can do this. I used to climb everything when I was a kid.'

She pulled herself up and looked back at the parked cars. Nobody got out to try and stop her. On the other side of the rattling fence, nothing moved inside the library. She was just hoisting herself all the way up when her phone vibrated in her pocket. She stopped. 'If this is Dad, I swear, I'm going to scream.'

She dropped down and took out her phone. An unknown number. She put it to her ear. 'Hello?'

'Beth Krush?'

'Who is this?'

'Lisa Wainwright, Organised Crime. We need to talk.'

'I'm busy right now.'

'What would your gynaecologist say if they saw you climbing that gate?'

Binoculars all around. Where was she?

'I've never been one to pay much attention to doctors.' Krush tried to keep her voice calm, while she looked around in fright, trying to see the hidden officer.

'Keep looking,' Wainwright said in her ear. 'Cross the street. Walk up thirty paces. I'm in a grey BMW. Bring your buddy.' She hung up.

Krush lowered the phone. 'What are *they* doing here?'

'Was it your dad?' Jeff said.

'Same difference. Come on. Stay behind me and keep your mouth shut.'

78

Neil drove too slowly in his old blue Volvo, keeping an eye on the speed dial. In the back, Claire tried to keep her father calm as he flailed about.

'Whose car is this?' he shouted. 'Where are they taking me?'

Claire stroked his hair and shushed him. 'It's alright. These are friends. Try to stay calm.'

'What happened to my arm?' He picked at the makeshift bandage around his elbow.

'You had an accident. Don't worry. It's fine. Just leave it.'

Stray, in the passenger seat, watched the buildings pass as they headed inexorably towards the tunnel. 'This is crazy. We'll never get him inside.'

'What?' Neil said. 'You were thinking of walking into the tunnel on foot?'

'I don't know what else we can do.'

'Where am I?' Slate shouted from the back seat.

'There's a guided tour,' Neil said, a wary eye on the rear-view mirror. 'They take you down in a lift and show you the passages under the car deck.'

'Oh. I never knew,' Stray said.

'I've been on it twice.' Neil sounded proud.

'Why?' Stray said.

'The tunnel's a historic part of Liverpool. You know it's the longest road tunnel in the country?'

'Ah, civic pride.'

'You have to pay to get in though,' Neil said. 'Do you have any money?'

Stray could have cried to think of the dirty money from the gangster that he had wasted.

'Hold on.' Claire reached into her dad's pocket and pulled out a thick wad of banknotes in an elastic band.

Slate looked at it. 'Where did… is that mine?'

Neil whistled. 'That'll buy plenty of tickets.'

'Who is he?' Slate said. 'Where is he taking us?'

'Just stay calm.' Claire put the cash in her pocket.

'I have to get out!' Slate fumbled at the door handle, trying to escape, but the door was locked.

'This reminds me of family holidays,' Neil said. 'We used to drive down to France with the girls in the back of the car. That was when they talked to each other, but they only bickered. I thought at the time things couldn't get worse. "It'll get easier when they grow up," I used to tell myself. "Things will get better, they have to."'

79

Krush crossed the street, sensing watching eyes in the cars parked along both sides. When she reached the grey BMW, the back door opened before she had a chance to knock.

'Get in,' Wainwright said.

She climbed inside and slid along the cream-coloured upholstery. The car smelled new. It was a relief to sit back on the fresh leather. Jeff got in beside her and put on his seat belt for some reason. The child locks on both doors clicked into place.

In the driver's seat, Wainwright was wearing sunglasses. Beside her, a man watched the library through binoculars.

Wainwright leaned over the back of her chair. 'What are you doing, Krush?'

'I'm looking for someone.'

'You can't be here.'

'Why not?'

Wainwright hesitated. 'You just can't.'

'Those men in the cars, they're not looking for birds. There's some gang business going on here. What is it?'

'I can't tell you.'

'Well then. If you'll excuse me. I've got work to do.' Krush tried the handle, but the door was locked. 'Let me out. You can't keep me trapped in here.'

'Will you quiet down?' Wainwright said. 'There's a sensitive operation in place. You'll spoil everything.'

'They're in the library, aren't they? What's happening in there? This is Heart of the City, it must be.'

'For God's sake, Krush. You know everyone at the station calls you a pain in the arse, don't you?'

'I take it as a compliment.'

'Yes, it's Heart of the City. Do you even know what that means?'

'Is Iris Slate in there?'

'I don't know.'

'What *do* you know?'

'She's probably inside, yes. We can't get involved. Our strategy is to stay out of this.'

'Stay out of what?'

'All I know is, it's a kind of a sit-down. This is neutral territory. The different gangs are meeting to try and broker a peace. You see why we can't do anything. We can't take sides. We have to wait and see what happens. There have been peace talks before, but these are the most serious in years.'

'And if there's bloodshed?'

'There won't be. They've given hostages. The wives of the gang leaders are downstairs, locked in the basement. There's Marge Gilchrist, Dawn Looney, and whatever dumb girl is married to the leader of the kids.'

'And Iris,' Krush said. 'She's there too. Damon Slate is mixed up with these gangs. It's because he wants to buy the land and redevelop it.'

'Well, take a look around.' Wainwright waved a hand in the direction of the derelict shops. 'Everything's collapsed around here. With the gang war, nobody wanted to build, nobody wanted to invest. The mayor wants an end to that.'

'Even the mayor's involved. Is his wife under the library too?'

'Don't be ridiculous.'

'And so, what…' Krush stared at the library. It was totally still. She could not imagine anybody inside. 'They're just going to talk it over and make friends?'

'They have to. They're in there now. Ron Gilchrist and Wayne Looney went inside five minutes ago.'

'How long's it going to take?'

'As long as they need. It's been going on a few days. You understand what's at stake. The mayor has picked this area to headline his urban regeneration scheme. Investors are ready to open the tap and let the money flow. God knows, the Marsh needs it. But the gang violence has to stop first.'

'And what if the investors and the gangs are the same people?'

'That question isn't part of my job.'

'There's going to be killing,' Krush said. 'I can feel it. It's too tense.'

'They don't have weapons. The kids are mediators. They're guarding the entrance. They won't let Gilchrists or Looneys inside with a weapon. The kids act as go-betweens in the Marsh. It's all been figured out. There are no weapons. They can only talk. And anyway, their wives are downstairs as hostages. These men may be dangerous, but they're not going to put their wives in harm's way.'

'Bullshit,' Krush said. 'This is obviously a trap.'

Jeff squirmed in his seat. 'Can I go?'

'No,' Wainwright said. 'Sit tight, both of you. We're just here to watch, understand? Whatever happens, we don't get involved. Those orders come all the way from the very top. We only watch. That includes you, Krush. I hope you brought your binoculars.'

80

Claire led her father through the door of the dock building. Neil stayed behind in the car, having already seen the tunnel twice.

Stray straightened his clothes and hair, tried to keep his eyelid from twitching, and approached the cash desk. 'Three adults for the tunnel tour, please.'

The woman behind the counter peered at the wad of notes in his hands.

'Is he alright?' She nodded at Slate, who was leaning on Claire to one side.

'Oh yeah, he's just tired.'

'Is he...' She leaned forward to whisper. 'That's Damon Slate, isn't it?'

'I appreciate your discretion,' Stray whispered back. 'Mr Slate would rather keep out of the public eye.'

'Yes, well, after what happened. Is that why...' Her eyes narrowed. 'Can I ask the purpose of this visit?'

Behind his back, Stray heard Slate's panicked voice as he started up again – 'Where am I? What am I doing here?' – and Claire's soothing hushes.

The woman behind the counter was called Kylie, according to her badge. She was perhaps in her mid-fifties. Stray knew how to deal with people. There were some you had to deal with through deception, and others you had to deal with through openness. Some you had to befriend, others you had to keep at a distance.

'Full disclosure,' he whispered. 'I'm Mr Slate's doctor. I'm a psychiatrist. We're trying to get to the bottom of the memory problems my patient has been suffering. I can't disclose medical information, you understand. The public is not aware of the full story. I can only tell you that a trip in the tunnel is necessary for my patient to process certain, erm, traumatic experiences. Obviously, this is all confidential.'

'Oh, of course.'

'Could you, do you think – could you help us? Mr Slate would be extraordinarily grateful if you provided this service on his road to recovery. He counts on your complete trustworthiness.'

'Well, I do try to always be trustworthy,' Kylie said. 'Alright.' She checked over her shoulders. 'There are no other visitors at the moment. I'll take you down myself, and I'll make sure no other groups go down until Mr Slate is finished.'

'Thank you, Kylie. You can't imagine how important this is to all of us.'

* * *

The metal door of the lift closed over, sealing them inside.

'Where am I?' Slate said. 'Where are you taking me?'

He struggled against Claire's grip as she tried to stroke his shoulder.

'Shush,' Claire said. 'Just be calm.'

Kylie looked alarmed. She reached for the button but did not press it. 'Are you sure about this?'

'Yes,' Stray said. 'Don't worry. Everything's under control.'

'Who's he?' Slate said.

'That's the doctor,' Claire said. 'Remember? He's going to help you get your memory back.' She smiled weakly at Kylie.

'Well, if you think it's for the best.' Kylie pressed the button and the lift jerked into motion.

They descended.

Slate was red-faced and shivering.

'I think maybe your father needs to go to hospital,' Kylie said.

'Who are you?' Slate asked her.

The lift cabinet rattled and shook as it dropped.

'What do we do now?' Claire said. 'This isn't going to work, is it?'

Stray shifted around in the cramped lift. 'I'm going to put you to sleep, Mr Slate, alright?'

'Who are you? Where are we? Where are we going?'

'It's alright, Dad, relax,' Claire whispered. She rubbed his hair.

The lift stopped at the bottom of the shaft, and the door opened.

'Listen to my voice,' Stray said. 'Just listen. You're going to sleep now. You're going to sink, and as you sink, I want you to float.'

81

'Will you sit down?' Marge said. 'You're making me nervous.'

Eleanor came away from the door where she had been banging without any response. She dropped into the free chair at the table.

'Don't worry, girl.' Liz tried to smile. 'This is all weird, but it's almost over.'

'You came down here looking for Iris?' Marge said. 'Why? I don't get it.'

'She's been missing four days.'

The other women looked at each other in confusion.

'But her husband knew where she was,' Marge said. 'They all know where we are. They're the ones who brought us here.'

'Why would they do that?'

'You really don't know much, do you?' Liz chuckled. 'I'm amazed you managed to find your way here at all.'

'We're here to guarantee the peace,' Marge said. 'That's the way my husband puts it. Ron Gilchrist. You'll have heard of him. He's one of the leaders of the city.'

Eleanor looked at the women. 'You're hostages.'

'That's not the word we use,' Liz said.

'What word do you use?'

Liz shrugged. '*Wives*, I guess.'

'So, you four are supposed to stay down here while your men… do what?'

'Make peace,' Marge said.

'Make peace… about what?' Eleanor asked.

'What else do you make peace about?' Marge said. 'War.'

Eleanor stared at Dawn Looney. 'Are you alright?' she asked her directly.

Dawn flinched. 'Me? I just want to go home. The sooner this is over, the better.'

'That's nice, isn't it?' Marge said. 'Here's me thought we were bonding. A bit of girl-time for a change. Crumpets and card games. There's champagne as well.' She nodded towards a crate in the corner. 'But it's warm. There's no fridge.'

The horrible implication of Iris Slate's words were beginning to tighten around Eleanor's heart. She needed to stay calm.

'Let me get this straight. You four have to stay down here until they make peace upstairs? The idea is, they can't hurt each other up there because you're all down here, like… guarantees of good faith?'

'Well, there's five of us now, darling,' Marge said. 'Although I don't know whose good faith you represent.'

Eleanor jumped up. 'There's no other way out of this cellar, is there?' She ran to the side wall and ran her hands along the surface, seeking… what? A crack, a fissure.

'There's a toilet room back there,' Marge called, 'but I don't recommend it. Full of spiders.'

'Don't worry,' Liz said. 'This is almost finished. I don't know what's taking them so long. But that's men for you. They've probably gone fishing. They'll talk it out and make friends. They'll shake hands, and we can all go home.'

'Sit down,' Marge called over as Eleanor moved to the back wall, running her hands along every surface. 'There's no way out. Come on, sit down. Play a hand of cards. I'm glad you're here; four players is better than three, and that one's no use.' She tipped her head towards the curtain.

'What do you prefer, rummy or blackjack? We'd play poker only we don't have anything to gamble with except crumpets, and we're running out of those.'

Eleanor dropped into the chair and held her head in her hands.

'Relax,' Liz said. 'It's not so bad. We've got bottled water and a kettle, and as much instant coffee as you can stomach.'

Nobody responded.

82

They watched the library in silence. Looking through a borrowed pair of binoculars, Krush examined the tops of the shelves that were visible through the dirty windows. A thick layer of dust covered everything, but it was possible to make out the different-coloured spines of the books, if not their titles.

She had always loved libraries. During one long summer of childhood, the last simply happy period of her life, she had read all the Sherlock Holmes books from the local library, taking them out one at a time. By the time she finished *His Last Bow*, the summer was ending. Even in the ignorance of youth she had dimly perceived, it would never come again.

No human figures could be seen inside the library. They must be sitting down out of view somewhere. Whatever was happening in there was silent. After a while like this, watching the stillness, the surrounding world became motionless – the trees, the rubbish, the scaffolding, the police officers, and gangsters with their binoculars.

The late afternoon was dying, turning the westward windows golden, and she felt the tension crest. With no idea what she was looking for, Krush swept the binoculars away from the library, letting the focus blur as it crossed the ragged sky and the backdrop of buildings. The circle of the lens wandered through a group of budding trees surrounded by mouldering crates. She caught a flash of movement. A bird was perched on a branch in an old, sick elm tree. Just a tiny thing with bright eyes.

It seemed for a moment nothing could take place to break the spell of quiet. Until it tore. Engines sounded in the street. The bird took flight.

'What's that?' Wainwright swivelled in her seat. She dropped the binoculars as a jeep turned the corner up ahead and came speeding down the road towards them.

'Drive,' Krush said. 'Drive, now.'

Wainwright hesitated at the wheel. Behind them, another jeep raced up the street from the opposite direction.

'Drive!' Krush kicked the seat in front of her, but the others were frozen as they watched.

The first jeep screeched to a halt outside the parked 4x4 up ahead, occupied by the man with the tribal tattoos on his neck. Gunfire echoed from every side at once.

Wainwright screamed and ducked down. Jeff grabbed the locked door handle beside him and shook it uselessly. Krush was unmoved. She stared unblinking.

The white VW, occupied by the kids, pulled out from the street but stalled. The second jeep smashed into its side in a burst of glass. Screams filled the street. Three men jumped out of the first jeep. They wore black hoodies with their faces hidden behind masks of King Charles III. This jarring detail distracted Krush's rapt attention – just for a beat – from the fact that they carried assault rifles. They opened fire along the side of the parked 4x4 and the crashed VW.

Wainwright and the driver watched stupefied. The second jeep, its bonnet crumpled from the impact with the VW, reversed too fast with a screeching of tyres.

'It's turning around!' Krush shouted in the back seat. 'We have to go now! Go! Go!'

Wainwright snapped to life. She turned the key in the ignition. Krush put on her seat belt. Beside her, Jeff, was weeping.

'This isn't right,' Wainwright said. 'They promised it would be a clean job, no unnecessary bloodshed. They promised.'

'And you believed them?' Krush said. 'They'll kill us all. We're witnesses to the massacre.'

'It's my fault,' Jeff wailed. 'It's because I botched the killing, isn't it? They told me to deal with him, but there was no time, and I panicked. He knew about the plan. I had to torture him to find out what he knew. He wanted to save Iris. He would've told Slate. I dumped him in the park, as if the kids did it. But I forgot about the shoe. I shouldn't have left it in his hand.'

'It's too late for confessions,' Krush said.

'I always fuck everything up. My dad used to say that about me when I was just a teen. He was–'

The jeep smashed into the front of the BMW. A wave of force flooded through the metal frame as the windscreen shattered, firing glass through the interior while Krush ducked down behind the driver's seat. Somebody screamed.

'Drive!' she shrieked. 'Just go! Go!'

She smelled blood. The man in the passenger seat rolled forwards over his seat belt. One arm hung down limp over the gearbox.

Covering her ears as machine-gun fire ripped through the air, she glanced between the front seats and saw Wainwright, unconscious beneath a patina of broken glass. She could not see the rest of her body, but blood came seeping down her arm.

Jeff, hollering beside her, shook the locked door handle so violently it might snap.

The gunfire stopped. Krush risked a glance out of the window and saw three men in black circling the car with rifles raised.

83

In the cellar, muffled gunfire came from all sides at once. Boots tramped overhead and the library shook down to its foundations. A whirl of limbs and screams, the women ran behind the curtain divider, as if it offered any safety. Eleanor banged and kicked on the door, but it would not open.

She ran back across the room, through the curtain, to find the others huddled together in the corner around Iris.

'Why are they firing?' Eleanor shouted. 'You said this was a peace talk.'

Liz sobbed. Dawn hugged her, shivering, her eyes horrified. Marge grabbed at their few belongings – clothes, towels, and bags – looking for anything that might protect them. Nothing would. Iris lay curled up against the wall, unmoved, as if she could not hear anything.

Above their heads, the gunfire stopped. For a long moment the five women froze, listening for a movement.

'Is that it?' Marge whispered. 'Have they finished?'

Eleanor closed her eyes, trying to pinpoint any sound through the ceiling. 'If it's a shoot-out between three sides, they might have taken positions. Most will be dead. They'll have been taken by surprise. If there are any survivors, they'll be hiding behind cover now.'

A man let out a sound, part scream, part groan, just above. She knew that noise, it was somebody dying.

'But… why are they shooting each other?' Marge said. 'This was supposed to be about making peace. Isn't that the whole point? Otherwise, why are we four down here?'

Eleanor pointed at Dawn Looney. 'Do you know her?'

'Me?' Dawn's frightened eyes welled with tears.

'Sure, that's just Dawn,' Marge said.

'But how well do you know Dawn Looney? Are you old friends?'

'We don't exchange Christmas cards if that's what you mean. But Dawn's been married to Wayne for over a decade. Everyone knows Wayne and Dawn.'

'What are you trying to suggest?' Liz said.

Dawn said nothing to defend herself. Her face was crumpled with despair.

Eleanor pointed at her. 'Are you sure, are you *certain* that's really her? Look closely. Haven't you noticed, she's hardly said a word this whole time?'

'I'm just quiet, that's all,' Dawn said, but her voice wavered and cracked.

Liz dried her tears and looked again. She shook her head. 'I don't know. I've only been married to my fella for a couple of years. I've met Dawn once or twice. Enough to recognize her. She looks like Dawn to me.'

'People can look similar.' Eleanor struggled to master her fright. 'People can look almost identical, but there's always a tiny difference, even between identical twins, you can always tell which is which. Look at her! Marge! You've known her ten years. Is that Dawn Looney? Are you absolutely certain?'

'I don't know who *you* are.' Marge turned on Eleanor. 'That's all I can say. You're a total stranger. Everything was going fine down here until you showed up. Now it's turned to shit.'

Marge grabbed at her, and Eleanor pushed her away. 'I told you, I'm a police officer. I've got nothing to do with what's happening up there. I just want to keep you alive. That's all.'

'You're a lying cunt.' Marge grabbed a fistful of Eleanor's hair and pushed her back. She was heavy and strong. 'How do we even know you're police?'

'Get off me!'

'It's true,' Dawn said in a quiet voice.

'What?' Marge span around.

'It's true. I'm not who you think.' Dawn sobbed and swallowed back tears and managed to bring out the words. 'Six months ago, they found me. I'm an actress. A failed actress. Never been in anything. They found me in a catalogue. They told me it was a special role. I'd need to do a Scouse accent, they said. I've always been good at accents. They offered five hundred thousand quid. I couldn't turn it down. I was broke. I had no idea…'

Her accent had changed. She sounded cockney now.

'What?' Astonishment showed on Liz's tearful face.

'I'll kill her!' Marge pulled back her fist to strike, but Eleanor grabbed her from behind.

At their feet, the fake Dawn Looney made no move to protect herself. She wrapped her arms around her chest and stared up at the ceiling as gunfire started again.

Marge did not register it. 'I'll kill her. I'll kill her.'

'Stop it!' Eleanor held her tightly. 'Stop. Think a moment. All of you. If that's not Dawn Looney… this was always a trap. The Looneys aren't here to make peace. They're here to kill off the leaders of the Gilchrists, the kids, Damon Slate too. They're taking over everything, not just the territory; the construction firms, the land deals, all of it. They'll kill us too. All of us. The actress included. We're witnesses. We're all going to die just as soon as they finish mopping up the last survivors upstairs.'

'But… but…' Marge tried and failed to find the words.

Liz and Dawn hugged each other. Iris still lay curled in a ball, eyes blank, indifferent to the world.

Eleanor stood over them. 'We have to get out of this cellar.'

84

'You've been in this lift before,' Stray said. 'You've been here before. Smell it. Take a breath through your nose and smell it. Touch the wooden walls. Remember.'

'I've been here before,' Slate mumbled, deep in the trance.

'Let the memory come back to you,' Stray said. 'Don't force it. Let it come.'

From outside the lift, Claire and Kylie watched in silence. Stray would have preferred to be alone with his patient, although he had never been above a certain showmanship. Let them watch; let them be amazed.

'I'm in the lift,' Slate whispered. 'Why?'

'Don't worry about why. Just go back. Go back into the memory. When you exit the lift, you're going to remember what happened next. Are you ready? Take a breath now. Stay calm. Sink. Sink lower. Let yourself be guided as you float. Walk into the memory.'

Stray stood aside as Slate took a hesitant step forward. Eyes closed, he walked slowly out of the lift while Claire and Kylie scurried out of the way.

Stray kept pace behind him. 'Where are you now?'

'I'm walking down. I'm following the directions I was given. I go right.' His hand found the wall and kept contact with it as he wandered blindly in that direction.

'Good. That's good.' Stray stayed close but did not touch him. 'Keep following the directions you were given.'

He tiptoed behind as Slate, more confident now, followed the corridor around a turn and reached a metal staircase leading down. Claire and Kylie crept after them, keeping their distance. Claire reached out instinctively with fright when she saw Slate start down the staircase with his eyes closed. Stray shook his head at her, and she held back. Thank God, she was willing to trust him, he thought. He hardly believed in himself. It had been a long time since he did anything like this.

But it was working. Slate reached the bottom of the staircase and turned left, while the others crept behind him, straining not to make a sound.

Stray followed along a concrete passageway. The sound of speeding cars above their heads was frighteningly close.

'Who gave you these directions?' Stray said.

'It was a message. He said it was dangerous to talk. The only safe place was down here. The only place nobody could spy on us.'

'But… who?'

Slate stopped. 'He's here.'

'Who?' Stray gestured for Claire and Kylie to stay back.

'My wife's lover.'

'He's here now?'

'He's waiting for me.'

'What does he want?' Stray said.

'To save Iris.'

'Can you see him?'

'He's come out of the shadow.'

'What does he look like?'

'Ugly. He's so ugly. He's a liar. Iris could never love a man like that. She has everything she wants. She's rich. She's mine. How could she? But… he's holding her shoes. He says, these are her favourite shoes.'

'Shoes? Why?'

'He brought them as proof. Proof Iris loves him. Proof he's telling the truth.'

Stray signalled to Claire. He pointed frantically at her feet until she got the idea and removed her shoe, a simple, black slip-on. Stray grabbed it from her and put it in Slate's hand.

'You're holding her shoe now,' he said.

Slate stroked the shoe. 'I'm holding it. I think, *how sad*. I never knew she had a favourite shoe. And then I know, he really does love her, like I never managed.'

'What does he say next?'

'He says they're everywhere. They're spying all the time. They're listening. They have bugs in our homes. Hidden cameras. The Liverpool KGB. They know everything.'

'Who does?'

'The Looneys, of course. That's why we're down here. It's the only place in the city where their spies can't hear us. He has a friend who works in the tunnel. "Don't worry," he says. "The camera footage will be deleted. It's safe." He's wearing a tunnel police uniform. He's snuck in here before. I understand then. This is where Iris came to meet him. This was their secret place, under the river.'

'And now?'

Slate hesitated. 'He's scared. He's scared like crazy. They're going to kill him, he says. As soon as they find him, they'll cut him up.'

'Why?'

'Because he knows the truth. Heart of the City is a trap, he says. It's not peace talks at all. They're going to kill the Gilchrists and the kids. Iris will die. We'll all die, me and the others. Mann is part of it. He's working with the Looneys. The mayor as well. The police are on their side. There's nothing to stop them. They'll take control of the whole construction business in Liverpool, and all the land.'

'And what do you say then?'

'Nothing. It feels like… something cracked. I grab him. We fight. Something cracked in my brain. I'm alone. I'm shaking. I panic. I can't remember anything. I don't know where I am. I'm holding this shoe.'

'And your wife's lover?'

'I'm alone. I'm in a tunnel. I'm holding a shoe. Where am I? Why am I here?'

Stray turned to Kylie and Claire. 'That's it. That's the whole of his memory. He had that meeting in the tunnel. He must have started to panic. A massive anxiety attack, combined with a spike in blood pressure. His brain overloaded. To protect itself, some functions shut down, including short-term memory.'

'But...' Claire stammered. 'What about Iris? What did it all mean? A trap? Heart of the City? Who's going to die?'

'Iris...' Slate said. His eyes wide open, he seemed to awaken from a dream. He looked around with amazement. 'Iris... where is she?'

Claire leapt and embraced him. 'Dad, are you awake?'

'Where is this?' He looked at Stray. 'You're the doctor?'

'I'm the doctor, yes. I'm sorry about your arm, that was... amateurish.'

'I heard your voice in my dreams. It was the strangest thing.'

'You lost your memory. We brought you here to bring it back.'

'I lost my memory again? Shit. Not today. Today's the most important—'

Claire clung to him as she sobbed. 'Dad! What's happening? what did you do? Where's Iris?'

'Heart of the City.' His voice was dry. 'What time is it? Is it too late?'

85

Krush cowered down behind the driver's seat and listened to the approaching feet. The locked door rattled by her ear. She forced herself to look up and face the man who was about to kill her. Their eyes met. Although his face

306

was hidden behind the mask, she could see his brown eyes were youthful. He raised the machine gun. She pulled herself up straight to let him see her baby bump. Did he notice? He hesitated with the gun aimed at her heart. She closed her eyes. All that remained was not to flinch.

A single shot broke through the windowpane and buried itself in flesh with a deathly thud. Silence. She opened her eyes. The man, on the other side of a bullet hole in the glass, swayed and capsized.

'I'm sorry,' Jeff said, apparently addressing the dead.

She had forgotten he existed. Too shocked to speak, she turned and saw the pistol in his hand.

'God,' she said. There was no time to say another word.

Over the top of the driver's seat, she saw the two other gunmen around the left-hand side of the car.

Her voice returned. 'Behind you!'

Jeff ducked down. Gunfire exploded all around the car and the frame rattled with bullets. She buried her head beneath her knees and waited for the world to end. When it did not end, she dared to glance across at Jeff, who cowered so close, his knee touched hers.

Somebody knocked on the window. She looked up and saw Tommy Presley, covered in blood, a rifle in one hand, the other hanging limp.

Jeff checked over the seat in front of him where Wainwright's body was sprawled, then reached through the gap and released the child lock on the rear doors. 'Come on.' He opened his door and slipped out.

Krush found that her legs did not want to move. The door opened beside her.

'You alright?' Presley said.

She shook her head.

'Get out, before anyone else comes.' Presley gave her his hand. 'I'm police, undercover. We've never been introduced. I don't spend time at HQ.'

She crawled out into a scene of carnage. Five damaged cars, smashed together and ravaged with bullet holes. The kids' white VW was stained with gore. She could not bear to look inside. Multiple bodies lay twisted on the ground in pools of blood among shattered glass.

She grabbed Jeff's arm. 'Whose side are you on?'

He hesitated. 'I don't know.'

'There are no sides anymore,' Presley said. 'We're police, that's all.'

'I was never much of a police officer,' Jeff whispered.

He scooped up a rifle from one of the corpses. A spray of bullets hit the side of the car and they threw themselves down.

'They're firing from inside the library,' Presley said.

'We have to get in there, somehow.' Krush peeked over the top of the bonnet, but another round of bullets rattled the metal frame of the vehicle.

'Are you alright?' Presley was staring at her feet.

Confused, Krush looked down and saw a trickle of blood seeping out of the bottom of her trouser leg into her sock.

'What the fuck?' A dark, sticky patch soaked into her crotch. 'Not now. No. This can't be happening.'

Pain like a knife cut through her belly and she sank to her knees.

'What do we do?' Presley said.

Krush tried to speak but all the air was sucked out of her lungs.

Gunfire sounded in the library. A scream broke through the windows.

'There are still some Gilchrists alive in there,' Jeff said. 'They'll be torturing them.'

Another long, gurgling scream pierced the grey sky and broke off. Stillness returned to the stricken road.

The ringing of a phone was the most absurd noise.

'Is that… yours?' Presley looked around.

She managed to pull the phone out of her jacket pocket. For once, she only wanted it to be her father calling. 'I don't believe it.'

'Who is it?'
'It's Damon Slate.'

86

Huddled against the back wall of the cellar, Eleanor held onto the others, and listened. Another round of firing ceased. Each time they thought it was over, the shooting started again. It was further away this time. The silence that followed brought no relief, punctuated with screams and broken shouts. Finally, even those died down.

'It's quiet now,' she said.

'Have they really stopped?' Marge raised her head from Eleanor's shoulder. 'They must have run out of bullets, right?'

'Maybe they all killed each other.' Liz was still so young, absurd hope came to her easily.

Lying on her own, facing the wall, Iris spoke up. 'They killed the last survivors. Now they'll come down here and kill us. They're not in a rush. They know we can't get out.'

Eleanor's imagination balked. No way to escape; no way to fight. At best, she could try to plead for their lives.

'Come on.' She got up.

'What are you doing?' Marge said.

'We have to barricade the door. It's all we can try. If we can hold out long enough, the police must turn up sooner or later, with all the guns firing.'

Paralysed by fear or hopelessness, Dawn and Marge did not move. Liz got up, legs wobbling, and helped push the table across the door. They piled it with every box and piece of furniture to hand. In the quiet, Dawn's sobs were rhythmic and pathetic.

Footsteps came down the stone steps leading to the cellar. A chilling sound. Liz let out a scream and clamped her hand over her mouth. The others stayed silent. Eleanor felt their shaking through her skin, or perhaps it was her own shaking.

The bolt was pulled back. A key turned in the lock. Another set of footsteps sounded overhead.

Liz gripped hold of Eleanor. 'What do we do? What do we do?'

There was no answer to this.

'In here.' Liz ran to the toilet room, as if that might protect them.

The cellar door rattled. Eleanor pushed against the table with all her weight, while somebody beat against it from the other side.

'Open up!' a man's voice shouted. 'It's time now. Don't be scared. We're not going to hurt you. Step away from the door. Let us inside.'

Marge and Dawn got to their feet. Between them, they lifted Iris, who allowed them to lead her over to the little toilet room. There was hardly room for all of them inside, but they clung together. Whimpering, their eyes locked on Eleanor, waiting for her to do something.

The door shook. The man shouted to somebody else in the stairway outside. 'They must have barricaded it. Fucking bitches. Help me knock it down.'

She would have to beg for their lives, but as she tried to think of something to say, she could only think, *I found Iris first.* At the funeral, Beth Krush and all the others from the station would have to acknowledge it.

'Come on,' the man was saying. 'One, two, three!'

The door jolted and the table vibrated, scattering cups and plates, as they threw their shoulders against it from the other side. Eleanor gritted her teeth and pushed.

The cellar rumbled. The walls quivered. Behind her back, she heard the women scream. A hiss of brick dust in the air. The pipe of the toilet burst, sending a shoot of water out. The cellar door heaved inwards; it was almost open. A man's hand came through the gap and reached behind, trying to find what blocked it.

'Goddamn it,' he said.

'Eleanor!' Liz cried.

She turned around to see – what? What was happening back there? She did not dare to release the edge of the table. The women cowered under a fountain of toilet water, too afraid to leave whatever shelter they imagined. But there was something… a hole in the wall… and now a man. This was finished then. They were coming for them, somehow, from both sides.

'One, two, three!' The door slammed against the table as she hung onto it.

A screaming confusion of bodies behind her.

'Shit.' A man crawled out through the streaming toilet water. 'Help me, for God's sake.'

The women dragged him out, coughing on dust and spraying water all over the place. She knew him. Even as he was, she knew him, with a powder of brick plastered with blood on his face. Tommy Presley got to his feet. He pulled out a pistol from his back pocket.

'What?'

He silenced her with a finger to his lips.

The men counted again. 'One, two…'

'Get out of the way,' Presley hissed.

She dived aside.

'…three!'

The table scraped across the floor as the door opened inwards. A man in a tracksuit grabbed a rifle strapped around his shoulder. Presley's shot hit him between the eyes. Before he hit the ground, his friend, stood behind, was dead as well.

Eleanor looked back and saw Liz disappearing through a small gap that had been opened up in the wall of the toilet. Marge climbed in after her.

'What's going on?' Eleanor asked.

Presley looked around the edge of the doorway and up the stairs as gunfire and screams sounded overhead.

'Seems Iris had a boyfriend,' he said. 'Romantic type. He stole equipment from a different job, dug a tunnel from the abandoned building next door. He did it at night. This must be what they mean when they talk about love.'

Epilogue

Behind her desk, Carver set down the file with a sigh. 'I know what you're up to, Rose.'

'I just want the best thing for the police.' She adjusted the sling around her shoulder. The bullet had gone through the top of her arm as she was fleeing the library shoot-out, taking out a clump of flesh, without harming any organs. Still, the sling gave her a certain status around the station, along with the bravery award the new acting mayor had bestowed on her. Officers passing in the hall gave her a nod of respect, or a thumbs-up, or just a smile.

She had been reinstated as a detective, after Dr Shepherd's psychological report was rejected. It turned out he was on Slate's payroll as well. He'd been trying to undermine her after she was put on the murder case in the Marsh.

Carver read aloud from the file. 'This informant has provided vital services to the police. In particular, his involvement saved several lives at the "Heart of the City" crime scene.'

'It's all true,' Eleanor said.

'What's also true is several people were killed in the process of all these cases,' Carver said.

'That's not the fault of my informant. He... or she... was not even present at Heart of the City.'

'Indeed. How convenient. And this informant, code name Seagull… I won't ask where you cooked that one up.'

'It's just a cover name.'

'You really believe he… or she… needs to receive living expenses courtesy of the taxpayer?'

'He or she provides a critical service to keep the taxpayer safe.'

'I know exactly what your Seagull spends his money on.'

'The results speak for themselves. This one informant has been key to the resolution of more major cases in the last year than any other source on the books. Maintaining a reliable network of informants has always been essential to good police work.'

'Don't get cocky, Rose. You know the rest of our informant handler team is opposed?'

'That's why I brought it to you.'

Carver muttered to herself. 'I spoke to Beth Krush. She's corroborated everything in the file. We also spoke to Claire Slate. She gave us a detailed account of what happened. It seems that your Seagull's actions helped save the lives of all the hostages at the library. I'm going to approve this informant. He'll be taken on the books with expenses paid. You'll be his go-between. As you conveniently make clear in the file, he wouldn't work with anyone else except you anyway.'

'You'll approve it?'

'For a probationary period. We'll reevaluate in six months. And, Eleanor, I want receipts for all those expenses. The taxpayer cannot be billed for drugs, got it?'

'One hundred percent.' She could not hold back a smile, even at the risk of annoying her boss.

'Oh, Eleanor, watch your back. Just because the newspapers called you a "hero", don't get too big for your boots. Some members of HQ are dead against this move. I had to push it through. If things go wrong, you'll take the blame. You're making enemies on this force.'

* * *

Damon Slate took out a deck of cards and laid them on the table. 'What do you say, Detective, one more hand?'

'It's too late for that,' Krush said.

'Oh, come on. You know you owe me a game. I bet you Iris would turn up alive, and she did.'

'Little thanks to you.'

'I always had everything under control. It just got a little… tense, that's all.' He shuffled the cards and turned over the ace of hearts. 'If I hadn't lost my memory, everything would've been fine.'

Krush ignored this. 'You asked to see me. Why?'

'I wanted to apologise. Honestly, I never intended for any of that to happen. I never wanted anyone to get hurt. What the Looneys did was pure treachery. I had no idea. All I ever wanted was to build. I want to make this city beautiful and liveable for everyone.'

'Save it for the jury. I'm not interested.'

'But it's you I want to talk to, not any jury. I wanted to check everything was OK. You know, with your, with your…' Slate pointed at her belly.

She put one hand out to shield it in a reflex action. 'The baby was premature. He lives in a little box now. He's not allowed out. Like you.'

'A boy? How wonderful. What's his name?'

'None of your business.'

'I'm glad you weren't hurt, truly I am. Liverpool needs you, Beth Krush.'

'Is that it?' She stood up.

'I've instructed my people at the casino. You'll have free premium membership for the rest of your life.'

'I won't be going back to your casino.' She crossed the prison cell and was about to knock on the door for the gaoler to let her out.

'You're going to walk out, like that? Can't we be friends; can't you even pretend?'

'I'm a police officer. I don't maintain friendships with the prisoners I put in jail.' Still, she hesitated and did not knock.

'Ah, don't worry about that. We both know, I'll walk out of here free. We've had this conversation before. I told you last time, I have the best lawyers, and I always have a trick to play.'

'Well, your lawyer is dead this time. I saw him lying on the floor, covered in his own blood.'

'He betrayed me. I don't pity him.'

'Ron Gilchrist is also dead. Wayne Looney is in a max-security prison, awaiting sentencing. You'd better watch out you don't cross paths with him.'

'It's nice of you to feel concern.' He shuffled the deck and turned the top card. Again, the ace of hearts.

'I think you've run out of tricks.' She knocked on the door.

'Relax, Detective. Stop taking things so seriously. All this, life, it's just a game.'

If you enjoyed this book, please let others know by leaving a quick review on Amazon. Also, if you spot anything untoward in the paperback, get in touch. We strive for the best quality and appreciate reader feedback.

editor@thebookfolks.com

www.thebookfolks.com

ROUGH SLEEPER (Book 2)

Detective Eleanor Rose tricks her way through a
psychological evaluation and rejoins the force whilst a
serial killer dubbed The Binman terrifies her city. He is
suffocating his victims with a refuse sack and discarding
their bodies like trash. She is determined to catch him but
is in danger of succumbing to the madness gripping the
world around her.

FREE with Kindle Unlimited and available in paperback!

Other titles of interest

THAT CARE FORGOT
by James Warren

Junior attorney Rebecca Holt isn't too happy when given the pro bono case of a convicted murderer. Yet Nick Malone isn't really interested in his parole hearing, rather he is obsessed with a serial killer who terrorized New Orleans in the 1990s. When Malone reveals his secrets, Rebecca is faced with a life-changing decision.

FREE with Kindle Unlimited and available in paperback!

MURDER IN THE NEW FOREST
by Carol Cole

When a woman's body is found on the ground next to her horse, it seems an unfortunate accident had occurred. However, DI Callum MacLean, newly arrived in the picturesque New Forest from Glasgow, suspects differently. But hunting a killer in this close-knit community, suspicious of outsiders, will be tough. Especially when not everyone in his team is on side.

FREE with Kindle Unlimited and available in paperback!

Sign up to our mailing list to find out about new releases and special offers!

www.thebookfolks.com

9 781804 622827